Second edition.

A Foreign Shore:
Clothes Make a Man

by

Forrest Johnson

Illustrations by

Liz Clarke

Cover by

Tania Kerins

ACKNOWLEDGMENTS

Thanks to Dorothee Eren and Dieter Manderscheid for reviewing the manuscript, and to the Wordos group for their criticism. Special thanks to Liz Clarke for her numerous questions and suggestions (Heraldry? OMG, I forgot about heraldry!), and also to Tania Kerins, a brilliant young artist, who among other things, decided to change the the subtitle and improved it.

Second Edition, December 2015

ISBN-13: 978-0615812526 (Forrest Johnson)

ISBN-10: 061581252X

"What is the use of a book, without pictures or conversations?" - Lewis Carroll, *Alice in Wonderland*

1: Raeesha

On the day before the battle, Raeesha got up shortly after dawn and put together the bundle of things she'd gathered: a few small coins, some jewelry, a blanket, a water flask, leather sandals, a knife, five flatbread cakes wrapped together in a piece of cloth and her one great treasure, a book of poetry.

Most of the other women were still in bed, nursing their heads and other parts still sore from the night's celebrations, but the younger ones were peering through the window screen at the men as they rode out. There was a quiet fluster of girlish voices as they whispered to each other the name of one champion and the next, sometimes with admiring or indecent comments.

A little while ago, I was just like them.

These were her only friends: the sisters, aunts and cousins she'd been raised with. A few days ago, they'd all been crowding around her, hugging her and saying how lucky she was. Now, she felt a cold, dead certainty she'd never see any of them again, and if at some future date, one of them should glimpse her from a distance, she'd probably just look the other way.

She was only sixteen, but the years weighed very heavily on her as she went downstairs to the last place one would wish to be on such a day, the laundry room. It was a dark and ill-smelling place, well known to her. She passed the drying room and the baskets of fresh laundry which awaited sorting and went straight to the pile of dirty clothes, which had been hastily dumped there, untouched and forgotten amid the furious preparations.

What foul and ill-fitting rags shall I wear on this day of days?

Picking through the laundry, she found a pair of baggy black pants, not too long, a dirty shirt of coarse brown cloth, a bit too large, and a shabby old padded silk vest, which had probably once belonged to some uncle or the other. Examining her dim reflection in one of the wash basins, she thought she might easily pass for a servant boy. But there was one problem: the long braid of dark hair which hung almost to her waist. She took the knife.

And now, she didn't want to do it. She'd reached the point of no return, and it seemed impossible to step out into the blank unknown, with no one to catch her. She'd lose everything . . . but what did she really have? The contents of the bundle spoke for themselves. And as for her home, her friends, her family, she'd never see them again anyway . . .

I'll never have another chance!

She cut the braid. It didn't want to yield at first, and she cursed as she sawed at it. With the last stroke, she saw she'd cut her hand. A trickle of blood was running down to mingle with the braid of hair which she'd grown since childhood.

For a moment, she ignored the blood and just stared at the braid. She'd never seen it like this before, lying in her hand like a dead bird. What would Mother say? She would be shocked. She was easily shocked for a woman who had borne eight children, and so far as Raeesha could tell, hated every minute. She was city-born and found everything at Jasmine House unspeakably rustic and crude. Her mother wouldn't approve. She never approved of anything.

Why should I care what Mother thinks?

The braid felt oily and disgusting. She threw it in a corner, like a snake, and examined the

wound. It was only a scratch, a nick to the fleshy part of her thumb. With a good bandage of clean cloth, it would be fine in a day or two. There was cloth all around her. It took only a minute to rip the hem off someone's shirt and tie it around the wound.

Thinking again, she ripped up the rest of the shirt and wrapped the rags around her head, in place of a hat, as she'd seen the boys do.

If I saw myself now, carrying a basket or a load of firewood, I wouldn't pay the slightest attention.

Now began the dangerous part. Down a narrow corridor was a small door, which opened into the courtyard. It was locked, but she'd filched the key from the drunken housekeeper the night before. There was some kind of ruckus in the courtyard. Standing on tiptoe to peer through the narrow slit window, she witnessed a strange and repugnant scene:

A mob of peasants was in the courtyard, each in the coarse white clothing they wore. More were being herded in every minute, soldiers pushing and shouting at them. And another group of soldiers grabbed them as they entered, adding them to lines of woeful men chained together by the ankles.

So this is how one recruits an army.

Men talked so eagerly about weapons and fighting, she'd imagined they were all in love with it. Plainly, some of them were not. But she had no time to sympathize with the peasants. They were only Chatmaks anyway, and at the moment, they were simply an obstacle between her and the gate. How was she to get out?

She stared at the weeping, groaning, praying, cursing bustle of men for some minutes before it occurred to her that she could walk right through it. She saw no one who might recognize her. She didn't look like a peasant or a soldier. She looked like a servant boy carrying a bundle, no unusual sight. There was no reason to detain her. If questioned, she could just say she was bringing some things to her master at the camp, a plausible story.

Slipping out the door, she adopted the trudging walk of a servant with a heavy burden and a long way to go. She thought it might be dangerous to look people in the eye, so she concentrated on their feet, the sandals of the peasants and boots of the soldiers, moving around them as required, until she almost bumped into a pair of nicely polished and expensive black boots which were squarely in her way.

Suddenly, she was staring him in the face, a face she knew very well. It was Hussni, the captain of the watch, a tall and intimidating presence. He looked down impassively on her from over the long black beard which spilled out onto the shining metal armor.

Gods help me!

"Pardon me, effendi," she said meekly, adjusting the burden on her shoulders. Time seemed to freeze as Hussni contemplated the ragged little figure. Then, he stepped aside and let her pass.

Suddenly, she was outside and completely lost. All her plans had only brought her to this point. Where to go? The road to the southeast passed miles and miles of farmland before it eventually forked. One road went south, to the city of Kafra.

The last place I want to be! There stands the palace of Amir Qilij, with its high walls and iron bars! Anywhere but there!

The other fork rose to the escarpment. And then, there were over a hundred miles of wild country before it reached a lonely outpost, the fortress of Barbosa.

Evil den of witches and demons!

She couldn't go there. She couldn't even take a step in that direction, before Hussni noticed and called her back to ask where she was going. The only possible way to go was west to the sea, where they were dragging the miserable peasants, where her father and his men were already far ahead of her.

Abruptly, it occurred to her she'd left the braid of hair lying on the floor in the laundry room, where they were certain to find it. It was too late to go back for it now. She'd just have to put as many miles as possible between herself and Jasmine House. She started down the road at the brisk walk of a servant who fears a whipping, if he arrives too late.

The countryside was green, but turning brown. It was near the end of the summer. Passing a village, she saw almost no one in the street, only a woman drawing water at a well. Those peasants who had escaped conscription were lying low, hoping to avoid notice.

The foreigners must have picked the time of the harvest to invade. They knew the peasants would bitterly resist recruitment, and the fields would be full of grain to plunder, or to burn, if that was their wish.

But they'll have to defeat us first, and that may not be so easy.

The day was getting hot, and her little bundle seemed unbearably heavy. A little after noon, she came to a bridge. She left the road and crawled under it, to have a snack in the shade. Suddenly, she was staring a strange man in the face: a Chatmak peasant, from his clothing, a little older than she, his eyes wild with fear.

He's hiding from conscription. He sees I'm a Bandeluk and is afraid I'll betray him.

Moving slowly, she opened her bundle and offered the fugitive a piece of bread. He took it cautiously and began at first to nibble, then to chew with vigor.

The soldiers surprised him. While they were chasing someone else, he got away and hid in the first hole he could find. He has nothing but the clothes he's wearing and is hungry.

They sat awhile and stared silently at each other, while chewing on the bread. On the bridge above them, they could hear many feet passing, and sometimes the hooves of a horse or the wheels of a cart. Raeesha realized her feet were sore.

I've been walking for miles in these rough sandals, and I'm not used to it.

She took off her sandals and dangled her feet in the rivulet under the bridge. Then, she leaned back and rested her head on the bundle, staring up at the rough stones.

I didn't plan this very well. Is this going to be my life from now on, to hide under bridges and share bread with outcasts and fugitives? I'm Sheikh Mahmud's daughter!

And a moment later:

No, I'm not Sheikh Mahmud's daughter, I'm nobody, not even as good as this wretched peasant. He has a home and family somewhere, I have nothing and no one. There is no place in this world for me.

These thoughts made her restless. If she had any place in this world, it was not here. Perhaps the people in Jasmine House had already noticed her absence and were searching for her. Maybe Hussni remembered the strange boy he'd seen at the gate. She couldn't afford to stay here any longer.

Above her head, the footsteps came and went. She waited for a pause, then grabbed her bundle and climbed back on the road, leaving the silently staring peasant behind.

It was almost dark by the time she got to the camp. She had long since passed the shuffling lines of dejected peasants. She joined a group of mules and porters, who were bringing in supplies. No one paid her any attention.

The camp was huge, like a city, but with tents, she thought. There were over a thousand people there, not only her father's men, but those of all the landowners of the district, just about every able-bodied man who could be ordered or cajoled or whipped into coming. Some soldiers were still putting up tents, but most simply sat around waiting for supper. A number of lively card games had started.

Someone was playing a flute. She thought she recognized the music:

> *They sent me to a foreign land,*
> *With jackals for company,*
> *Do not try to understand,*
> *And do not wait for me.*

A depressing song, a bad omen. Suddenly, she felt afraid.

Her feet hurt. She was hungry and in need of rest, but she couldn't stop here. Someone might recognize her. She continued in the only plausible direction, to the west, from whence she could already hear the sound of the sea.

Soldiers were everywhere, big sweaty men in mail. There must have been a hundred just to feed all the horses. Another bunch was setting up some objects shaped like giant kettles behind the dunes. Others, messengers she supposed, rode hastily back and forth on foaming horses. Officers yelled at everyone, and some cracked whips.

I feel sorry for the foreigners. If they knew what a big army was waiting for them here, they'd never have come.

Dodging soldiers, she hurried toward the dunes, and before she expected it, was staring at the sea. She gasped. The setting sun had turned the whole sky red. The towering grey clouds were all tinged with red, the waves that advanced toward her in endless rows were soaked in redness. It was as if a huge river of blood was rushing at her.

This can mean nothing good.

Appalled, it took her a moment to notice the slight figure, about her size, standing to one side in the dunes. Before she could hide, he turned, and in the same moment, they recognized each other.

"You!" they both exclaimed in astonishment.

It was her brother Rajik. He was a year younger than she. They'd played together as children, but for some time he was no longer allowed in the women's quarters, just as she was seldom allowed out.

To hide her surprise and confusion, she went on the offensive: "Rajik, what are you doing here, you reckless child! Don't you know you'll be whipped if Father finds you here?"

That's how Mother would say it.

But Rajik stood his ground. "I should ask you that question. You of all people should not be in this place of men. You are putting our family's honor at risk!"

Now he sounds like his father!

"I asked first! Answer the question!"

"Fine, I snuck away because I wanted to see the foreigners. Now you!"

It was no good lying to Rajik. He was clever, and if he told anyone she was here, she might be killed. She'd have to take him into her confidence.

"Brother, I am in trouble, and you must help me. Look!"

She removed the makeshift turban, revealing her short-cropped hair.

Rajik gaped at her. "But . . . but why?"

"Because there's no other way. Because Father wants to marry me to the Amir, Qilij the Cruel, and no dog should have such a fate."

"But Qilij is a rich and powerful man!"

"And fifty years old, and two wives already, and several children older than I am!"

Rajik spoke slowly and loudly, as if he were talking to an idiot or one hard of hearing: "But he's a rich and powerful man!"

"He killed Samia the courtesan, had her whipped to death because of some stupid flower a soldier gave her!"

"It was a token of love! She betrayed him!"

"And what of Nazif the stable boy? He didn't fasten a horse's girth tight enough. Bang went the Amir, down in the mud, in all his fine clothing. He hit the boy just once with a stick, and that was the end of him!"

"He was . . . he was . . ." While Rajik was searching for words, Raeesha brought out her strongest weapon:

"Look at me, brother! It's too late to go back! I have cut my hair and cannot put it on again!"

"But our whole family will be ruined!"

"What is done is done. Look there." She pointed to the west, where the last glowing redness was fading from the sky. "The foreigners are coming. They'll be here soon, and then who knows what will happen? We could all be killed. And the Amir could be killed. Perhaps the foreigners will overrun the whole district."

"That will never happen!"

"This may happen or that may happen, but one thing will *never* happen, and that is I will marry Amir Qilij!"

They yelled at each other in the darkness until they were hoarse. Then they began to shiver in the cold sea air and, feeling hungry and afraid, found a sheltered spot in the dunes, shared some of the bread, and presently fell asleep.

Raeesha was the first to waken. The light was dim, but she could hear the tramping of many feet, and the sound of horses. She shook Rajik to wake him up.

"We have to move. The soldiers are coming. They'll find us here. You'll surely be whipped, and I may be killed!"

"Whuhuh?" Rajik sat up and rubbed his eyes. Raeesha took his hand and dragged him away from the menacing sounds, toward the beach, and there she saw something she could never have imagined.

At first, she thought there was a low bank of clouds over the sea. But as the sun grew brighter, she saw they were not clouds, they were sails, hundreds and hundreds of white sails, with brightly colored banners speckled among them. They stretched as far as she could see, almost from one edge of the horizon to the other.

"The foreigners are here! You wanted to see the foreigners? There they are!"

They both stared as the rising sun touched the top sails, turning them to gold. For a moment, they forgot where they were, and Raeesha at first mistook the glowing red dots for another reflection. But as they grew in size, she realized they were flying toward the shore, gaining speed as they travelled. At first faintly, she could hear

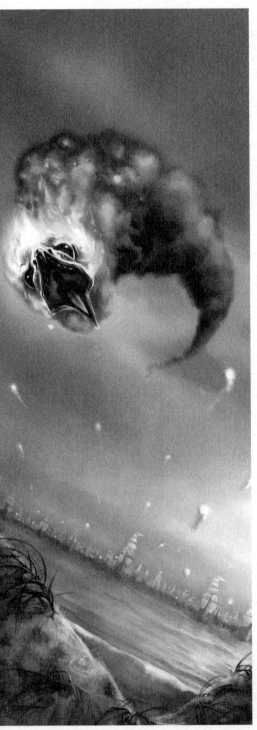

a high-pitched screeching.

BOOM!

Something struck one of the dunes about fifty feet away. Suddenly, the air was full of choking, sulfurous smoke. Sand rained down on them.

"What was that!" she said.

"A fire-demon! They're throwing fire-demons at us! Look out!"

Raeesha had just time to turn her head and observe a ball of fire rushing at her, and in the middle a strange, inhuman face whose open mouth emitted one loud unbroken screech.

That was when Rajik pushed her down in the sand and fell on top of her.

2: Singer

They'd gotten about half way to shore when Capt. Hinman's head exploded.

He was standing as high as he could on the prow, to get a better look at the shore bombardment, and giving one of his spontaneous lectures on tactics to the available audience, which was his adjutant, Lt. Singer, the quartermaster, Sgt. Pennesey, the chaplain, Father Leo, and old Dr. Murdoch. Indifferent to military glory, all four were crouching as low as they could in the madly rocking boat, along with everyone else who was not obliged to row. Every few seconds, a screecher would go whizzing over their heads, or one of the enemy springers would send up a huge fountain of spray nearby, making them want to crouch even lower.

Hinman didn't call them cowards, though there was a superior kind of smirk on his face as he informed them there was no chance of being hit: "Look, the screechers are aimed well over our heads, or there would be no possibility of reaching the shore. And the enemy has nothing but indirect fire weapons which are only good for killing fish. Look at that!"

Singer raised his head just enough to peer over the gunwale, catching a glimpse of screecher flying past, not more than ten feet away, looking like an airborne bonfire and wailing like a lost soul from hell, which he guessed it probably was. It flew in a straight line toward its target, which was a row of sand dunes with the crimson-silver Bandeluk flag visible above them, still almost half a mile away. A little puff of sand marked its impact. Squinting, with the sun in his face, Singer saw no enemy soldiers anywhere. They must have been sheltering behind the dunes, a very sensible thing to do.

"What a waste!" Hinman shook his head in the manner of a schoolmaster correcting a persistently dull child. "We came equipped for a naval battle, whereas the Bandeluks are ready to fight us in the field, and neither is really prepared for an amphibious invasion. Now if . . ."

KAKAKRUNCH!

The boat shook and Singer stared stupidly at his left arm, wondering why it was suddenly spattered with blood, but then Hinman's body fell over on him, blood still pumping from the arteries in the neck and making a mess of Singer's fine linen surcoat. Hinman's bearded head was nowhere to be seen.

He looked at Sgt. Pennesey, a small, sad-faced man with a droopy mustache, who seemed almost as dumbfounded as Singer was. "Seventeen," Pennesey said loudly, as if this was a crucial piece of information he should report at once. Dr. Murdoch merely grimaced at the corpse. Father Leo had closed his eyes; his lips were moving in prayer.

Behind them, the rowers had stopped rowing, and were simply clutching their oars, those who hadn't lost theirs over the side. The boat was ankle-deep with water, which was quickly getting deeper as they turned sideways to the swells.

What would Hinman do? He'd stand up and yell something and get us moving again.

Singer stood up and yelled, as loudly as he could: "IDIOTS! KEEP ROWING! TURN US TO SHORE!"

They were soldiers, used to taking orders, but they hadn't much nautical experience, and so it took a few minutes before they were straightened out and moving toward the beach again. Singer had the ones without oars use their helmets to bail out the boat.

(He later determined an unusually accurate, or maybe just lucky, springer had landed in the middle of Boat Seventeen, scattering pieces of wood, together with the remains of ten soldiers, three sailors and a couple days worth of supplies, in all directions. One of these fragments, he never knew exactly what, had collided with the late Capt. Hinman's head.)

With Hinman's unexpected death, there was no one left to take charge but Singer, who was more of a glorified secretary and errand boy than a soldier . . . but that didn't matter anymore. He had to stay alive, which meant keeping the rest of the people in the boat alive, and so found himself standing in the prow as Hinman had done, trying to project an air of confidence, while concealing the fact he actually had no idea what he was doing.

Hinman would probably look around coolly and assess the tactical situation.

So that was what Singer tried to do . . . and damn it, they were falling behind the other boats, which would soon pile up on the shore, small groups of confused men, waiting for a leader who wasn't there to give them orders.

"FASTER!" Singer yelled. "GET THIS THING MOVING! WE'RE DEAD MEN IF WE DON'T GET TO THE SHORE!"

The situation on the shore, when he got there, was almost as bad as he'd imagined. Lt. Fleming had managed to collect most of his hundred crossbowmen, and Lt. Pohler had lined up almost all of his spearman, but they were over a hundred yards away from him, and further than that from each other. The majority of the thousand-strong Halland Company were scattered in small clumps or milling around, looking for someone to give them orders.

One good thing: The enemy hadn't yet decided the bombardment was over, that it was safe to come and drive the invaders from the beach. It wouldn't take them long to figure it out, though.

Singer fished around in the blood and the muck in the bottom of the boat until he found something which he prayed hadn't been washed overboard: Captain Himman's heavy, gold chain of office. He put it on his own neck, the solid weight giving him a new feeling of authority.

"RAISE THE FLAGS!"

The soldiers scrambled to erect the flagpole, which was in two 7-foot sections, and before long the blue-and-white Halland flag was fluttering where everyone on the beach could see it. It was soon joined by the silver-black Free State banner.

"SOUND ASSEMBLY!"

Kyle the bugle boy let out some notes on his trumpet. No one appeared to notice.

"LOUDER!"

Kyle, a plump orphan whose main asset was a good pair of lungs, blew with all he had, and, without waiting for orders, repeated the call.

Now, everyone noticed the flags and was moving in that direction, Fleming and Pohler's men double-timing it in good order, the rest a mob.

"FALL IN! FORM THREE LINES! SPEARMEN FORE!"

The soldiers, even those slow on the uptake, needed no further instructions. The Halland Company was quickly turning from a herd of bewildered men into its familiar shape: four groups of a hundred spearmen, the crossbowmen standing similarly behind them, and two hundred halberdiers, divided in groups of forty, behind that. There were gaps in the lines – already, eleven men were at the bottom of Massera Bay – but the gaps were soon closed.

Those without a place in the formation gathered behind him: mainly the headquarters staff, Pennesey's cooks and clerks, Father Leo, Dr. Murdoch, Kyle the bugle-boy and Sgt. Littleton, the engineer. Littleton, with a couple assistants, was trying to assemble one of the big siege crossbows, a heavy tripod-mounted weapon which could fire a three-foot iron bolt about half a mile.

"Up there, sir," said Kyle, pointing.

Singer caught his first glimpse of the enemy. With the sun behind him, it at first looked like an armored giant ten feet tall. But as his eyes adjusted, he saw the man was mounted on a warhorse. An extravagantly plumed helmet added to the illusion of enormous size.

The Bandeluk complacently surveyed the Halland Company from a dune two hundred yards away, stroking his mustache as if trying to choose the best method of exterminating them, out of several attractive possibilities.

Singer grabbed the nearest crossbowman by the shoulder. Blaine was it? Yes, definitely Blaine. "See if you can knock that jackdaw from his perch."

"Yes, sir!"

Blaine (or was it Halverson?) took aim. The range was long for the light Hallandic crossbow, but there was a coiled spring in the stock which could re-cock it, if the first shot missed.

The first shot hit, but bounced off the Bandeluk's breastplate of heavy metal scales. Nothing worried, he waved contemptuously at the invaders, and turned his horse to descend, without haste, from his position on the dune.

The second shot caught him in the back, where the armor was thinner. He fell forward, clutching the horse's neck. The frightened horse soon carried him out of sight.

"Good shot, Blaine!"

"Eckhard, sir."

"Yes, good shot, Eckhard, good shot!"

Lt. Fleming, a thin, hawk-nosed man, looked behind him to see who had opened fire. Seeing Singer wearing Hinman's gold chain, he smirked and seemed about to say something . . . but then he changed his mind.

There was a dazzling flash of light from many polished helmets. Up in the dunes, where the Bandeluk officer had been a moment before, there were hundreds of lancers. They paused only a second before advancing out of sight, behind the next row of dunes, and were immediately replaced by another line of lancers.

"Oh gods," said Singer. "PREPARE TO RECEIVE CAVALRY!"

As they'd practiced many times, the spearmen grounded their shields and crouched behind them. There was a spike on the butt end of their twelve-foot spears and a slot in each shield to hold the spear steady. The crossbowmen, standing behind the shield wall, shuffled around as each man sought a clear line of fire.

The first cavalry line was now cresting the nearest dunes, about a hundred yards away, and a third line had appeared behind the second. There must be over a thousand of them, Singer estimated.

"HOLD YOUR FIRE! HOLD IT!"

A lot of nervous hands rested on the triggers of the crossbows, but none went off. The Bandeluks in the first line were picking up speed now in the hard-packed beach sand, beginning their final gallop. They let loose a loud and intimidating war whoop.

"AIM AT THE HORSES!" yelled Singer, and shortly, when the lancers were about fifty yards away: "FIRE! FIRE AT WILL!"

Four hundred crossbows went off at once. Over half of them buried themselves in horseflesh. Suddenly, the air was full of the dreadful, shrill sound of screaming horses.

The remaining lancers in the first line now had two bolts each aimed at them from point blank range, and most went down. In front of the shield wall, the beach was strewn with fallen, screaming, kicking horses and their armored riders, who were trying to get to their feet or calling desperately for help. It was a hellish, chaotic scene, one which both stunned Singer and pleased him: The next wave of horsemen would have to get past their fallen comrades.

On the other hand, the crossbowmen had shot their bolts and would need a minute before they could fire again. There was nothing now that Singer could do but watch. The fight was in the hands of lieutenants and sergeants and individual soldiers.

Should I draw my sword? No, the men will know I'm afraid. Then, they will be afraid.

If the fallen riders of the first line had expected their comrades to aid them, they were cruelly disappointed. The second line, full of zeal to get at the enemy, rode down everything in the way, causing almost as many casualties as the crossbows had in the first place.

Being charged by cavalry is one of the most frightening things a soldier can experience. The Halland Company could only brace themselves and wait as the line of hungry lance points came down on them.

Every one of the lancers knew this: The shield wall was just an inch thick. A charging horse could easily knock it over, and then they'd be among the helpless crossbowmen, who were still cocking their weapons.

But their horses knew only this: For some insane reason, they were running headlong into a solid, four-foot wall bristling with spears. They began pushing each other in order to get to the ends, or else to one of the small gaps which had been intentionally left in the formation. Cursing, the lancers struggled with their reins, but the horses were stronger.

As the second line approached the shield wall, it was no longer a neat line of charging lancers, but a mob of riders trying to control their horses, which were bunching up and running into each other.

Many tried to stop at the last moment, and the riders went tumbling. A few tried to jump over and were impaled. Those who made it through the gaps or around the ends of the formation had to face the waiting halberdiers.

The halberd is a weapon which has a spear useful for poking at horsemen and also a hook for pulling them from their saddles and also a pole ax for chopping through their armor. All three were much in use. It was more butchery than battle.

The lances were too bulky to be good for much except charging. Some were dropped, and the lancers drew their swords, swinging at anything within reach. Others dropped their shields instead, and tried to use the lances two-handed. But the spearmen now stood up, and extending their weapons, began forcing them back.

Where's the rest of the cavalry?

The third line of Bandeluk lancers, presumably not the most valorous of the lot, were standing immobile, on the nearest row of dunes and staring at the melee. A lancer had only one effective tactic, the charge, and there was nowhere to do that now.

Meanwhile, the crossbowmen, one by one, were readying their weapons. First one lancer and then another fell; their armor couldn't withstand the bolts at such short range.

Whoever was in charge of the Bandeluks came to a conclusion. A whistle sounded, and the whole mob of horsemen, those who could still ride or run, turned and, following the third line, disappeared behind the dunes. An exuberant cheer went up from the Halland troops. They'd suffered hardly any losses, and already the battle seemed won.

"FORM UP! KEEP YOUR POSITION! THE FIGHT ISN'T OVER! HALBERD MEN, TAKE CARE OF THE WOUNDED!"

The halberdiers advanced to take care of the enemy wounded, which did not mean medical attention. Dr. Murdoch, on the other side, was already seeing to their own wounded, who were surprisingly few. Sgt. Littleton was still single-mindedly trying to assemble his siege crossbow, paying no attention to the rest of the battle.

What a bloody, ugly mess! Are all battles like this? I think I picked the wrong profession!

What followed was an appalling silence. The men shifted uncomfortably, waiting for the enemy to come back. Some glanced over their shoulders, to see who was giving orders, but the blood-spattered surcoat and chain of office told plainly why Singer was in charge. When he saw Singer wearing the chain, Lt. Pohler turned an angry red, but he was too good a soldier to raise objections in the middle of a battle.

Singer glanced out to sea, to estimate how soon the second wave would be there. Most of them seemed hardly to be moving, but a small group of boats was pushing ahead with astonishing speed.

Who are those guys?

His own men were getting restless. With the wind behind them, it was impossible to hear what was happening on the other side of the dunes. Singer was about to call for a volunteer to go scouting, when the horsemen reappeared. This time, they were in two groups, right and left, and both out of bowshot.

"FORM A SQUARE!"

The Halland Company pulled back into one of its well-practiced formations, this time with the spearmen facing in four directions, halberdiers on the corners and the rest in the middle. All of them, that is, except for Sgt. Littleton, who had finished bolting together the beams of the tripod and was struggling to lift the crossbow assembly onto the swivel of his siege machine. Singer grabbed him by the collar and hauled him, protesting, away from his project.

The lancers lined up to the north and south of them on the beach. They now had a perfect area for a charge, and each group was facing only a fraction of the invaders' strength. But they didn't charge. Stuck in the middle of his square, Singer could barely make out what they were doing.

The enemy's plan soon became apparent. A line of spearmen, at least a thousand strong, appeared on the crest of the distant dunes and began shuffling slowly down the slope. These men, Singer could see, were dressed in white and had no armor, only their spears and large, rectangular shields.

"HOLD YOUR FIRE!"

It would be useless to shoot at those heavy-looking shields at long range. But the long line of enemy infantry, if nothing stopped it, would swamp the Halland Company. As Singer watched, a second line of infantry appeared behind the first.

Shit! Now we're done for!

Similar thoughts were obviously crossing the minds of the men in the ranks, which shifted nervously as a third row appeared behind the second. Military discipline and tactics counted for very little against such numbers.

As the first line of infantry crested the nearest dunes, Singer noticed there were others behind them, driving them forward with whips. It was then he had one of his rare strokes of brilliance.

"SECOND GROUP CROSSBOWS! AIM AT THE MEN WITH WHIPS! REPEAT, AIM AT THE MEN WITH WHIPS! FIRE WHEN READY!"

Hitting such elusive targets at that range was difficult at best, but when a hundred men took their best shots, some were going to hit. One by one, the crossbowmen facing the oncoming infantry loosed. Many shots flew over the heads of their targets, and some struck the spearmen instead. (Singer noted, to his relief, the shields were not nearly as heavy as he'd thought.) But here and there, the men armed with whips went down, and the enemy spearmen began to hesitate.

When they saw they were being targeted, the whip-wielders took shelter behind the spearmen. For this, the crossbowmen had a ready answer: A bolt struck down a spearmen, and a second shot was then aimed at the man hiding behind him. Seeing his shield was scant protection, one spearman simply dropped his weapons and fell on his face, and soon the rest followed his example.

The second row of spearmen, as they encountered their prone comrades, fell to the ground in imitation, and the whip men behind them were left without protection, dancing around, cursing and swinging their useless whips before more prudently taking cover behind the dunes.

Looks like we may survive after all . . . what's that?

He turned his head just in time to see the lancers on his left side charging directly at him. He had just time enough to yell:

"RECEIVE CAVALRY! FIRE AT WILL!"

Then five hundred horsemen were all around them, galloping furiously, but staying just out of spear range. Here and there, the jittery crossbowmen took one down.

What the hell are they doing?

The lancers surged around them, as water in a stream flows around a large stone, and then they were gone, moving as fast as they could to their comrades on the other flank. These were attacking some boats which had just landed.

The second wave! It's here!

But there were only handful of men who had landed so far, and they'd surely be overwhelmed by the horde of cavalry which was descending on them. Singer turned to the men on his right.

"OSGOOD! BEECHER! ADVANCE! GIVE THOSE MEN SOME SUPPORT!"

Pohler was glaring at him now, his scarred face furious. This was extremely risky, breaking up his defensive square by detaching two hundred men, but if the landing failed, they'd all die anyway. Singer sent some halberdiers to fill the gap temporarily.

Peering into the distance, he could see the desperate fight. A small group of friendlies were clustered around the landing boats. They looked like women in green armor.

Women? Has the Prince gotten amazon warriors from somewhere?

Mounted Bandeluks were swarming around them, poking with their lances. As he watched, one of the women grabbed a lance by the sharp end, yanked it from the owner's hand, and proceeded to swing it around like a club, unhorsing one rider after the other.

How is that possible? Oh, gods, those aren't women!

He remembered now the rumor he'd heard from Pennesey while they were on the ship. He hadn't believed it, but now he did: The Free State of Westenhausen, assessed five hundred pikemen for the expedition, had offered instead fifty demon infantry.

These, then, were the notorious *fui* demons. Who else could withstand a thousand armored cavalry with less than a hundred infantry?

In the open, the *fui* demons, dangerous though they were, might have been ridden down. But, as he saw, they'd hauled in the boats and turned them over to make a kind of fort the lancers rode furiously around, but couldn't penetrate. Piles of dead Bandeluks and their horses filled the gaps between the boats.

Clever, too, the cursed things!

The Bandeluks were drawing back for another charge when they were hit unexpectedly by a shower of crossbow bolts, and Osgood's hundred spears came at them from behind. Cursing and shouting, they retreated into the dunes.

That looks like a victory! We won!

A little while before, he'd been ready to die, but now the surviving cavalry had retreated in disorder, and the infantry was still prone, not even daring to raise their heads.

Is it really over? Gods, I hope so!

He sent a runner to retrieve Osgood and Beecher and ordered the rest of his men to occupy the dunes. While they were doing that, a runner came over from the *fui* demons. His men eagerly stepped aside when it passed, and Father Leo made a warding gesture, which it ignored.

Singer had never seen a *fui* demon so close before. This one was about seven feet tall, but wider in the hips than the shoulders. He could see why he had, from a distance, mistaken them for women. Of course, women were not covered with green scales, nor did they have tails.

The demon was dripping dark red blood from a gash on its left arm, a wound which it didn't seem to notice. It stared at him through the eyeholes of an ornate silver mask, which reminded him, insanely, of the face of Narina, the goddess of mercy. From behind the mask came a buzzing sound, like angry bees trying to make conversation:

"You are *bzzz* leader here?"

Oh good, it speaks Akaddian, as do I, how convenient.

"Yes, I am Singer. Who are

you?"

"I am *bzzz* called Twenty *bzzz* Three. What *bzzz* are your orders?"

"That's a good question. Take your men, uh, troops to Prince Krion. He should be somewhere south of here. Tell him the northern landing zone is secure, and ask for further orders."

"Yes *bzzz.*"

The demon went springing away, leaving deep claw marks in the sand. Singer tried to forget about it and turned his mind to other matters.

There was no more fight left in the enemy spearmen, and to all appearances, there had never been much. He could see now they were chained together at the ankle.

To keep them from running away, how very practical. But it also kept them from advancing, after the first ones were shot down. Not too smart after all.

They were still lying on the ground, some of their white garments spattered with blood, and many bearing the marks of whips on the back or shoulders. Singer had never seen a more miserable and dispirited bunch. The whip men had fled, which was wise of them, because he'd gladly have killed them all.

"Sgt. Littleton! Find something to get these chains off!"

Littleton fiddled a moment with one of the tools he'd been using to assemble his siege crossbow, before taking something more useful from the belt of a dead whip man.

The captives were talking softly to each other in some language Singer didn't recognize. He approached the nearest one, addressing him in Bandeluki.

"What is your name?"

The man only stared at him, nonplussed. He tried the next one.

"What is your name?"

"Harim, oh master."

"I am not your master. Call me Singer."

"Yes, oh singer."

"Where are you from?"

"Fallingstone village, oh singer."

"What will you do when you're free?"

"I will go home, oh singer."

"Do that, but take this with you." He handed the man a spear.

Harim shook his head. "The masters will kill me if they find me with a spear."

Singer pointed toward the beach, where the corpses of hundreds of Bandeluks were visible. "Those were your masters. They're dead. Today, you are a free man. Take the spear."

Reluctantly, Harim took it.

He's going to throw it into a ditch, the first chance he gets.

"Harim of Fallingstone village, I'm coming to visit you someday. And if I find you don't have a spear, you will be whipped. Do you understand?"

"Yes, oh singer."

"But if you have a spear, neither I nor anyone else will whip you ever again. You understand?"

"Yes, oh singer."

Littleton freed him. Singer watched a moment as the pathetic figure stumbled away, using his spear as a walking stick.

How did we ever get into a war with these wretched people?

Singer detailed Pennesey's men to help Littleton gather up the tools and free the other captives. Then he picked up a whip and cracked it in the air, noticing many of them winced. In his best Bandeluki, he yelled:

"LISTEN! I AM SINGER. I AM SENDING YOU HOME. BUT YOU WILL NOT BE ALLOWED TO GO UNLESS YOU ARE CARRYING A SPEAR OR A SWORD. IN THE FUTURE, ANY OF YOU WHO DO NOT HAVE A WEAPON WILL BE WHIPPED BY MY SOLDIERS."

He cracked the whip again for emphasis. There was a lot of whispering in the strange language as those captives who couldn't hear or couldn't understand what Singer said had the new policy explained to them.

This is awful. Now, I'm threatening them with a whip. It was easier dealing with the demon.

He was detailing Doctor Murdoch and some volunteers to bandage the wounded enemy spearmen, when someone else came running up, a crossbowman.

"Message from Lt. Fleming, sir! He needs you in the enemy camp!" He pointed toward a place behind the dunes, where the colorful Bandeluk tents were visible.

Fleming! Of course, he'd be the first to the enemy camp!

(Years before, when Singer was still a boy, Pohler and Fleming had participated in the storming of the pirate stronghold at Mirajil. Pohler had returned from the campaign with much glory, many scars and a fine collection of weapons, and had since made a meager living as a swordmaster. Fleming, however, had returned with a mysterious, heavy box, and shortly thereafter bought a prosperous tavern near the barracks. They hated each other, in the way only old comrades can.)

It was not far to the camp, where he observed a crowd of crossbowmen surrounding a half-grown boy, who was swinging a scimitar around and cursing them in Bandeluki. He was dressed like a servant, and his hands were blistered and cut, as if he'd been working in the kitchen.

"We have a prisoner," Fleming informed him pleasantly. "But I can't speak that awful language, and I can't get him to drop the sword, and I don't have the heart to kill the poor wretch."

You mean, you didn't find much in the tents and you want me to persuade him to tell us where his master hid all the loot.

Approaching the Bandeluk, Singer told him in his own language to drop the scimitar, but the wild youth only turned and slashed at him. With a single motion, Singer drew his own sword and knocked the scimitar flying.

"Your life is a gift, boy, don't throw it away."

The boy drew a curved knife. "I take no gifts from my enemies, who have slain my brother!"

Well, I got him talking anyway.

"There's nothing you can do for your brother. Your mother is already weeping for one son. Don't make her weep for two."

This had an unexpected effect on the youth, who fell to his knees and began crying like a girl. "I have no mother or father or sister or brother! And no home! The only one who cared for me was my brother, and he is dead."

"So you thought you'd end it all? We're not in that business. We don't kill children. What kind of monsters do you think we are?"

This only made him cry louder.

This is really a hard one. I know how to fight the Bandeluks, but what am I to do with weeping children?

Soldiers were coming from all directions to stare at the spectacle. One of them was Sgt. Pennesey, who tapped him on the shoulder. "I could probably find him something to do in the kitchen, if you please, sir. I can speak a bit of the language."

"Well, that sounds good, but teach him a few words of Hallandish. And try not to get stabbed."

"You aren't going to interrogate him?" Fleming seemed almost insulted.

"Where's the hurry? He's just some kitchen knave. What we need to do now is call roll, station sentries, move up the supplies and reinforcements, lay out a camp, take inventory of the spoils . . ."

Fleming's face was getting red. "Wait, a minute, who do you think you are . . ."

"WHAT THE HELL IS GOING ON HERE?"

It was Lt. Pohler, and he was even angrier than Fleming.

"Who told you to play captain?" Pohler seemed about to grab the golden chain from Singer, who took a step back.

"It was just temporary . . ."

"It's getting too damned permanent for me. Take that off NOW!"

Singer was ready to do that, but then Fleming grabbed him by the shoulder.

"So you can put it on, you mean? What gives you the right to do that?"

Uh-oh, serving under Capt. Pohler would be a nightmare for Fleming.

"It goes to the senior officer!" Pohler replied.

"You aren't the senior officer, just the oldest one, and in any case, no one is entitled to promotion without . . ."

Singer, who had been standing there, listening to them argue, noticed it was getting dark. The officers were coming in to hear the loud argument, and the soldiers they were supposed to supervise were milling around, each one on his own. Now, it was his turn to get angry.

"SHUT UP, THE BOTH OF YOU!"

Pohler and Fleming were momentarily startled, and just stared at him.

"I don't care who gets to be captain, but we're wasting time. All we need to do is assemble the officers and take a vote . . ."

At this point, a *fui* demon surprised everyone by appearing on a nearby dune and running into the center of the milling crowd of soldiers without pausing for them to get out of the way. There was a series of loud *CLUNKS* as armored figures went down right and left, followed by the ominous *SWISH* of many swords leaving their scabbards.

It was Twenty Three. Singer could see the wound on its left arm, now almost healed.

Oh great, they regenerate too! Does the other side have any of these?

Paying no attention to the circle of drawn weapons, the demon went straight to Singer. "Prince Krion *bzzz* congratulates *bzzz* Capt. Singer, *bzzz* and urgently requests *bzzz* his presence *bzzz* in his tent."

3: Krion

My officers are such idiots!

The landings had gone well enough. The flat southern shoreline provided the enemy with no cover from the initial bombardment, which drove them inland. But then, before he had advanced a mile, more and more enemy reserves began showing up, eventually numbering about thirty companies, so he was forced to break off the advance and form up his troops (though many had not yet landed) in battle array.

The Bandeluks had evidently expected a landing on the ample beaches of the southern shore and had concentrated their troops there. Their numbers were almost overwhelming. Krion's line was in danger of being engulfed on both flanks, when his father's elite cavalry, the Twelve Hundred Heroes, as they called themselves, rode down some negligible infantry and charged straight into the enemy camp, which they paused to loot.

This left a large gap on Krion's left flank, into which the Bandeluks poured a regiment of heavy cavalry. Krion had nothing to respond with except for his own personal guard, the Brethren. They were the best soldiers in the world, in his opinion, but they were badly outnumbered. The Bandeluk cavalry drove them back.

Meanwhile, the inhuman Ragmen, who he'd counted on to break the enemy center, had run into a company of mercenary pike, which didn't stop them, but slowed them down considerably. On the right flank, his brother Clenas had enmeshed the Royal Light Cavalry in a long, indecisive skirmish with some enemy lancers. It looked like the invasion of the Bandeluk Empire would be over before it began.

Krion threw himself and his staff into the fight where the line was weakest, on the left flank. As he hoped, this gave some spirit to the Brethren, who rallied around him and began pushing the enemy back. However, the rest of the enemy cavalry, by its sheer numbers, threatened to surround him.

At this point, when the situation was most desperate, he noticed the banner of Westenhausen ahead of him, in the enemy's rear. It was getting closer.

Westenhausen? What are they doing here?

He remembered only a small group of auxiliaries from Westenhausen, who were supposed to be landing with the rest of the Free State Contingent, miles to the north. But now, they were less than a thousand yards away and apparently advancing toward him.

Or have they gone over to the other side?

While he was pondering this question, a huge Bandeluk officer tried to take his head off with a scimitar. He parried the swing and thrust the point of his sword in the man's face. Thereafter, the Bandeluks were coming at him from all sides, and he was too busy to consider the tactical situation.

Meanwhile, the Bandeluk commander, who was surveying the battle from a small hillock, came to a fateful decision. He couldn't see what troops bore the Westenhausen banner, but he presumed it was at least a company. Behind them, where the sun was approaching the horizon, more of the Prince's soldiers – it was hard to say how many – were landing on the shore.

In this situation, he gave what seemed a prudent order: Of the three cavalry squadrons on his right flank, one was to continue pressing Krion, the second was to turn and face the Westenhausen forces, and the third was to pull back and prepare for a charge.

In theory, this was very sound, but he hadn't taken into account the exuberance of his elite soldiers, who thought the battle already won and were outdoing each other in their efforts to get at the Prince. All three formations were mixed together in great confusion. Two of his messages miscarried, and only the third, ordering a withdrawal, reached the intended officer, who shrugged and sounded the recall.

Retreating Bandluks now got in the way of those still trying to attack, and many who noticed an enemy flag in their rear and their own comrades withdrawing, joined what swiftly became a rout. But this disorganized mass of cavalry hadn't retreated very far before encountering the Twelve Hundred Heroes, still in the Bandeluk camp. The Heroes hastily stuffed what loot they'd collected in their saddle bags and mounted up to face the enemy.

The Bandeluk cavalry, threatened on three sides, now fled in all directions. This further disheartened the enemy pike, who were already alarmed by the discovery their weapons could impale the Ragmen, but not kill them. They left their pikes in the bodies of the still-advancing Ragmen and joined the retreat.

On the Bandeluk left flank, away from the rest of the battle, enemy lancers had been furiously trying to engage Clenas' light horse, which fired arrows at them and scampered away when they charged. Seeing the Bandeluk line dissolving, the commander there decided to pull back his own intact force, in order to protect his retreating comrades. However, this meant the lancers had to expose their thinly-armored backs to the enemy, a maneuver fatal to many of them. The Royal Light Cavalry pursued, but without Clenas, who had fallen from his horse.

Recovering from the frenzy of close combat as the last of his Bandeluk attackers fell, Krion saw the situation had completely reversed itself: The enemy line was broken, the Bandeluks were fleeing, and his forces were advancing triumphantly.

At this moment, he turned to see one of the lizardy *fui* demons, bearing the flag of Westenhausen. Another approached, saluted, and in its buzzing voice said: "Capt. Singer *bzzz* of the Halland Company *bzzz* wishes to report *bzzz* the northern landing zone *bzzz* is now secure *bzzz*. He awaits *bzzz* further orders."

Capt. Singer? Who in the name of all devils is he?

Krion only dimly remembered a baby-faced Lt. Singer who clung like a leech to the shoulder of Capt. Hinman.

Hinman must be dead, then, and the Hallanders have appointed a new captain without my permission. I should probably punish them for that, but all things in good time. Right now, I need a hero. Let's hope he looks the part.

"Congratulations to Capt. Singer. I urgently request his presence in my tent."

Victories are the kind of honey that attracts a lot of flies.

Gleeful, victorious officers streamed into his tent, in anticipation of honors and promotions. His brother Clenas strutted about with his arm in a sling, as if he'd been wounded. The greybeards (as Krion thought of his father's old officers) were clustered around Gen. Basilius, commander of the Twelve Hundred Heroes, loading him with praise for breaking through the enemy line and then turning to attack from the rear.

Krion slapped everyone on the back as they came in and gave them a hearty "Well done!" But inwardly, he thought:

What a lot of useless twits! Clenas is worthless as a command-

er. He couldn't even stay on his horse. And Basilius nearly got us all killed with his greed for loot. I can't give undeserved rewards to my own brother without insulting everyone else, and the best reward I can give Basilius is not to sack him on the spot. Still, a hero must be found.

His staff historian was probably already writing a narrative in which his personal courage, plunging into the enemy ranks, had turned the tide and saved the day. The fact he really had no control over the army, outside of his Brethren, after the initial dispositions, was not the kind of thing that historians were paid to write.

And certainly not that our ever-glorious army was rescued from destruction by a tiny group of demon auxiliaries from one of the puny Free States.

Meanwhile, he needed to pull the reins on his officers and lower their expectations a bit.

Or perhaps more than a bit.

"Gentlemen! Friends! There is no time for celebration! We've driven the enemy back, not destroyed him. We'll meet him again, and perhaps quite soon. When the final battle is won, there will be time enough for parades. What I urgently need to hear from each of you, is a report on your troops' condition and your counsel as to our next course of action."

I have to go through this stupid thing every damn time.

But it always worked: Instead of clamoring for honors and promotions, the officers had to go through the awkward business of reporting their losses and compete with each other to demonstrate their strategic brilliance. All agreed a rapid advance on Kafra was called for, but each emphasized the important role of his own particular troops.

Clenas proposed the Royal Light Cavalry should lead the van, a task for which it was particularly well suited. Basilius responded the Royal Light Cavalry had done nothing to deserve such an honor, whereas tradition and precedent (here his argument grew long and tedious) entitled the Twelve Hundred Heroes to go first. There was a muttering of approval from the greybeards.

These fools are more afraid of eating each other's dust than losing a battle. Light cavalry is obviously better for the mission, but the greybeards won't admit this, if it means yielding to Clenas. I need a distraction!

At this moment, a young man entered the tent, clad in the reinforced light chainmail and sallet favored by the Hallanders. His surcoat was splashed with blood – not his own, Krion noted. He might have been taken for a common soldier, except for the golden chain of office around his neck. Though broadly built, he had the innocent and timid look of a lamb which has wandered into a den of wolves.

There was a slight stir in the room, as a dozen renowned commanders, resplendent in their polished armor, turned their heads to stare at him. He pulled himself to full attention and said: "Lt. Singer reporting as ordered, sir!"

Well timed. Now let's see how well you play your role.

"At your ease, Singer. You are not to call me 'sir,' because I am not a 'sir,' I am Prince Krion. And so long as you're in my tent, you may call me Krion. This, by the way, is my brother, Prince Clenas, our second in command, and I'm sure he prefers to be called 'Your Highness.'"

There was a twitter of amusement. "Just 'Clenas,' thank you," said Clenas, embarrassed.

Pardon, me, brother, but a joke at your expense seldom goes amiss. Perhaps you should stop sleeping with other men's wives and develop a healthy interest in boys, like our dear brother Chryspos.

"The other introductions will have to wait. And, incidentally, you shouldn't refer to yourself as a lieutenant when you're wearing the insignia of a captain and filling that office. I take it the esteemed Capt. Hinman is no longer with us?"

"He died in the boat before we landed. I temporarily assumed his position."

"What position you assume, if any, is for me to decide. But first, tell us of our trusty Free State allies. I hope the landings went well?"

"Well enough, sir . . . uh, Krion. The Halland Company landed first, a thousand strong, and was immediately attacked by a force of about a twelve hundred Bandeluk lancers. They were shortly thereafter reinforced by approximately three thousand spearmen."

A murmur of incredulity came from the assembled officers.

"That sounds like very long odds."

Come on, let's hear it. Tell them what a hero you are!

"They were just a local levy, mainly reluctant conscripts, poorly trained and equipped. We killed three or four hundred men. When

the second wave began landing, the lancers fled, and the spearmen surrendered. I paroled them and sent them home with their weapons . . ."

There were several gasps of consternation.

"Wait a moment, Singer. You sent home three thousand armed enemy soldiers? How do you know they won't attack us again?"

"They were not Bandeluks, but some local tribe the Bandeluks had rounded up and chained together."

Oh, the Chatmaks. I was wondering when they'd show up.

"The Bandeluks were driving them around like cattle, with whips. I believe these peasants are much more of a threat to them than to us."

"But the Bandeluks have been defeated. This leaves us with three thousand armed and potentially rebellious peasants at our back."

"Or three thousand potential recruits, depending on how they're treated. We can, in any case, hardly afford to leave a large garrison, while the breadth of the Bandeluk Empire lies before us. And the region would be worthless without peasants to work the soil. These peasants can help supply our army, which is in a foreign land and far from its bases."

Oh, well played! I believe you

show some promise!

Nonetheless, Krion frowned, as if disapproving, and stroked his chin thoughtfully while the generals watched. Of course, he had already made his decision.

But let them wonder about it a moment longer!

"That's not exactly what I'd have done. Arming the peasantry is a dangerous expedient at best. But I'm reminded of one of my father's favorite dictums . . ."

Pay attention, you greybeards! I am my father's son!

" . . . 'Keep your friends united, and your enemies divided.' These Chatmaks will be of no further use to the Bandeluks, and might be some help to us. This shall be one of your responsibilities in your new post as general and commander of the Free State Contingent. I'd intended this position for the late Capt. Hinman, but as you've demonstrated your worthiness in battle, the promotion belongs to you."

It's either you or that ass Rendel!

Krion thought he detected a blush of maidenly modesty in the young Hallander's cheeks. "But this morning, I was only a lieutenant!'

I feel that way all the time, but I try not to show it.

"We were all of us lieutenants, and some not long ago. You've commanded a force of one thousand in battle, we shall now see if you can manage five. If you consider yourself unfit, you can board the next ship back to Halland, but if not, I am hereby putting the lives of five thousand men in your care, and more importantly, I am giving you my trust and confidence."

"I fear the more senior officers may not share your trust and confidence."

Very likely not.

"They'll have to. Take off that old pot." – He pointed to Singer's helmet. – "And leave it in the kitchen. Here is a real helmet, one of my own, which you shall wear with pride and honor."

From the wooden case, where it had lain all along, he produced a shining golden helmet, in the form of a lion or some other legendary beast. Its ruby eyes glared menacingly, as Singer timidly took it from the Prince and placed it on his own head.

"It's damned heavy," he complained.

Gentle, comradely chuckling came from the assembled officers, but not from Lessig, captain of the Covenant Sappers.

(Years before, during the Covenant War, Lessig had been the first of the aristo leaders to surrender. He was rewarded with an estate outside Eloni and a commission in the Akaddian army, but he was still a Covenant man, through and through.)

Poor Gen. Singer, you don't know the ladies of Covenant melted down their gold jewelry for this loving gift in tribute. How very upset they'd be to see a Free Stater strutting about with it on his head! But a bit of rivalry between our allies may keep them from conspiring against us. Sometimes it's a good thing to divide your friends as well as your enemies.

"This is the lightest of the burdens I'm laying on you today. The honor of Akaddia rests on your shoulders. Treat it with care.

"Now bring him a mirror, so he can see how splendid he looks."

The helmet had its intended effect. Staring into the offered mirror, Singer gaped, as if failing to recognize himself. Now, no one would mistake him for a common soldier. He was a truly commanding figure, as the ruby eyes and golden fangs of the helmet gave his every expression a forceful character.

It would take a brave man to question the authority of an officer who wears such a helmet, especially as it's my own.

One by one, the royal officers came forward to congratulate Singer and shake his hand. Last and most reluctantly came the greybeards, who were obviously fuming to see another of the Prince's "new men" promoted above them. Last of all was Lessig, who only managed to mutter "well done," before turning away.

You were also somewhat tardy in coming forward, dear Lessig, when I was nearly surrounded by 2,500 heavy cavalry, and your troops were assembling on the beach. If you're a secret anti-royalist, you may have to bear my disfavor quite awhile longer.

"Gentlemen! It is right and proper you should praise Gen. Singer for his services on this day. But I must bring you back to the business at hand, our advance into enemy territory.

"The Royal Light Cavalry shall leave before dawn to conduct a reconnaissance and clear the road of stragglers."

Even Clenas shouldn't have any trouble with riding down a few helpless stragglers. He's just the man for the job!

"The remainder of our troops must be ready to march at sunrise. We shall form two columns of two: The Brethren shall have the place of honor on the right, with the Twelve Hundred Heroes to their left."

You couldn't object to that, Basilius, you old war dog? No, you can't.

Then, as his aides feverishly took notes, he recited the place of every unit in order of march, with the Covenant Sappers coming last and charged with guarding the baggage.

Is there any real place for the Sappers? Not yet, at least.

"Any questions? Does everyone know his place in the order of march? If there are no questions, you're dismissed. Try to get some sleep. We'll be leaving quite early in the morning. Gen. Singer will remain while we discuss our position in the north."

The officers filed out. Singer had meanwhile taken off the heavy golden helmet and tucked it under his arm, as he'd seen the other officers do. He was standing self-consciously near the entrance, waiting for the Prince to say something. Krion took him by the arm and led him to the map table.

"Show me the disposition of your troops."

"As well as I can. I didn't actually have command of most of them until a few minutes ago, and the cavalry, last I saw, had not yet landed."

"That's not your fault. We needed the barges for the southern landing zone. What is your current position?"

"The Halland Company has occupied the enemy camp *here* and is taking inventory of the captured supplies and equipment. The other troops have bivouacked nearby, except for the Westenhausen demons, which have been assigned to take a forward position, a village about *here,* which was visible a few miles to the east."

"You don't want the demons in your camp? I don't blame you, but isn't such an exposed position dangerous?"

"Dangerous for any Bandeluks who run into them. The main enemy force is broken and scattered, and the survivors are not likely to seek further combat with the *fui* demons. Frankly, I have reservations about mixing demons with my own troops, at least until they get used to each other."

Which will be never.

"Sound reasoning! I assigned the Free State Contingent to this small bay on the assumption the Bandeluks wouldn't waste a lot of effort defending it, and I'm glad I was correct."

Because you'd all have been slaughtered if I were not.

"It is, however, of some strategic importance. Until we capture a major port, there's nowhere else to unload supplies."

Singer frowned. "I saw only a few fishing boats. There are no docks or quays, and the harbor is too shallow for large vessels."

"Then I'd better get my engineers to work right away. Tell me about the local labor force."

"If you mean the, uh, Chatmaks, I think they'd be surprised and pleased if anyone offered them some decent pay, instead of driving them to it with whips."

And since you sent them home with their weapons, whips would be out of the question.

"Very well, my staff will make a survey of the available resources, including labor and of course food. You will be responsible for security."

"Five thousand men sounds like a lot for a security detail."

"You may find restoring order to a conquered province will tax your resources. And there isn't much time. You were quite right when you said we can't afford to leave so many troops behind in a garrison.

"In a few days, two weeks at the most, you'll leave behind one company to keep the natives in line and march eastward. Your mission is to take the enemy fortress of Barbosa, *here*."

"I don't see how a few hundred men can control an entire province."

The easiest way is to devastate it, but too late for that.

"Their main responsibility is simply to keep the supply lines open. If your Chatmaks are so friendly, you can recruit some for a militia. They sound like people who are used to taking orders. In any case, you're only responsible for security. The administration of the province is for me to worry about."

Come on, you oaf, it's an easy task. The fighting is the hard part.

Singer was studying the map, and not looking very pleased at what he saw. "What's this line *here*?"

"An escarpment. Ask your Chatmaks how to climb it, if it's an obstacle."

"After the escarpment, it looks like at least a hundred miles of wild terrain before we reach Barbosa. And I don't see any roads."

"Tell your soldiers to pack thirty days rations."

"That doesn't leave much for a siege."

"So don't besiege it. Take it by storm or a ruse. Be clever."

Why do I have to think of everything?

Singer was biting his thumb. It had probably occurred to him if he failed to take Barbosa, his men would be stranded two hundred miles deep in enemy territory without provisions.

Which is why I'm giving the mission to someone expendable, not my own troops.

"What do we know about Barbosa?"

"It's an old stone fort left from the Kano-Indo Wars. Probably in bad repair. I doubt the garrison will give you much trouble."

"But why is there a fort there at all? It's sitting in the middle of nowhere."

"I can't tell you that. The main thing is, we can't allow the enemy to maintain a base on our flank which could threaten our supply lines."

"Understood. But what is this area *here,* labeled 'Madlands'? It looks like a complete blank."

You would notice that.

"The geographers couldn't tell me much about it. It appears to be an empty wasteland. My advice would be to stay out."

"That shouldn't be too hard, since there seems to be a chain of mountains in the way. Anything else I should know?"

"Nothing I can tell you. Talk to the locals if you want better information."

And don't trust maps made by people who were never there.

After Singer left, he took a moment alone to stare at the map and reflect on the progress of the campaign. It was going as well as could be expected. Of course, the Bandeluks had been waiting for them on the shore, evidence of some extraordinary feat of espionage, or far more likely, treachery on the allied side.

My dear brother Chryspos, was it you who betrayed me, to clear your path to the throne? Or was it one of our lukewarm friends in Covenant? Or was it someone from the anarchic Free States?

It didn't really matter who had betrayed him. The main thing was, he was ashore now, and the Bandeluks were fleeing before him. Whatever schemes someone was spinning behind his back, the army was firmly in his hands. And when he brought home an imperial crown, a royal one could not be denied him.

The one thing outside his control was the Free State Contingent and the attack on Barbosa. It hardly mattered whether they won or lost, but it was imperative the attack be made. It would be reckless to leave an army of unreliable Free Staters, who might any day become suspicious of their allies, in his rear. It all depended on the newly-fledged Gen. Singer, he wearing the golden helmet, something which had many consequences, but the main one being it marked him as the Prince's man. That precious, golden thing would hold him like a chain.

But he hardly knew Singer. He'd only seen him once before. What kind of man was he really? He turned to a corner where a figure had been standing the entire time, shunned by all the officers. It looked like a rag doll, if rag dolls were six feet tall and carried heavy, double-bladed axes. Krion didn't have to come very near to smell it.

(He had once dissected a Ragman, and found nothing but rags inside. Some were fine and silky, some coarse and stiff, but all smelled like something dead. He was not interested in repeating the experiment.)

"You heard all that?"

"Yes, I heard." The Ragman had a voice like a small child's.

It always sounds like they're mocking me.

"What do you think of our new general? Is he loyal?"

"He is a reluctant tool, but without guile. He will do you great service. But . . ." Krion waited for it to go on, but the Ragman remained silent.

"But what?"

"I felt something strange."

What would a Ragman find strange?

"That's why you're here. You can sense things I can't."

"I do not know what it is or how to express it."

"Try harder. How do you think I'd describe it, if it were me?"

The Ragman looked at him thoughtfully for a moment. "You would be afraid. It was fear."

Krion had never heard them use that word before.

4: Rajik

Rajik awoke. He was lying face down on the ground. Someone was saying. "See, he's twitching again. The burns are serious, but not lethal."

His back was on fire. He tried to say something, but his mouth seemed to be full of dust, and he couldn't move. Then a goatskin waterbag was placed in his mouth and some bitter-tasting liquid was poured down his throat.

" . . . some of this, not too much at once, you may choke," the mysterious voice was saying. Despite this warning, he sucked greedily on the waterbag, until he felt his body getting numb and he could no longer raise his head . . .

. . . now, though no time had passed, he was lying on a blanket on a rough wooden surface, which was jerking roughly up and down, causing dreadful pains in his back. He turned his head enough to see the wheel of a cart slowly spinning . . . He was about to ask where he was, when it suddenly no longer seemed important, and he laid his head down again . . .

. . . now, he was on a carpet in a tent. His back was still burning, though not quite as fiercely as before. His father, Sheikh Mahmud, was sitting on a stool in front of him. He tried to speak, but this throat was raw and nothing would come out but a soft moan.

He'd never seen his father looking so angry. He held a braided black thing in his hand, which he held up to Rajik's face, so close he could smell the faint odor of a woman on it. "Tell me about this," his father said.

Rajik could only make a croaking sound. Furiously, his father raised the braided black thing and lashed down, striking his tormented back. . . . Rajik felt an unbearable rush of pain, as his father raised the whip again . . .

. . . some time must have passed, because it was darker now. The pain was not so bad, but his head felt groggy, and there was a bitter taste in his mouth.

"Found your tongue?" His father was looming over him like a

threatening giant.

"Yes," was all he could think to say. He tried to raise himself up, and by a ferocious effort managed to achieve a kneeling position, but was unable to stand. His legs had no strength, and he felt incredibly dizzy.

His father said nothing, but merely held out the braided whip, which he now saw was the hair of a woman.

"That must be Raeesha's hair," he guessed. His voice was hoarse and croaking.

"And how do you know that?"

"I saw her on the beach. She had cut her hair."

"And what were you doing on the beach, in the company of your sister?"

"We met each other by chance."

His father struck him in the face, not too hard, with the whip.

"That is for lying. You were seen together, both disguised. You sneaked away about the same time and went directly to the same place."

"By chance! I only wanted to see the foreigners!"

"Is that how she persuaded you to help her?"

"I never did! I told her to go home!"

"Was that before or after you cut her hair?"

"She did that herself!"

"And you did nothing to stop her?"

"Please believe me Father. I swear I didn't know what she was doing until I met her on the beach."

"Then you should have killed her at once, or at least reported her treachery to me!"

This was too much for Rajik. His voice was failing again. The more he tried to say something, the worse it got. Nothing came from his mouth but a rasping sound, like wood being sawed.

"That will be enough for now," his father said. "I'll tell them to bring you something to eat. We'll speak again in the morning. Try to think of some better answers, or at least some better lies. Don't expect to convince me little Raeesha did this all by herself."

With that, he left.

When he awoke, he was still in the tent, but now he was wrapped in blankets. The sun must have risen hours ago. The pain in his back was now a throbbing ache. He reached back to touch the tender flesh, and when he looked at his fingers, they were covered with a watery fluid that smelled like pus. The blankets were also smeared with it.

Apparently, he was going to live . . . if his father let him. At the moment, he felt terribly hungry; the soup they gave him last night had left a great vacancy in his stomach. He crawled out of the tent, looking for something to eat.

He was standing in the woods somewhere, on one of his father's hunting preserves, he guessed. There were scrubby little pine trees everywhere and tents scattered around in no particular order. Dozens of soldiers were sitting around idly, and most turned to look at him as he emerged: Some eyes glared at him with fierce resentment, and some softened with pity, but most were blankly indifferent.

They were defeated men. He could see it at once. Their clothing was torn and disheveled, and they hadn't washed or shaved in days. Their armor was dinted and unpolished. Several were nursing wounds. One man struck the ground over and over with a dagger, in manic repetition. The others paid him no attention.

They didn't go home because they have none. The foreigners have taken it. And if they have no home, neither have I.

Not willing to break the silence, he simply rubbed his stomach to show he was hungry. One soldier pointed toward a tent which looked like all the others. Inside, he found a pile of stale, dry bread. He broke open a loaf and sampled it, discovering it tasted no better than it looked. But his hunger was stronger, and soon he was cramming handfuls in his mouth.

Chewing was hard work. As he ate, he tried to make sense of what had happened: In the space of just a few days, he'd snuck away from home in disguise, been attacked and nearly killed by a fire demon, lost his home, been accused of treachery, and whipped with his sister's hair.

How many of his family were still alive? Alim, Hisaf and Umar had ridden out with the soldiers. If they weren't here, they were probably dead. And the women were dead or worse, if the foreigners caught them. It was a lot to take in. He felt like crying, but he knew men don't cry.

If my father sees me crying, he'll be angry. I must not cry!

At this point, a soldier stuck his head in the tent and said his father wanted to see him. He grabbed a loaf of bread to take along, but then realized this would make him look childish, so he left it with the others.

As he approached his father's tent, he saw Umar come out, clad in armor, and without pausing to look around, walk away. Rajik didn't dare to call to him.

That's one, at least! Did Alim and Hisaf also survive?

His father was waiting in the tent, studying a map of Chatmakstan. He didn't look up as Rajik entered. He kneeled and waited for his father to speak.

His father was wearing a robe of red silk, embroidered with gold. He wore a white turban, decorated with a ruby the size of Rajik's thumb. He'd shaved his chin and trimmed his mustache. His manner, though, was pained and uncomfortable, and he grimaced as he traced something on the map with his finger.

"Look here," he said. "We're about a day's ride northeast of Jasmine House."

Rajik nodded. He knew the place slightly. His father had a lodge not far away, "the Fox Lair," where he sometimes went hunting. Why didn't his father go there?

If he's not in the Fox Lair, he's afraid of being seen.

The thought his father was afraid was unsettling.

"Are you feeling well?" Rajik also found this question disturbing.

Yesterday, he didn't care!

"Yes Father, I'm better now."

He wanted very badly to ask about his brothers, but instinct told him it was better just to be silent and answer questions. There was no telling what might provoke his father into another rage.

"Good. I have something for you to do, but first, I must explain a few things:

"Your sister is a whore. She's living now in Jasmine House with the foreigners. Doubtless, she's found a lover, or more likely, several."

Rajik felt his face turning red. This shame was really too much to bear.

"I have told Umar to take care of your sister, so that need not concern you. I am no longer interested in what you were doing with her on the beach. It is my highest duty now to rescue what remains of our family's honor. To this end, I must use every tool that comes to hand.

"You have seen the men outside?"

Rajik nodded.

"There are about a hundred left, though I haven't yet counted today. Many have deserted. I send out scouts, good and trusted men. Most do not return.

"The foreigners gave weapons to the peasants. The whole province is armed against us. No place is safe, and it's only a matter of time before they find us here.

"The women and children have fled to Kafra. I'd go there too, but there's an obstacle."

He loosened the red silk robe, exposing white bandages which crossed his chest.

"I was wounded in the back. You know what that means?"

Speechless, Rajik could only nod.

My father bears the mark of a coward! No wonder the men are deserting!

Loyally, he said, "I too was wounded in the back."

His father snorted contemptuously. "You're only a boy, and the little burns on your back are of interest to no one, least of all to Amir Qilij. That's why I want you to bear a message to him. Since I can't go, this falls to you."

He gave Rajik a letter with a red, wax seal. Rajik could feel his heart pounding.

My father still loves me! He's entrusted me with this important message!

"You must get to Kafra before the foreigners encircle it. You're young and clever, you will find a way. You must go directly to the Amir. Do not stop to visit your uncle. This message is for the Amir only, you understand?"

Rajik nodded.

"Good. Abdul-Ghafur has charge of the horses. Take the fastest he has. Leave now, without delay."

"I won't fail you, Father!"

"You have already failed me. See if you can repay me for that."

Kafra was almost two hundred miles away, so a few preparations were necessary. Rajik threw some of the bread in a sack, and grabbed a water bag and a blanket as well. There was no time to change his clothing, but he found a leather jacket and a cap in one of the tents and put them on. Lastly, he stuck a long, curved knife in his belt, and took a short horse bow and a quiver of arrows.

Then, he went looking for Abdul-Ghafur, an old man who had tended the family's horses since before he was born. He found him sitting by a stream among the horses, who he loved more than his own children.

Rajik showed him the sealed letter. "My father has given me an important message! Saddle the fastest horse!"

Abdul-Ghafur looked at him skeptically, stroking his thin, white beard. "That would be Sea Wind, your father's favorite. Are you sure he wants you to take him?"

"Yes, and without delay! This is urgent!"

Even if demons were striking him with flaming whips, Abdul-Ghafur couldn't be hurried. He continued talking as he saddled the dappled horse. "This is a stallion, boy. They're temperamental. He'll bite you if you offend him, and may throw you off and run away if you're not skilled."

"I am as skilled as any man here!"

Abdul-Ghafu looked like he had something to say about that, but instead, he merely bowed and offered Rajik the reins. Without another word, Rajik mounted and rode off.

He hadn't gotten many miles before he wished he'd stopped to look at that map. He had never been to Kafra but once, and that was years ago, in a coach with his mother. It was somewhere to the southeast, he was sure. But it was almost noon, and the sky was cloudy, so how could he be sure he was going the right way? He should look for someone who could give him directions, but the people here were Chatmaks, who would only lie to him, or perhaps even kill him for the horse.

He stopped and pulled out the letter. It seemed like a very small thing to carry such weighty information. If it was so important, why did his father give it to him instead of some soldier? Perhaps there was nothing important at all. Perhaps it was just a trick to get rid of him.

"The women and children have fled to Kafra." Am I also a child?

The thought was unbearable. He wanted to rip open the letter. Maybe it was only a letter of introduction, placing him in the care of the Amir.

Am I an orphan then, to live on the bread of charity?

He scrutinized the letter to see what information he could glean from it, but, except for the red seal, it was unmarked. He held it up the light, in hopes of seeing the writing inside, but the thick parchment and the cloudy sky frustrated his efforts.

It's wrong for my father to send me to Kafra.

He should have sent Umar, his elder brother. Umar was honest and slow-witted. He could never kill Raeesha. If the foreigners questioned Umar even half as sternly as his father had questioned him, he'd begin stammering and contradicting himself, and then they'd cut his throat. Poor, gentle Umar would die, and his treacherous sister would just go on whoring.

He didn't debate the matter with himself more than a minute before he stuck the letter in his sash and took the one road he knew very well, the road to Jasmine House.

It was only a few minutes later he saw the dead man. He was lying face down the road, in a puddle of drying blood. The crows had gotten his eyes. They flew away, cawing indignantly, as Rajik rode up. Sea Wind felt stiff between his legs, made nervous by the smell of blood.

He studied the corpse for a moment. It was a young man, not more than thirty. His clothing and possessions were gone. There were no wounds visible, so they must be on the front. By the cut of his hair, Rajik guessed he must have been a Bandeluk.

Was this one of my father's scouts? Perhaps a deserter?

Rajik looked around, but saw no one. Probably, the dead man had also seen no one, until they jumped from behind a bush and stuck a spear in him. In the distance, he could hear the crows, who were waiting impatiently to return to their feast.

Perhaps they'll have my eyes too, before long.

Maybe going to Kafra was not such a bad idea, after all.

Shall I then forsake my brother, merely because I'm afraid? And why should I fear death, when it lies in every direction?

He gave Sea Wind a light slap with the reins, which was all it took to move him to a brisk trot.

Catching Umar was not terribly hard, because Umar was moving at a slow pace. Cresting a small hill, Rajik could see him plodding along in the distance.

He doesn't want to kill his sister; this makes him ride slowly. He's a big man, but he acts like a child.

He urged Sea Wind into a canter. He was just coming within hailing distance, when he saw Umar ride past a hedge, and suddenly there were spearmen running at him from all directions. Then, Umar had his sword out and was slashing at them, but they encircled him, trapping him between their spear points like a wild boar.

No, brother! You can't die when I'm so close!

Umar lunged at one of them, but the others came at him from the sides, and one stabbed the horse in the haunch to make it rear. Then, Umar had a spear in him, just where the shoulder armor meets the breastplate, and he was falling.

As one of the attackers raised his spear to finish off the wounded man, Rajik's arrow struck him in the throat. And while the others were looking around to see where this arrow had suddenly come from, a second one struck another of them between his ribs. Then, they were running and jumping the hedge and abandoning their spears in their haste to get away.

Cowardly peasants! Come back, so I can kill the rest of you!

By the time he reached Umar, there was no sign of the Chatmaks. Umar was getting slowly to his feet, clutching his wounded side. Blood streamed from beneath his armor. He stared at Rajik in astonishment.

"Are you well, Umar?"

"Do I look well? They almost got me this time."

He was fumbling one-handed at the straps that held his breastplate in place. Rajik dismounted to help him. The spear, he saw, had struck deep underneath the collarbone, but missed the lung. He scavenged some cloth from one of the dead peasants to bandage it.

Umar watched stoically while the wound was cleaned and bandaged. "If you're ever wounded, don't lie down," he told Rajik in a brotherly way, "because the blood will drain faster from the wound."

"I'll try to remember that," Rajik said. He'd stopped the bleeding, but had no way to sew up the wound. There was going to be an ugly scar, and it was open to infection.

"That was some good shooting. Who taught you to shoot like that?"

"You did."

"I remember now. And Raeesha wanted to shoot, so I took her shooting too."

"She was better than I was."

"And boastful about it. She was always an impudent little rascal."

Umar sighed heavily, which made him wince.

"Don't talk so much, brother, you'll break open the wound."

But Umar couldn't stop talking. That was just how he was. "We could have used you on the beach. The foreigners had crossbows that made a joke of our armor, and we had nothing to shoot back with. Everyone thinks the bow is an unmanly weapon."

"I was on the beach, brother, but a fire demon knocked me down before the battle started. How did it go?"

"Bad, very bad. We left hundreds on the beach and hardly did anything at all to the foreigners. Father was wounded right at the start, or it might have gone differently."

"And Alim? And Hisaf? What happened to them?"

"Alim was in the first line. I saw his horse go down, and I didn't see him after that. They shot the horses, the bastards!"

Umar was still outraged about the horses. Like Abdul-Ghafur, he was a great horse lover.

"But Hisaf? What about him?"

"He was younger, so they put him in the third line, and he survived the first attack. But then, the demons came, and we scattered in all directions."

Hisaf is alive? Hisaf was always the cleverest and the bravest of us. If only he were here, instead of dull-witted Umar!

Umar kept on talking: "Those demons were ten feet tall! They were throwing men around like turnips! Our weapons did nothing to them, but they killed a man with every blow!"

The bandaging was done now.

"How do you feel?"

"How do you think? It hurts like hell. Father told me to go kill Raeesha, but I don't see how I can."

Now my childish brother is happy because he has an excuse to turn back, but I have a better idea.

"Then I have good news for you. Father wants you to take this letter to Kafra."

Umar took the letter and stared at it, mystified. "Really? What is so important about this letter?"

"If you want to know, you'll have to go back and ask him. He said it was very urgent. You have to get to Kafra before the foreigners encircle the city, and deliver the letter to the Amir in person, no one else."

"I don't know how I can do that. My horse, you can see, is lamed."

"Take Sea Wind. He'll get you through."

Umar stuck the letter in his sash. "Very well, but what about Raeesha?"

"Don't worry, I'll take care of her."

"Are you sure? That's a very serious thing for a boy like you. I can hardly believe Father would give you this task."

Telling lies was something Rajik could do without much trouble. "He says the foreigners won't suspect me because I'm so young. And Raeesha trusts me because I saved her life on the beach. It will be no trouble to cut her throat in the night and then sneak away."

Umar frowned, doubt rising on his face like a dark cloud before a storm. "C-cut her throat? Th-that is not what he told me!"

"Of course not, brother, that was only a manner of speaking. He said you'd instruct me."

"Oh," said Umar, relieved. "Wait a minute."

Fishing around in his saddle bag, he pulled out the length of braided hair Father had shown him before. "You are to strangle her with this and leave it tied around her neck as a token. You understand?"

"Yes, leave it to me."

The braid felt somehow slimy in his hand, like a snake. He clenched it firmly, as if it were trying to wriggle away.

You won't get away from me, treacherous Raeesha!

5: Erika

"Wonderful! My own brother-in-law is a general!" Rosalind was practically jumping up and down with joy, clutching the letter as if it were made of diamonds.

"He is a general, but he isn't your brother-in-law quite yet," Erika reminded her.

"But you're engaged! That means you'll be married soon, and that means PRINCE KRION will come to the wedding!"

"Stop yelling. 'Soon' is relative, and I don't think we should make any plans for Prince Krion."

"But it says here the Prince gave him a golden helmet and put him in charge of a whole province! The war must be almost over!"

"The Prince has a lot of helmets. Singer is only in charge of security; I doubt he gets to keep the tax revenues. And the Empire has many provinces, more than the Prince has helmets, I should think."

Rosalind's jubilation could not be dampened. "He must see Prince Krion every day!"

"I don't know about that," said Erika, "but the important thing is, he said he'd give it all up if he could come home to me. That sounds very sweet, doesn't it?"

How am I to cure my baby sister of this passion?

It had been a mistake to share the letter with Rosalind. She was the biggest royalist in Tideshore. Having once glimpsed Prince Krion at a parade, she couldn't imagine marrying anyone else. She had a plaster bust of him in her room, surrounded with candles and fresh flowers, as if it were the shrine to a god.

"It sounds incredible! Nothing ever happens here, and now . . ."

There was a knock on the door. The maid stuck her head in.

"Miss Erika? Your mother wants to see you in the store right away."

Erika had known this was going to happen. There was a ship from Covenant in the harbor, and doubtless merchants on board, and doubtless they had business with her father. She'd already spent most of the morning grooming and had put on the dress she wore for such occasions, which was a low-cut affair of blue satin that showed off the lacework and her own buxom self to good advantage.

As the only presentable young woman in the establishment, it was her duty to fetch the bolts of cloth visiting merchants came to examine, and to be gawked at and sometimes furtively handled like the merchandise. It was quite useless to whine or protest: As her father liked to say, "The only important thing is the price."

Coming downstairs, she was somewhat relieved to recognize the visitor as Moullit, a cheerful, middle-aged man, who sometimes made familiar remarks, but was otherwise no trouble. Her parents had already offered him tea and engaged him in polite conversation (which was, since he spoke no Hallandish, in the Akaddian language). She waited for them to finish speaking.

Moullit was saying: "Ever since they declared a Protectorate, our money has been flowing into the royal coffers and our young men into the army. A terrible state of affairs, except it has created a fashion craze among the girls, who all compete with each other, as it were, for the last fruit on the tree . . . oh, hello, Erika, how you've grown."

He means "filled out," not "grown".

She curtsied. "I'm happy to find you well. How may I be of service?"

"As I was explaining to your parents, I'm mainly interested in the silks, satins and laces. And perhaps some velvet, if you have any."

"I'll see what we have."

Not very damn much! Except for the laces, we have to import it all ourselves! I guess the shipment from Kafra didn't come in, or he wouldn't be begging off of us.

Going behind the counter, she checked the bins. There were only four bolts of satin and one of fine silk, and it had been lying there for ages because it was a particularly disagreeable shade of purple. There was no velvet at all.

She laid the silk and satin out on the counter, then went back to pick out some lace, which was in good supply. Choosing three bolts of the first grade and two of the second, she threw in a bolt of fine damask linen, and carried the load to the counter, where Moullit was critically examining the satin and silk.

"You understand, I had expected a better selection than this," he was saying. "I hope I didn't come all this way just for a few oddments!"

"You know how hard it is to get anything out of the East these days," her father said. "And with trade suffering as it is, our local customers have already picked out the cheaper weaves. Frankly, I'd despaired of finding a buyer for these bolts, which you can see are of the highest quality. If you want to take them off my hands, I could let you have the lot for 150 krones."

Sheer robbery! My father can sell a kitchen rag for a gold thaler, and convince you he was doing you a favor!

Moullit chuckled softly, as if he'd just heard something funny. "Of course, that is an extravagant price, but perhaps we can come to an agreement. Let's see what else your charming daughter has brought us."

Erika spread out the laces on the counter, leaning forward slightly, so Moullit would have a good view of her breasts.

The only important thing is the price!

Her mother held out some lace between her fingers to show how light it was. "The rose point is a specialty of ours. We employ three families of lace makers, just for this alone. You'll find no finer lace on the entire coast, or even in the whole world."

Moullit nodded agreeably. "I'm sure you're right, but as it happens, the duchess lace is particularly in demand right now. I don't suppose you have any?"

Erika briefly exchanged glances with her mother. They both knew there was no duchess lace in the bins and probably none for sale in the whole city.

"We don't get much call for that here," her mother said. "Because, you know, it's so similar to rose point, which is more economical and, besides, much more durable. Go see what we have, Erika. You may have to open a crate or two before you find it.

"Oh, look, the silly girl has mixed things up again. She's brought out some of our linen, though you didn't request it. So long as it's here, why don't you just have a look . . ."

Knowing her presence in the showroom was unwanted for the moment, Erika went poking around in the bins, creating a rustle and bustle to show she was working, and she even pried open two of the crates. She found exactly what she expected to find: a fortune in unsold linen, sorted by color and grade, enough to supply most of the city with sheets and tablecloths.

When she ventured back into the showroom, Moullit had finished transacting his business and was once again engaged in small talk: " . . . completely dried up. The army is still buying, of course, but that's all broadcloth, bunting, sailcloth, duck, melton and sacking, sold on bulk contracts, and you have to know Duke Claudio if you want one."

"Duke Claudio sounds like a good man to be friends with," her father commented.

"He might be, if he weren't so very insistent on collecting his own personal share, and that quite takes the profit out of the business."

Sighing, Moullit turned to her. "Oh, I take it you found no duchess lace?"

Erika displayed her empty hands. "We're entirely sold out."

"Well that's too bad, but not entirely unexpected. As it happens, I've reached an agreement with your father for the purchase of your entire stock of silk and satin, and besides, ten bolts of the rose point."

"And the linen?"

Moullit looked sad and sentimental. "There was a time when I could have filled a ship with it, and sold every scrap, but now, our tradesmen are running around in coarse homespun, and there isn't much call for linen, unless you

girls decide that linen blouses are back in fashion. Why don't you take counsel with the other young beauties and let me know what you decide?"

Laughing at his own joke, he went out the door.

With Moullit gone, her mother called in the maid to remove the tea service, then said, "That went quite well, Erika. We will be hard put to lose you, when you're married."

"That arrangement appears to have hit a snag," her father said. "We may need to make other plans."

I do NOT like the sound of that!

"I'm not sure what you mean."

Her parents looked at each other anxiously. Her mother spoke first:

"Your young man is at war now, Erika."

Erika silently pointed to the sign on the wall that said, "All sales are final."

"That's a very good principle, but in this case, there's a problem with delivery. We don't know when he'll be back, or even if he will."

"He's with a thousand other Hallanders who don't have the Prince's favor nor the rank of general. I think the odds of his return are quite good."

Her father spoke: "He may well return when the war is concluded, but if you paid attention to your geography lessons, you know the Bandeluk Empire is huge. It would take nearly a year to march across it, let alone conquer the place."

"I can wait a year, and I can wait longer, if necessary."

"I'm sure you can, but there is another matter you may not have considered. The bulk of our trade is in fine linen, for which there's now very little demand, especially as all contact with the East has been severed."

"Perhaps *General* Singer can help with that. He is in charge of a whole province, you know."

"I'm afraid Chatmakstan is a miserable, dirt-poor place which presents no opportunities for linen merchants. Nor can it furnish the imports we need."

"I don't see what that has to do with my marriage."

Her father sighed and looked at her soulfully.

This is bad news. He puts on that face when he has to cancel a big order.

"I can't spare your feelings any longer. To put it bluntly, we're being driven out of business. Already, we have had to lay off several of our weavers, skilled craftsmen it will be hard to replace. And some of them have already found positions with Houghton. The man hardly knows tweed from tulle, but he does have excellent connections in Akaddia, and his business is thriving."

"I'm not unaware of our situation, father, but I still don't see what it has to do with my marriage."

Now, her mother spoke up: "We have had the offer of a merger. Houghton needs our lace makers, and we need his connections. It does, however, require a marriage to join our two houses. You know Houghton's son, Brandworth?"

"Brandy? You want me to marry Brandy? He's my second cousin! And he's a sot! He drinks through his weekly allowance by Thursday, and then he tries to borrow money from me. From ME!"

She couldn't have been more outraged if someone had offered two krones for her maidenhead.

Her mother tried to soothe her: "Many a man has put aside the excesses of his youth when he assumes family responsibilities."

"A young rake may become a family man, but a sot who marries is just a married sot!"

"There is another problem you may not have considered. Marriage to a promising young lieutenant is one thing, but a general is something else. His marriage is no longer in his own hands. It's a matter of state. The Prince will want him to marry some noblewoman, or maybe even a princess."

"He just sent a letter saying he'd give it all up, if he could just come home to me!"

"But he can't, that's the point," her father said. "He can't marry anyone, so long as this war is going on, and if he's victorious, the Prince will elevate him through marriage to some noblewoman, a proposal he cannot possibly refuse."

"He's a free citizen of Halland and can marry anyone he chooses!"

"He was, but now he's entered the Prince's service, and the royals seldom give up anything, once they've taken possession."

He held up a clenched fist for emphasis.

What's the use, they're both against me!

"I can't marry Brandy anyway, until the engagement is announced and a suitable time has passed."

"That's only a matter of a few months, and as for the engagement, we can announce it tomorrow."

"I give up! Announce what you want, but I shall always love Singer!"

Then, she heard a soft crying sound. It was her sister Rosalind, standing at the top of the stairs. She must have heard the whole argument. Tears were running down her cheeks.

"How COULD you!" Rosalind said in a choked voice. "How COULD you!"

She ran off to her room, where her constant lover, the plaster bust of Prince Krion, awaited her.

"I'm afraid your sister is taking this rather badly," her mother said. "Perhaps you should have a word with her."

"I'll see to her as soon as I've put away the linen."

Upstairs, Rosalind was lying face down on the bed, soaking the comforter with tears of rage and disappointment. Erika let her lie there and went to her own room, where she began hurriedly packing a bag. She was almost done, just trying to squeeze in the tortoise shell brush set, when Rosalind appeared at the door, red-eyed and runny-nosed.

"What are you doing?"

"Nothing much, just going to see my husband, that's all."

"What? You said you were going to marry Brandy!"

"I lied. It comes with the profession."

"But how will you cross the ocean?"

"Ships sail over it every day. How do you think the letter got here?"

"That costs money."

"We had a big sale today. I managed to pinch it, just before Father locked up."

"You STOLE it?"

"Stop yelling. I prefer to see it as an investment. Do you want your brother-in-law to be a general who can introduce you to the royal family, or do you want me to marry Brandy, so he can introduce you to all the local tavern keepers?"

Rosalind stared at her, agape, and blinked just once before exclaiming, "This is wonderful! Take me too!"

"I'm afraid I can't do that. You're much too young, and you have no husband waiting on the other side."

"If you don't take me, I'll tell mother!"

That's a bluff if I ever heard one.

"That would mean I shall have to marry Brandy, and your future husband will be some butcher or cobbler."

"Then you must promise to do something for me."

She went to her own room for a moment and came back, holding a gold ring which bore a golden heart.

"Wasn't that Aunt Gwyneth's?"

"She gave it to me, and I want you to give it to Prince Krion, when you see him."

"Are you sure he's interested in receiving gifts from thirteen-year-olds?"

"Just give it to him, please."

"As you wish. Any words for Prince Krion?"

"Tell him I love him."

"He shall hear of it, I promise."

"Wonderful!"

Rosalind gave her a hug.

I'm clearly wearing the wrong dress!

The low-cut blue satin was drawing a lot of unwanted attention in the harbor area, where ladies of quality were seldom seen. "How much for a night with her?" a sailor openly wondered.

"More than you could possibly afford!" she answered brazenly. There was a general chuckling among the spectators.

They're not laughing at me, they're laughing at him, so why do I feel so ashamed?

Arriving at the harbormaster's office, she found it deserted, except for a clerk, who was entering things in a ledger. She dropped her bag in front of him and cleared her throat, assuming he'd stand up to greet her, but he only glanced, disinterested, in her direction.

"When is the next ship departing for Chatmakstan?"

Tell me it is soon!

He merely pointed his thumb to a chalkboard on the wall, which had a list of ship names, with particulars, such as home port and cargo. She found it confusing. Sailors reckoned time in "bells" rather than in "hours," she knew, but she'd never understood the details. And no ship was listed with the destination "Chatmakstan."

"Perhaps you'd care to assist me?" She laid a silver krone on the desk.

That caught his attention. He stood up and offered an obsequious smile. "Sorry ma'am, I was a bit occupied. What you're looking for would be the 'Princess Zenobia,' out of Kingshaven. She'll be shipping with the tide, that is, about 2 bells . . . I mean, 5 o'clock. The listed cargo is 'provisions.' The military doesn't give you a lot of details, and we don't ask."

"I see the destination is 'Massera Bay'. That's in Chatmakstan, I take it?"

"Yes'm. That's where they say it's going, anyhow. The military again, you understand. Who knows where it will end up. Wherever the army is, would be my guess."

"And where can I find the 'Princess Zenobia'?"

"Right now, at Wharf Three, but she won't be there much longer. They've been loading her all day."

"Thank you, you've been most helpful."

There were several ships at Wharf Three, but only one of them was loading cargo. The 'Princess Zenobia' turned out to be a three-masted schooner, rather old, but it gave the impression of being seaworthy.

I guess I can expect no luxury accommodations here.

The figurehead, she noticed, was in the form of a woman wearing a golden crown, but little other clothing. Presumably, this was the princess herself.

I assume we'll be the only women on board, your Highness, but I hope to make a less slatternly impression than you do.

A number of large, sweaty men were carrying sacks up the gangway. An officer stood at the top, checking each item off a list as it arrived. She pushed her way to the head of the line.

"I'd like to speak to the captain, please."

The officer looked her up and down, obviously confused by her sudden appearance. She was not on his list.

"The captain, if you please?"

"You'll find him on the quarterdeck, talking to the pilot."

The quarterdeck is the one in the rear, or the "stern" as I think they call it. Why do they have to give everything such peculiar names?

There were two men talking to each other on the quarter-deck: One was a grubby little man with a disreputable-looking pipe clenched in his teeth, the other a tall and athletic-looking fellow sharply dressed in a pea jacket.

"Captain?" she said to the taller man.

"Yes, mum?" said the grubby, little man.

"Ah. I wish to book a cabin."

Slowly and thoughtfully, the captain took out his pipe and rapped it against the railing, sending sparks and ashes flying everywhere. He then stuffed it in a pocket.

"We have none. This is a cargo vessel with military supplies. We're not allowed to carry passengers."

"But I have military supplies! Prince Krion ordered his winter uniforms from the Wartfield trading house. I am to deliver them for the fittings."

The captain scratched his head and stared at her bag. "That doesn't change the fact we have no cabins. Try the next ship."

Tugging his sleeve, she drew him aside and spoke softly in his ear, taking care he should get a good whiff of perfume.

"The Prince requested me *personally,* you understand? He urgently requested I attend him *personally.*"

"Oh, I see. Yes. Well, I guess you can have my cabin, then. I'll just have to bunk with the mates."

The captain's cabin was as small, grubby and unkempt as the man himself, with dirty blankets on the bunk and articles of clothing on the floor. There was a table bolted to the floor and some stools, similarly bolted, next to it. An enormous, ancient-looking sea chest was in one corner. Except for a basin and a shaving mirror near the door, it was otherwise unfurnished.

Looking out the window, she could see the prow of the next ship and a couple sailors, who were peering curiously in at her. She reached automatically for the curtains, but found there were none.

"Well, it's a snug little nest, but I guess it will have to do," the captain said. "I'll send the cabin boy to clean it out for you."

I wish you'd do something about the reek of tobacco, while you're at it.

"You are most kind."

"Oh, one other thing, we hold the captain's mess in here, evenings. I don't suppose you'd mind?"

"I will be most pleased to receive you and your officers."

When the captain had gone, she examined the gold ring her sister had given her. It was a perfect match for the one Aunt Gwyn had given her years ago, which she was wearing on her right hand. There was nothing special about either of them, that she could see, no ominous inscription or secret compartment for poison or anything of the sort. It was a very ordinary-looking ring.

"Give this to your true love and no one else," Aunt Gwyn said.

As Erika remembered her, Aunt Gwyneth was a rather dotty old lady with a great deal more money than sense. She'd married a wealthy sorcerer in Westenhausen, and as the years began to subtract from her natural charms, invested a small fortune in magical glamours that made her look younger than she actually was. This, however, excited the jealous suspicions of her husband. One day, while Aunt Gwyneth was out trimming the roses, she suddenly vanished in a stinking cloud of smoke, and that was the end of the story . . . or so Erika had thought.

What if this ring is enchanted?

She slipped her own ring on and off, without noticing any change. She was about to try on Rosalind's ring, when something warned her the experiment might be foolhardy.

Well, I can't do anything about this. Prince Krion will have to sort it out, if there's a problem. He has lots of sorcerers and people working for him.

She stuffed the ring in her purse and turned to inspect herself in the mirror.

I'll be seeing Prince Krion, and a lot of other men, I know, but I have to keep my mind on my one real chance.

She removed her hat and practiced kissing herself in the mirror.

You're irresistible. How could he not fall for you? Clearly a seller's market for this commodity, and it would be a shame to lose it in a fire sale. After all, the only important thing is the price.

6: Raeesha

Hallandish is a terrible language.

The first words she learned were "wash the dishes." There were a huge stack of them on the table, and more were piling up on the floor. And the things these foreigners ate! Today it was some awful meat paste that, to judge by appearances, had already been eaten once and regurgitated. That, together with sliced tubers fried in lard and some vile-smelling stuff that looked like poisonous weeds, but was probably just pickled cabbage.

Even the Chatmaks eat better than this!

The least-edible remnants of this meal had to be scraped off of each plate, which was then dunked in hot, soapy water, wiped, rinsed, then wiped again and stacked. Once she'd finished all the plates, the cook would give her a plate with the same repulsive meal, but cold and congealed into goo. Then, he'd tell her to sweep up, and when that was done, she'd start over with the plates. At the end of the day, she'd go to her bed, which she'd made herself out of old sacks laid on the kitchen floor of her own home.

It had been like this for six days. On the second day, the cook, a fat man who smelled of rancid grease, had pressed himself against her and put his hand in her pants. She whirled and drew her knife, but he had already stepped back, surprised by what he'd found in her pants. They'd simply glared at each other without saying anything. The look they exchanged was enough: "You keep my secrets and I'll keep yours." And that was the end of that . . . or so she hoped.

Things could be worse.

And they probably would get worse, when the foreigners left. The Chatmaks were strutting around everywhere with swords and spears, and any Bandeluk who failed to get out of their way fast enough received the butt end of a spear or worse. It was not that the remaining Bandeluks were doing anything provocative. The only ones left were those too slow to flee, mainly women, children and elderly men.

This is what it means to be a conquered people: washing dishes, sleeping on the kitchen floor, being groped by strangers, and pushed around by the rabble.

It was still better than marrying Amir Qilij.

The foreigners were multiplying. There were now many more than on the first day. There must be several kinds, she guessed, because they carried different banners and had different kinds of armor and weapons, but all spoke the terrible, guttural Hallandish or some variant of it.

She'd sometimes seen Singer, too, after he'd threatened her with his sword on the first day, but he no longer took the time to speak to her. Now, he was known as "the General" and wore a golden helmet, and all the foreigners hurried around doing his bidding.

General or not, he'd better play no more tricks on me!

At this moment, as she was scraping a dirty dish, she felt a hand on her shoulder, and thinking it was the cook again, turned and reached for her knife. But it was not the cook, it was the General himself staring at her from beneath the ruby eyes on the golden head of the king panther that formed his helmet.

Ignoring the knife, he said, "You speak Chatmaki?"

"Yes, effendi."

"Don't call me that. My proper rank is general. Come with me."

Singer went to the courtyard, where there was a lot of shouting and hubbub. A line of spearmen were trying to hold back a big crowd of Chatmaks, who were screaming at them.

"What are they saying?" Singer asked.

"They keep shouting, 'Great Lord, Great Lord.' I guess that's you, General."

"Find out who they are and what they want."

Raeesha knew how to deal with Chatmaks. She stepped forward and clapped her hands as loudly as she could, yelling, "SILENCE! Anyone who speaks without being called on will be whipped!"

Suddenly, it was quiet. She could hear people shuffling their feet and whimpering to themselves. She picked out an old man, who looked to be one of their elders.

"You! What is your name and where are you from?"

When the old man opened his lips, a flood of woes came out: "They killed my son! And my nephew! And then they burned . . . OW!"

Raeesha had grabbed his nose and twisted.

"Answer the question! Who are you and where are you from?"

"I am Faisal of the Seven Pines village. We've walked all this way without food . . ."

"Silence!"

She turned to Singer and said, "They're from Seven Pines. That's about three days east of here, quicker by horse. Their village was attacked and burned. Some were killed. They've walked here seeking assistance."

"Who attacked them? How many?"

Raeesha repeated the questions in Chatmaki.

"Bandeluks! Hundreds of them! They seized the women and took . . ."

"Silence!" Turning to Singer, she said: "He says the village was attacked by hundreds of Bandeluks, but I don't think he stopped to count."

Singer stroked his chin. "No, that may be an exaggeration. What about all those weapons I distributed? Didn't they defend themselves?"

After another translation, she reported, "Those who raised weapons were the first to die. The rest fled."

She stepped closer to Singer and said softly, "General, these people are not soldiers. If you give them weapons and tell them to fight, they'll probably just be killed."

"I can see that. But I don't need you to give me advice right now. Just translate. Were the Bandeluks on horses? How were they armed?"

When Raeesha turned back to the group of Chatmaks, she saw it was turning into an angry mob. A woman in back pointed at her and screamed, "Look how the Bandeluk is whispering in the ear of the Great Lord! He is plotting to kill us!"

Now, several of them were picking up stones. Singer said something loudly in his own language, and the spearmen lowered their weapons. All at once, the angry mob was a panicky mob. Many fell to their knees, and the rest took a couple steps back, preparing to flee.

"The hand that throws a stone will be severed!" Singer yelled.

When Raeesha repeated these words, a remorseful, whimpering moan arose from the group. Those who hadn't kneeled did so, and those kneeling put their faces in the dirt. The ones who had picked up stones tried, inconspicuously, to roll them closer to their neighbors, who promptly shoved them back.

"Listen!" said Singer. "I offer you my hospitality! You may stay in the courtyard tonight. I'll see that you're fed. Tomorrow morning, I will ride forth and do justice to those who attacked you!"

Raeesha repeated this speech word for word, and the Chatmaks seemed relieved. They began spreading out in the courtyard, looking for the best spots. Some, she saw, were clutching bundles of possessions, but most had nothing. The stragglers of the group, mainly women dragging small children, came wandering in and asked what had happened.

She turned back to Singer. "General, I believe they'd be grateful for a distribution of blankets, but you may have trouble getting them back again."

"I'll see what we can do. Step into my office."

The "office" was simply a small room near the entrance, formerly the home of the doorkeeper. It contained a table, two chairs, a campaign chest and a cot. A map of Chatmakstan was pinned to one wall.

So this is the home of the Great Lord?

Singer closed the door. "What's your name?"

"Rajik."

Forgive me brother, you don't need the name anymore.

"Rajik, you have twice pulled a knife on me. Do you know how to use it?"

Raeesha nodded.

"Then stab me. DO IT!"

Raeesha raised the knife, but it just hung there, trembling, in the air. Singer watched complacently.

"Stab me! I'm the one who killed your brother!"

Now, she was stabbing, but somehow, the knife was in Singer's hand, not hers, and he was pushing it hard into her stomach. For a moment, she thought she was dead, but then she realized he'd turned the knife at the last second, to strike with the hilt.

She took a step back and leaned on the table for support. Singer had knocked the air out of her. The knife clattered on the ground.

Singer said, "Never draw a weapon unless you're going to use it, and you better know how to do that. If you want to stab someone, do it like that, quick and underhanded, straight to the gut and up to the heart, and they won't know what hit them. But make sure they aren't wearing a mail shirt," – He thumped his chest for emphasis. –

"because a knife like that won't get through."

He stood and stared thoughtfully at her for a moment before saying, "I'm transferring you to my personal staff. You'll be an aide-de-camp. That means, you'll stick close to me and do what I tell you."

She stared at him in alarm.

Does he know?

"It also means you'll have your own room and no longer have to wash dishes. Go to Pennesey and he'll equip you. We're riding out early in the morning. Be ready."

"Please General, tell me. Did you really kill my brother?"

"The war did. It killed a lot of men on that day and many more yet to come. But who killed him in particular, I have no idea. I never drew a weapon until I met you, and I have never killed a single soul."

"How could you tell such a lie!"

The General smiled down at her indulgently, as if she were a pouty child. "All warfare is based on deception," he said.

"He wants you to ride with him?" Pennesey shook his head doubtfully. "Well, let's see what I have."

A warren of small rooms in the back of Jasmine House, formerly the servants' quarters, had been converted, pro tem, into an armory. Neatly sorted piles of weapons and armor lay where the servants had once spread their mats. Pennesey stopped before the first room, which was full of swords and daggers.

He tugged at his mustache. "Don't tell me you can use a sword, because you can't. Are you any good with that knife?"

"I've had lessons."

I had one, anyway.

"That kitchen knife is no good, you want one of these." He picked out a thin, straight dagger, and drew it from the sheath, admiring the sharp, polished edges.

"Foot long blade, double edged, diamond in cross section, sharp as a needle. This will find the chinks in any kind of armor ever made. We call it a 'misericord' or mercy dagger. Take good care of it, because I don't know when we'll be getting any more."

Raeesha stuck it in her sash, next to the curved knife.

"Any other weapons?" Pennesey asked.

"I can use a bow."

"Fine, pick one out. I recommend the covered quivers, because you'll be bouncing up and down on a horse. I don't suppose you know how to ride?"

"Well enough," she lied.

In the next room were bows of several kinds, from simple hunting bows, to the big ones carried by foot soldiers. She picked out a short horse bow, of Bandeluk make, and strung it.

"Wait," said Pennesey, "you're turning it the wrong way."

"No, this is the right way."

The bow was now bent in the opposite direction, the ivory nocks curving back outward. She tried pulling the silk string, but it cut her fingers. She poked around among the quivers until she found a thumb ring and drew the bow as far as she could, which, despite her slender arms, was a long way.

Pennesey watched skeptically. "If you're done playing with that toy, we'll look at the armor."

A couple doors down was a room with different sizes of chain armor. He selected a shirt and handed it to her. It was so heavy, she almost dropped it. She needed both arms just to hold it, and walking around all day in it would be torture.

"Too heavy," she said simply, and handed it back.

"I was afraid of that."

Another room held doublets, padded gambesons and surcoats. He poked around until he found a heavy leather jacket with some thin metal plates riveted to the front.

"Try this on. It used to be Kyle's, but he got too big for it."

The jacket covered her arms to the elbows and her legs almost to the knees. It was heavy on the shoulders, but she liked the smell and feel of the oiled leather.

"I'll take it."

"You'll want a sword belt with that, to put the weight on the hips, not the shoulders."

He showed her how to use the belt, then proceeded to the next room, which was full of helmets. "Pick one."

Impulsively, she took a splendid, big helm with a feathered crest and put it on her head, but it was heavy and she could hardly see anything.

Pennesey chuckled. "That belongs to the Illustrious Knights.

The show-offs use it for jousting. Try one of the helmets."

The first helmet was too big, as was the second. Finally, on a shelf in the back, she found a battered old helmet of the pointed Bandeluk kind with a mail skirt to protect the back of the neck. More important, though, was what it lacked: padding. It was intended to be worn over a tightly-wound turban, as large or small as the user pleased.

"This will do."

"That's an ugly old piss-pot," Pennesey said. "But it's probably better than nothing.

"Speaking of which, you need something to protect your neck." He jabbed at her throat with his finger. "A blow there could end your career in a hurry."

The iron collar he gave her made her feel like her neck was in a vice. "I can't possibly wear that," she said, taking it off.

She picked out a light collar of Bandeluk make, with two attached plates, protecting the shoulders. "This one, I can live with."

"I'd like to cover those skinny shins with some greaves, but I don't think I have anything to fit. Maybe you can find some boots. Same problem with the wrists, but there's a pile of old Bandeluk equipment in back. It won't hurt to have a look."

She finally found a leather ar-

cher's bracer which covered her left arm from wrist to elbow.

Pennesey looked up and down, finally saying, "I'm afraid that's the best I can do for you. Try to stay out of any fights, would be my advice."

"Thanks, I'll do that."

The armor and weapons made her feel powerful. She went to the hall mirror and had a look at herself.

Here stands a mighty warrior!

The only weak point she could see was the leather sandals she'd been wearing since she escaped Jasmine House. They were getting worn and plainly wouldn't last much longer.

Maybe I could find my brother's old boots? I think I saw them on a trash heap in back.

To leave Jasmine House, you had to pass through the dim courtyard, which at the moment was full of Chatmak refugees, making themselves as comfortable as possible on their borrowed bedding. The nearest ones turned to inspect Raeesha as she entered.

"Oh look, here comes that effeminate young Bandeluk, who was so rude before. Now, he thinks he's a great warrior!"

Effeminate?

That word stung. If she looked effeminate to the dumb Chatmaks, what did the General think of her? As she picked her way through the crowd of Chatmaks, she reflected on it.

What made her effeminate? There was something about the way Pennesey had touched her throat that suddenly made her feel vulnerable. She rubbed her neck. What was so special about it? Men had thick necks with a bump in the middle which moved up and down when they talked . . .

And beards! How could I forget something so obvious!

Pennesey was checking her for a beard. Now, there were at a least two of the Halland Company who knew about her disguise. Her secret wouldn't last much longer at this rate! So far, she'd escaped notice in the kitchen, but now she'd be parading around in front of everyone.

False whiskers or a mustache would never work; if she suddenly sprouted a beard, any fool would know what had happened. But what if she just rubbed her chin with charcoal every morning? Then, it would look like she'd shaved.

She went out into the street and immediately had to step aside for a sentry who was walking his post near the entrance.

Look at him! He is a man! He doesn't step aside for anyone!

The sentry was tired, she could see by the way he walked, but his back was straight. He seemed confident, afraid of no one. And look how he walked! Legs apart, heels first, then toes. Raeesha walked behind him, imitating his gait, until he turned and glared at her. She gave him a comradely wave as she walked past.

That is how men do it! They have deep voices full of authority and the proud stance of an eagle! They have bold eyes that make you look away! They defer to no one!

Practicing her new walk, she went around the corner, searching for the trash heap. It didn't take long to find it. The foreigners had simply tossed everything they didn't want out a window. But then, the villagers had come and picked through the heap. The colorful shawls and dresses had disappeared first: She'd seen fat, coarse peasant women wearing them in the street. Fine linen shirts and pants hadn't lasted much longer.

There was still a pile of castoffs, old clothing and rags which even the Chatmaks didn't want. She poked through it until she found a pair of old boots, about her size.

I don't know which of my brothers left these, but I thank the gods he did!

She took a few steps in the boots. They seemed to fit. Then, she lay back on the rubbish pile and looked up at the stars. She suddenly felt very much alone, as if there weren't a single person who knew about her or cared.

Gods help me! Who am I, and what am I doing here!

7: Singer

Gods help me! Who am I, and what am I doing here!

Lying on his cot not far away, Singer was having similar thoughts. Everything was going wrong. He felt like crying.

He'd divided Chatmakstan, with the help of a map, into six districts, assigned one company to each (with the *fui* demons in reserve) and instructed them to take charge of the local authorities and restore order. The problem was, he knew hardly anything about Chatmakstan, and his subordinate officers knew even less. And none of them were prepared for this situation.

There were no local authorities. The Bandeluks had run things their way, which meant they lived in nice, big country estates, while the Chatmaks lived in squalid villages. If a Chatmak needed something that was not available in his village, he'd have to apply to his local landowner, who might or might not grant the request. Usually, the Chatmaks handled their own personal affairs without consulting anyone.

Now, most of the Bandeluks had fled, and their fine estates (those not physically occupied by his troops), had been looted. The Chatmaks ran around, taking what they wanted, and frequently disputing ownership with each other. A lot of feuds and quarrels among the Chatmaks, long suppressed by the Bandeluks, were resurfacing.

He'd done what he could. He'd established outposts and patrols. He'd consulted village elders. Usually, they just said, everything is fine here, go away, those people in the next village are up to no good.

Then, on the way to the next village, he'd find a dead man lying the road. There were no witnesses and no evidence, just the corpse of someone who had been robbed and killed. He'd summon the village elders to the spot and they'd all say: we don't know him, never saw him before, don't know who killed him, it was probably someone from the other village. Or a crowd of wailing loved ones would arrive, accusing someone or the other, but always without proof.

What sins have I committed, ye gods, that you punish me this way! I'd rather sweep the streets of Tideshore than be a general in the army of Prince Krion!

At best, he controlled Jasmine House and the adjacent villages. The rest of the district was left to fend for itself, most of the time. He doubted his subordinates were doing any better. From the spotty reports he received, probably not as well.

The Thunder Slingers, for example, were from the city guard of Kindelton, and were used to police work, but they couldn't speak Chatmaki and had no horses to pursue fugitives. The Illustrious Knights, on the other hand, were hobby-soldiers drawn from the aristocracy of Tremmark. They exercised their martial skills on the tourney field and were prone to settle their personal differences with duels. A less suitable force for the occupation of Chatmakstan could hardly be imagined.

The village of Seven Pines, now that he'd found it on the map, was near the border of the district assigned to the Knights and that of the Slingers, though more on the Knights' side. However, the villagers knew nothing of the lines he'd drawn on the map. They simply came to him directly, ignoring his plan.

The Halland Company was very good at what it did, but chasing bandits through the hills was not one of those things. For this reason, he'd recalled Baron Hardy's Company of Gentleman Adventurers from the Southwestern District, which was mostly peaceful, because it was mostly unpopulated.

Baron Hardy was a military contractor who had offered his services to the Free State of Dammerheim, which preferred hiring mercenaries to risking its own citizens. Exactly what he was the baron of, nobody knew and nobody cared. The Gentleman Adventurers were, by reputation, a rowdy bunch, but the important thing was, they had horses, and they could get things done. Singer wanted to get more familiar with them.

I still don't know my own subordinates!

The administrators Prince Krion had promised had never shown up. The Prince only wanted to move supplies down the road to his army at Kafra. He'd sent some engineers to dredge and build docks at Massera Bay, but they were only interested in their assigned tasks. They'd requested men for work details, but Singer had none to spare.

It took me a week just to find a competent translator! And that from my own kitchen!

To top it off, he still hadn't appointed a new captain. Fleming and Pohler were the obvious candidates, but they hated each other. Fleming was an easy-going tavern keeper and popular with the men, but he couldn't be trusted with the pay chest. Pohler was a strict disciplinarian and little loved, but generally quite reliable. At the moment, they were both off running outposts, while the harmless but rather ineffectual young Lt. Ogleby, a teacher by profession, served as his adjutant.

He's the only one I can spare from the real work. I probably got my own job the same way. Hinman never appointed a second-in-command.

Pennesey devoted himself to inventorying and cataloging the captured equipment, of which there was a great deal. Littleton, though, was obsessed with his latest project, to bring irrigation to this part of the province. His project couldn't be completed in less than a year, but Littleton would not be dissuaded.

I don't know how to get him to abandon his new love. Tie him up and gag him, maybe.

Next week, he'd have to leave Chatmakstan in whatever state it was and make a seemingly-pointless attack on a remote imperial outpost. The best he could do in the mean time was clean out a few bandits, who might endanger the Prince's supply line, whereas the general misery and disorder wouldn't. And then, he'd have to leave one company behind.

Gods help the poor bastard who gets stuck with this mess!

Troubled thoughts and dreams kept him from getting much sleep, and when the officer of the watch rapped on his door before dawn, as he'd been ordered to do, Singer illogically cursed him for it. Kyle, doubling as his batman, had polished his armor and laid it out, and now helped him with the buckles.

There never was any more uncomfortable clothing than metal armor. I'll be grateful when I no longer have to wear the stuff.

He was halfway through his breakfast when a soldier came in to announce Baron Hardy had arrived and was awaiting orders. He left the uneaten remnants where they were and went to see.

Rajik was already in the courtyard, holding the reins of his horse.

"The stirrups are too long. Take them in a couple notches."

"Yes, sir!"

You don't know much, but you seem eager to learn.

Hardy was waiting outside with his six hundred horsemen formed in two columns, lancers to the right and horse archers to the left. Their gear was motley, as each man wore what he pleased or could afford, some with heavy breastplates and some merely in their shirts, but all wore a cap or helmet with a long yellow plume. A Standard-bearer carried a banner with the symbol of a golden sun on a blue field. Squinting, he could see it also bore a motto: "Second to none."

Baron Hardy was a tall blond man of middle years. His beard spilled out over a shining breastplate which bore the golden sun. He saluted as Singer approached.

"I see your motto is 'second to none,' but you are second to me, I hope?"

"Indeed sir, they do say a nobleman born comes before an appointed officer of any rank, but it would be small-minded of me to insist on antique protocol." Changing the subject, he added, "That's a nice helmet you're wearing."

"Glad you like it. This is my guide and translator, Rajik. He'll be coming with us today."

"Your friend Rajik looks rather like a Bandeluk."

"Good guess."

"Well, then, we must do something to fix that. Come here, lad."

With Singer translating the Hallandish, Hardy took Rajik's pointed helmet and fastened a yellow plume to it. "You're now an honorary member of Baron Hardy's Company, and there's no more danger of being taken for one of the enemy."

Rajik saluted, as Hardy had done a moment before.

"Are you a man of much military experience?" Singer asked.

"Indeed sir," Hardy answered, "I've earned my pay with the sword since I was a youth, patrolling the hinterland of Tremmark against the wild Moietians. Then, when I came into my estate, I founded my own company and took employment with the aristos in Covenant, until the royalists sent them packing."

"I hope you were paid in advance."

"That I was. We fought for the aristos as long as they were paying us, but not a day longer."

"Then I hope your present employer has deeper pockets. But I think we've wasted enough time with chatter. Let's go."

As they rode eastward along the road, Singer asked Rajik the names of villages, streams and other landmarks. He was pleased with the peaceful look of the countryside. Women in bright clothing were working in the fields. The men, too, had a more prosperous look. They waved their swords and spears at the passing soldiers, not out of hostility, but to show they were complying with the new regulations.

Any Chatmak men without weapons would be lying low until we've passed.

Daring young women sometimes also waved at the soldiers, but ran giggling away if anyone waved back, as Rajik regularly did. The young Bandeluk seemed to be having a great time, despite complaining of saddle sores.

Poor Rajik wouldn't have had much experience riding horses.

A little before noon, they came to Lt. Fleming's outpost, which was in an abandoned Bandeluk villa. Fleming came to the gate and saluted.

"Anything to report, Lieutenant?" said Singer.

"Nothing much, sir. A bunch of Chatmaks came through from the east early yesterday, but I couldn't understand what they were jabbering about, so I just waved them on. We haven't had any luck finding a translator."

"Well, keep looking."

It would take a huge stroke of luck to find anyone in this place who speaks Hallandish or Akaddian. What are we going to do?

A few hours later, they entered the Northeastern District, which, according to the map, was controlled by the Illustrious Knights. However, there was no sign of outposts or patrols.

They're probably off somewhere playing at chivalry, damn them!

Singer turned to Hardy: "You must know a lot about the Tremmark nobility. How would you rate them as soldiers?"

"Honestly sir, I wouldn't call them soldiers at all, or they wouldn't have to hire professionals like me. They lay out a fortune for knightly gear and warhorses and spend a lot of time practicing with the lance, but have no concept of tactics. They're all preparing to fight in wars that ended a hundred years ago. Point them at the enemy and tell them to charge and they'll ride down anything in the way, unless it's pike – which is the bane of cavalry – but don't try to recall them, because that would mean a rout, assuming they pay you any attention at all."

"This was also my impression."

It was evening when they arrived at Seven Pines, and Singer soon wished he were somewhere else. The whole place stank of death. Corpses were lying everywhere, some still clutching spears. In other cases, the spears had been used to display the owners' severed heads. The buildings had been set afire, but the mud brick walls resisted burning, and only the roofs were missing.

Rajik was no longer having fun. The youngster turned pale, muttering, "This is like the day my brother died."

"If you ride with me, you'll see a lot more like it," Singer said.

The field of corpses disturbed him too, though it was not his fault. He hadn't killed all these people. He'd only failed to protect them, and no one could have done more.

Prince Krion would probably just shrug it off with a c'est-la-guerre, so why can't I?

"If you want to be useful, look around and tell me if you find any clues about the attackers."

Rajik clearly found the order distasteful, but obediently dismounted and began studying the hoof prints which were everywhere.

"This is what happens when untrained militia is matched against professional soldiers," Hardy commented.

"Yes," said Singer, "but why do you think they did it? This place looks a lot like the other villages we've been passing all day, so why destroy it?"

"To pick up some provisions and a bit of loot. Or maybe one of the Chatmaks insulted someone. Bandeluks can be touchy about their honor."

"Or maybe it was revenge. There have been a lot of revenge-killings lately."

While they were speculating, Rajik came back and reported: "They were Bandeluk-shod horses. I'm not sure how many, twenty or thirty, perhaps. They came from the northwest and left riding southwards."

Singer tried to conceal his disappointment. Rajik was obviously no great tracker. Singer had known all that a minute after entering the village.

"There was something else." Rajik held up two arrows. "I found this near one of the bodies. And this is one of my own."

"They look identical," Singer said, passing them to Hardy, who agreed.

"They were both made by a man named Rahat. He lived near Jasmine House and worked for Sheikh Mahmud."

"So this was done by Sheikh Mahmud's men?"

"Either that, or by deserters from his following."

Singer translated this for Hardy, and there was a brief silence as both men digested the information. "This seems to raise more questions than it answers," Hardy finally commented.

"Yes," said Singer, "but it doesn't really change anything. We're chasing bandits, and it doesn't matter which ones. Let's find someplace to camp, preferably a good way upwind from here."

In the morning, Seven Pines looked just the same, except the corpses were more visible and therefore more repulsive. Animals had chewed on some of them, and many were bloating. Big, fat flies were buzzing everywhere.

"Nothing for us to do here," said Singer.

They spent half the morning going up a zigzag path in the hills to the south, arriving finally on a crest overlooking the southern plain. In the distance, they could make out a thin blue line, which was the sea.

"Nice view," said Hardy. "Looks like our bandits were heading for that compound over there."

It was one of the walled estates built by the Bandeluks. As they came within about a mile, the tracks suddenly turned to the east.

"It seems they changed their minds," said Hardy.

"There's the reason," said Singer, pointing to a small group of soldiers standing outside the compound. "This must be an outpost of the Thunder Slingers."

"So the bandits weren't looking for a fight."

"Not with anyone who could fight back."

A few hours later, the tracks led them to a Chatmak village. A drum sounded as they approached, and the men of the village quickly gathered together in front of it, spears at the ready.

"This bunch has gotten organized," said Hardy.

"The village hasn't been burned," Singer observed.

"Look, sir!" said Rajik. "One of them is a Bandeluk!"

It was true. Someone dressed in Bandeluk armor was walking back and forth, inspecting his men and probably giving them some words of encouragement.

"That's damned strange," said Singer. "Maybe it's a Chatmak dressed like a Bandeluk."

"Or maybe the rest of them are Bandeluks pretending to be Chatmaks," said Hardy. "Could be an ambush?"

Singer looked around, but there was little to see except fields full of stubble from the grain harvest. "Pretty damned clever if they can pull that off. But if they want to fight six hundred horse with only a hundred or so militia, they're more courageous than I thought."

"I doubt they're expecting any trouble from the Free Staters. More likely, assembling the militia is just a precaution."

"I'll send Rajik to find out."

Singer felt bad about sending Rajik alone into a dangerous situation, but the two Bandeluks seemed to greet each other like old friends. Before long, they were having a lively discussion, and Singer thought he could make out

smiles and expressions of surprise. He felt a bit relieved.

"I wish I could hear what they're saying," Hardy said.

"Even if they were standing next to you, it wouldn't help. You ought to study the language."

"Indeed, sir. I have tried, but it's devilish hard. Did you know, they actually write backwards! It's true!"

"Believe me, I know all about it."

Now, Rajik came back, bubbling over with news.

"It's Ebrahim! He was the one who gave the flower to the courtesan Samia!"

"I have no idea what you're talking about."

"He's a marked man! Amir Qilij put a price on his head! He's been living among the Chatmaks for two whole years!"

"That's interesting, but it's still not what I wanted to know."

"Oh, the bandits? They're in a pit over there." Rajik pointed to a heap of fresh-turned earth.

"Ebrahim appears to be a resourceful fellow. I'd like to have a talk with him."

"That was quite a wild adventure," Ebrahim was saying, as they sat on some worn cushions in his modest home. Singer had never been in a Chatmak house before. He found it cramped and dim, but impeccably clean. A woman, visibly pregnant, was brewing tea by the fire.

"I was sure no one knew about us," Ebrahim continued. "But what do you think, one of Qilij's other women was jealous and told him, and poor Samia was arrested. There was nothing to do but run for my life. My comrades looked the other way. Then, they were ordered to chase me down, but my horse was faster.

"There was nowhere to run. The whole province was raised against me. I rode until my horse was exhausted and then I went to a Chatmak village and begged them to hide me. And they didn't know me, but they all knew Qilij, so they hid me from him. At no small risk. You know, Qilij would surely have burned this place if he'd found me here.

"It got myself some of the white Chatmak clothing, changed my hair and let my beard grow, and soon I don't think my own mother would have recognized me. And I've been here ever since."

The Chatmak woman brought four steaming cups of sugary

tea.

"This is Tamira," Ebrahim said. "I used to think the Chatmaks were stupid, but this one calls me stupid every day."

"You're also a big liar," Tamira said, serving the tea.

"You should be grateful for that, my dove. If I were not a good liar, Qilij would have impaled me, and I'd never have married you!"

"He would have," said Tamira. "And me too, if he'd caught you here. Qilij the Cruel is the worst man in the world."

"I've heard that also," said Rajik.

"This is all fascinating," said Singer. "But weren't you going to tell me about the bandits?"

"There's not much to tell," said Ebrahim. "They came charging in, expecting a bunch of helpless peasants, and we pretended to flee, but when they were in the middle of the village, we turned and attacked from all sides. Not many escaped."

"And you organized all of this?"

"It was not so hard. Once I saw Qilij was defeated, and the Chatmaks all had weapons, I insisted on drilling them. At first they hated drilling and were full of excuses, but now they're all quite keen on it. There's not much to do here after the grain harvest anyway."

"Any sign of Sheikh Mahmud?"

"I didn't ask their names. Maybe he was one of those who ran off. He was not among the dead. Anyway, why are you asking me this? I've already reported it all to Capt. Stewart."

Singer felt like kicking himself. He'd set up these pacification districts and, when the first crisis came, totally ignored them. There was probably a report waiting for him back at Jasmine House.

"We were pursuing them from Seven Pines. They murdered a lot people and burned the village."

"If I'd known that, I'd have killed them twice as dead!"

"I think you killed them enough. Are there any other Bandeluks left in the district?"

"A few, mostly old people. We leave them alone, and they leave us alone. Most of them have fled to Kafra, but if I were them, I'd have stayed and taken my chances with the foreigners."

"Why is that?"

"Because Kafra, my beautiful city, which was so full of fair-scented young women . . .HEY!" Tamira had boxed him on the ear.

" . . . has become a pesthole. The streets are crowded with refugees, and half of them are sick, and I'm sure most of them would get out if they could, but it's too dangerous."

"So, the Prince has the city hemmed in?"

"It's not that. If they want to go, no one stops them, but the city is in the middle of a lagoon, and there's no way out but to swim, and some have escaped, but twice as many have drowned!"

"That doesn't sound like a good deal for anyone. Qilij is determined to fight to the bitter end?"

"Yes, because he expects no mercy from the foreigners, and none from his own people, if the foreigners spare him. But he'll take the whole city down with him rather than give it up. Only a handful have escaped Kafra, and only one made his way in, and he died anyway."

"What do you mean?"

"Ah, I should have explained that if you want out, you can try your luck, but if you want in, the foreigners will stop you, or just as likely, the Amir's men will kill you for a spy."

"But someone got in? How was that?"

"A crazy story, and I'm not sure I believe it myself, but if you want to hear it, this is what Javid the peddler told me: There was this big fool who was one of Sheikh Mahmud's sons . . ."

Rajik broke in: "Which one? Alim? Hisaf?"

Ebrahim looked surprised. "You know these men? No, it was Umar, a big ox of a man, but a simpleton. His father had given him a letter for Amir Qilij, and he was determined to deliver it, no matter what.

"He hid himself near one of the villages on the shore and waited until the foreigners patrolling the area had gone away, then he tried to trade his horse for a boat. But what do you think, all the boats had been burned, on orders of Amir Qilij!

"Then, he traded his horse, armor, weapons and everything he had just for a goatskin and an empty bottle! He put the letter in the bottle and sealed it, then waited till dark and filled the goatskin with air so it would float, lay on it and started paddling across the lagoon. The foreigners spotted him anyway and, because he wouldn't stop, they shot arrows at him, but it was dark, so they only hit the goatskin. Umar couldn't swim, and he sank like a stone.

"But what do you think, the water there was shallow. When his feet touched bottom, he pushed himself back up, took a gulp of air, then went down and pushed again. The foreigners were still shooting, but they could only see his head bobbing up and down, and by the time they shot at it, it was gone.

"He crossed almost the whole lagoon that way, but then he was in the mud and could wade some, though he was very tired and besides that wounded and bleeding. But he made it to the place of the washerwomen, and he called to the guards not to shoot, because he had an important message from Sheikh Mahmud.

"Then, they wanted to take the letter, but he wouldn't give it up, said he had to give it to Qilij personally. So, they woke Qilij up in the middle of the night, and when he read the letter, he had the man impaled!"

"No!" said Rajik, much affected.

"Because the letter, what do you think, said, 'This is my son, who has betrayed you to the foreigners and sold your bride to be their whore. Do with him as you please.'"

8: Krion

My officers are such idiots!

He'd taken a break from the siege to study the mirror that reflected whatever the ruby eyes on Singer's golden helmet were looking at. The mirror gave everything a reddish tint, but that couldn't be helped.

From what he'd seen, Singer was wasting his time, riding around the countryside, going to unimportant places and talking to unimportant people about what were (doubtless) unimportant things, when he should be preparing for the march on Barbosa.

Why did I give him two weeks? I should only have given him one!

Singer had not learned to delegate authority, or else he wouldn't be running around, trying to do everything himself. Annoyed, he put the mirror back in the box and pulled out another.

This time, the tint was green. He was looking at a technical diagram of some sort. It took him a moment to recognize the dam he'd ordered Capt. Lessig's sappers to build upstream, in order to drain the lagoon. Evidently, Lessig was on the job.

Lessig looked up momentarily, and Krion caught a glimpse of some subordinate, who was apparently answering a question. Lessig returned his attention to the diagram, making an "X" through part of it and penning a note in the margin.

Krion frowned. It would be nice to hear what was being said, or at least to read what was being written. He'd have to talk to his staff sorcerer, Diomedos, about that sometime.

Even more serious, he had no way of knowing whether the plan for a dam was good or bad or even calamitous. What if it burst when his men were crossing the lagoon? He'd lost his chief engineer on the beach, and the rest were busy at Massera Bay, so he'd just have to trust Lessig for the time being.

I have to trust someone, but I'd like to know whom.

He put Lessig's mirror back in the box and took out Gen. Basilius'. Now, the picture was dim and strangely distorted, because it came from the small obsidian eyes of the eagle on the crest of Basilius's helmet. All Krion could see was a blanket and part of a cot.

He left his helmet off again! Does he know something?

It was certainly strange Basilius so often left his helmet in the tent, especially because it was a gift from the King, and even more so because Basilius had a bald head which was prone to sunburn.

Damn! If I ordered him to wear his helmet, or published some regulation to that effect, it would only confirm his suspicions.

Krion reached back to scratch the place between his shoulder blades which always itched when there were conspiracies afoot. It had plagued him, on and off, for years, but lately it seemed much worse than usual.

If Basilius was conspiring with someone, perhaps that person was wearing a helmet. Krion checked his other mirrors, but none of his senior officers was doing anything outlandish, nor was Basilius visible in any of the mirrors.

The only important officer without one of the special helmets was Prince Clenas. That was partly because it was a serious matter to lay enchantments on a royal prince, but mostly because no one suspected Clenas of anything but being a lecherous young twit. Everyone knew Clenas was here as punishment, because he'd gotten the chamberlain's daughter pregnant.

Krion had forbidden women in the camp, but Clenas had invoked his privileges to commandeer one of Bandeluk villas overlooking the lagoon for a headquarters, and he was busily turning it into a love nest. With the light cavalry scattered around on patrols, there wasn't much for him to do anyway, Krion reflected.

At this point, one of his aides, Mopsus by name, came in. "There's a woman at the gate who wants to see you, my Prince."

"Why are you bothering me with this? I gave orders no women were to be allowed in the camp!"

"She says she's the wife of Gen. Singer."

"Tell her to go home. She's wasted the trip. Gen. Singer is not here. He's on campaign."

Krion pulled out Basilius' mirror again. The scene in the tent hadn't changed, except now he could see an insect of some kind nosing about on the cot and inspecting the blanket.

Basilius would be upset to see that!

Assuming he was around at all, of course. The Twelve Hundred Heroes had been assigned to guard the northern road against counterattacks, but he really had no way of knowing where Gen. Basilius was at the moment.

All this spying made him feel uneasy. What reason did he really have to suspect Basilius? His sudden breaking formation on the beach had placed Krion in grave danger. He'd put it down to greed for the loot in the enemy camp, but what if it were something more?

Basilius had served his father loyally in many campaigns, though he'd been heard to say he never gotten anything for it but the scars – which was a huge exaggeration – but plainly he was not content with the rewards which had been lavished on him.

Basilius had also been heard to say the four princes of Akaddia, all together, were not worth half of their father. That didn't sound good. Supposing, just supposing, Krion had died on the beach, who would have benefitted?

Not Clenas, obviously. He was too young and impractical. No one would support his bid for the throne, if he were to make one. Clenas was just an idle skirt-chaser.

His older brother Chryspos was a more serious contender. Despite his sexual habits, he'd managed to ingratiate himself with many of the Akaddian nobility, simply by hovering about the court and running errands for the King, who relied on him more and more in old age. Chryspos' business was influence peddling, and business was good.

However, Chryspos and Basilius couldn't stand each other. They were always seated far apart on state occasions. It had been like that for years, ever since an incident between Chryspos and one of Basilius' nephews. A conspiracy between the two would be unthinkable.

That left only Vettius, the eldest brother, who had forsaken all ambition. He devoted himself exclusively to his country estate, his wife and his ever-growing family, and had often been heard to remark the capital was a cesspool of vice and corruption. Vettius might serve as someone else's puppet, if he were compelled, but he wasn't likely to hatch a plot on his own.

Aside from the four princes, the only plausible successor to King Diecos would be his son-in-law, Duke Claudio. The amiable Duke, Krion's brother-in-law, was mainly occupied with skimming every penny from the Exchequer, with which the King had foolishly entrusted him. Claudio didn't want the throne. He didn't care about anything but money.

But what about his wife, Krion's sister Thea? She was older than her brothers and as a child had often said if it weren't for prejudice, she'd become king. But that was a child speaking, and now she had two children of her own. Thea loved dressing up for public events, and when there were none, she'd invent one. Plainly, she'd enjoy playing the queen, but would she really kill her own brother for the sake a gaudy crown?

Damn me! I shouldn't be vegetating in my tent like this! I'm fighting ghosts!

He'd come to conquer the Bandeluks. Whatever plots might be brewing, he'd deal swiftly and effectively with them when they surfaced. The power of the state was in his hands, and he wouldn't give it up lightly. The army needed his attention, so the wicked fantasies would have to wait.

He stepped outside, to where Mopsus and another aide, Bardhof, were waiting. "Saddle my horse and yours too, both of you, I'm making a tour of inspection. Pick out ten Brethren for an escort, whoever is on duty."

Krion didn't like to be kept waiting, nor was he. Within five minutes, the whole group was ready to leave. Krion was famous for his surprise inspections, the terror of his officers, so his sudden decision to leave the camp didn't cause any consternation.

The road outside the camp was, as usual, crowded with sutlers, most of them selling things like fresh fruit, grilled goat meat and beer to soldiers who were not content with their rations. In one corner, someone had set up a cock fight, and the betting was heavy. Most of the vendors were westerners who had sailed, bribed and smuggled their way to follow the army, but a minority were locals attracted by the sound of clinking coins.

Before long, they'll be renting out their sisters, and I'll have to crack down.

As his escort cleared a path through the crowd, he heard a shrill, feminine voice: "YOUR HIGHNESS!"

Standing next to his horse was a prim-looking young woman in one of the beribboned travel suits fashionable among the bourgeois. She was a very unlikely figure to see in such a place.

Is this the same one who tried to barge in on me before?

"Your Highness! I am Erika, the wife of Gen. Singer! I urgently need to see him on family business!"

Family business? Where does she think she is?

He was stuck. Tradition required him to be gallant to the ladies, at least so long as anyone was watching, and a lot of people were.

"My apologies, madam. Military duties require my immediate attention. If you will present yourself at the gate tomorrow, I will receive you then."

"I'd be most grateful."

Now she's made me break the rule against women in the camp!

Women were so needy and importunate, and on the battlefield quite useless. He thought he'd escaped them, but they'd followed him even here.

Leaving Erika behind, a problem for tomorrow, he followed the road until it forked. One way led down to the beach where he liked to gallop his horse for exercise. He chose instead the shore road, which passed a small hill, one of the outcrops which dotted the southern plain. He left the guards below and rode up with his aides to have a look at the city.

Kafra was a beautiful city, as grand as any in Akaddia. Refugees described it as a dismal place stinking of sewage and unburied corpses, but from a distance, it had lost none of its charm. He could clearly see the exotic-looking walls, domes and towers, covered with blue and green tiles. Sunlight reflected off the gilded dome of the Amir's palace. Above everything floated a red and white banner.

This city is mine! It belongs to me!

Basilius wanted to storm the place, which would be, as he described it, a quick and easy assault. All they had to do was bombard it with screechers, while moving some warships laden with troops up the channel.

That was much too risky, Krion thought. If the Bandeluks managed to sink even one vessel, the channel would be blocked, and he would be defeated.

I have never been defeated! I will never be defeated!

Besides that, he refused to bombard the city. He wanted it intact. The makeshift docks at Massera Bay wouldn't supply his army for very long, nor could he anchor his ships offshore through the winter. He needed a real port, and he would have one.

As he was riding down the path which wound behind the hill, his horse suddenly stumbled, and he was flung headfirst over its neck. He made a grab for the bridle, but missed and landed on his back on the hard, stony path, still clutching the reins in one hand.

"My Prince!" yelled his aides in unison and rushed to his side.

He was momentarily stunned, but soon pulled himself to his feet (thus avoiding the indignity of being helped) and began brushing himself off. "Now how the hell did that happen?"

Bardhof, the young officer he'd gotten to know in the Covenant campaign, picked a horseshoe from the path. "He's lost a shoe. Look at it!"

"I see. It is a horseshoe. So what?

"The nails have been filed down. They're barely half the normal length!"

There was a brief silence, as Krion studied the horseshoe and reached some conclusions. "This shoe was certain to come off. If I'd gone for my usual morning gallop, I could have been seriously injured, perhaps killed."

"Someone is plotting against you, my Prince!" said Mopsus, who liked to point out the obvious.

"Yes indeed, but we must keep it to ourselves for the time being. If I go back to the camp like this, everyone will know what happened. Go find me another horse, and be quick about it!"

As Mopsus hurried back to

the road, Krion gave the horseshoe to Bardhof. "Put this somewhere safe. Don't lose it; it's evidence.

"I want you to look into this for me. Talk to the grooms. Find out if anyone was hanging around the stables lately.

"Also, speak to Clenas' officers. Don't tell them what happened, but find out if Clenas' horse lost a shoe on the beach. I know he fell during the battle, but I don't know why. Go now!"

"Yes, my Prince!" Bardhof saluted, and he was gone.

For a minute, Krion was left standing alone on the hillside. The truest, best royalists he had were Covenant plebs, he reflected. Besides, Bardhof was intelligent and capable, and would have been promoted long ago, if he could have been spared from the staff. Bardhof would surely find out whatever was to be learned.

Mopsus returned quicker than expected. He was leading a splendid dappled stallion. "My Prince, you may not believe this, but some peasant was actually using it to pull a cart full of melons! I gave him three gold thalers for it."

Krion studied his new horse. It was indeed very fine. "You cheated him. It's worth at least five, perhaps even more."

This is excellent! The beast must have strayed from the battle-field.

"Put the saddle on him and a halter on the other. We'll leave it at the next outpost."

The next stop was Fort #5, one of several forts he was building to encircle the city, obstacles to a sally or to a relief attempt. Construction was behind schedule. Capt. Parsevius complained there was a shortage of building materials.

"You see, my Prince, the work on the scarp is nearly done, but we haven't nearly enough timber for the palisade. I've sent out foraging parties, but they were able to find very little. Unless we start demolishing villages, I don't know where the timbers may be found."

"If you demolish the villages, you'll get nothing but mud bricks and an arrow in the back. There's hardly a tree to be found here, unless someone planted it, and the Chatmaks value their olive trees more than their wives.

"I don't want you wasting any more time with foraging. I'll publish a decree offering a bounty on timber. The locals will bring us what we need from the hills, or wherever they can steal it."

This war is a lot more expensive than I expected. Let's hope Amir Qilij has a fat treasury!

"By the way, what are those men doing? Are those embrasures?"

"Yes, my Prince. Gen. Basilius said this would be a good position for bombarding the city."

"He is in error. There will be no bombardment. Fill them in."

Does Basilius think he's my schoolmaster? Or did he assume I wouldn't be alive to countermand him?

The rest of the day went on like that. In one place, there was a shortage of stone, in another, a shortage of labor. In a third place, he found an officer had embezzled the funds intended for construction work and had the man arrested.

I hate sieges! If I'm not doing it, it doesn't get done!

His chief engineer had chosen a very bad moment to get himself killed. Perhaps he'd promote Lessig to the position, if the dam turned out well.

Toward evening, he reached Basilius' headquarters, which was in the foothills next to the winding road that led to Barbosa. The guard at the gate told him Basilius was not there. He was on patrol.

"Would that be him then?" Krion pointed to a party of mounted, hooded men, who were slowly working their way down the road.

"I believe so, my Prince."

Krion studied the group as it approached. If this was Basilius, he was in disguise. The usual trappings of heavy cavalry were not visible. The hooded men were wearing breastplates under their cloaks, but these were smeared with something that blocked any reflections. The clanking of the armor was muffled in some way, as were the horseshoes. They were dragging two captives behind them.

This is a side to Basilius I haven't seen before. Why is he sneaking around like this?

As the men drew closer, the lead rider threw back his hood, exposing a bald head. He saluted. "Forgive me, my Prince! My men are not prepared for an inspection."

"No apology is necessary, General. This is not a parade. What have you been up to?"

"A bit of reconnaissance, my Prince. I went up and had a look at the plateau. It's a bleak and dreary place, and almost impassable. I don't believe we'll face any serious threats from that direction."

"Excellent. Who are your prisoners?"

"A couple of Bandeluk stragglers. The fat one claims to be a sheikh or some such. He offered me his weight in silver if I let him go."

"If he really has those funds available, he must be someone important. Mopsus, ask him his name and where he's from."

Krion had chosen Mopsus for his staff because he was fluent in Bandeluki. He now addressed the prisoner with some polite words and got angry shouting in response.

"He refuses to answer, and he calls you a thief. He says you're riding his horse, Sea Wind."

"Tell him I paid gold for it. Repeat the question."

The prisoner had another fit of angry shouting.

"He just keeps cursing someone named Rajik, who he says betrayed him twice."

One should not speak this way to princes.

"Tell him he's a fool, if he trusted someone who had already betrayed him once."

Krion turned to Basilius. "Your prisoner is uncooperative. Put him to the question. Find out whatever he knows about the imperial army, its location and what it's doing."

Basilius grinned in a way that always gave Krion a slight chill. "You can rely on me, my Prince."

"And do try not to kill this one."

Narina forgive me, but I do need people on the payroll who enjoy this kind of work.

9: Rajik

"Is being called Lt. Ogleby. May being helping you?"

Inwardly, Rajik was fuming, but he stayed polite. The guards had tried to ignore him. They just stared blankly at him when he spoke. Finally, they'd called this tall, gawky young officer, who spoke Bandeluki so poorly.

"I'm looking for my sister Raeesha. We were separated a week ago, on the day of the battle, and I haven't seen her since. I was told I might find her here."

"Raeesha is being female woman? Is no being female woman here, is all being military soldier."

"Have you seen Raeesha? She's a woman about my age. She recently cut her hair short."

"Is having seeing many, many female woman. Short hairs on woman is no being seeing. Is being something what jokish, yes? Good luck, young dog."

Rajik turned red, but said nothing. He simply walked away.

"Young dog" is probably a nice endearment in whatever stupid language he normally speaks.

Next to Jasmine House was the home of Nabil the smith, but the house was looted and empty. Even the blacksmith's tools were gone; nothing remained but the anvil and forge. It was the same in Khalid the potter's place: there was nothing inside but the heavy potter's wheel and the kiln.

The door to Rahat the fletcher's house was standing open, so he didn't bother to go in. One door remained closed, the shop of the widow Mubina. Rajik went in without knocking, as he had many times in the past. A bell attached to the door announced his arrival.

Immediately the odors welcomed him, the anise, cardamon, cinnamon, garlic and the others which were familiar to him since childhood. Blocks of sugar and salt, bags of tea and spices stood in rows on the shelves. Fresh herbs from Mubina's own garden hung over the counter, behind which sat Mubina herself, smiling as she always did, as if there were no war and no demons, as if his father had never whipped him, as if he'd never seen his brother struck down with a spear, as if he had not come here to kill his sister.

"Rajik! I'm so happy to see you! I didn't know whether you were alive or dead! How is your esteemed father?"

"He was well, the last I saw him. He fought very bravely against the foreigners, who came at him in overwhelming numbers with their demons, until he was forced to retreat. He's now gathering men to his banner and will surely drive them into the sea!"

"This is wonderful news! Just look at my poor little store, hardly anyone comes in, and still the shelves are half empty! It has been almost two weeks since the last shipment from Kafra! If this war doesn't end soon, I shall be ruined!"

And why are you not already ruined? Because no one wants to rob a harmless old Bandeluk woman? Or because no one wants to try it while she's within screaming distance of the foreign garrison? Who knows what they might do?

"Grandmother, you must help me. I'm looking for my sister Raeesha. I haven't seen her since the day of the battle, and I've looked everywhere."

Mubina seemed perplexed. "I haven't seen Raeesha in quite a long time. When she was a child, she used to come in often, but when she became a woman, she was penned up in the women's quarters, and I was seldom invited there. I heard she was pledged to Amir Qilij. Is she not in Kafra with the others?"

"No, she became separated from the others and hasn't been seen since. I fear something may have happened to her."

"To our little Raeesha? No, that cannot be!"

"Could the foreigners be holding her prisoner?"

Mubina seemed surprised at the question. "No, I don't think so. If they were abducting girls, I'd have heard of it. One of them came in yesterday and bought some tobacco. Look at the strange coin he gave me!"

She brought out a silver coin and laid it on the counter. It had the symbol of a crown stamped on it, besides some strange lettering

"It it good silver. I checked. It was even a good price. But what am I to do with this strange foreign money?"

"I'm sure you'll find someone who wants it. Is there anyone here who can help me?"

"I don't know. The ones left are mainly old people who don't get out much. Sometimes they come into the store, but no one has said anything about Raeesha."

Maybe she's dead, after all. Why do I feel so relieved? I'm getting childish, like Umar.

"Wait," said Mubina, remembering something. "There was a boy working for the foreigners in the kitchen. He was also named Rajik, but he was a stranger. No one here had seen him before. He rode off to the east with a bunch of foreigners a couple days ago."

"Another Rajik? That is strange."

"Hmpf. I've known several Rajiks. Most of them are dead now, I suppose. This one was about your age, but I didn't see much of him. He mostly stayed in the kitchen."

This is confusing. Is Raeesha still pretending to be a boy? If so, can she also be whoring herself to the foreigners?

"Did you see this Rajik? What did he look like?"

"I only saw him from a distance. He didn't come in here. He was about your size, I think. When he left, he was on a horse, with armor and weapons like a soldier. He had a yellow plume on his helmet. They all did, except for the General. He wore a golden helmet."

It was hard to imagine his sister Raeesha wearing armor and carrying weapons. But she'd fooled a lot of people into thinking she was a boy, so maybe she'd deceived the foreigners too. Surely a whore wouldn't dress in this way? But then why ride off with the foreigners? Working in the kitchen was something he could understand, if they forced her to do that, but if she was just a slave, they'd surely not have given her armor and weapons!

Nothing makes any sense. Maybe she really is dead. Maybe this new Rajik is a spy or a traitor. I should find out!

He spent the rest of the day in the village, talking to everyone he could, but no one had seen Raeesha, and no one could identify the other Rajik. For the most part, the Chatmaks wouldn't speak to him. Whatever information they might have, they kept to themselves.

In honor of his visit, Mubina killed a chicken and cooked it up with some rice and raisins and spices. It was the first real meal he'd had in a week, and he found himself trying to praise Mubina's cooking while stuffing more of it in his mouth.

"My, you're hungry!" Mubina said. "Sheikh Mahmud really is in a bad way, isn't he?"

"I'm afraid so," Rajik admitted, shame-faced.

Mubina sighed. "Your father and his men were always parading around in their fine armor and weapons, and I thought they were invincible, but now they've left me stranded, like a fish dying slowly on the beach! Whatever shall I do?"

Rajik said nothing. He avoided her gaze.

"One thing, I can do, at least. You can sleep here tonight, but where you go after that, I can't advise you. I really don't know what happened to Raeesha."

Lying on a mat in Mubina's store, Rajik had trouble falling asleep, despite the satisfying meal in his stomach. Trying to piece together what had happened was going to be difficult. His father had said Raeesha was whoring with the soldiers in Jasmine House, but no one here had seen her. Tomorrow, he should go east and look for the stranger Rajik. It was the only clue he had.

What a disaster this war was! His family was totally ruined! All were dead or scattered; not a single one was left in Jasmine House. And not only them, the whole Bandeluk people had been driven from their homes. Where now would someone shoe his horse or buy a jar for water? Soon, Mubina too must shut her door, and then where would they buy tea, a necessity for even the poorest? In all Chatmakstan, there was hardly anyone left who could even read and write!

The foreigners thought they'd won, but all they had was an empty sack. What did they think they were doing, those mighty princes and generals? They'd spoiled everything, so there was nothing left to steal! They must be mad, these foreigners!

Morning found him staring at the long road eastwards and trying to think of some clever plan. The stranger Rajik had left three days ago, mounted, armed and in the company of many foreign horsemen. His chances of chasing him down and interrogating him didn't look very good.

He had no horse, and stealing one would be too big a risk. The foreign soldiers were everywhere, and the Chatmaks hardly even needed the excuse of a stolen horse to strike him down. He couldn't overtake the stranger anyway, unless he stopped somewhere, and his chances of approaching him would be better on foot.

Perhaps he should disguise himself as a Chatmak. Fooling the foreigners would be easy . . . but fooling the Chatmaks would be almost impossible. They'd know him at once by his accent and his mannerisms. If they caught him in disguise, they'd assume the worst. But a stray Bandeluk boy looking for his family might escape their notice.

His only chance would be to travel as quickly as he could on foot and not linger longer than he must in any one place. Mubina had given him three flatbread cakes, which would last a day or two. After that, he'd have to scrounge for food. The date harvest was in, but the olives were ripening on the trees. Most of the grain had been harvested, but there were still stalks here and there. It wouldn't take long to gather a handful of grain. He still had his bow, and he could down a bird or a rabbit without much trouble. Or, if he got hungry enough, it wouldn't take any skill to make a chicken or some vegetables disappear from a peasant's garden.

Nothing stands in my way, I only need to take the first step.
He took it.

A little after noon, he overtook a patrol of foreign soldiers that must have left Jasmine House at dawn, while he was still sleeping off his big supper. The day was warm. They looked very hot and sweaty in their metal armor, their spears and shields clanking with every step.

What do they think they're doing, marching around like this, where everyone can see them a mile away, and any child can outrun them?

The soldiers didn't seem interested in him, but he still gave them a wide berth as he passed. A little later, he came to Birdsong village. As he was getting very thirsty, he asked a woman who was getting water at the well for a drink, but she just stared at him insolently.

Fool! All I want is a drink of water!

He tried to take the jar, but she screamed and struck at him with it. He dodged nimbly away, and the jar hit the side of the well. There was a loud *BANG* and pieces of jar flew in all directions. This attracted the attention of everyone in the village, who stopped what they were doing and began cursing him.

"Look! Look! One of the masters is back!"

"Come to molest our women, master?"

"Or do you want to put us in chains and whip us!"

Meanwhile, the first woman was still screeching. Outraged at

the loss of her jar, she picked up pieces of it and flung them at him. He backed cautiously away, raising his hands to show his peaceful intentions, but it was too late. When he saw the villagers were picking up stones, he turned to run.

He only got three paces before the first stone hit him.

His father was hitting him on the head with an iron chain. He cried and pleaded, but his father wouldn't stop.

He was lying in a bed. His head was throbbing. Raeesha was sitting next to him and holding his hand.

"You're alive," he said.

"And you, gods be praised. I thought you died on the beach, and then I found you, but it looked like you were dying, your head was broken, and the doctor didn't know if you'd ever wake up, sometimes they don't, but you're back now and . . . I talk too much," she said, trailing off.

"My head hurts."

"Oh, the doctor gave me some pills. Don't move, he said not to move your head."

She gave him a pill and some water to drink. He could only lie there and look at her. Her hair was still short, but now it was tangled and dirty. Her chin was smeared with something black. A heavy jacket concealed her body.

If she's playing the whore, she isn't making much money.

"You look awful."

"Better than you, by a long way. The doctor says you should try to sleep."

The pill was making him sleepy, but he didn't want to sleep, his father was waiting somewhere with an iron chain . . . no, that was just a dream, he was getting confused . . . of course, he was confused, his head was broken . . . but if it was broken, why didn't it hurt . . . because of the pill of course . . . what was in the pill anyway . . . it didn't matter, nothing mattered . . .

When he opened his eyes again, Raeesha was still there. She looked like she hadn't slept in days.

"My head hurts."

"You want another pill?"

"Not now, later. Where am I?"

"Jasmine House. Some soldiers found you at Birdsong village. The Chatmaks were trying to kill you."

"I will burn that village."

"You've never seen a burned village, or you wouldn't say that."

"What have you been doing?"

"Trying to stay alive. They all think I'm a boy named Rajik. I gave them that name because I thought you were dead. I told them your name is Hisaf."

This is too much!

"You're not taking my name! I've lost everything else, but I'm not giving up my name!"

This outburst seemed to frighten Raeesha. She just sat there, staring at him, saying nothing.

She doesn't want to provoke me. She's afraid I'll get excited and injure myself.

That reminded him his head hurt. The pain was making him cranky. He should take a pill. But not yet.

"I can't use that name. Hisaf may still be alive. Umar said so."

"Umar. Yes. Well."

"Tell me."

"Tell you what?"

"About Umar. I said his name, and you looked like I beat you with a stick."

"Later."

"Now."

Raeesha sighed and looked away. "Umar is dead. Amir Qilij killed him."

"What? He was alive a few days ago. I spoke with him."

"He is dead now. He was carrying a message from Father to the Amir. When the Amir read the message, he had him impaled."

"What? Why?"

"The message said the bearer was a traitor who had sold the Amir's bride to the foreigners."

No! Father! It was not I who betrayed you, it's you who be-trayed me!

"Give me a pill. Then go and sleep. I'll be fine here."

He closed his eyes as if he were already falling asleep. His sister must not see him crying.

When he opened his eyes again, Raeesha was gone. There was some food on the table: bread and cheese, some dates, and a pitcher of goat's milk. Slowly and carefully, in order not to injure his head, he sat up and began eating. It was a simple meal, and he'd eaten many like it before, but none had tasted nearly as good.

The gods have spared me again. But why do they make me suf-fer like this?

The clothes he'd been wearing had been cleaned and left on a chair. He put them on. Looking around the room, he found his satchel under the bed. He poked around in it until he found the long braid of black hair, which he stuffed in his sash.

There was a foreign soldier walking by as he stepped into the hall. He stared at Rajik, noticing the white bandages which covered his head.

"Ra-ee-sha," he said slowly and carefully, but the soldier only stared blankly at him.

He tried it again: "Ra-jik." This time, the soldier nodded and pointed down the hall, toward the entrance of Jasmine House.

They really do think she's a boy named Rajik!

There were several small rooms here. The door to one of them was open, and inside sat Raeesha, polishing a big pair of boots. He touched her lightly on the shoulder.

"You should be in bed!" she said. "Your head was broken like an egg!"

"Then I'll go to bed. But first, I wanted to give you this." He handed her the braid. "Father wanted you strangled with it. If you see him again, you can give it back to him."

"I'll just throw it out. What I should have done before. Why should I care what Father thinks?"

"Everyone needs a family."

"Then I need a new one. The old one is trying to kill me."

"You're lucky, *everyone* is trying to kill me!"

"Then you should try to make some friends."

"I would, if I could find any."

"The foreigners saved your life."

"Only *after* they tried to kill me!"

Why do we keep arguing about nothing? She's the only one left who cares about me, and I can't talk to her!

"Those are nice boots."

"They're the General's. He says I'm an 'aide-de-camp.' It's a kind of personal assistant."

"Why are you helping our enemies?"

"They're Father's enemies, not mine. They never did anything to me."

"They will."

"Nothing nearly as dreadful as what Father has already done."

Another stupid argument. Just shut up!

He saw a map on the wall and went to look at it. Chatmakstan was stuck between the ocean and the barren Area of Effect. The only way out was through Kafra, and it was besieged. He couldn't stay here, and he couldn't escape.

"What are we going to do?" he finally said.

"In a few days, the army is marching on Barbosa, and I'm going with it."

"Across the Area of Effect? That's crazy!"

"Caravans cross it all the time."

"Once or twice a year. There's almost no water, only enough for a few camels."

"The General says we're going to cross it, so that's what we're going to do."

"And you're going to show him the way? You've never even

been there."

"I've been as far as Sour Spring."

"Great! You travel one day and come to Sour Spring, and then you tell the General, 'I'm sorry, but this is as far as I can take you, I have no idea how to get to Barbosa!'"

"That's easy, you just follow the caravan trail around the edge of the plateau. If you don't fall off the edge, you come to Barbosa."

"You say it's easy, but you've never even tried it!"

"And you think it's impossible, but you've never tried it either."

Why do we have these stupid arguments!

"What do you want in Barbosa, anyway?"

"I don't know. When the General says, 'Go!' no one asks why."

"The Witch will just turn you into a big mushroom or something."

"She might think twice, if I have five thousand armed men with me. How many can she turn into mushrooms?"

"They're *men* and she's the *Witch!*"

"Then it's lucky they have a woman with them."

"It's too dangerous. I'm coming with you."

"And *you* will protect me from the Witch? You're a *man* and she's the *Witch!*"

"I'm going, and you can't stop me!"

"You're a stubborn donkey. You just had to go look at the foreigners, and how did that work out?"

"I saved your life! I did see the foreigners, and I came home, and I survived!"

"Yes, yes, things are going very well for you. But the doctor says you shouldn't move around until your head is healed."

"It's better already. Don't worry about me, I'm fine." He turned to stomp out the door, but the sudden motion made him dizzy, and instead of striding away manfully, his knees folded and he fell to the floor.

10: Hisaf

He had another corpse on the line. He tugged gently, then with vigor, hoping to pull it free, but the precious fishhook was hopelessly stuck, and he was forced to haul it in. The fishermen to his right and left, knowing what was to come, stepped back, so for the moment, he stood in the middle of a broad, empty space on the jetty.

Last time, it was a stocky, middle-aged woman, pale as if carved from marble, eyes staring blindly and mouth frozen in a permanent scream. She was one of the newly dead. They were not much trouble. Removing the hook from where it was caught in her skirts was no difficult task. Then, he had only to push her back in, using one of the oars that were lying around. Oars were plentiful, now that the boats had been burned.

This corpse was lighter, so presumably a child. As it came closer, he could see the yellowish tinge of a corpse that had been in the water for a long time. There were large reddish patches, where crabs and fish had stripped off the skin.

A boy. He was nearly naked, his hands raised as if in prayer. The hook was in a bad place, under the scalp. Now, he'd have to touch that stinking mat of hair. First, though, he needed to get rid of the crab that was still clinging to the corpse's ear.

Drawing his knife, he struck the crab with the flat of the blade, causing it to fall into the shallow water around his feet. It began scurrying into deeper water, but before it had gotten very far, someone from the crowd of onlookers waded in and caught it. Crabs were food.

Disgusting!

There was no time to reflect on the morality of eating crabs taken from corpses. He still had the unpleasant task of freeing his line. He sawed at the scalp with his knife, until a patch came loose, then used the knife blade to scrape it off the hook.

He took an oar and began shoving the corpse back into the water. He wanted it deep enough to be out of sight, otherwise, he'd have to look at it for the rest of the afternoon and possibly the next day. At one time, he couldn't have done this without lacerating his feet, because the water was full of shellfish, urchins and other sea creatures. But now, everything which could possibly be caught, cooked

and eaten had been stripped away, so the sea bottom was bare.

Looking out over the water, he could see bodies floating here and there in the lagoon. They were not a problem. He could always cast his line between them. It was the bodies that lay on the bottom, so they couldn't be seen, that were the problem.

Back on the jetty, he checked his fishing gear and the day's catch, two small, foot-long fish. Nothing had been stolen. He was, however, out of bait. To get more, he'd have to cut up his fish. It didn't seem worthwhile, so late in the day. Already, the other fishermen were crowding around, hoping to get in a lucky cast before the carts came.

He held up the fish and inspected them. They were a disappointingly small offering for the twenty hungry people crowded into Uncle Davoud's home. Still, it was the only fresh meat they had, so perhaps he should be grateful. He sighed and began trudging down the long jetty to the shore.

The jetty, he was constantly reminded, was not built for fishing, but to keep out enemy vessels. It was made of loosely-fitted blocks of stone, very rough and uneven, and in places, slippery. The best fishing was on the far end, so he had to get up early and navigate the whole length every day, trying to find a place before the other fishermen came.

The far end, naturally, was also the place where they dumped the corpses.

He felt achingly tired. Not that he'd been doing anything very strenuous, it was just the constant hunger that made everything so difficult. The one small loaf of bread a day, which was the standard ration, was hardly enough to keep even a small child alive. Simply standing in one place for ten hours drained his strength to the limit.

He'd left just in time to avoid the carts. As usual, there were several of them being pushed toward the jetty by exhausted-looking people with despairing expressions on their faces. Amir Qilij had exercised his cruel sense of irony by forcing the foreign residents to collect corpses.

Things could be worse. I could be pushing a cart.

With the ghastly carts behind him, he increased his pace. His stomach told him it wanted to put the fish in the family stewpot as soon as possible. What else went in the stewpot depended on chance: Sometimes it was an onion from the garden, sometimes only a handful of dandelions. Once, there was a rat.

And, of course, there would be wine to drink. Uncle Davoud was a wine dealer, and he still had an impressive cellar. The family was drinking it dry, being suspicious of the well water. So far, none of them had gotten sick.

Every morning before dawn, Uncle Davoud got up and hid a bottle of wine in the trash behind Ferran the baker's house. Every evening, someone threw a sack containing four small, stale bread rolls over the garden wall. These, too, went in the stewpot. Drinking that watery cup of fish soup was the high point of his day.

Before long, he came to Tanner Square, a part of the city that always smelled bad, even before a mob of refugees had set up tents where the leather merchants had once hawked their wares. There was, he noticed, a young girl with a rash on her face next to the fountain, just sitting and staring blankly into space. Everyone was giving her a wide berth, as she was obviously sick and possibly contagious.

Probably, her parents were dead or dying, or she wouldn't have been left by the fountain. Or perhaps, she'd been expelled from her home as soon as they noticed the symptoms. Hisaf had seen more and more orphans and abandoned children in the streets. Sooner or later, they all ended up in the carts. . . except for a few who vanished into dark corners.

The cats and dogs had long since disappeared.

Not wanting to pick his way through the crowd of street-dwell-ers on the main avenue, he took Draper Street, a side road that ran along the edge of the city. This was one of the richest parts of Kafra, and he'd once envied the wealthy merchants whose mansions, look-ing out over the lagoon, competed with each other in splendor, but now it was stinking and crowded with refugees, like everywhere else.

Before he'd gone very far, a woman in a flimsy silk dress came out of a doorway and bumped into him, whispering, "Hello, hand-some! Would you like to spend an hour with me?" He merely shook his head and brushed past her. It was no good getting outraged. A woman with hungry, crying children would do what she had to do.

Draper Street eventually connected to Dock Street, which ran in to Heroes Square, one place that Hisaf would gladly have avoid-ed. There were a few militia men standing here: not the dreaded pal-ace guard, but unhappy conscripts forced to carry a spear while their families went hungry. Hisaf might have been one of their number, had not the watch commander received the timely gift of a case of wine. The militia had no interest in Hisaf, they waved him through with only an envious glance at his fish.

What a waste, forcing tinkers and cobblers to stand around with a spear, doing nothing! They'll be sneaking off for a nap, first chance they get.

There was not much here worth guarding. Even the homeless refugees avoided Heroes Square, which stank worse than Tanner Square, or any other place in Kafra. The smell of blood and guts here was even worse than the corpses in the lagoon.

Where once had stood a single impaling stake, there were now ten. Blood was pooling under each of them, and the flies, which were everywhere, came here in companies and regiments. In front of each victim was a neat little sign which gave his offense. Most said something like, "I stole bread," but today, he noticed one that said, "I was a cannibal."

Involuntarily looking up, he saw a young man about his own age, but with a plump, well-fed appearance. Someone had a grudge against this one: They'd cut off his right hand and stuffed it in his mouth, before skewering him through the stomach, where it took a long time to die.

I guess fresh meat is not that hard to find. Rather expensive, though.

Some of the victims were marked, "I was a traitor." This happened more and more, because Amir Qilij would not believe it was possible to defeat his invincible army without some treacherous plot. At first, the foreigners had come under suspicion, then people working for foreigners, then anyone with foreign relatives or connections, and now, it was anyone at all.

Suspects were always guilty. They were tortured until they confessed, and they seldom failed to implicate other suspects. The spacious dungeons under Amir Qilij's palace were full of miserable captives waiting their turn to be tortured and impaled. The executioners couldn't handle them all, so ten people or more were often packed into cells intended for only four.

So far, Uncle Davoud had avoided the stake, despite his sizeable import business, because he had the privilege of supplying the palace with wine. No matter what else happened, deliveries of wine to the palace must not be interrupted.

Still, palace officials sometimes came by and demanded bribes for striking his name from the list of suspects. These were, Hisaf believed, the same ones who had put his name on the list in the first place. Everyone in the palace was corrupt to the soles of his shoes. Uncle Davoud always paid. It was his privilege to pay with silver and wine, rather than with blood.

What will become of us when the wine cellar is empty?

Suddenly, the answer was literally staring at him in the face. It was his own brother, Umar, looking down at him from an impaling stake, his face full of incomprehension and despair. Hisaf thought he had been taken down. Leaving the corpse up for three days seemed like an unnecessary insult. Hisaf felt he'd already suffered every possible injustice and humiliation, but this went over the limit.

I must find some way to kill Amir Qilij!

11: Erika

This is not going well.

Prince Krion was being unhelpful. He'd created a gracious impression when she met him at the gate, but now he was brusque and almost surly.

"You simply must understand Gen. Singer is otherwise engaged," he was saying. "As you can see from the map, Barbosa is almost two hundred miles away. This is hostile territory and nearly impassable."

"And yet, you have apparently ordered my husband to cross it."

"At the head of a considerable army. If I were to assign you an escort, it would require at least a hundred cavalry, which I cannot spare. Besides which, you've refused to tell me why your visit is so urgent."

"I am not at liberty to do so without my husband's consent."

"Then you will have to wait until the campaign is concluded."

"Such a delay might have grave consequences for your loyal officer and for his family."

Krion was getting seriously annoyed. "I did not wish to raise the subject, but I've made some inquiries, and I am reliably informed Gen. Singer is unmarried. He has no family."

Erika felt a blush spreading across her cheeks. "We are betrothed! The banns have been announced and officially registered!"

"Which, even if true, is still insufficient ground for presenting yourself as his wife. I have been entrusted with conducting this war by my father, the King. It is a matter of the gravest import, on which the future of my country and yours depends, and I have no time to meddle in the love interests of my subordinates, even if" – he glanced suspiciously at her midriff – "it may be a case of impending fatherhood."

Erika could only stand there with her mouth open, appalled.

This is totally outrageous!

"Mopsus!" said the Prince, and a young officer immediately appeared. "Escort this young woman to the gate. In the future, it will not be necessary to announce female guests. Simply inform them I'm occupied with important military affairs."

With her own hopes sinking, Erika suddenly remembered her promise to Rosalind.

"One moment, please, Your Highness!" Reaching into her purse, she pulled out the ring and handed it to him. "My sister Rosalind wished to give you this."

Krion glanced at the very ordinary-looking ring in his hand. "Yes? Well?"

"She's quite smitten with you."

Distracted, Krion slipped the ring on his finger. "She and a thousand other unbalanced young women, who are zealous to take charge of my personal affairs. Good day, madam."

Next to the gate was a wooden bench, apparently provided for messengers and other minor functionaries to cool their heels. As she had nowhere else to go, Erika sat down on it. She took a handkerchief from her purse and starting wiping away the tears which were streaming down her cheeks.

This is an impossible situation!

The stress of the ocean voyage had proved to be only a mild foretaste of the overland trip: She'd spent days bumping up and down on wagons, lying to drivers and supply officers, and bribing guards, besides continuously fending off one amorous young man after another, by now too many for her to count. It had taken all her charm and most of her money to get her this far, and the prospect of going back, empty handed, to face the wrath of her parents was more than she could bear.

If only I had some poison, I'd take it!

Someone quite near was clearing his throat. She looked up, blinking away the tears, to see a young man in a gorgeous uniform, obviously an officer of some sort.

"I'm terribly vulnerable to crying ladies," he said. "And to find one in such a place as this excites my curiosity to the utmost. I'm Capt. Nikandros, chief of staff to Prince Clenas. How may I be of service?"

"I am Erika, the wife of Gen. Singer. I've travelled a long way to see my husband on some urgent personal business, but Prince Krion informed me that he's not here and unlikely to return in the near future, and he ejected me summarily from the camp. Now, I'm stranded here, nearly destitute, without the means either to support

myself or to return."

Nikandros clucked his tongue sympathetically. "I apologize on behalf of Prince Krion. He has a rather abrupt way with the fair sex. If you want my advice, you should seek an audience with my superior, Prince Clenas. He's a friend to the ladies, and likes nothing better than playing the gallant rescuer. At the very least, he won't turn you away so brusquely as his brother.

"I'm on my way to his headquarters now. You may accompany me, if you wish."

Prince Clenas? Isn't he the infamous young profligate and seducer? But it seems I have no other choice! At least, Nikandros seems nice enough.

The only transport available was one of the clumping, bumping supply wagons. This one contained sacks of navy beans, the taste of which was already familiar to Erika.

Nikandros rode alongside the wagon, making conversation: "You know, the army employs a great many dispatch riders. It would require no miracle to send a message to Gen. Singer. His last headquarters were near Massera Bay."

But I was just there!

"I thought he was with Prince Krion! And then the Prince told me he was at someplace called Barbosa!"

"He departed just a short time ago. It's possible a messenger could still catch up with him."

Stupid, stupid! Why did I have to stick with the fable about the winter uniforms? If I'd just told the truth, I might be in the arms of my husband now!

"I must write him a letter at once!"

But how am I to explain this? If I tell him I'm with Prince Clenas, my plans will be ruined!

As she wrestled with this problem, the wagon began climbing a rise where a road led up to an impressive two-story building, crowned with six cupolas, and surrounded by a low wall. Looking over her shoulder she could see all the way across the lagoon to Kafra. It was a huge city, at least twice the size of Tideshore. The sun glinted brightly from the tiled roofs and towers, and from the golden dome.

So this is where the silk comes from!

The bumpy ride came to a bumpy end. Nikandros dismounted and helped her to the ground.

"Pray excuse me a moment, Madam. All visitors to the headquarters must be registered with the main office there." – He pointed to small building near the entrance to the compound. – "I shall return shortly."

Erika, though distracted by her own problems, noticed the guards had saluted very smartly to Nikandros, and the groom who took his horse had bowed as if to royalty.

This is a stroke of luck, to find a protector who's such an important person. But why does he have to be with Prince Clenas?

Waiting for Nikandros to return, she paced nervously back and forth, composing the letter to her husband in her mind. She had only planned on a joyous reunion. Explaining her presence at Kafra would be tricky. And of course, there must be no mention of Prince Clenas.

When Nikandros returned, his manner was apologetic: "Madam, I fear you will think very little of me. I am forced to explain that a short time ago, Prince Clenas received orders to conduct a reconnaissance some distance east of Kafra, and I can't be certain when he'll return. In the meanwhile, you're welcome to enjoy the hospitality of the Royal Light Cavalry, in one of the rooms we reserve for visiting officers. And if you'll step inside the office for a moment, we'll see about dispatching your letter."

Clenas isn't here? What a relief!

Sitting at a rough wooden table in the headquarters, she began to write out the letter she'd mentally composed:

> Dearest Singer!
>
> I rejoice at the news of your promotion! There will be no need for you to resign it to see me, as I have come to you! Temporarily, I've been placed under the protection of Capt. Nikandros, an officer in the service of his Highness. I may be found at his headquarters, which is located in a two-story building with six cupolas, on a hill by the lagoon, just north of the main camp. No time for further news, as I must scurry to post this letter. Please reply by return messenger. Waiting with anxious anticipation, your adoring,
>
> Erika

She took a moment to study her prose. Surely, the letter would bring him, as soon as he could, to this place, and they'd be reunited. Any entanglements with Clenas could be left for the future. She sealed the letter and passed it to Nikandros, who gave it to a dispatch rider.

"Hikmet, our major domo, will see you to your room," he said

Hikmet took her bag. He was a Bandeluk man of middle years, well dressed and of dignified bearing. Erika had often seen men like him in her family's shop.

As soon as they were out of earshot, she addressed him in his own language: "Tell me, effendi, how did you become a servant to these Akaddians?"

He looked at her for a moment in astonishment, before grinning. "You shouldn't call me that, so long as I hold this lowly position. The truth is, I'm the owner of this property, or I was until the foreigners confiscated it. I begged to be allowed to stay in the capacity of a servant."

"It's a very nice home. You hope to recover it after the war?"

"It's my home. If I abandon it, I have nothing. My family is small, and is allowed to sleep on mats in the kitchen. My wife is a very good cook. You'll sample her food this evening."

"But what were you before the war?"

"I was a silk merchant."

"Really! Do you know the Wartfield trading house? I was employed there until recently."

"I sent House Wartfield a shipment of Recaih satin just last year. Here is your room." He left her bag on the bed and bowed politely before leaving.

Erika caught her breath.

What kind of a trap is this?

The room was sumptuously over-decorated with thick carpets on the floor. Silk hangings showed men and women engaged in romantic activities. The ceiling was painted to show a rose garden in which young boys and girls played naughty games. In the middle was a gilded double bed, covered with silk sheets and embroidered cushions.

And this is supposed to be a military headquarters?

Her first thought was to check the door to see if it was locked. It was not, and she felt a bit safer when she saw there was a solid bolt on the inside. She then picked up a pillow and examined it. Someone who wore too much perfume had laid her head there not long ago. She checked the sheets, but they'd been freshly changed; there seemed to be no evidence of debauchery. She pulled open some drawers, but they were all empty, except for the lingering scent of perfume.

I wonder who my predecessor was? Some local woman? Hikmet's unfortunate wife or daughter? Would he have warned me, if I were in danger?

Going to the window, she saw she had a fine view of the lagoon and of Kafra.

Where are the other people who lived in this big house? Gone to Kafra? Are they looking back across the water at their home?

She sat down on the edge of the bed and assessed the situation. Nikandros was a procurer, or at least he expected a reward for recruiting young women like herself. They were apparently not planning to hold her by force, because neither the door nor the window was locked, and the low wall outside would be easy to scale. But if she fled, where would she go?

My husband is coming here, sooner or later. I saw the messenger leave with the letter. But will he be here before Prince Clenas returns?

The safest course would be to remain where she was. At least, she was in no immediate danger of being ravished; she'd just have to deal with that contingency when it occurred. She began dressing for dinner.

The dining hall was a long room with a raised platform on one end. On the platform was a table set for two. Nikandros was waiting for her, wearing a uniform even more splendid than the previous one.

"We'll be dining alone. Prince Clenas has taken the rest of the staff with him," he told her.

"My compliments on your uniform," she said. "I hope that the prince will not be jealous of your finery?"

Nikandros laughed. "Not in the least! Clenas likes to dress up his staff in the finest clothing available, so as to create an impressive display. His own uniforms are even gaudier."

Really? Even a prostitute would feel silly wearing all that braid!

"Dressed as you are, I must assume that you've distinguished yourself in many battles?"

"Unfortunately not, staff officers are drones on the battlefield. I was assigned to diplomatic duties during the Covenant War, and since we landed, I have only engaged in one battle. Then, I barely held my own against the Bandeluks, who outnumbered our small force.

"The battle went on for hours. I was principally concerned with dodging their lances, as they came at us again and again. At one point, when it seemed that I'd surely be spitted, fate intervened, and I was thrown from my horse. It was badly shod. If not for the luck of a bad horseshoe, I wouldn't be here today.

"Ah, I see they're bringing our dinner."

The meal which Hikmet had promised turned out to be shrimp and oysters fried together in olive oil, with diced vegetables and many spices. Suspicious of drugs, Erika tasted the wine carefully, but it seemed perfectly normal, merely a good vintage of scopolo. The food, on the other hand, was full of red pepper, which could encourage heavy drinking and licentiousness.

But only if I allow it to. I must simply moderate my consumption, and all will be well. If this is a seduction, it's a tame affair. Nikandros plays by the rules.

Dessert was a confection made with candied dates. Erika ate it eagerly, especially because it moderated the burning taste of pepper.

Having eaten, Nikandros rang a small bell, summoning Hikmet, who supervised the removal of the plates. Erika was ready to leave, but Nikandros said, "If you'll be patient a moment longer, Hikmet has arranged a small entertainment for us."

Three musicians entered the lower hall: a lutist, a drummer and a man with a brass horn. Nikandros leaned close to comment: "I'm told these men played for the Amir himself."

"And yet, they didn't flee to Kafra."

"They fled *from* Kafra, taking the opportunity to put some distance between themselves and Amir Qilij. They were once a quartet, but one of them managed to offend the Amir in some way."

Erika settled back to enjoy the music.

The lutist began strumming an adagio, a pleasant, simple tune, accompanied by soft drumming. It spoke of lazy summer days, innocent childish pleasures, country dances. But just as Erika was beginning to feel a bit sleepy and thinking this was all there was, the horn broke in with a soft, disharmonious note that faded slowly away. The lutist paused briefy, then continued in forte, as if to drive away the intruding horn, but it soon returned, louder and louder, and a duel developed with the adagio. The wailing, sorrowful horn suppressed the cheerful lute and played a brief finale before it, too faded away. The drummer, who had been pounding out a beat, unnoticed, in the background, continued by himself for a moment, before ending on a single, heavy stroke.

"That's charming," said Erika. "What do they call that?"

"I'm afraid I've never mastered their language, or they mine," said Nikandros, throwing the musicians three gold thalers. "But I'm told we can expect another performance."

Now a woman came out, dressed in dark silk.

"She's lovely, but not nearly so lovely as you," Nikandros said.

So! Things are getting a bit warmer!

The dark woman began singing, accompanied by the musicians. Erika had never heard the song before, but the theme was familiar:

Without you, the birds can't fly,
Without you, the rivers run dry,
You're gone, and I don't know why.
Come, come, come, come home to me!

Are there demons that would pain you?
Or soldiers to detain you?
Or high walls to constrain you?
Come, come, come, come home to me!

If demons, let us bash them!
If soldiers, let us thrash them!
If high walls, let us smash them!
Come, come, come, come home to me!

Erika applauded. "That was some fine singing," she said in Bande-luki. The woman smiled and nodded.

Nikandros threw her a gold thaler. "What did you tell her?" he whispered.

"Only that she sang well."

He must have told the truth when he said he couldn't speak Bandeluki. It's clear he wouldn't have chosen this song if he could.

The woman took her coin and left. Then a man and a woman dressed in white came out.

"Peasant dancers, very skillful," said Nikandros.

The musicians began playing a simple, rhythmic tune in lazy tempo. The dancers, beginning from opposite sides of the hall, approached each other and passed with a stately glissade, as if each were alone in the room.

Having passed, each looked back over the shoulder at the other. They reversed direction and approached again. This time, the man drifted toward the woman, while she drifted away, so that they circled, and each returned to where they'd begun.

Now the music shifted to allegro, and the dancers quickened their step. As they approached each other for the third time, the man took the woman's wrist and spun her around. She broke free and fled around the hall, in a series of graceful leaps, while the man pursued, step for step.

The music became feverish and the dancing passionate. The

man kept rushing at the woman, but she eluded him until he finally fell to one knee, as if exhausted. With this, the music broke, but resumed in a different key. The woman now approached the man, took him by the hand, and they shared an intimate pas de deux as the band performed its finale.

I can see where this is heading.

Nikandros whispered to her, "If you're in the mood to step on the dance floor yourself, I happen to know a number of . . ."

How do I escape this nuisance . . . Wait! What are they wearing?

As the dancers presented themselves for the expected payment, she had a better look at their costumes, which were sewn from a coarse fabric she'd never seen before.

She stood up and said, in Bandeluki, "Please step closer. I'd like to inspect your costumes."

The peasants only gaped at her, uncomprehending.

They aren't Bandeluks! What are they then?

She reached over and rang the bell to summon Hikmet.

"Madam! What are you doing?" said Nikandros, as she left the platform and walked up to the male dancer, rubbing the fabric of his shirt between her fingers. Hikmet soon appeared beside her.

"Please ask this gentleman to remove his shirt. I'd like to examine the fabric."

Hikmet said a few words in a language she'd never heard before, and soon the shirt was in her hands. She tore a strip from the hem and began teasing apart the threads.

"What is this? I've never seen it before!"

"They call it *pamuk*," said Hikmet. "It's a coarse fabric suitable only for peasant garb or sacking. You haven't seen it because the export market is nil."

"What are you two jabbering about?" said Nikandros, much put out.

She switched from Bandeluki to Akaddian long enough to mutter, "Don't forget to pay the dancers. Show them some of your famous princely generosity."

Meanwhile, she'd untwisted some of the threads and held them up to a candle flame for a better look. She exposed one thread to the flame and watched while it burned.

"The fabric is coarse because it's homespun," she told Hikmet, "but the fibers are both fine and strong. We could make some excellent cloth from this, light but durable."

Hikmet shook his head skeptically. "But why go to so much trouble, when we can simply import silk from the eastern provinces?"

"We *can't,* that's the point. This cursed war could go on for years and meanwhile, the market is starving for eastern fabrics!"

"I see what you mean!" said Hikmet excitedly. "This *pamuk* grows like a weed all over Chatmakstan. If we could only get our hands on some looms . . ."

"And a bit of capital . . ."

"I demand to know what is going on!" said Nikandros loudly. The evening was not going the way he'd planned it.

"I doubt our conversation would be of much interest, your Highness. Unless, perhaps, you're not content with being the laughingstock of your nation and would rather be known as the richest prince in Akaddia."

12: Raeesha

"That's the damndest thing I've ever seen," said the General.

"There are damnder," said Raeesha.

"Not that I've seen," insisted the General, shaking his head.

They'd been riding all day, with the army behind them, southward along the edge of the escarpment. Raeesha had pointed out several places where one could climb up, but none that could accommodate horses. Now, they'd come to the Stairway, a long series of steps which had been cut from the stone, running up the side of the cliff, over a thousand feet.

Singer stared at it. "Why would anyone build such a thing? You said there was nothing up there but some ruins."

"I don't know, General. It was the ancient Kano people who built it. I guess they had a good reason."

"I'm trying to imagine the amount of work it took to remove so much of the cliff face. They must have needed thousands of workers."

"According to the legend, they did it all in one night. They used demons."

Singer stroked his chin thoughtfully. "That's an interesting story, even if untrue. Let's go see what's on top."

The stairs were only wide enough for a single horse, and riding would have been reckless. They dismounted and led the horses, but they hadn't gotten many steps before Singer said, "We won't make it to the top if anyone up there is trying to stop us."

"Don't worry, General, the Stairway is not guarded. There's nothing on the other side that needs guarding."

"A good theory, but I'll feel better about it when we reach the top."

Singer was the first one up. As he got his first view of the Area of Affect, he said, "You weren't joking!"

Behind them was Chatmakstan, with its fields, villages and the numerous streams which twisted down to the sea. Ahead was something else entirely. From the top of the Stairway, all one could see was a valley, sloping down from the edge of the escarpment

for about a mile, before rising toward a high, rocky ridge, which stretched to the right and left into the distance. A second ridge was visible behind the first, and in the evening light, it was still possible to discern a third, behind that.

"It's like that all the way to Barbosa, except for the ruins in the middle," said Raeesha.

"You still haven't told me much about the ruins."

"I've never been there, and I don't know anyone who has. All I know is what I was told, it's some ancient Kano city, abandoned now for a thousand years."

There was no water to be seen, and not a single tree anywhere. Singer reached down and plucked some of the fragrant, knee-high shrubs, which were growing everywhere, and offered them to his horse, which merely snorted.

"There's no grazing between here and Sour Spring, and not much on the other side," said Raeesha. "Not even camels will eat these plants. There are some antelope around, but not enough to feed an army."

"Go back down and tell Baron Hardy to camp below the Stairway tonight and graze the horses all he can. We'll save some on the water and grain if the cavalry is the last to ascend.

"Can you explain that to

him?" he added in Hallandish.

"I now more good," said Raeesha in the same language.

"That will have to do. I'll wait here for the first infantry to arrive. This is going to take some thought."

As dawn rose over the barren, rocky landscape, most of the army was still waiting to ascend the Stairway. A seemingly endless line of soldiers, carrying their weapons and packing all sorts of supplies and equipment, gradually emerged at the top, before making camp and waiting for the rest to arrive.

The General told Raeesha, "While we're waiting, ride down to Sour Spring and tell me what you see there. . . . Well, what are you staring at me for? Get on your horse and go!"

Trotting down the caravan trail seemed like a nice outing, at first. Simply sitting astride the horse was pleasant enough. Saddle sores were no longer a problem. It was a warm day, but she had the wind in her face and felt fine.

After awhile, though, she began to feel lonely and a bit frightened.

This is the Area of Effect! Gods know what can happen here!

She remembered the stories she'd heard: Ghostly armies assaulted ruined cities in the moonlight. People got lost and were found years later, entirely turned to stone. Monsters had been reported: lions and other fantastic creatures.

Quit being so nervous! Men are brave! If you're scared by fairy tales about lions, how are you going to deal with a real menace like the Witch?

The emptiness of the land was reassuring in its own way. One mile of caravan track looked a lot like the last.

There's nothing to be afraid of. It's just an empty desert that any fool can . . . WHAT'S THAT!

Something had suddenly jumped up from the bushes. It shot away, quick as lightning, to the ridge, where it disappeared between two rocks.

It was just an antelope. Men are brave! Don't jump at every sound!

Soon, she was no longer nervous. The trip was just hot and boring. There was nothing to see, nothing to do. She wished she'd brought more water.

About noon, she came to Sour Spring. It was as if something had made a hole in the landscape, obliterating a ridge line and leaving a big depression with a large, shallow pond at the bottom. There was grass everywhere, and she could see a little circle of tents.

Tents!

Those were Bandeluk tents, and the Bandeluks themselves soon appeared, ten of them, dressed as soldiers. All stood to look at her as she approached.

Men are brave! Ride right up to them!

Entering the camp, she dismounted, just as if she were back in Jasmine House. One of the soldiers stepped forward.

"Olgun, sergeant, Kafra Light Cavalry," he said.

"Rajik, private, Sheikh Mahmud's Home Guard," she replied without blinking.

Olgun was a tall man, broad-shouldered and fiercely mustachioed. He grinned down at her. "If you're looking for your boss, he passed us about a week ago. He was running for Kafra like a scared rabbit. I told him there was no way to get through, but he wouldn't listen."

"He's a stubborn donkey, like the rest of his family. I'm not looking for him. He abandoned us in a fight with some Chatmaks."

Olgun laughed. "Chatmaks! Great warrior, he!"

"You wouldn't laugh if you'd seen them. They've gotten courage from somewhere. They surrounded us with their spears in a village, blocking the way out. I cut down the man in front of me and got through, but I was almost the only one. Sheikh Mahmud was long gone. I won't follow him anywhere, if I have the choice."

Olgun nodded sympathetically, as if he'd heard the story before. "You're plucky, for such a little fellow. Where did you get that nice jacket and the strange dagger?"

"From one of the foreigners. He won't be needing them anymore."

"Neither will you, I fear. You're not out of trouble yet!"

"When the foreigners landed, Amir Qilij sent us to collect his newest bride from Jasmine House, but we couldn't find her. Meanwhile, foreign troops overran the province, and there was no going back to Kafra. Qilij would probably just impale us, anyway, if we returned without the girl. We've been stuck here ever since. There's nothing to eat but antelopes, and they're very shy."

"You don't want to go to Kafra," Raeesha said. "It's a pesthole full of hungry refugees and surrounded by foreign troops. Qilij just sits in his palace, waiting for the city to fall.

"You should thank the gods that you're free of his service. I had a little disagreement with him myself, and I was lucky to escape. He probably still has some fools out looking for me."

"You're not Ebrahim? No, he was a much bigger man."

"Ebrahim is still alive. He was hiding among the Chatmaks. He joined the foreigners, and they made him a sergeant in their militia."

"Tricky bastard! Probably found a girl too!"

"He has. But that doesn't help us. We're sitting in a trap here. I just came from the Stairway. There's a whole army of foreigners coming this way."

"Really? What do they want here?"

"Only the gods know. They're foreigners. Maybe they're looking for some way to outflank Kafra and break into the homeland provinces."

"They'll never make it through the Area of Effect!"

"Unfortunately for them. Unfortunately for us, they don't know that yet."

Olgun took off his helmet and wiped the sweat from his face. "Then it's up with us. There's nowhere to run, unless we want to try our luck with the Witch of Barbosa."

"If you ask me, it might be better surrendering to the foreigners. At least, they won't turn us into anything unnatural. We might make out like Ebrahim."

With this, the other soldiers, who had clustered around to hear the conversation, broke in, all talking at once:

"That would dishonor us!"

"Would you rather be impaled by Qilij?"

"Or fed to the Witch's lions?"

"Maybe we can get through to the Madlands!"

"A clean death in battle would be better!"

One wanted to fight, another to abandon the horses and climb down the escarpment, a third to go to Barbosa. But most wanted to surrender. Eventually, the frenetic discussion tapered off, as the idea took hold.

"This would appear to be our fate," said Olgun, putting his helmet back on. "Gods help us!"

There was now a large camp of over a thousand foreigners spread out around the Stairway. "You said there was a whole army. I thought you were exaggerating, but now, I believe you," said Olgun.

"I don't see any cavalry. It's not too late to turn back," Raeesha said.

"To where? They'll catch us sooner or later."

As they approached the camp, a group of foreign soldiers came out, forming a line to block them. The Bandeluks reined in. "Who are these?" said Olgun.

"They're called Thunder Slingers. We always kept clear of them. Best you stay out of range. I'll go forward alone. If I don't come back in an hour, do what you think best."

Olgun clapped her on the shoulder. "By Savustasi, you're a brave one, for such a little fellow!"

Getting past the Thunder Slingers didn't take long. She simply shouted the word "Peace!" in their own language. They called forward a hard-bitten man with penetrating eyes, Capt. Stewart, who, ignoring her Hallandish, practiced his limited Bandeluki on her.

"Who you?"

"I'm Rajik, a personal aide to the General. I'm returning from a scouting mission to Sour Spring with prisoners."

"Oh. General's Bandeluk. You go him."

She was waved on through.

Finding the General was not so easy, as the camp was now quite large. She had to lead her horse past some strange soldiers, heavily armored, who stopped pitching their tents to stare at her, but she walked on by as if it was nothing unusual, and no one tried to stop her.

When she found the General's tent, it was surrounded by demons, seven feet tall, a frightening spectacle.

Men are brave! The demons haven't attacked, and they won't! Ignore them!

The demons were holding a prisoner, casually, as a man might hold a struggling rabbit, so as not to injure it. He was yelling angrily at the General, who stood there calmly in his golden helmet, and took it without protest.

Raeesha was surprised to see the prisoner was a foreigner. He was exercising his voice in Hallandish. She couldn't make out more

than a few words: "Impossible . . . brute . . . disaster . . . betray . . .
forever . . ."

My vocabulary is getting better, but I don't think even a Hallander could understand him, the way he's yelling.

Seeing her, the General threw a dismissing gesture in the direction of the prisoner. A demon promptly stuck a rag in his mouth.

She saluted. The General addressed her in Bandeluki: "Excuse the fuss. When we have a moment, I'll introduce you to Sgt. Littleton, our engineer. I was just explaining my plan for crossing the Area of Effect to him. What did you find at Sour Spring?"

"There was a squad of Bandeluk cavalry. I persuaded them to surrender. They're waiting for us south of the camp."

"I'll mount up."

Olgun and his men were where she'd left them. Their relief at seeing her again was obvious, but they seemed intimidated by the General. As the dying rays of sunlight reflected from his polished armor and golden helmet, he looked like the very god of war.

The General spoke first: "I understand you men are here to surrender?"

"Yes, effendi," said Olgun.

"Then dismount."

No one moved. Raeesha could see what they were thinking: This was the final step. Dismounted men can't run away. On the other hand, here is an important enemy general, fallen into their hands. Amir Qilij would probably pardon them if they brought back his head, and give them a generous reward besides.

Before this new idea could germinate any longer, she seized the moment and dismounted. The nearest soldier dismounted as well, and the rest followed him.

"Make a pile of your weapons," said Singer, full of confidence, as he always was.

Again, there was a moment of hesitation. Raeesha threw her bow and quiver on the ground, followed by both of the knives she carried. The others added their weapons. Soon, there was a big pile of swords, daggers and bows, topped off with the gruesome war axe that belonged to Olgun.

"Those of you who wish to leave your weapons on the ground may do so. You may mount your horses and go home or wherever you please."

There was a quiet moment as each man looked at his weapons. They all knew it wouldn't be easy to cross the Area of Effect without provisions and without a bow for hunting. And then, how could they fend off the vengeful Chatmaks? And where could they go? Did they still have any homes to return to?

One soldier, the youngest, said, "Excuse me, effendi. My father is a bailiff at Willow Lodge. I'd like to go and find him."

"Go then."

There were many sorrowful looks as the young man rode away, but no one followed him. The chances of finding his father at Willow Lodge didn't seem very good.

"Anyone else?" said Singer.

No one budged, though several lowered their heads, as if ashamed.

Mark those men. They're the most honorable and the most dangerous.

"Those who wish to enter my service can take their weapons back. We'll make a place for you in the camp."

Raeesha fished through the pile for her weapons, and the others followed her example. Whatever was to come, it would be better to face it with a weapon in the hand, and a foreign master was better than none.

One sword was left on the ground. Raeesha leaned over to pick up the light, curved blade. "I lost my scimitar in a fight with the foreigners, but the foreign swords feel strange in my hand, and I'm not sure I can use this one. It's not much like the scimitar."

Olgun looked at it. "Oh, Arif's old shamshir. A good blade, watered steel. That takes more skill than chopping people up with a scimitar. I'll give you a lesson sometime."

"I would be grateful."

Back in the General's tent, Littleton was sitting next to a folding map table, studying it and sipping from a wine bottle as if nothing had happened. He started to address Singer as he entered, but the General silenced him with a gesture.

Turning to Raeesha, he said, "Sgt. Littleton will be building a road across the Area of Effect."

"General, that is over a hundred miles!"

"We will be employing the *fui* demons, which may not be ideal for the task, but much better than a crew of human workers. So far, the *fui* demons have never failed at anything they've attempted. In the meanwhile, the army will camp at Sour Spring, if you think it will hold us."

"For a week perhaps, or maybe longer, if you're careful not to muddy the water."

"I'll have to look out for that. I congratulate you on the successful completion of the recent mission. I'm promoting you to head scout."

"But General, I didn't know we had any scouts!"

"We do now, and they seem more willing to follow you than to follow me. You'll be leaving with them tomorrow for the ruins. Report to me what you find there."

The ruins! What have I gotten myself into!

"General, I've never been there. And there's no water."

"If we knew what was there, scouting would be unnecessary. You should pack all the water you can carry, and grain for the horses.

"You told me the ruins were an abandoned city. Whoever lived there had water. If there is no water now, it must be because the water level has fallen. Take a pick and shovel with you. Look for a well, a dry spring or lake bed. That's where you'll find water."

"And if we don't?"

"Then you should return and report that."

Raeesha thought it over.

This is not a little romp to Sour Spring. This is a long and dangerous mission!

And shortly, after that:

The General trusts me! He's put men under my command, the advance guard of the army! I must not disappoint him!

She thought of something else: "General, the men will desert if I tell them where we're going."

"Then don't tell them."

"Shouldn't they swear an oath or something?"

"They have already broken one."

"Ah. Very well, sir. We'll be needing some more of the yellow plumes."

"See to it."

When the sun rose, the General's camp was much larger, but

the yellow plumes were with Hardy's company, still at the bottom of the Stairway, which was full of troops. However, the Invincible Legion had blue plumes on their helmets, not so long and flouncy, but for Raeesha and her scouts, they worked just as well.

Over breakfast, Raeesha explained the mission to Olgun and the others in this way: "The General is sending us to scout the area northeast of here."

"Really?" said Olgun. "What is to the northeast?"

"He doesn't know, which is why he's sending us to look."

"I know what is there," said Navid, a leathery-faced old veteran. "Plenty of rocks and scrub and nothing else."

"If we're lucky, that is all we'll see," said Raeesha. "But the General didn't expect to find you here, and he doesn't want any more surprises."

"It's better than being sent to fight our own people," said Olgun. "Yes, let us go have a picnic in the desert. Where's the harm?"

"Maybe we can shoot another one of those antelopes," said Yusuf, who had been complaining about the food the foreigners had given them.

Raeesha's method of getting over the ridge was simple: She followed the tracks left by antelopes. The first set of tracks led to an opening in the stones which was too narrow for the horses. The second went up a slope that quickly became too rocky and steep to be passable. But at the third place, a great boulder had rolled downhill, leaving a gap the horses could pass through, though carefully and only one at a time.

"I told you," said Navid, as he surveyed the next valley. "It looks just like the place we left."

"And that's good," said Raeesha. "What were you hoping to find?"

"A wine dealer would be nice," said Yusuf. "Or maybe some pretty girls."

"I'd settle for just a water hole," said Raeesha.

"Ha! Now you're really dreaming!" said Olgun.

The second ridge line was easier to cross than the first, and the third was easier still. They were getting more clever about finding ways to cross the ridges. By noon, when they stopped to eat and water the horses, they'd crossed five of them.

"Hey!" said Raeesha. "Don't let them drink all the water! We have to make it last!"

"Really?" said Olgun. "How long are you planning to stay out here?"

"When the food and water are low, we'll head back."

"Then why so strict? We aren't going to find anything out here anyway."

"When we go back, the General will just give us another mission, maybe not so easy as this one."

"I see what you mean. The foreigners are mad to come here at all, and only the gods know what they plan to do next. Easy on the water."

By sunset, they'd crossed a dozen ridges, but the horses were getting tired and balky. They camped on the floor of a valley, a patch of desert that looked much like all the rest. Raeesha told the men to gather all the dry brush they could to make a fire, but it just produced a big cloud of choking smoke, and quickly burned down to a few embers, barely enough to make tea.

"This is not a fun picnic," said Yusuf.

"You could be enjoying the Witch's hospitality," said Navid. "I hear she loves plump youngsters like you. They're so very tasty when she fries them up with a bit of garlic."

"We're alive, and that's the only thing that really counts," said Raeesha.

"We could just camp here and go back when the water is gone," said Yusuf. "No one is going to come and check on us."

"I am checking on you now!" said Raeesha.

"And why should you care?"

Quick! Think of something!

"I've been noticing things," she began vaguely. "We're going up and down all day, but more down than up."

"So?"

"I think we may be getting closer to water. See, the plants are bigger now."

Are they? I think they are!

Navid pulled out his dagger and dug a small hole. He reached in and rubbed some dirt between his fingers. "There's no moisture here, just dry, cracked soil."

"If it's cracked, that means there *was* water here!"

"In the spring, maybe. Not now."

"If there *was* water here, then there may *still* be water downhill, and that's where we're going!"

Sitting around the dying campfire and sipping their lukewarm tea, Raeesha could see a new idea was taking hold: Men who have spent time in the desert didn't need to be told water was important. And searching for water would be more interesting than simply loitering in this bleak campsite.

The next morning, Yusuf shot an antelope and immediately wanted to cook it, but there would be no time for that until evening, so he had to ride around all day with a dead antelope slung over the pillion. His complaints were frequent.

A few ridges later, they found the road. It was made out of cobblestones and ran down one ridge line, across a valley and up the other side, ending in a blank cliff.

"What in the name of all devils is this?" said Olgun. "Why would anyone build a road here?"

There was a silence. No one seemed to know the answer to this question.

Think of something! You're the boss. You have all the answers.

"No one would. The road is older than the cliff. It was once flat and straight. Then these ridges popped up and ruined it."

Olgun removed his helmet and wiped his face. "That sounds impossible. How could such a thing happen?"

"Who knows how. This is the Area of Effect. Maybe that was the effect. Anyway, they didn't put a road here just for fun."

"We must be close to the haunted ruins!" said Yusuf.

"Maybe, but we're not there yet. Meanwhile, let's see where this road goes. It's headed in the right direction."

The brush was getting thicker, the plants greener. By evening, they were riding along the road, which was easier than pushing their way through the undergrowth. The ridges were also lower and easier to cross. Having found a relatively open place for a campsite, Raeesha sent the men to gather some firewood, a harder task now, because the plants were not so dry.

While they were doing that, she asked Olgun for a lesson with the shamshir. "This is a very light weapon," he began. "But for a little fellow like you, it might be the best thing . . . Hey! Your ears are pierced!"

"Yes, I got drunk one night in Kafra and made a stupid bet with a friend. Are you going to show me how to use this thing?"

Olgun shrugged. "Some friend! . . . With the scimitar, you're just chopping people, mostly with a downward stroke, and you don't care much what you hit, because it will always do damage. But the shamshir takes a more delicate hand. Hold it like this. It's important that the little finger press firmly on the pommel, because you'll be drawing the blade across your opponent's body.

"The edge won't penetrate heavy armor, so pick some place which is unprotected. The face is good, because your opponent will draw back, which throws him off balance, and he may even close his eyes, which means you can hit him anywhere.

"Even better is the throat, a cut there always kills. But of course, that depends on what kind of armor he's wearing. Since you have a nice iron collar, I'll show you. You must stand perfectly still, so I don't cut you by accident."

Raeesha felt a sharp prick of

fear.

He's going to draw that big, sharp blade across my neck!

"Now you're closing your eyes, which is a very good example of what *not* to do. I'll try it again, and this time, watch closely."

The high-pitched squeaking sound, as metal touched metal an inch from her throat left her nerves tingling.

I don't think I'll ever get used to this!

Which was followed by:

Men are brave! If they can do it, so can I!

"You saw how that works," Olgun was saying, as if he were a master of penmanship, "from directly under your opponent's right ear, downwards toward his left shoulder. Now try it on me, in slow motion."

Olgun was wearing a heavy iron collar over a mail shirt, but it looked like it would be very easy to nick his chin, or even take off an ear. She drew the blade very slowly across the collar, as requested.

"Now, you're making two mistakes. First, you're too timid. Secondly, you're not looking me in the eye. You must always look your opponent in the eye, because the eyes will tell you what he's going to do.

"I have more to teach you. There are parries and feints, and the point attack, and a special trick for cutting the wrist. But the main thing is to practice the basic stroke over and over until it's automatic.

"In a cavalry skirmish, enemies will come at you from all directions, one after the other, as fast as a swarm of bees. Hesitation means death. There's no time for fancy sword work. Whoever strikes first is the winner, and there is no second prize. If you do it right, you may end the battle with a bloody sword in your hand, and not know whose blood it's or how it got there.

"When we have the opportunity, I'll find a practice post, so you can repeat the motion until you do it without even thinking. Now, I'll show you how it works from the other direction . . ."

Not thinking, yes! If I stop and think about any of this, I'm lost!

The eight men had brought back a surprisingly small amount of dry wood, but the pieces were bigger now, and Raeesha thought she could cook the antelope if it were cut into strips. She brought out one of treasures she'd put aside for such occasions, a bag with samples of the spices which were prized by every Bandeluk.

"This is not bad," said Olgun, savoring the roast antelope. "How did you learn to cook like that?"

"A soldier does what he has to do," she answered vaguely.

With a good meal in their stomachs, the men grew moody and thoughtful. Navid was moved to sing:

> There were seven soldiers who rode for Khuram Bey,
> They came o'er the mountains and into Hillineh.
> "Oh, why have you come here, you soldiers of the Bey?
> Have you come to rob us, or have you run away?"
> "We have not come to rob you nor have we run away,
> We've come to see your master, the lord of Hillineh."
> "What news do you bring him, what news from Khuram Bey?"
> "That we soon shall tell him, to you we will not say."
> They came to the palace, there they found their way,
> And stood before the amir, the lord of Hillineh.
> "We have a memento, a token to convey,
> The head of your brother, who slighted Khuram Bey."
> Do not look for them, the soldiers of the Bey,
> They have left their bones in the land of Hillineh.

"What a cheerful song! I feel better already!" said Yusuf.

"Khuram Bey sounds worse than Amir Qilij," said Lufti, a young man who hadn't spoken much before.

"There's no one worse than Amir Qilij," said Raeesha.

"You've never met my father-in-law," said Olgun.

Raeesha brought out a second treasure, a bag of dates, and passed it around. But now, the melancholy had set in. The men were all thinking about their homes and their women, and wondering if they'd ever see them again.

A wind suddenly came up and scattered sparks from the fire. The men backed away until each was sitting alone in the dark. It was starting to get chilly.

Olgun finally asked the inevitable question: "When are we going back? The water is half gone."

"I still want to see where the road goes."

"What does that matter? We could die of thirst in this desert."

"I don't think so."

She drew the curved knife and dug a small hole in the ground, as Navid had done the night before. "See how moist it is! The soil clings to your fingers!"

Several men dug out their own samples.

"He's right!" said Lufti.

"I was once a farmer," said Navid. "I have often seen soil like this, and no water for miles."

"Then why are the plants so tall and green?" said Olgun.

"The water is only a short distance under our feet," said Raeesha. "Why do you think we brought a pick and shovel? We could probably dig a well right here, but it would be easier to travel a little further, and then we'll have no trouble finding water."

"What for?" said Yusuf. "We're running straight into the cursed ruins, and no good can come of that."

"I wouldn't mind seeing the ruins, just once," said Lufti.

The others simply stared at him.

Raeesha brought out her strongest argument: "Comrades, we are not covering ourselves with glory! If your grandchildren ask what you did in the war, what will you say? 'I was a henchman for Qilij the Cruel . . .'"

"I would not put it in those terms!" said Olgun.

"'. . . but then I changed sides and joined the foreigners . . .'"

"I'm still not happy with that deal!"

"'. . . until we cowardly deserted . . .'"

"That is *not* what I meant!"

"I'd rather say, 'I took part in an expedition that crossed the barren Area of Effect and rediscovered the marvelous ruins of the ancient Kanos.' That would be a story worth telling!"

"What makes them so marvelous?" said Yusuf. "I always heard they were full of ghosts and monsters."

"You heard that from someone who had never seen them," said Raeesha.

"If there are ghosts and monsters, I want to see them!" said Lufti.

"I am forty-two, and I have never seen any ghosts and monsters," said Navid skeptically. "I'm not afraid of ghosts and monsters."

"Because you've never seen any," said Yusuf.

"And you have? Bah!"

"We're not looking for ghosts and monsters, we're looking for water," said Raeesha. "And even if there are ghosts and monsters, why should we run away? If there are ghosts and monsters, let them run away from us!"

The fire had burned down, and the moon was rising, large and red, over the nearest ridge. They all turned to look at it.

"A red moon means clear skies tomorrow," said Olgun.

"I call that a good omen," said Raeesha. "Let's look for water until noon. If we don't find any, it won't be too late to turn back."

After two ridges more, they saw the foundations of a building next to the road. There was not much left, only some rows of heavy field stones, enough for a big farm or perhaps a small inn.

"I see ruins, but I see no ghosts or monsters," said Navid.

"Look, there is a well!" said Lufti.

They all rushed to see, but the well was full of earth and stones. It was no more than four feet deep, and it was dry.

"So, there was water here," said Olgun.

"What I've been telling you!" said Raeesha. "Let us go a little further."

The ridges were getting lower and gentler. The road crossed over the next one without breaking, as it had before. As Raeesha crested the hill, she dropped the reins. The horse stopped anyway. It too was staring in astonishment. The men pulled up beside her. All sat there and gaped. They sat for a long time on their horses, simply staring

Olgun removed his helmet and wiped the sweat from his face. "So, I guess we found them," he said.

13: Singer

I hate this! Why do I have to do this?

It was the high holy day of Theros, the god of war. Observance was obligatory. Attendance was obligatory. A homily from the commanding officer was obligatory.

But faith is not obligatory. That's good, because I don't have any!

Father Leo had set up his wooden field altar, with its folding legs, and a small gilded statue of Theros prominently displayed, along with the ritual objects: a sword, shieldand helm. He was preaching a long sermon, recounting the legendary deeds of Theros, which everyone knew already.

I hate you, Theros!

Judging from the expressions on the five thousand upturned faces, many of his men felt the same way. The lucky ones were too far away to hear Father Leo's droning voice.

I don't know you guys, and you don't know me, but at least we agree about this! What a stupid way to waste a perfectly nice day!

His mother had been devoted to Narina, and had dragged him to the temple twice a week, rain or shine. He could still remember the tedious ritual when he, as a small child, was dedicated to the service of Narina. His mother had also wanted him to sing in the choir, and he'd done that until his voice broke.

But when she died in pain after a long illness, Narina was nowhere to be seen. His tearful prayers had made no difference at all. His father dumped all the pious images of Narina his mother had collected into the harbor and sent him off to the military school at Eloni. Still, some residue of his mother's devotion lingered in him. Narina probably *should* exist, even if she didn't.

But Theros was a bully and a braggart. All of his deeds were bloody. Theros should *not* exist, even if he actually did.

Why do we deceive ourselves this way?

Theros was the patron of soldiers, and many claimed to have been saved from death by his hand. (On the other hand, those who were not saved didn't give any testimony.) Prayers cost nothing, and sometimes, there was nothing else to do.

Even I pray sometimes. I'm just a fool like all the others!

Father Leo had wound up his sermon and was giving the benediction. Singer bowed his head to receive the blessing of Theros.

" . . . in the sure knowledge that his divine hand will support and defend us always. Amen."

Finally! Now it's my turn.

He began his prepared homily. "It is fitting and proper, on this occasion, that we should reflect on the virtues of Theros, courage, loyalty and . . ."

Damn, what was the third one?

He'd known this all his life, so why couldn't he remember it now? Suddenly, he felt dizzy. There was a ringing in his ears. He couldn't speak.

Five thousand upturned faces looked at him in surprise and alarm as he put his hand on the altar to steady himself and accidentally knocked the ritual sword to the ground. A bad omen. And then, stumbling, he stepped on it. A worse omen.

There was a collective gasp from the audience. Those in the rear craned their necks to see what was happening.

"Are you all right, sir?" whispered Father Leo.

"Mmm . . mmm. . . mmm. . ." was all he could say.

The mass of faces before him was filled with consternation and reproach. He was losing these men, their faith in him was ebbing away before his eyes.

I must speak! Theros, or whoever, I'll say whatever you want, just let me speak!

"LISTEN TO ME!"

Did I say that?

"I HAVE SOMETHING IMPORTANT TO SAY!"

I don't know what it is, but it better be good!

"YOU HAVE BEEN LIED TO! WE ARE ALL HERE BECAUSE WE WERE LIED TO! WE WERE TOLD THE BANDELUKS WERE PREPARING TO ATTACK US, THAT WE MUST TAKE ARMS AND DEFEND OURSELVES!

"BUT NOW WE ARE HERE! AND WHERE ARE THE SIEGE WEAPONS AND THE INVASION BARGES THAT THE BANDELUKS WERE PREPARING AGAINST US? WHERE IS THEIR MIGHTY ARMY OF INVASION? SO FAR, WE HAVE SEEN ONLY LOCAL FORCES, HASTILY SCRATCHED TO-

GETHER!

"AND IT IS TOO LATE TO CHANGE THAT! THE SHIPS THAT BROUGHT US HERE WILL NOT TAKE US BACK UNTIL THE WAR IS OVER! WE HAVE BEEN SWINDLED, BULLIED, BETRAYED AND LEFT TO FEND FOR OURSELVES IN A FOREIGN COUNTRY!

"BUT I WILL TELL YOU ONE TRUE THING! I AM IN THE SAME POSITION THAT YOU ARE, AND I AM NOT GOING HOME UNTIL YOU DO! WHATEVER POWER I HAVE IS FULLY AT YOUR DISPOSAL! I HAVE NO OTHER GOAL THAN TO SEE EVERY ONE OF YOU SAFELY RETURNED TO YOUR HOMES!"

He stopped yelling and stared blankly at the audience, who just stood there, waiting to hear what else he might have to say. But there was nothing else. Whatever had opened his mouth had closed it again.

Because he could think of nothing else to do, he bent over, picked up the ritual sword and waved it above his head with a flourish. The audience exploded into cheers, five thousand men yelling at the same time: "SINGER! SINGER! SINGER!"

What just happened? Why did I say that?

The little statue gleamed on the altar behind him, forgotten.

That evening, a courier brought in a letter from the Prince's camp at Kafra. To Singer's great surprise, he smelled a lingering trace of perfume.

> Dearest Singer!
>
> I rejoice at the news of your promotion! There will be no need for you to resign it to see me, as I have come to you! Temporarily, I've been placed under the protection of Capt. Nikandros, an officer in the service of His Highness. I may be found at his headquarters, which is located in a two-story building with six cupolas, on a hill by the lagoon, just north of the main camp. No time for further news, as I must scurry to post this letter. Please reply by return messenger. Waiting in anxious anticipation, your adoring,
>
> Erika

Of all the damned things! Now what do I do?

"Wait a minute while I write a reply," he told the courier and went into his tent to sit down and think it over.

Erika was a nice-looking girl, neat, well-spoken and presentable, and she came from a good family. All in all, an excellent marriage choice for a young officer. But now, she was showing a new character, one he didn't like at all: That she should cross the ocean in pursuit of him, intrude in a military camp, present herself to his commanding officer and summon him to Kafra while he was on campaign went far beyond the normal behavior expected of brides-to-be.

This raised a lot of questions he didn't even want to think about: He'd never heard of any Capt. Nikandros and he had no idea what troops were stationed at the headquarters where she'd so blithely deposited herself. A young lieutenant could perhaps get a few days leave to check up on his crazy girlfriend, but a general with 5,000 troops, to whom he'd just pledged total commitment, could not afford to take any vacations. On the other hand, telling her to go away would mean breaking the engagement, which would involve a loss of dignity and some complications on the home front. This situation was totally out of control!

What if she shows up here? That could ruin me!

The best he could do was to delay things and try to keep her at a safe distance, without breaking any promises or making new ones:

> Dearest Erika!
>
> I am thrilled to hear from you, as I have longed for you every day since we parted! Alas, I am engaged with a relentless foe, deep in enemy territory and pressing forward, as best I can, in the face of bitter resistance. Behind me lies only a wasteland littered with the graves of fallen comrades, ahead are unknown and perhaps insurmountable dangers. If only I were a bird that could lightly fly to Kafra, I would leave this very instant! But if I do not return, think well of me, your ever-faithful,
> Singer

He paused and read the letter. Perhaps he'd over-done things a bit. (Did people still say "alas"?) But some brassy fanfare would be necessary temper her immoderate passion. Maybe she'd do the sensible thing and return home. Anyway, she wouldn't come, stumbling over the "graves of fallen comrades," to visit him here, amid so many "unknown and perhaps insurmountable dangers." If he had more time, he'd have polished it more, but he could already hear them assembling for the evening roll call. He'd lend a fresh horse to the courier. Perhaps the letter would reach poor, foolish Erika before she caused him any more worries.

"Those are some impressive ruins!" he said

Rajik nodded. The view from the last ridge was truly amazing. The ruins extended into the far distance, where the other side of the ridgeline, which circled the area, was dimly visible. In between the streets were roofless stone structures, piles of rubble, isolated chimneys, broken towers, in short, ruins of every kind. Ruins even poked out of the lake, two or three miles across, which lay in the center.

"We rode around the lake," said Rajik. "It's brackish, but it's fed by a number of small streams, enough for your army. There's plenty of grazing."

"Any signs of life?"

"A good number of antelope. I don't think a human being has been here in a hundred years."

"And all this was built by the ancient Kano people?"

"Yes, General. It looks like their work. So far as I can tell, there were three of four cities around the lake, but it rose over the years, drowning parts of them."

"Why was it abandoned?"

"Some kind of a disaster, I think. An earthquake, perhaps."

"We'll have to puzzle that out later. Baron Hardy is not far behind me. It will take a couple days to move the rest of the army down the road. In the meanwhile, we need to assign bivouac areas. You said you found a place for my headquarters?"

"Yes, General, over there." Rajik pointed to a large stone structure that stood out prominently amid the wreckage.

As they rode up to the building, Singer saw it had a high, domed ceiling which had survived the centuries, one of the few buildings which still had any roof at all. It stood on a rise, a short distance from the lake shore and just a few steps from a creek. Rajik had chosen well.

"By the way, I'm promoting you to sergeant. Your duties will be the same, but you'll be entitled to a sergeant's pay . . . at the next pay day, that is. Right now, no one has much use for money, except of course for gambling, which I don't encourage."

"Yes, sir." Rajik seemed to be bursting with pride, but added. "I think my men are entitled to some reward as well. Riding here across the desert took a lot of courage."

"Well, I can advance them a week's pay, if that makes them feel better."

"It might."

Their horses were ascending a series of steps, which led to two huge, gaping doorways, open to the dim emptiness within. Singer peered inside, but, except for scattered pieces of rubble on the floor, there was little to be seen.

"I think it must have been a temple," said Rajik. "There are some tombs in back. Or maybe it's just an assembly hall. I didn't find any idols."

"Not all temples have them," said Singer.

This seemed to confuse Rajik. "What do they worship, then?"

"Pagans worship all sorts of things, the sun, for example."

"Paralayan is the sun god. He's just a big ugly idol, like all the rest."

"He's your sun god, we don't have one."

How superstitious they are, to worship material things, like the sun! A real god embodies divine principles!

"Which god is this one here?" he said, pointing to a shape like a centipede, about three feet long, which was been scratched into the stone wall beside the door.

"I don't know, sir. It's not one of ours," said Rajik, touching it with a finger. "These marks are fresh."

"One of your men must have made it."

"No sir, they were with me the whole time, and I haven't seen this before."

"When were you here last?"

"Three days ago."

"And you've seen no one here?"

"No, sir. Littleton and the demons came through awhile ago, but they didn't stop here."

There's something awful strange about this!

He dismounted and studied the thin layer of dirt on the floor. There were many Bandeluk tracks, but above them, more recent, were two parallel rows of indentations, each about an inch wide, penetrating into the soil.

"What do you make of this?"

"I've never seen anything like it before." Rajik scraped away some of the soil with a knife, revealing a cracked marble slab, scratched with similar markings. "Whoever did this has sharp toe-nails."

"Assemble your men. Search the building. Find out where the tracks go."

The Bandeluks didn't like this order. One kept saying "Ghosts and monsters!" portentously, until the rest told him to shut up. After half an hour, they came back and reported.

"The tracks come from an opening in the back and return in the same direction," said Rajik. "We were not able to follow them after that. The rocks are too hard. Otherwise, the building is empty."

Meanwhile, Ogleby had ridden up with the rest of Singer's staff: two clerks stolen from Pennesey (who was still back in Jasmine House, having been promoted to a lieutenant of the militia), four messengers, who were wounded men assigned to light duties while recuperating, and Kyle, who he'd made his aide-de-camp. Besides that, he had only the Bandeluks, whom he'd christened the Scout Corps, but were generally known among the men as the Blue Bandeluks.

"Will we be camping here, sir?" Ogleby asked.

That's an excellent question!

"How big is the rear entrance?" he asked Rajik.

"It's just a normal-sized doorway."

"Have your men block it up with stones, and any other ground-level holes bigger than your helmet. When you're done with that, assign two men to guard the main entrance, and two more to watch the horses. You'll be sharing this building with my staff."

"Yes, sir!"

After supper, Rajik gave an improvised Bandeluki lesson to Singer's men, which was followed by a Hallandish lecture by Ogleby. Singer, who knew both languages perfectly well, wandered out the door and stood by the entrance, surveying the ruins.

We seem to have found the downtown area. Anyway, there are a lot of big structures here.

It was hard to tell what some of the ruins were. Several resembled smaller versions of the building they were camped in. Temples to lesser gods, perhaps? One was surrounded by what had once been a high wall. A palace? An armory? A prison? It was impossible to say. Most of the buildings had no obvious function: There was nothing left but a few unconnected walls, or a heap of rubble where the walls had been. In other places, there was a row of columns and no other sign of a building.

Some future scholar is going to make a fine career exploring, mapping and classifying these structures, and puzzling out their mysteries. But not now; there's no point in speculation. I just hope my own people leave behind something better than a big pile of stones in the desert.

He lingered by the door, enjoying the evening air. There was no point trying to sleep yet. More and more, his nights were spent tossing and turning, sometimes almost to dawn.

From down the road, he could hear the faint sound of voices from the ancient stadium Baron Hardy had taken over. Because of the lights and occasional applause, he supposed the Baron was staging some sort of competition or amateur entertainment as a morale-booster.

No need to worry about that. The Baron knows what he's doing, if anyone here does.

He turned his attention to the centipede drawing, which was only dimly visible in the twilight. He used a finger to trace the lines.

Rajik was right! These are sharp lines, and I can feel loose grains of stone. This can't be more than a day old!

Who had left this thing? Someone who expected him to come here, obviously. Who could know where he'd set up camp? It would have to be someone who was here already, hiding in the ruins and watching the Scout Corps.

But what kind of message was this: "Beware the centipedes?" "I, Mr. Centipede, am awaiting you?" "This place is sacred to the Centipede God?" And what was he supposed to do with this message? Run away before the centipedes got him? Wait for Mr. Centipede to show up? Make an offering to the Centipede God?

A waning moon was creeping up over the horizon, throwing a

pale, ghostly light on everything.

It's no good standing here, waiting for something to happen. Time for bed!

Someone touched him lightly on the shoulder. Startled, he turned and saw it was only Rajik.

"General, I'd like to speak with you privately."

"Very well." He told the guards, "You men can go in. We'll call you when we're done."

He and Rajik were left, looking at each other in the moonlight. Rajik was standing a bit too close. He took a step back.

"You really mean to do it?" said Rajik. "You're really going to Barbosa?"

"Those are my orders. Littleton and his demons are already working on the road."

"But what about the Witch?"

Oh, the legendary Witch of Barbosa. The Bandeluks keep talking about her as if she really exists.

"I'll have to deal with her when I meet her."

"That may be too late."

"Then what do you suggest?"

"Send someone else. Do not set foot in Barbosa yourself. The Witch has magics that make men her slaves."

"I'm told there's a garrison there."

"A small one, and all of them are eunuchs. For hundreds of years, nothing but eunuchs."

"What about the caravans?"

"They don't go in. They leave their goods outside."

They must be serious about this.

"Rajik, what you describe is an enchantment, such as any sorcerer can cast. I am the leader here. I can't hide for fear of magical trickery."

"The Witch is not a sorcerer, she's the Witch. She's a thousand years old, and you have no chance against her. No man who was lured into the Witch's arms was ever seen again."

This sounds like more Bandeluk superstition . . . What's that!

Down by the creek, the horses were in a panic about something, and the guards he'd left there were shouting. He drew his sword and ran that way as fast as he could, Rajik behind him.

The horses, though hobbled, were neighing frantically and

trying to get away. Two had already fallen. A young Bandeluk ran around, waving a sword and yelling, "I saw it! A monster!"

"Put away your sword and see to the horses!" Singer told him, and without waiting to see if he obeyed, ran to the creek.

A second Bandeluk, as he watched, was hastily drawing a bow. He heard the soft *plunk* as the arrow sped away toward some unknown target, followed by the metallic sound of an arrowhead striking a stone. The soldier drew a second arrow. Singer turned to see what he was aiming at, but there was nothing visible in the moonlight, only stones and the vague shapes of stone buildings.

The archer, too, had lost sight of whatever he was shooting at. He lowered his bow.

"Go get the men!" said Singer, and turned to run in direction the soldier had been shooting. Though his heart was pounding, he had to slow down and pick his away over the uneven ground. Ahead stood a number of small buildings, probably the tombs mentioned by Rajik, who was still behind him. He could hear the footsteps hurrying to catch up.

Lying among a pile of boulders, he saw the arrow the Bandeluk had fired. But, as he reached down to pick it up, he felt something else that was long and thin, sharp on the end and cold to the touch. It was not an arrow, and it was abruptly wrenched from his hand.

And then, suddenly, it loomed above him in the moonlight, a centipede taller than a man. Dozens of sharp claws, a row on either side, reached for him.

Demon!

He jabbed it automatically with the sword and felt the point strike something hard. The demon dropped from its threatening posture and, falling to the ground, scurried away among the rocks. He chased after it.

"GENERAL! COME BACK!" Rajik was yelling in a thin, girlish voice.

But he couldn't go back while this thing was on the loose. As it approached a small building, he saw it rear up and then disappear into a hole. The building, he saw, was an ancient tomb. The hole was left from a piece of rock which had broken off from the stone slab blocking the doorway.

The hole was too small for him. He stuck his sword in it, but there seemed to be nothing on the other side. "Go get the pick and

shovel," he told Rajik, "and some torches."

A few minutes later, a big, muscular Bandeluk named Olgun was pounding the door with a pick. It took only three blows to smash it into pieces. Singer threw a torch inside, illuminating a small space with three man-sized niches on either side and a small stone table or altar on the end. There was no sign of the demon.

Cautiously looking around with the help of a torch, he saw nothing in the niches except dust and debris. The altar held two ancient candlesticks, green with corrosion, and a ceramic bowl. There was a painting of some kind on the wall, but dripping moisture had long since effaced it. As he stepped forward for a better look, torchlight glittered on something in the bowl. He pulled it out.

The mysterious object from the bowl was a silver bracelet in the shape of a centipede, with sapphires for eyes. It shone as if freshly polished. The open jaws formed a clasp. Experimentally, he put it on his wrist. The jaws of the clasp closed, so they were biting its own tail. When he tried to open them again, he found they were stuck.

There was a space behind the altar. As he inspected it with a torch, he saw a big crack in the floor. Thrusting the torch in as far as it would go revealed nothing, just a hole extending deep into the earth.

Looks like it got away.

He wasn't sure whether he felt upset or was just happy to be alive. The demon could probably have killed him, if it had tried a bit harder.

"Give me a hand, here," he told Olgun. Grunting and heaving, they slid the stone altar over the crack in the floor.

"Take what men you need and fill this tomb with stones, the heaviest you can find. Don't go to bed until you've done this, or we may have another visitor."

He studied the silver centipede bracelet, but there was no obvious way to remove it.

Damn! I'll have to find some butter or grease so I can slide it off.

The sapphire eyes of the centipede seemed to be twinkling with amusement.

"They told me this was going to be a walk-over," Singer said.

"Indeed, sir. My experience is they generally say something of the kind," Baron Hardy replied.

They were looking at the walls of Barbosa, a fortress that lay at the foot of a desolate mountain pass. Its walls were ten stories high. A row of Bandeluk archers was visible behind the parapet, waiting for someone to come within range. Pretty soon, someone would have to.

"The story is, those men are all eunuchs," said Singer. "There's supposed to be a Witch living here, and the Bandeluks are all terrified of her. They say she can overpower men and bend them to her will."

"Unless they're eunuchs?"

"Apparently."

"I like the affliction better than the cure. If she's so dangerous, why do they surround her with soldiers and fortifications? Are they trying to keep her *in* or us *out*?"

"Good question. Why don't you ride over and ask those fellows?"

"Honestly, sir, my Bandeluki is still rather poor."

At this point, Ogleby rode up beside them.

"Did Littleton do an inventory of the siege equipment?" Singer asked.

"Yes, sir. We have four siege crossbows and fifty rounds each. Littleton is assembling them as we speak. Besides that, there are a thousand six-inch nails for the construction of scaling ladders and two hundred twelve-inch spikes for siege engines."

"That makes me wish we had some timber," said Singer. "There doesn't seem to be any in the neighborhood."

"Indeed, sir. We should have foreseen this," said Hardy.

"And then done what about it? We'd have had to fell a small forest, then transport it up the Stairway and across a hundred miles of desert."

"We could have brought enough for a battering ram."

Singer studied the gate. It was a heavy, two-story, iron-bound affair, and to all appearances, it had rusted shut and settled into the ground at least a hundred years ago. There was a small doorway built into the gate so that people could actually get in and out.

"Could have, would have, should have, but this is the situation we've got," he said.

"No portcullis or gatehouse, no moat or drawbridge," said Hardy. "They don't understand the art of fortification."

"Small difference it would make, so long as their enemies are poorly equipped as we are."

As they were speaking, a three-foot iron bolt, launched from a nearby hilltop, flew over the intervening space and struck one of the towers, knocking off a piece of stone the size of a man's head.

Singer told a messenger, "Go tell Littleton to stop wasting ammunition. We aren't ready to assault this place."

"He's probably just getting the range," said Hardy. "But look, they respect our weapons."

The Bandeluk archers had disappeared. They were crouching behind the parapet.

"If we could persuade them to keep their heads down, we could try scaling the wall," Singer said.

"'Try' is the correct word, sir," said Hardy. "It's like the escarpment, but without any stairs."

"I believe the Halland Company could sweep those battlements clean in ten minutes."

"Yes, it's too bad we left them twenty or thirty miles behind. I wouldn't count on my horse archers doing as well, at least not without some siege mantlets."

"Another useful piece of equipment we don't have. Maybe we should concentrate on what we *do* have."

"Indeed, sir. At the moment, that would be six hundred cavalry and four siege crossbows. Sieges have been done with less."

"By people who had a lot more time than we do. The garrison has had plenty of opportunity to send for reinforcements."

That ended the discussion for a minute. They sat and stared at the wall. There was nothing else to do.

I'm going to have to think of something. This old castle in the middle of nowhere was completely unimportant until I built a road to it. Now, it could decide the whole war!

"The Thunder Slingers should be here later this afternoon," he said suddenly.

"So?"

"I think we have everything we need. By tomorrow, Barbosa belongs to us!"

"I must have missed something."

"I sincerely hope that you have."

Capt. Stewart arrived at the head of the Thunder Slingers about an hour later. A hard taskmaster, he'd crossed the desert at forced march.

I'm glad I'm your superior, rather than you mine, but still, I wouldn't trade you for anyone else. Now, your men are tired and sweaty, and they deserve a rest, but I have other plans for them.

"Captain, have your men drop their packs and deploy in combat formation opposite that wall. Stay out of bow range until you receive my order."

A man of few words, Stewart simply saluted and went to give the order.

As the Thunder Slingers took up their positions, Singer sent a messenger to Littleton and told him to fire at will. Iron bolts began crashing into the walls of Barbosa, doing little damage, but causing the Bandeluks to take cover.

Singer then told another messenger: "Tell Stewart to advance and direct his fire on the battlements. Tell him to use his special stones."

The Thunder Slingers took their name from the special sling-stones they carried, in addition to the usual lead ones. These were drops of volcanic glass containing gas bubbles. When they struck anything solid, they burst with a pop, scattering fragments of black glass in all directions and leaving a foul smell. They were of no use against heavily armored enemies, but good for panicking horses.

As the Thunder Slingers fired, Singer could hear a distant *pop pop pop* of stones exploding and some shrill screams, as the Bandeluks abandoned the wall.

I guess eunuchs don't have much staying power.

Singer sent a messenger to Littleton: "Tell him to cease fire. Tell him to get his 12-inch spikes and some hammers and meet me at the wall."

To Hardy, he said, "Now, we have to move fast. Get your men down to the wall."

While Hardy was bringing up the cavalry, he rode down to Stewart's position and told him to cease fire. Then, he went to inspect the wall. Close up, it didn't look as solid as it had from a distance. The wall was about the same age as the ruins. It was made of blocks of a reddish stone common in the area. He could see numerous cracks and fissures, which had appeared over the centuries, and some old attempts at repair.

He picked a crack between two large stones, about knee height, and stuck his dagger in. Then, he used his sword hilt to pound it in as far as it would go. He stood on the dagger hilt, and it didn't budge.

"That looks like the waste of a perfectly good dagger," said Hardy, who had just ridden up.

"Tell your men to dismount and shoot anyone who shows his face. The ones who don't have bows should clash their shields and make all the noise they can. We don't want anyone to hear what we're doing."

Now Littleton arrived. He had the demons with him, some carrying sacks that gave a metallic clank when they moved.

"Give me a hammer. Count 40 of those spikes and put them in a sack."

To Ogleby, he said, "Call for volunteers. See who else wants to scale Barbosa."

After twenty feet, he stopped and looked down. There were still only two volunteers hammering in spikes, and they were the last two he'd have chosen: Littleton and Kyle. He needed Littleton on the siege crossbows, but his maniacal-obsessive nature wouldn't allow him to ignore such a challenge. Kyle was too young; Singer had hoped putting him on the wall would shame someone else into volunteering, but it hadn't worked. The older men saw this for what it was, a desperate gamble.

Only a madman or a child would try something like this!

It was a good thing he'd told the Scout Corps to go search the area, or Rajik would probably have volunteered as well.

At fifty feet, one of the spikes came loose, just as he put his weight on it. He looked down in time to see it falling a terrifying distance to the ground. For an instant, he was frozen with fear. Then, he closed his eyes and pressed his face against the wall.

It's what they always tell you, but dummies always forget: Don't look down!

Hanging by one hand, he fished around blindly with his feet until he found the previous spike and stepped on it. Then, he dared another downward glance.

Everyone was staring at him, over a thousand pale faces with open mouths, waiting to see if he would fall. They had stopped clashing their shields.

"KEEP MAKING NOISE!" he yelled and reached for another spike.

At seventy feet, he belatedly decided climbing a sheer wall while wearing fifty pounds of armor was not one of his better ideas. He allotted himself a minute's rest and looked over to see how the other two were doing.

Littleton was pounding spikes like he was in a race to the top, and he was nearly even with Singer. He had the advantage of less armor, and he'd also worked out a system for hanging the bag with the spikes below his feet and pulling it up with a short rope when he needed more of them, so he wouldn't have to constantly haul the spikes around.

I wish he'd shared that idea before.

Kyle was way behind. He looked tired. If he fell, it could kill or cripple him. Singer was about to yell at him to turn back, but then he hesitated.

I'm taking some crazy risks. What right do I have to tell the kid he can't?

At ninety feet, he checked the sack and saw he had only three spikes left. It looked like he still had about twenty feet to go. He must have underestimated the distance. Also, he'd dropped a spike. It was time to reassess the situation.

He'd been putting the spikes too close together. He needed a good grip on the last spike for leverage, before he could hammer in a new one. But there was, he saw, a crack in the wall here that ran almost all the way to the top. If he jammed his fingers in the crack, he'd have all the leverage he needed. First, though, he'd have to stand up, full length, on the last spike.

Pulling himself up on the tiny foothold caused sharp pains in his hands, arms and shoulders. He teetered there a second before quickly thrusting his hand into the crack. Made it! As he shakily drew himself to full height, he estimated three more such efforts would bring him within reach of the top.

A few minutes later, he was standing on the last spike, and he was stuck. Whoever built the fortress had capped the wall with a smooth, curved piece of hard stone, intended to deflect grappling hooks. It overhung the edge two or three inches. Reaching around as far as he could, he felt nothing but smooth stone. There was no way to get a grip.

His right hand, wedged in the top of the crack, was becoming numb. On his flailing, useless left arm, the silver centipede (he hadn't managed to remove it) seemed to be giving him a disappointed look. "How did I get stuck with this loser?" the little blue eyes seemed to say.

This is BAD!

To his left and down about ten feet, Littleton had run out of energy. It took all of what he had just to cling to the wall, and he plainly wouldn't be doing that much longer.

Kyle was nowhere in sight. Singer hoped he'd given up and gone back down while he still could. In their exhausted states, neither he nor Littleton had any chance to do that.

Behind and below him (he dared not turn his head), his men were chanting "SINGER! SINGER! SINGER!" in a premature celebration of his ascent. Their voices, however, were getting a bit thin and uncertain, as they saw he'd reached the top, but wasn't going anywhere.

That one fallen spike has murdered me!

He had only one choice left, and it was a bad one: He could let go of the wall with his right hand, gather whatever strength he had in his trembling legs and jump. Possibly, there was a handhold, just out of reach, that he couldn't see because of the curved stone that was blocking his progress. If he could just get his fingers into that, purely hypothetical, joint or crack, then he still had a chance.

Narina help me!

He was about to begin this last, near-hopeless effort, when something grabbed him by the left wrist. Surprised, he automatically pulled back, but whatever had a grip on his arm was stronger. It dragged him over the top of the wall, to the walkway on the other side, where he collapsed.

For a moment, he thought that his mother's beloved goddess Narina, her face blazing with divine glory, was looking down on him, but then he saw it was only the sun reflecting from the silver mask of one of the *fui* demons. From the thin, pale scar on the left arm, it must be Twenty Three. It seemed to have a fresh burn on its right hand, where the palm was black and blistered. As always, it ignored the wound.

"Is *bzzz* the General *bzzz* well?"

He was wretchedly tired. His joints were all on fire. There was no feeling in his right hand, which was dripping blood. "Yes," he said. "Yes, he is."

He looked around. A dead Bandeluk was lying nearby. Another *fui* demon was hauling Littleton over the parapet. A third was pulling a rope, which probably had Kyle on the other end. To his left and right, more demons were joining them on the walkway.

"You didn't tell me you could climb walls!"

"Our *bzzz* assistance was *bzzz* not requested."

"Then you didn't have to do it. You could have stayed where you were. No one would have blamed you."

"That *bzzz* would have *bzzz* been incorrect."

My demons have a code of ethics! Or is it just etiquette?

"What you did was correct. Now send someone down to open the door."

"It is *bzzz* being done."

Cheers from the other side of the wall confirmed that the door was open.

He turned his attention to the dead Bandeluk. Was this one of the eunuchs? It was a small man, quite beardless, dressed in armor much too big for him. He was leaning against the parapet as if deep in thought. A trickle of blood ran down his cheek like a red tear. Some fragment of glass or stone had penetrated his right eye and gone through to the brain. Singer removed the helmet, and a mop of black hair fell out.

This is a woman!

He picked up her left hand, which was resting next to a curved bow. The hand was still warm. Neither it nor the right hand had any of the calluses he'd expect of a swordsman or archer.

This is just a maidservant pretending to be a soldier. They were bluffing!

Below him, he could hear many footsteps entering at the gate. Someone had given the order to storm the castle. When he looked to see how they were doing, he noticed at once there was a second wall behind the first one, higher and equipped with a gate just as immovable as the other.

"Are we *bzzz* to attack?" asked Twenty Three.

He imagined the group of *fui* demons swarming over the wall and into a castle defended by women.

"No, the battle is over. We must give them a chance to surrender. That is correct."

"Yes, *bzzz* very correct."

Did that thing just give me a pat on the head?

14: Krion

My officers are such idiots!

They were always pestering him with unimportant details. Today, it was Lessig, who had showed up unannounced, demanding he approve plans for a diversion canal, which he said would drown a local village. Krion had told him that, since he had no technical expertise, there was no point in examining the plans, they'd just have to do, and if he was going to drown a village, he should evacuate the population somewhere.

Yesterday, it had been Basilius who had bothered him with the request for a council of war, to plan the final assault. Krion had simply said there was no point in a council, until the preparations were complete, and it would be he, not Basilius, who called one.

Mopsus had also become an annoyance, with his complaints over the disappearance of Lt. Bardhof and demands for an investigation. He couldn't waste his efforts on an investigation every time one of his junior officers made himself scarce because of some affair of the heart or gambling debts. Nonsense!

The last time he'd checked on Gen. Singer, he almost dropped the mirror, because he'd found him looking down into an abyss from an immense height. He'd hastily put the mirror back in the box. It was no good trying to supervise Singer from such a distance. He'd just have to wait until the siege was over, when he could give him either a commendation or a decent burial.

Besides that, there was a huge pile of reports from various officers, concerning enemy troop movements or the price of timber, or something else equally boring. He glanced at the latest one, from Clenas, which was titled, "The Economic Exploitation of the Occupied Areas," and was written in a woman's hand. As usual, Clenas was making a fool of himself, chasing all over the countryside, trying to impress his latest love interest. At least he wasn't creating a fuss in Krion's tent, but only sending in reports which could safely be ignored.

He threw the report from Clenas on top of the pile. In the corner, he noticed the attendant Ragman was looking at him strangely again, something it was more and more prone to do. Why in the world did he have one of those monsters spying on him in his own tent?

"Go back to your camp," he told it. "I don't need you here. You're just stinking the place up. I'll call you when I want you." The Ragman left without a word, but not without a backward glance.

Now, at last, he had some privacy! He went to the section of the tent he'd curtained off, his own personal space, and removed the cloth from the easel. Immediately, he felt better. *She* was here, resolute and unafraid, her lips slightly pursed, and with that playful look in her eyes, which was so familiar to him from his dreams.

He'd hated art lessons when he was a child, but now all of it was coming back to him, and even more. He was a better artist than any of his teachers. Already, he'd burned the first crude sketches of his great love. They were unworthy of her. Now, with the help of his paint brush, he could actually see her, or *almost*, as she appeared in his nightly dreams and daily reveries.

"My beloved Rosalind," he breathed, "soon, this war will be over, and I shall return in triumph and claim you as my bride. And I shall build the palace, greater than any before, that I promised, and the multitudes will give you their obeisance, as I already do."

He raised his hand to kiss the golden ring, that wonderful love token, which had been blessed by the touch of her fingers.

15: Rajik

Lying in bed was painful. His head was sore. His back was sore. His whole body was sore. And now, he had bed sores. He'd have to get out of bed, but he couldn't risk another fall. He'd thought he could just do what he wanted, but he was wrong, and now he was worse off than before. Raeesha was gone, and most of the foreigners with her, and he was almost alone in the big, empty house. He'd seen no one for days but the foreigner who came with food and to change the bandages. And he spoke no more than two words of Bandeluki.

Jasmine House had always been full of life. There were brothers and sisters and cousins running around, laughing and playing games, and wise elders offering words of advice or reproach, and flocks of servants bringing food and clean clothes. Now, it was like a ghost house: There was only the occasional sound of strange boots in the hall and distant voices speaking a language he didn't understand.

This must be what it's like being dead.

But he was not dead. They'd knocked him down, burned him, struck him with whips and with stones. They'd done everything to kill him, but he was still alive. He'd won, and he'd keep on winning. He'd do whatever he had to, to stay alive.

He got up and looked at himself in the mirror. He looked bad, all thin and pale, his head still covered with bandages. Gingerly, he began unwinding them. What he saw only made him feel worse: They'd shaved his hair, or parts of it, so they could sew up the gashes, which were still red and tender. The hair he still had was patchy, and it stuck out at strange angles. Not even his skull was the right shape anymore, there was a place, still painful to touch, where it bulged inwards instead of outwards. Also, two of his teeth were missing.

You're an ugly boy, Rajik. But you're still Rajik!

The hair would grow back, or at least, most of it would. In the meanwhile, he'd have to wear a cap. He started to put on his clothes.

The hall was empty, and he saw it had not been swept for some time. Voices were coming from a room near the entrance. Moving quietly, he stepped closer to hear what they were saying.

There were three men inside, two foreigners and one Bandeluk. He couldn't understand what the foreigners were saying to each other, but one of them was translating it for the Bandeluk:

" . . . out of mail shirts. There's nothing left but the leather jerkins, and they won't last long either."

"I thought we requisitioned a load of mail shirts."

"We did, but they're raising new companies in Akaddia, and the militia has no priority."

"Do the Illustrious Knights have anything to spare?"

"Maybe, but they aren't sharing. They only send us things for repair."

"Useless twits. We'll have to make do with what we can scrape together locally."

"Chatmakstan is a poor province. There aren't many local craftsmen."

"But it is a whole province. There are hundreds of villages. Surely we can find something."

"If we had the money, maybe. Singer didn't leave us with much of a budget, just enough for the HQ."

"How are we supposed to do anything without money?"

"We don't have to equip everyone right away."

"Yes, I'm more worried about the level of training. Three days training is not enough. A new group is coming tomorrow, and the last lot can't even march in step."

"We need more instructors."

"You mean more Bandeluks. The Chatmaks have no military experience."

"How are we supposed to recruit more Bandeluks, when we're fighting a war with them?"

"What about the sick one, Hisaf or Rajik or whatever he's called?"

"I thought Rajik was the other one."

"He's too young. I might make him an errand boy, or add him to the kitchen help . . ."

Too many people have been making plans for me! Maybe I should make some plans for them!

The guards at the gate had changed. Now, they were Chatmaks armed with spears. They glared contemptuously at him, but said nothing as he passed.

Mubina's door was locked. He stood a moment on the stoop, dumbfounded. This had never happened before. He began knocking, first politely, then loudly.

Finally, a thin, tired voice from within said, "Go away! I have nothing to sell!"

"It's Rajik, Grandmother. Open the door."

The door opened. "I'm sorry, Rajik, but as you can see, the shelves are bare. What little I have left, I must save for myself."

"Perhaps I can help you, Grandmother. What is it you lack?"

"Everything. But mostly salt, sugar, tea and tobacco. When they saw there was a shortage, people rushed in to buy, and now there's nothing left."

"But you must have a lot of money from so many sales."

"Yes, but what am I do with it? I can't eat money."

"Give me fifty piasters, Grandmother, and I'll see what I can do."

"What are you going to do with fifty piasters?"

"Trust me. You've known me for many years. If I can't help you, I'll give you your money back. You can't lose."

He knew only one foreigner in Jasmine House who could speak Bandeluki, a man named

Pennesey. He went into the back, where Pennesey had his office, and found him sitting at a desk, writing things on pieces of paper. He laid his bag of piasters on the desk.

Pennesey looked at him skeptically. "What is that?"

"That is money. You need money, yes?"

He took one coin out of the bag and put it down on the table. Pennesey picked it up and looked at it, feeling the weight of the silver in his hand.

"So, I see you have money. Now what?"

"I need to purchase certain things, namely salt, sugar, tea and tobacco."

"This is not a store. This is a military base."

"Then I'll have to take my money and go somewhere else." He reached for the bag.

"Wait a minute. We have some things in surplus. When the army marched away, they left a lot of supplies sitting here, unneeded, subject to spoilage and pilfering. According to regulations, it's lawful to sell the surplus."

"Would this include salt, sugar, tea and tobacco?"

"It would include salt and sugar. For tea, I'll have to check with the kitchen. We have no tobacco to sell; the last thing a soldier parts with is his tobacco."

"Then perhaps we can come to an arrangement."

A few minutes later, he was back in Mubina's shop. There were two foreign soldiers with him, lugging heavy sacks. "I've brought your salt, Grandmother. The sugar will be here shortly. Also, one box of black tea. For these items, I paid twenty-five piasters. I'm retaining two piasters as a commission and returning to you twenty-three piasters."

He counted out the money and put it on the counter, as Mubina watched with her mouth agape. "How did you do this miracle!"

"It comes from knowing the right questions and who to ask. I can obtain more for you when this has been sold."

"Then I'm saved!"

"There are also some quantities of spices, especially red and black pepper."

"I will buy both!"

"Tobacco is not available here, but I'm told it can be obtained through the depot at Massera Bay. One need only fill out the necessary forms. Also, certain sundries such as soap, buttons, needles and thread, boot polish, and so forth. We'll need to prepare a list."

"Rajik, you are performing wonders!"

"No, I'm trading on the black market. It's best if we don't call any attention to this trade, or it may dry up and vanish."

And probably get us all hanged!

The next day, he got a requisition form from Pennesey and went to Massera Bay, with a cart and a Chatmak driver, to pick up some tobacco and sundries. When he returned, Mubina had already sold the supplies he'd delivered the day before, and he had to get more from Pennesey. Meanwhile, his commissions were starting to add up to a tidy sum, which he hid under a loose tile in his room.

When he visited Mubina on the following day, there was a line at her door. People had come from the outlying villages, walking for hours to fill a small jar with salt or tea. He noticed there were some Bandeluks standing in line with the Chatmaks, a new experience for them.

Get used to it, friends!

Someone he recognized was coming out the door, Husam, a man a few years older than he was, the son of an overseer on one of his father's farms. He waved, but Husam turned his face away.

"Husam! It's me, Rajik!"

Husam just quickened his pace.

He ran after Husam and took him by the arm. Husam turned to face him and backed away. Rajik could see he was afraid.

"What are you scared of? You know me!"

"But your father . . ."

This man deserted from my father. He's afraid I'll betray him.

"I'm finished with my father, and he with me. Jasmine House has new masters."

"But what are you doing here? Why are you not in Kafra?"

He still thinks I'm a spy or an informant.

"Kafra is a trap, a prison. There is no going to Kafra. The war has passed us by, Husam."

"So what do you want with me?"

He's still suspicious. But he has a point. What do I want with Husam? He belongs to my past.

"We must help each other Husam. We're in a dangerous place. If we don't help each other, no one will."

He removed his cap, displaying the wounds on his head.

Husam was taken aback. "I didn't know it was so bad with you, Rajik. Truly, I did not."

He replaced his cap. "I had a little argument with some Chatmaks. I won't make the same mistake again."

"Where I live, the peasants all know me. They're no problem. But I have to be careful with strangers. And I'm afraid Sheikh Mahmud will come back, or the foreigners will find me."

"You shouldn't worry about the foreigners. They'll do you no harm. I'm living under their roof."

"Truly?"

"As true as truth. How are you getting along?"

Husam looked troubled. "My father disappeared when the foreigners came. I don't know if he's alive or dead. I'm living with my mother. We have only a small garden. I do some work for the neighbors now and then. The Chatmaks worked for us, but now I work for the Chatmaks!"

"At least you can work."

"Only sometimes. And at the end of the day, I'm lucky to get a loaf of bread or hunk of cheese for my trouble."

"You're not a farmer, Husam. And you have no fields. You must find something else to do."

"What then?"

"Keep your eyes open. I myself have become a trader. Mubina's shop is open thanks to me."

"Truly? You're more clever than I am. I'm all alone with nothing to trade."

"Something is bound to turn up, I'm certain of it! And when it does, I'll call on you."

"Truly?"

"Truer than the truth!"

Two days later, he was back in Pennesey's office.

"I've done a survey," he told the officer. "In this area, I know of twelve Bandeluk deserters living alone or with relatives, or else protected by Chatmak families. Of course, that's only part of them. If I keep looking, I can find more."

"And?"

"You need military instructors. I can recruit these men, or most of them, for only a small commission."

"Deserters are not what I'd call reliable people."

"Sometimes. These deserted from your enemies. Maybe they had a good reason."

"How do I know they're competent?"

"Because I'll vouch for them personally, and because you'll be paying me three piasters for each one you hire, none for those you reject. How can you lose?"

Pennesey glanced at the locked drawer which was now heavy with silver piasters. "I think we can afford that. But there's something else more urgent. I will pay you *ten* piasters if you can find a skilled blacksmith or farrier, and ten more for a skilled leatherworker, and *twenty* for a weapon smith. And if you can find one of those Bandeluk sorcerers who were throwing demons at us on the beach, you can name your own price."

Today, it's raining piasters!

He put on a face of deep skepticism. "I think the sorcerers have all fled to Kafra, or even further, but they left behind their equipment, which was looted, with everything else, by the Chatmaks . . ."

"No sorcerer, no piasters!"

"No sorcerer, then. As for the rest, we shall see."

The next day he was in the Old Mill village, trying to find a retired swordmaker who had settled there with a Chatmak girl. He had to use a few coins to loosen the tongues of the local peasants, who were being surly, and didn't like strangers poking around in their affairs.

While he was talking to one of the elders, an expensive coach with four horses and four outriders pulled up and two foreigners got out: One was dressed like an important general or maybe even a prince. The other was a blonde, the first blonde woman Rajik had yet seen. He stared at her in amazement.

Foreign women are very bouncy!

She walked up to the village elder and addressed him in Bandeluki, which he didn't understand.

"May I be of assistance, *Lady*?" he said. The last word was in Hallandish.

"You may," she said in Bandeluki. "We're looking to purchase some *pamuk*, carded but not yet spun. We haven't been able to find any."

"I'm sorry, *Lady*. The *pamuk* harvest is not in. Carding and spinning are done at the same time, so you won't find any for sale. If you can wait a week, I can probably find some."

She looked at him doubtfully. "Who are you, may I ask?"

"I'm Rajik, an assistant to Lt. Pennesey at the headquarters of the Free State Contingent at Jasmine House."

"Then you've probably have met my husband, Gen. Singer. My name is Erika, and I have the honor of introducing Prince Clenas of Akaddia."

Rajik bowed to the prince, who had plainly understood nothing of what was said, and merely nodded in response. He looked completely bored.

"Forgive me for the discourtesy, *Lady*, but I'm not used to meeting foreign princes."

"You did fine. Perhaps you have some news about my husband. I haven't seen him for months, and his last letter was most discouraging."

"Gen. Singer left over two weeks ago. I believe he's near Barbosa, but I don't really know. You might ask Lt. Pennesey, or better yet, Capt. Pohler, the head of our local militia."

"I'll do that. But at the moment, I'm more concerned about the *pamuk*. Do you think you could obtain some for me?

"Certainly, how much did you want?"

She gave him a sharp, appraising look. "How much do you think you could deliver?"

"I don't know, *Lady*, the crop is small. A hundred pounds? Two hundred?"

She sighed, an elegant sound, conveying helplessness and frustration. "We were hoping to obtain at least eight tons, more if it can be arranged."

His jaw dropped.

That's half the pamuk *in Chatmakstan!*

"That is a huge purchase! To collect so much *pamuk*, it would be necessary to send messengers to all the villages, and I'd need at least a hundred piasters just to cover an initial purchase of one ton, besides which, there's the question of transportation . . ."

The *Lady* leaned forward, providing him with a breathtaking look down the top of her dress. He stood there staring dumbly, like a fish that's hit on the head.

"Tell me, Rajik," she said intimately, "if I were to advance you a hundred piasters right now, could you have a ton of *pamuk*, carded but *not* spun, waiting for me at Jasmine House in one week's time?"

Rajik swallowed. "I could."

"And could you arrange further shipments at the same price, one a week and at least seven in number?"

"Yes, *Lady*, I'm sure I could."

"Then we have a deal."

She said something to the prince, who counted out ten gold coins and gave them to Rajik. He stood there, just looking at the money in his hand, as they drove off. Heavy coins, these. He'd never held a gold coin before, he'd hardly ever seen one, and now he had ten of them!

I'm rich! Rich, rich, rich!

16: Lamya

Lamya was born into the family of a poor fisherman. Since he already had several children, he didn't greet the new daughter as a loving father should. In fact, he was tempted to drown her, but his wife persuaded him not to: "See how hard she's sucking. This one is hungry for life! She brings good fortune with her, I'm certain of it!"

The good fortune was long in coming. To be sure, her father caught many fat fish, but these went mainly to feed the rich people on the hill, and the money he thus earned paid the rent on their ramshackle old house. The burden of feeding the family fell to the children themselves: They daily went to the shore to take whatever the sea provided: crabs, oysters, mussels and clams, besides the edible seaweed that sometimes washed up, and driftwood for the fire. This, together with a bit of bread and a few vegetables from the garden, was their daily diet.

As the family grew, it was harder and harder to feed, and the children had to travel farther and farther to find enough to eat. As the youngest, Lamya inherited from an elder sister the undesirable task of digging for clams in the mud. With eight years, she was already dragging a bucket and a shovel almost two miles to the vast mud flat in an inlet down the coast from their home.

Every day, she faced the same struggle, wading through knee-deep mud to collect enough clams before the tide came in. When the clams heard the shovel, they'd dig themselves deeper into the mud, and so there was a race, one that Lamya was not certain to win. In the end, she had to pick up the bucket and run for the shore before the waves caught her. Then, she faced the wearisome effort of dragging the filled bucket, slopping with seawater, back home.

At ten years old, Lamya already hated her life, which was so full of drudgery.

Anything would be better than this!

She was digging after an escape-minded clam one day, when she had the idea she could calm it down by singing. Is that not what her mother did to her at bed time? Not knowing any songs which would appeal to clams, she made one up:

In the mud, it's dark and cold!
Don't be shy, you must be bold!
Come on out and see the sun!
Come with me, let's have some fun!

Much to her surprise, the clam popped out of the mud without any fuss. She put it in the bucket and tried the song on the next one. That clam yielded as easily as the first, and the third was the same. In no time, she'd filled the bucket.

When presented with the bucket, her mother said, "Finished already? Why don't you do that every day? Honestly, you do nothing but loaf around. Go fetch me some driftwood. The fire's getting low."

As she was dragging a heavy plank of driftwood, Lamya thought:

I better keep this singing trick to myself! If my parents find out, I'll only get more work!

The next day, after filling her bucket, she amused herself by collecting seashells and arranging them in interesting patterns. When she went home at the usual hour, she was neither scolded nor given extra work by her mother.

Before long, she could fill her bucket in a few minutes, simply by saying, "*Come with me!*" and she had a lot of time on her hands. For some weeks, she made castles out of sand and little boats from driftwood, which she released to sail about in the shallows, but eventually this all seemed rather childish and boring, and she began looking for new adventures.

Fooling clams was too easy. The clams were dumb. She tried singing to the shore birds, but they only stared at her. After many experiments, though, she discovered the light, trilling sound birds find irresistible. First came the little ones that run along the edge of the water, sticking their beaks in the sand, then the fat, lazy pelicans, and after that came the raucous gulls and terns, and finally she could lure even the big cranes and herons that wade in the shallow ponds.

She gave her new friends pieces of clam meat, sang to them and told them stories she made up about places far away and long ago. After awhile, they came without being called. Whenever they saw her on the beach, they'd come and flock around her.

She was sitting in the middle of her feathered audience one day, explaining how the waves always came from the west because that was the famous Land of the Waves, where giants went out daily to pound the ocean with their clubs, when all the birds, moving as one, suddenly got up and flew away. Looking around to see what had startled them, she felt a chill in her heart, as she first caught sight of the Old Woman.

The Old Woman was bent over and leaning on a cane. She was wrapped up in a cloak and hood, but the hands on the cane looked like they belonged to a corpse, and the eyes peering intently at Lamya were white, without any pupils. The Old Woman spoke to her without moving her lips:

You are my blood, my heart, my soul! Come with me!

Lamya came.

Over the years, she'd gotten used to the Old Woman's strange appearance and even her manner of speech, but the chill in her heart never left her.

"But they *killed* Deva!"

That was a misunderstanding. They thought she was a soldier. You look sweet, dearie. They won't kill you.

Lamya stared discontentedly at herself in the mirror. She was wearing a narrow-waisted black gown, covered with seed pearls set in astrological patterns, and black satin gloves. She had a silver coronet on her head, the high points of which looked suspiciously like the horns of some unnatural creature. It was decorated with polished bits of obsidian, as was the heavy, silver necklace.

"Sweet? I look like the queen of the witches!"

That is how you should look, dearie. In dealing with barbarians, one must assume a position of strength.

"You send me out, all alone, to surrender the castle to an army of barbarians, and you call it 'a position of strength'!"

I am sending you to lure them into the castle, where we can do with them as we please.

"Why don't you just summon a lot of demons and chase them away?"

They already brought a lot of demons with them when they came. One thing I have learned, in over a thousand years of experience, is not to be there when demons fight demons, because even

the victor won't be left with much. Trust me, dearie, this is the safer course.

Lamya knew she had no choice but to trust the Old Woman, who won every argument without ever opening her mouth.

Besides, I have plans for this General.

Lamya could guess what these plans were, but it was better not to think about it.

As she approached the main door, she found the servants waiting for her: All of the cooks, parlor maids, washerwomen and scullions, who yesterday were so afraid of being raped that they'd dressed up as soldiers, now pinned their hopes on her and crowded around to wish her well. She dismissed them with a reassuring smile and a nod. There was a barbarian general waiting for her outside, and she didn't want to test his patience.

Oh gods, just look at him!

The barbarian was waiting by the outer gate. He was dressed in polished armor that blazed with reflected sunlight, and he wore a golden helmet shaped like a cat demon. A soldier bearing a silver-black banner stood beside him, and beyond the gate were more soldiers, at least a thousand, in ordered ranks.

I don't think he'll be intimidated by my costume.

There was an awkward pause as they stood looking at each other, separated by the width of the courtyard. The General made no move. He was not coming to her, so she'd have to go to him. Behind her, the nervous servants closed the door. She could hear the bolt sliding into place.

That pretty well destroys my confidence!

Gathering what remained of her dignity, she began crossing the courtyard at what she hoped was a calm and stately pace. Details were becoming visible which made her even more nervous: The golden helmet was set with ruby eyes that seemed to be staring at her curiously. Instinctively, she made a warding gesture, and the rubies dimmed momentarily, before blazing up brighter than before.

On his left hand, the General wore a silver bracelet in the form of a centipede. Its blue sapphire eyes were following her, she thought, with amusement and disdain. "Don't you even try it, little girl," the eyes said.

The soldier carrying the banner was no soldier, it was a wild Bandeluk girl, armed to the teeth. She had a sword and two daggers in her belt, and a bow slung on her back. To judge by her hostile stare, she was ready to fight to the death for ownership of the General.

That's not a disguise! She really thinks she's a soldier! But why does this barbarian trust someone who has forsaken both her race and her sex? Does he even know what vipers are gathered around him?

The General spoke first: "I am Gen. Singer," he said in perfect Bandeluki.

"And I am Lamya, the housekeeper," she replied in the same language.

"That's some fancy get-up, for a housekeeper."

"What, this old thing? It was a gift from a friend," she said unconvincingly, adding, "Who is the young lady?"

The face of the "young lady" turned a bright red.

"I wish you hadn't said that," said the General. "I had a lot of trouble convincing her I really believed she was a man."

"I won't tell, if you won't," said Lamya.

"I think the joke has gone far enough."

"I believe you had a specific reason for calling me here?"

"If you're the one in charge, what I'm looking for is unconditional surrender."

"I'm afraid the best I can offer is the surrender of myself and the servants. The garrison disappeared as soon as they saw the demons. I'd give you my sword, if I had one."

"What about the soldiers yesterday?"

"The servant girls were afraid of being raped, so they dressed up like soldiers to scare you off."

"You can tell them nothing of the kind is going to happen. In a few minutes, I'll introduce Capt. Stewart, who will take charge of security here. You should report any breaches of discipline to him. Trust me, we take these things very seriously.

"I'll need quarters for him and his men, and also for myself and my staff."

"And the young lady?"

"What about her?"

"It may be a bit indiscreet, but I really must ask if she'll be sharing your quarters."

The General looked at the Bandeluk girl, who, if possible, turned even redder. "She'll require a separate room."

"I did the 'lure them into the castle' part. That went fine. When do we get to the 'do with them as we please'?"

That will take a bit of preparation.

The barbarians had run all over the castle, poking in every room and taking inventory of what they found there, particularly military equipment and supplies. The kitchen was inspected, as were the cistern and the granary. A list had been drawn up of everyone in Barbosa . . . with one exception.

"They know you're here. They're going to be looking."

For the Witch of Barbosa? That would be you, dearie.

Lamya snorted. "Dressing me up in a scary costume doesn't make me a legendary witch. Even the barbarians can see that!"

Exactly! The Witch is just a frightening rumor! You are the reality!

"You may fool the barbarians, but there's no way you can fool the Bandeluks. They know what you are."

Not one of them has dared to set foot in Barbosa, except for the girl, and anything she says can be dismissed as jealousy.

"She's jealous of me?"

She will be. She's clearly infatuated with this general.

"So, you want me to seduce the General?"

We're out of other options. He's resistant to the usual methods. Invite him to your room. Separate him from the girl and his jewelry, and then he'll be at our mercy.

"It sounds more like I will be at his. You have instructed me in many things, but not this. Life in an isolated castle full of women and eunuchs is not good training for romance."

You won't be without assistance. I have prepared a solution. You'll find a phial of it on the table behind you. It's quite tasteless. One drop will put him in a very agreeable mood. Two would suffice to make a great lover out of a eunuch. Three would render him insane, and four would almost certainly be fatal.

"So, do we go with the one or the two?"

Just one, dearie. If one drop does not suffice, we can always try it again with two.

"Very well, but I wish you'd told me about the trick with the eunuch before they all ran off."

"There is a time for casseroles, and a time to kill chickens," she'd told the chief cook. "Today, we kill chickens."

Usually, she didn't spend much time in the kitchen. But today, everything had to be perfect: Chickens were killed, cut up, fried and covered with a piquant sauce. Rice was rinsed and steamed. Vegetables were stewed. A glazed fruit kabob (the cook's specialty) was prepared. Everything was laid out in the great hall, fifteen places at the long table, with the General in the big chair at the head.

The Bandeluk girl was the first to arrive. She was still wearing the leather jacket and the pants she'd worn that morning. She had removed the other weapons, but still had a long, thin dagger in her belt.

"I have some nice dresses you can borrow," Lamya told her.

"Thank you for the offer."

What's going on here?

"The General said your little joke had fallen flat."

"I'm still a soldier until he says I'm not." She proceeded to sit in the General's place and taste everything on his plate. "I apologize, a necessary precaution," she said between bites.

"Perfectly understandable in the circumstances."

Thank goodness the wine is still being chilled!

"I didn't catch your name, by the way."

"Raeesha."

Raeesha, if that was her real name, stood behind the chair to the right of the General's, putting her hands on it to defend her place from any other claimants.

"That place is reserved for Capt. Stewart. Yours is at the end of the table."

"I prefer sitting here."

"Then perhaps you should take it up with Capt. Stewart." He was just entering, a thin, hard-faced man who stood by the door and scanned the room for hidden dangers before setting foot inside. He was still wearing his arming doublet and a sword. Nodding to Raeesha, he went to the General's place and started tasting the food.

"I just checked," said Raeesha.

Stewart merely grunted. When he was done tasting the food, he claimed the chair to the General's left.

This is not going as planned.

She moved to Stewart's left, before someone else claimed that place, and said, "Capt. Stewart! I hope you're enjoying our hospitality. Is everything to your satisfaction?"

Stewart nodded.

"I had some items I wished to discuss with your superior officer over dinner, specifically, the protocols for receiving your officers and men. We are not accustomed to . . ."

"Bandeluki no good," said Stewart.

Uh-oh.

In desperation, she turned for assistance to Raeesha, who helpfully said something in the barbarian language. Stewart's answer was brief.

"He says you should talk to Lt. Ogleby. Don't bother the General."

Everything is going wrong, wrong, wrong!

Next entered a tall young officer in a nice-looking uniform, Lt. Ogleby. He immediately went to the head of the table, as the first two had done. Stewart waved him off.

Raeesha said, "Lt. Ogleby, this is the housekeeper, Lamya. She would like some instructions on military etiquette."

"Is being most honored, beautiful hussy!" said Ogleby, taking the place to her left. "Etiquettes is being many, many important thing!"

Lamya stood there with a frozen smile on her face, as Ogleby launched into a garbled monologue about the military ranks, how to recognize them and the appropriate greeting for each. Meanwhile, the other barbarian officers were filing in, taking whatever place was open, and standing there, making small talk in their incomprehensible language.

Finally, the General entered, without, Lamya was pleased to see, the golden helmet. He'd taken the time to bathe and put on a uniform. The silver centipede sparkled on his left wrist. Its blue eyes seemed to wink at Lamya. "I know what you're up to, you naughty little girl!" it seemed to be saying.

The General sat down, and everyone else followed. Four servant girls came in with the wine. They were dressed in their best and were trying hard to please. No longer afraid of being raped, they seemed to be more worried about being ignored. Lt. Ogleby had offered the staff Hallandish lessons, and many had expressed interest in learning the obscure barbarian language.

With the General sitting next to Raeesha, the wine might have an unwanted effect, Lamya realized.

Let's see if I can abort this!

Desperately, she tried to catch the eye of Jessamina, the girl with the General's wine. The cup had a slight scratch on the rim to identify it, and Lamya had instructed her this glass, and only this one, was to be given the General.

To get up and give new instructions to Jessamina would create suspicion. If only the stupid girl would come her way! But no, she was going the other way around the table, and the pained expression on Lamya's face only seemed to confuse her.

As Jessamina set the drugged wine in front of the General, Stewart made a grab for it, but Raeesha got there first and, without pausing, stood up and raised the glass in a toast. Her speech was a babble of foreign words, but the other officers also stood and raised their glasses. All drank to the General, who remained seated, beaming amiably at the assembly. Lamya also stood and drank her wine, having first checked the rim of the glass.

Now we find out what that potion does to women! Something nasty, I hope! Maybe she'll grow a beard!

As officers sat, the General stood, making a speech in the same guttural language. Finally, he made a sweeping gesture toward Raeesha, who blushed. All the officers applauded.

"What did he say?" she whispered to Ogleby.

"Is being big honor! Raeesha is being new army flag-carrier!"

Standard-bearer! She plays him for a fool, is exposed and humiliated before the whole army, and he promotes her to Standard-bearer!

Raeesha's face was getting flushed, Lamya noticed. She'd loosened the collar of the leather jacket, and then the top button. She looked around the table at the men, seeing them with new eyes, and tugged absentmindedly at her short hair, as if trying to make it longer. Then, her eyes turned to the General and stayed there.

She's just a witless young girl, a transvestite! How can she beat me like this?

Raeesha made some witticism, raising one of the fruit kabobs, as if it were a banner. Everyone roared with laughter. The General leaned forward and wagged his finger in playful reproach. He reclaimed his wine glass, and Raeesha was too flustered to stop him.

The General raised his glass in a toast to Raeesha, and everyone joined, even Lamya, who could only watch as the General drank the tainted wine.

Those two can hardly stop looking at each other, and now I've given them a love potion!

You have failed me!

"I did exactly what you told me to do."

You completely mishandled it!

They'd been looking out the window at the southwest tower, where the lights in the General's quarters had just gone out. Lamya felt certain Raeesha's room would be empty tonight.

"I told you, I'm no good at these things. You're blaming your own puppet."

Why have I taught you so long, if at the first test, you are out-maneuvered by a teenaged girl!

"Perhaps because she's seen more of the world than I have. The social graces are not learned from musty old grimoires."

We're running out of time!

"Time? What does that have to do with anything? You're a

thousand years old!"

The stasis spell is becoming unstable!

"THE stasis spell? How could you let that happen?"

I have already told you many times, I don't have the key to that spell! I can't modify it in any way, the best I can do is reinforce it. It is old. It's falling apart, as am I. It takes all my strength to just hold it together.

"Why didn't you say something about this before?"

Because you were already as nervous as a cat in a kennel! And what could you have done about it? This was our last chance, and now it's gone!

"I wouldn't put it that way. The General is still our guest."

What if he is? He might as well be on the moon!

"You're much too devious. You always try to trick people into doing what you want. Even me. That is why your schemes fail. Maybe we can get at him in a different way."

And what would that be?

"Just let me handle it, dearie."

17: Erika

"Are you deliberately provoking me?" said Clenas. He was staring at her breasts, the way they moved up and down with the motion of the coach.

"Of course not!" said Erika. "Why would I do that? We're partners!"

The trip to pick up the first lot of *pamuk* was not comfortable for either of them. Prince Clenas had insisted on keeping an eye on his investment, and she was clearly part of the investment, but he'd become restless and peevish, and he had ways of sharing his discomfort.

"Then why are you dressed up like that?" he asked.

"This is my negotiation suit. We're meeting a supplier today, and I find business transactions go more smoothly when I dress this way."

"Your husband would *not* approve."

"Dear Clenas, you need not remind me of my vows. When my husband returns from Barbosa, he will find me compliant to his wishes."

"That is most odd. I've always found you to be obstinate and headstrong."

"You're a royal prince, but he is my husband, and so his authority is higher than yours."

"The women of my acquaintance don't seem to feel that way."

"Then perhaps you should seek a broader acquaintance. You will have to marry eventually, you know."

"A most depressing prospect. If she's like you, I may prefer suicide."

"I should think you'd want a woman *exactly* like me, who's good with money and faithful to her husband."

"I know how to handle money."

"My dear prince, you throw it around like a drunken sailor!"

"You should take note that I have been keeping careful records of my expenditures on this project, and they are considerable. Besides which, there is the inconvenience of falsifying reports and requisitions, bribing nosey officials, putting up with the whims of a pertinacious woman and a pretentious Bandeluk, and lowering myself to the status of a common tradesman."

Erika gave him her doe-eyed look. "I hope you don't imagine I am ungrateful for your efforts! Remember that, whatever the cost of your investment, it will be returned many times over!"

"So you keep telling me. But I have yet to hear exactly what this promised fortune amounts to, or when it will land in my pocket."

Time for some rosy projections!

"I hate to reckon up the profits beforehand, but you laid out ten thalers for a ton of *pamuk*, and by the time it's woven, dyed and delivered to market, it will be worth at least two hundred!"

"That would be a nice addition to the exchequer, but it doesn't amount to a great fortune. Besides, I have to deduct my expenses, and your share, and Hikmet's."

"Now you're thinking like a common tradesman! A *common* tradesman doesn't become wealthy. For that, you must think like an *uncommon* tradesman. You can expect a return of ten times your initial investment, and this is only the first delivery. There will be at least seven more, in time for the summer season."

Clenas leaned back and thought about it. "Eight hundred

thalers in all? I can pull more than that from my estates, in a good year. It doesn't make me 'the richest prince in Akaddia'."

"But that's only the first season! This *pamuk* is a light, strong fabric, and there's no competition. We can expect demand to increase in the second season, perhaps even double, and the price may increase as well."

Now, Clenas was stroking his chin. His mind was on other figures than hers. "Sixteen hundred thalers annually may not exceed Duke Claudio's revenues, but it would certainly bring me up to his level," he admitted.

Oh dear, he's already spending all those thalers!

"As I said, I do hate to reckon up the profits beforehand. A hundred things could get in our way, a plant blight or a shipwreck, or a new fashion craze, but I do not exaggerate when I say the *potential* profits are enormous. No risk, no reward."

His eyes returned to her bosom. "I am acquainted with the saying."

Rajik was waiting for them in front of Jasmine House, sitting on top of a big pile of sacks. Somewhere behind him, a blacksmith's hammer was ringing, saws were sawing, and a small bell announced the frequent arrival of customers at a local store.

"Those look like the sacks we use for horse fodder," said Clenas. "Ask him about that."

As they emerged from the coach, Rajik came down from the small hill of *pamuk* he'd constructed. He bowed respectfully to the prince, as he had before. "There are twenty sacks, each with a hundred pounds of *pamuk*, carded, but not spun, as you ordered. You can weigh them, if you wish."

"You can be sure we will," said Erika. "But where did you get those sacks?"

"Lt. Pennesey declared them surplus. After the cavalry left, we didn't need so much horse fodder."

Erika translated this for Clenas, adding, "This fits into our plans. When the wagons come tomorrow, we need only give them a manifest stating that they're delivering fodder to the Royal Light Cavalry."

"That should be easy to arrange," said Clenas. "Lt. Pennesey sounds like someone I'd like to know better. Let's check in on him."

Pennesey was sitting in his office in the back of Jasmine House, counting out stacks of coins. He stood to attention as the prince entered.

"At your ease, Lieutenant," said Clenas. "This is not an inspection, just an informal visit."

"I'm much relieved to hear it, sir," said Pennesey. "You've caught me preparing the weekly payroll. We're expanding our operations here, and the bookkeeping has fallen behind. I don't suppose you know where I could find a good clerk?"

Erika broke in: "Finding a clerk in want of a position wouldn't be hard back in Tideshore, but I'm not sure how one could be found in the wilds of Chatmakstan. If you like, I could check with some of my connections in the fabric trade. Even if I'm successful, though, you'd have to pay a premium for one willing to work here, besides covering the cost of transportation."

"I'm so desperate, I'd gladly pay twice the usual salary!"

"At that price, I'm sure one can be found. However, our real purpose here was to inspect the shipment outside. Has Rajik explained that to you?"

Pennesey nodded. "He has. The, um, horse fodder. Rajik is an ingenious lad. We depend on him a lot here. However, I wouldn't bring up the subject with Capt. Pohler, if I were you."

"Thank you for the hint," said Clenas. "How are things proceeding otherwise?"

"So far, we have about six hundred militia recruits with rudimentary training and equipment. They're still somewhat short of being a combat-ready force, but I'm pleased to report the incidence of banditry has sharply declined. Capt. Pohler can give you a more precise account of our operations. As you can see, I'm stuck back here, shuffling papers and counting coins."

"I'll speak to the good captain over dinner. Do you have any news of Gen. Singer?"

"None recent, sir. The last report was almost a week ago. He was camping in some ruins while his road crew was working. He reported a skirmish with a demon."

"A demon?" said Erika, much concerned. "Was he injured?"

"Thankfully, no. He struck it with his sword and it fled."

"That must have been a powerful blow!" said Clenas.

"I don't know what to call it. Very few people have survived demon attacks, much less put them to flight."

Dinner with Capt. Pohler was a very dull affair: salt pork fried and served with hard biscuits and the inevitable navy beans. To drink: a thin, sour table wine of no identifiable vintage.

"You should really get a better cook," Erika told him. "The local cuisine is really excellent. I'm sure Rajik could find someone."

"I refuse, on principle, to eat better than my men."

"Your men here are not many, and it would cost very little to improve their diets."

"And that money, great or small, would have to be diverted from legitimate purposes, which is also against my principles."

"I try to get by without too many principles," said Clenas. "In the end, they bury you together with your fine principles. What good is that?"

"The point not what they bury, it's what you leave behind. Right now, I am turning the Chatmaks from a worthless rabble into a capable military force. I found them wearing chains and being driven around with whips. When I leave, they'll be able to stand in the line with Akaddia's best!"

"Or against them, as the case may be. Do you think we can count on the loyalty of the Chatmaks?"

"It need not concern us, so long as the Bandeluk Empire remains a threat."

"Which won't be forever, I should hope. How will we justify our presence when the likes of Amir Qilij have disappeared into history?"

"That is not my problem."

"It is mine."

Lt. Pennesey, who had been picking without enthusiasm at his food, spoke up: "I'm much impressed with the resourcefulness of young Rajik. Young fellows like him are the future of this place."

"A pity, then, that he's a Bandeluk and not a Chatmak," said Pohler. "The Bandeluks are just about finished here."

"I'm not sure about that. The Bandeluk Empire may be finished. Their Emperor is, by all accounts, a useless and dissolute man, dedicated to the pleasures of the harem . . ."

Clenas threw him an offended look.

Better stay off that subject!

" . . . Their military is outdated, and their government can best be described as a despotic thugocracy. But the people themselves are intelligent and industrious, and skilled at many trades. The Chatmaks couldn't manage without them, and neither could we."

Pohler nodded reluctantly. "Sgt. Ebrahim is a real treasure. I wouldn't mind enlisting a few like him in the Halland Company, assuming they could learn the language."

"The language is a problem," Clenas said. "Anyone who doesn't know the language is at the mercy of the translator."

"My Bandeluki has gotten pretty good," Pennesey said. "And I'm picking up some Chatmaki as well."

"You should thank the gods you have that gift." Clenas looked around the table at the three Hallanders. "I never mastered any language but my own, and so I must rely on others to speak Akaddian."

"I wouldn't think that would be too much of a problem for a prince of Akaddia," said Pennesey.

"It wasn't, until Erika barged into my headquarters and started ordering me around. She's armed with three languages, and I have only one to defend myself with."

"This has been known to happen without the complication of foreign languages," Pennesey said.

Pohler had been looking gravely at Clenas without paying much attention to the talk. Now he spoke up: "May I ask you something, your Highness?"

I don't like the sound of that!

"Feel free."

"What are we doing in this miserable shithole?"

Clenas swirled the sour wine around in his glass for a moment before answering: "You can't possibly imagine how many times I've asked myself that question."

Erika was just getting into bed when there was a knock on the door. She threw on a robe and went to see who it was.

"Open up, it's Clenas!"

"Can we talk about it in the morning?"

"No, I need to speak to you NOW!"

She opened the door. Clenas was standing there in one of his fancy uniforms, the very picture of the handsome, young prince who was the subject of so many warm daydreams among Akaddian womanhood.

"I give up," he said. "I can't win this game. Marry me."

"I beg your pardon?"

"You were right. You're exactly what I need. So long as you're so stubbornly faithful to your husband, it might as well be me."

"The word 'husband' gives you no pause?"

"Please do not persist in that shabby pretense. You have no husband. Marry me."

"You must have a very low opinion of me. How would it look if I broke my engagement, while my beloved was off fighting at the front?"

"No different than a hundred similar cases I can think of. You are betrothed to a man who went off to war without making any provision for you, who has never visited you the whole time you were here, who has only sent you one letter, which you describe as most discouraging, and who's probably in bed with someone else. Marry me."

Perhaps, I've been keeping Clenas on too short a leash. But he's right, the leash on Singer is much too long!

"If you stop saying, 'Marry me,' I'll give it some thought. Why are you so determined to marry a woman you consider 'obstinate and headstrong'?"

"It is those particular qualities that endear you to me. It appears that you'll be entangled in my affairs for many years, you've already taken charge of my finances, you persistently scold me for my careless ways, and we're always fighting. We might as well be married."

"This is the *least* romantic proposal I've ever heard!"

"What does romance have to do with it? Romance just gets me in trouble. I'm good at it; everyone says so. But it doesn't help anything. It just landed me in Chatmakstan. Romance only clouds my mind with fancies. Whenever my judgment becomes clouded in this way, I can talk to you for just half a minute, and all the vapors are dispelled."

"We have been speaking for fifteen minutes already, and your words are as vaporous as before. We'll discuss this some more tomorrow." She closed the door.

Now what do I do?

It took a long time to fall asleep. The marriage proposal from

Clenas was both unexpected and very tempting. Not many women would turn down a prince, especially one who was so amiable, handsome, rich and sought-after. And there was a roguish excitement about him that the plain and earnest Singer lacked.

Clenas winks at all my faults, and he expects me to wink at his. We're not friends, we're accomplices! That's why he likes me!

But was the Erika that Clenas found so charming the same one Singer proposed to? What was it that had made her so set on marrying Singer? Her mind turned to the time they'd first met, at that dance. He was just one of many faces in the crowd. To be sure, he looked fine in his lieutenant's uniform, but no better than some other young officers who had attracted her attention.

He'd picked her out of a group of women who were gossiping together, just standing around in their silks and satins and jewelry, with their hair done up, and asked her to dance. And the other girls had giggled enviously when she said yes.

He picked me!

That was what made Singer irresistible: She was sick of living with her parents, and he had opened the door to escape. His interest in her had attracted her to him. Now Clenas had done the same thing, but he was here, waiting at her door, and Singer was so far away.

This is won't be easy.

She fell into a fitful sleep, full of dreams which she never dared describe to another person.

"You're doing it again!" said Clenas.

"Doing what?"

"Provoking me!"

They were again bouncing inside the coach, on one of the rough hill roads. Behind them, strung out along the road, were five wagons full of *pamuk*, disguised as horse fodder.

"Why would I do that? We were discussing a proposal of marriage!"

"You call this a discussion? You've done nothing but raise quibbles!"

"It's not a quibble to say you're a member of the royal house of Akaddia, and I'm a commoner from Halland."

"Everyone from Halland is a commoner. It's a republic. You

come from a perfectly respectable family. I checked."

"Your brother Vettius married a commoner, and there was a huge scandal. He was disinherited!"

"Why are you telling me about my own family? You think I don't know? Vettius was the heir presumptive, and he married a tavern keeper's daughter. That was the scandal. The daughter of a tavern keeper cannot be the queen of Akaddia. And he was not disinherited, he just gave up his place in the succession. I never really had a place in the succession, because no one expects me to become king. Anyway, they're all on the other side of the ocean and will learn about it afterwards, when they can only approve."

Am I joining the royal family or being smuggled in?

"What about your brother? Have you spoken to him about this?"

"Krion? No. He only cares for his war games. He's been hiding in his tent for over a week now, cooking up some new plan or other. He isn't likely to raise any objections."

"Why don't you at least tell me what I'm supposed to do? Does marrying you make me a princess? What exactly does a princess do?"

"It's not as if you're applying for a position at a foreign firm. Marrying me makes you my wife, and yes, your title is princess. Your duties are the normal ones expected of a wife, caring for the household and the children. There will be lots of servants to help with that.

"You'll have a big wedding, with all the military officers I can herd together and a nice tiara on your head, if we can find one here. You'll have to appear at state occasions, when we return to Akaddia, but you'll probably get tired of that in a hurry. Most of us do."

It's really that simple? Or is he concealing something?

"But what about our business, our partnership?"

"The only partnership you really need comes with a golden ring, which is a far more solid contract than what you have at present. Hikmet will have to manage the business for us, which should be no problem, once it's up and running. He can just set up a trading house in Kafra and ship up bushels of thalers now and then. He's rich, we're rich, everyone's happy.

"One rule that you *must* observe: A princess can't be seen engaging in commerce. That *would* be a scandal."

No more leaning over the counter in the fabric store? I don't think I'll miss that!

"It's a very attractive proposition. I haven't agreed to anything yet. Nor have I said no. But I won't keep you hanging much longer. It's possible that Gen. Singer is already waiting for me back in Kafra, or has at least sent another letter. That could alter the picture. But, in any case, you can expect a decision in a day or two."

If Singer finds out I've been sharing quarters with Prince Clenas, the engagement is definitely off! I can't afford to dither much longer!

"Life is short," said Clenas. "Let's pick a date that's sooner, rather than later."

He resumed staring at her bosom. "You're still wearing that damned 'negotiation suit'!"

"Am I? Oh, silly me!"

Gen. Singer was not waiting at Clenas's headquarters, but there was a large body of soldiers in the uniform of the Twelve Hundred Heroes. "You are Erika, the so-called wife of Gen. Singer?" said one of them, as she exited the coach.

"I resent the 'so-called,' but yes, that is my name."

"You are under arrest for witchcraft and treason."

While Erika stood there, dumbfounded, Clenas emerged from the coach. "Hold on, captain, what are you talking about?"

The captain saluted and produced an official-looking document. "Erika, the so-called wife of Gen. Singer was seen giving Prince Krion an enchanted ring, shortly before he fell into a state of bewitchment. I am to place her under arrest by order of Gen. Basilius, commander of the allied forces."

"And who made Gen. Basilius commander of the allied forces? Is he trying to usurp the authority of the royal house?"

"Gen. Basilius was appointed commander pro-tem by a military council convened yesterday, in view of the incapacity of Prince Krion."

"There are a number of things wrong with that, to wit, as second in command, I am in charge here, absent my brother. Also, such an appointment is not valid until it's confirmed by a representative of the royal house. Lady Erika cannot be charged with treason against Akaddia, because she's a citizen of Halland, and even if she did give my brother an enchanted ring, it is not evidence, per se, of witchcraft."

"All that is above my pay grade," said the captain stubbornly. "I only know that I have been ordered to arrest her, and I shall. Please step aside, sir."

"Who's going to make me?"

18: Singer

Narina's face blazed with divine glory. She looked down on him with eyes that were at once concerned and serene, kindly and distant, innocent and wise.

"I need you to do some things for me," she said.

Singer wept to hear her melodious voice, each word like a symphony. He'd have fallen to his knees, but he saw he was already there.

"I'd do anything for you," he said.

"There are some prayers that must be answered, minor miracles performed."

"I can't perform miracles."

"Nor more than I, and yet they happen every day."

"How can that be?"

"You said you'd never killed anyone. Was that true?"

A sin. It felt like he'd been struck with a whip.

"No," he said. "I gave the orders."

"Then you understand."

"Understand what? What am I to do?"

"What are the sacred virtues of Narina?"

"Prudence, candor and compassion."

"Then you know."

"Know what? Tell me what to do!"

But Narina's face was shrinking, withdrawing into the distance until it was only a small, glowing dot . . .

He was lying on his back in bed, staring at a bright dot on the wall, a narrow beam of morning sunlight that had penetrated the shutter. Raeesha lay asleep beside him. He closed his eyes, trying to return to the beautiful, golden dream, but it was gone, fading even as he reached for it. His eyes were running with tears, and he didn't know why.

Prudence, candor and compassion, that's all I remember.

They'd drilled those words into him every day for years. It was no wonder he had dreams about them. So why did he suddenly feel like he'd lost something incredibly precious?

I don't understand myself anymore. I must be going crazy!

Lying in bed, he stared at the little spot of morning sunlight, as it crawled across the wall. He thought about his recent behavior, and he found it totally unacceptable.

ITEM: Contrary to all the rules of war, he had enlisted captured Bandeluks into the army.

ITEM: He had committed a sacrilege on the high holy day of Theros.

ITEM: He had made a seditious speech before the whole army.

ITEM: He had chased a demon alone through the dark necropolis.

ITEM: He had nearly killed himself in an insane attempt to scale the walls of Barbosa.

ITEM: He had appointed a teenaged girl to be the army's Standard-bearer.

ITEM: Within an hour, he had bedded the same woman and made passionate love through most of the night, even though she was a subordinate, and he was engaged to someone else.

Looking at it objectively, his actions could only be seen as irresponsible. Totally inexcusable. He was out of touch with reality. If he were his own superior officer, he'd have dismissed himself a long time ago.

What in the name of all the gods can I do now?

There was no way to redeem all of this, or any appreciable part of it. The only honorable course was to resign. He had, after all, done his job, fulfilled his mission. It would be no disgrace to resign and seek other employment.

Anything but this!

But what about the girl? Leaving her in the position of Standard-bearer would be absurd, impossible. What if she became pregnant? He needed to find some excuse to send her back to Jasmine House, safely out of reach, until he knew whether or not he was a father.

Erika, of course, would have to be released from the engagement. She'd pledged herself to an ambitious, young officer, not an unemployed has-been. Also, he'd abandoned her and then betrayed her with another woman.

Raeesha was lying still beside him. He reached over to shake her and tell her of his decision, but his fingers encountered a hard, stony object. Surprised, he sat up in bed and looked at her. She was curled up and seemed to be asleep, but when he touched her body, it was as hard and rigid as a stone.

Is she dead?

"She'll be fine," said a voice coming from a dark corner. "It's only a stasis spell. I just needed to speak to you alone."

Reaching under his pillow for the dagger, he jumped out of bed and held the blade to the throat of someone he now recognized as Lamya, the self-described "housekeeper".

"Release her NOW!"

Lamya didn't seem to be surprised or afraid. "I should probably explain that the spell is keyed. That means, it can't be changed by anyone who lacks the key, which is usually a word or phrase. I'm the only one who knows the key to this spell, so if you kill me, she may be like that for centuries."

Singer pressed the dagger against her throat. "I don't have to kill you *entirely* to get what I want. A few sharp cuts should do the job."

Lamya was still unimpressed. Her green eyes stared calmly at him. "While you were asleep, I took a reading of your spiritual profile. Your egoism index was minimal, meaning you might threaten me with a knife, but you aren't going to use it."

"Don't put that theory to the test!"

"I just did," she said coolly. "Be reasonable. Your girlfriend is in no danger. I simply didn't want her interfering. She tends to be a bit over-protective.

"All I want is to talk a bit and show you some things which you've so far overlooked. This has a bearing on your responsibilities, General. Your army is in great danger, as are you and all of us."

"What do you mean?" said Singer, lowering the dagger.

"It would be easier to show you."

At the bottom of the stairs was a small chamber flagged with stone. No sentries were stationed here, because none were needed, it was just an open place at the foot of the stairs. Singer, who had put on his pants and a shirt, watched as Lamya used a finger tip to trace a symbol on one of the stones, which caused it to open like a trap door, revealing a darkened stairway underneath.

Lamya said, "Thousands of people have lived here without

ever knowing the castle is built on top of another structure which is much larger and more important. See for yourself."

"You go first."

"But of course."

A few steps down, she touched a lamp hung from the wall, causing it to fill the stairwell with light. Singer could now see she was standing on a small landing, looking up and waiting for him. Below the landing, the stairs stretched out of sight into the darkness. But he hadn't gone far before the stone slab which functioned as a trapdoor snapped shut above his head.

"Pardon me for not warning you about that, General," said Lamya reassuringly. "We can't have the servants stumbling on our little secret. Servants are so prone to gossip."

"Just show me what you're going to show me."

The stairs kept winding down, story after story, deeper into the earth. Lamya paused occasionally to light a lamp. Singer, who had been trying to count the number of landings, gave up at twenty.

This is deeper than the castle is high!

Lamya, meanwhile, gave him a lecture about the history of the place: "As you know, castles are built to guard strategic locations. The site for Barbosa was chosen in a mountain pass near the border between the Kingdom of Kano and the Indo Empire. This was contested terrain. In fact, all of Kano was coveted by the Indos, who claimed divine authority to reign over the entire continent. Am I boring you?"

"Not so far."

"Though badly outnumbered, the Kano people were protected by their mountains and by a powerful navy, which allowed them to bring in barbarian mercenaries from overseas. These, I expect, may have included some of your own ancestors."

"I never heard of that."

"Naturally not, they hadn't yet learned to read and write. Kano was also advanced in the art of sorcery, far more so than anyone today. Hence, they were able to deploy, in their defense, not only troops, but also ignoniums, dimidians, bellators and numerous other kinds of demons."

"You mean, like the screechers and springers, and these damned *fui* demons?"

"If that's what you call them. The Indos made many attempts

to invade Kano, but always without success. Eventually, however, they were able to improve their military sciences to the point of producing something they called 'wave effect generation,' a hugely destructive weapon. I'm not sure how it worked, but you've seen its effects."

"The Area of Effect?"

"That would be the most obvious example. They'd lost sight of their original goal, of conquering Kano, and simply wished to destroy the kingdom, which they imagined was an existential threat. And that's what it indeed became.

"Desperately seeking a weapon to deter the implacable Indos, Kano experimented with heretofore banned sorceries, summoning ever more powerful entities to its cause, until . . . well, you shall shortly see."

They'd reached the bottom of the stairs. There was a simple wooden door. Lamya drew an ordinary-looking key from her purse and turned the lock. The tiny *click* that this produced sounded ominously loud in the stillness. With an expectant smile, she opened the door.

On the other side was a stone platform, about a hundred feet across. Beyond that, everything was dark. Along the wall was a row of lamps almost as big as Singer himself, and behind them were curved mirrors. Lamya drifted from one to the other; as she touched each of them, a great beam of light appeared, revealing things that at first seemed impossible to understand.

Singer thought he was looking at a dark hillside. He was standing in a huge, vaulted chamber, and in front of him was a mammoth form, black as midnight, even where the light touched it. His eyes couldn't see the whole form at once, and only gradually did he understand the dark, polished surface he was looking at, shaped like a diamond and twice the size of his own body, was only one of an endless series of such shapes that overlapped each other like the scales of a serpent, and what he'd taken to be a hillside was a tiny part of some immense creature, which lay all coiled around itself in a vast pile hundreds of feet high.

What the hell is this thing? It's bigger than the whole castle!

Lamya came and stood beside him. "Behold Extinctor, the forgotten weapon of the ancient Kanos. It has been lying here for a thousand years, waiting for the command to go out and destroy na-

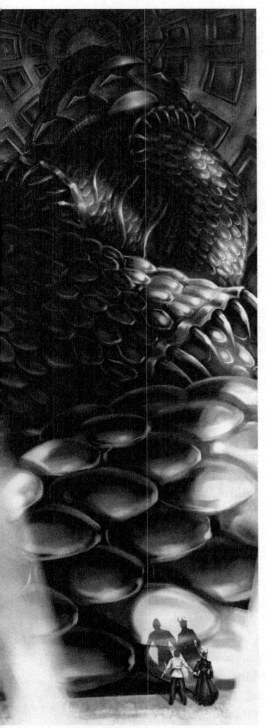

tions."

After gazing a moment at the huge demon, Lamya continued: "If Extinctor were to twitch its tail, the earth would shake. If it were to extend itself to full length, the castle would fly apart like a child's sand castle when it is kicked. But when Extinctor is released from stasis, the destruction will be far, far greater than that."

"You're threatening to use this demon against us?"

"No, no, no and no! Only a fool would use Extinctor as a weapon. This, unfortunately, the Kano people did not know until it was too late. You see, they didn't understand the full potential of what they'd summoned.

"Kano was under ultimatum from the Indos, who demanded its surrender. They had already demonstrated their 'wave effect generation' in a barren region, and were threatening to destroy the whole kingdom. Kano was desperate. They attempted a demonstration of their own weapon, which was not yet tested.

"For this, they summoned a smaller demon, of Extinctor's type, but only fraction as big, merely a hatchling of its kind. It was supposed a small demonstration of the new demon type might cause the Indos to withdraw their ultimatum.

"Because this demon came

from a distant dimension, conditions here were not compatible with its existence, and the sorcerers expected it would be destroyed in a great explosion. What happened, though, was far worse: Rather than submit to its own destruction, the demon drew on forces from its dimension and other intervening dimensions in an effort to create an environment more congenial to its existence. Within a minute, an immeasurable amount of matter drawn from distant planes was sucked into the target area, which was deep in Indo territory.

"Much of this material was harmless. But it also included elements which didn't exist here and could not, besides living creatures of many kinds, some themselves of great destructive power. In the process, the dimensional fabric itself was twisted, torn and mutilated. Up was down, left was right, day was night.

"The zone of destruction was far greater than expected, wider even than the Area of Effect and more complete. The Indo Empire was crushed. Retribution followed quickly, but it was their last gasp. Overnight, both civilizations ceased to exist."

"What happened to the Kanos?"

"Their power was broken, their great cities ruined or sunk into the earth or the sea. They were unable to resist, when, years later, a tribe of nomads, to whom no one had paid much attention, came and built an empire on top of the wreckage."

"You mean the Bandeluks? What about the Kanos themselves?"

"You're speaking to one. Today, they call us Chatmaks. We are few today who remember our ancient heritage. For centuries, the Bandeluks have watched over us, as we watched over the demon, one thing they had no wish to meddle with."

"And the Indos?"

"Possibly, some remnant survives, beyond the Madlands, but they need not concern us. No one has ever crossed the Madlands."

"That's some fascinating history, but what does it have to do with me? What is this great danger you speak of?"

"I put your girlfriend in stasis partly, as I said, because I didn't want her to interfere, but also because I wanted to show you how stasis works. Extinctor is under a similar spell, but far more powerful. This spell is a thousand years old, and it has grown very weak. We're doing what we can to reinforce it, but we are very few now, and we can't contain it for long. Extinctor will soon break free."

"'Soon'? When is 'soon'?"

"I don't know exactly. This has never happened before. I think we have at least a few weeks, perhaps as much as a year. Certainly, not more than that."

"What happens when it breaks free?"

"Again, I don't know precisely. The smaller demon destroyed the Indo Empire and created the Madlands, which remain uninhabitable. I'd estimate the destruction would be many times greater than that. I do not expect to survive, and neither should you."

"What do you plan to do?"

"I can do nothing. If I had the key to this stasis spell, I could release Extinctor harmlessly back into its own dimension. Unfortunately, that key is lost. The sorcerers who summoned Extinctor also summoned the smaller demon and they were engulfed in the chaos that followed."

"So there's nothing we can do?"

"Not quite. The sorcerers of Kano had tricks to extend their physical existence. We have evidence one of them may still be alive."

"How is that possible . . .?"

"As for what spell he may have used to prolong his life, there are several alternatives. The more puzzling question is, how he could have survived the destruction of the Indo Empire and how he could exist for so long in the Madlands. Come, let me show you something."

Behind them, by the door, was a table which held a jumble of objects unfamiliar to Singer. Above it, on the wall, were six small mirrors. Five of these were dark, but one seemed to glow with a pale, blue light. Lamya touched it, causing it to brighten momentarily, before returning to the same, faint luminescence as before.

"The man in question was named Shayan. He was wearing a monitor, similar to the one on your wrist."

Monitor? What does that mean? Is someone spying on me?

He looked at the silver centipede. Its blue eyes twinkled at him in the lamplight.

I need to cut this thing off, or at least pry out those gems!

The blue eyes stared at him complacently. "Don't even think about it," they seemed to say.

"It's still working," Lamya continued, "but it seems to be damaged and can no longer provide us with much useful information, beyond the simple fact that Shayan is still alive somewhere."

From the objects on the table, she selected a small, wooden wand, with a blue gem on one end. She pointed at the opposite side of the room and then swung her arm slowly to the left. Before it had gone very far, the blue gem began to glow, and then to pulse. She left it pointed in that direction for a minute.

"There is Lord Shayan, somewhere to the north, deep in the Madlands. We have sent at least a hundred expeditions to find him. None has ever returned."

"So you want to send another one? What good is that?"

"Possibly, no good at all. You led an army across the Area of Effect, a notable achievement, but the Madlands are far more dangerous, and there's no way to subdue them by military force. One might as well shoot arrows into a tornado or raise an iron shield for protection against a lightning bolt. Indeed, if inclement weather were the worst we had to fear, Extinctor would no longer be a threat. But we don't know exactly what dangers to expect in the Madlands. As I said, none of those expeditions ever returned."

"And still, you want me to risk the lives of myself and my men in this folly?"

"Not your men, just you personally. Military force is of no use. But, as I said, you and your men are already at risk. If you do nothing, I will die, and you will die, and they will die. I'd say you have nothing to lose."

"Why not just send some demons?"

"It has been tried. Conditions there are in constant flux. Travelling any distance in the Madlands would expose them to forces which could render them uncontrollable. Only men, those of the greatest fortitude, have any chance of success."

I was just thinking I'd disgraced myself, and now would be a good time to end my military career. If I don't return, at least that problem will be solved!

"What makes you think I can do this, when a hundred expeditions have already failed?"

"The odds are certainly against you. But we have been observing your recent career with interest, and there are a number of points in your favor: You were singled out for heroism, alone from the entire barbarian army. You crossed the Area of Effect, even where it was considered impassable, and camped in the lost city of Iram, which no one had seen in centuries. You scaled the walls of Barbosa. And there is the peculiar circumstance that you are resistant to sorcery. *T'eal m'ey!*"

As she spoke these last words, Singer felt a jolt throughout his body. The centipede bracelet suddenly felt warm, and its blue eyes blazed red, as if it were angry. His heart racing, Singer fumbled for his dagger, but Lamya hadn't moved. Her green eyes watched him as calmly at before.

"What the hell was that!"

"That, dear General, was a test. You passed, as I expected you would. If we could have forced you, we might have done that, but as we cannot, we must beg. But if I can't command you, I'm fairly sure no one else can, so your chances of survival in the Madlands may be better than one would expect. Besides, you'll have the assistance of an ally who can protect you from many dangers, and offer much helpful advice and good companionship besides."

"And who is this wonder-worker?"

"Me, of course."

19: Lessig

From the tower he'd erected for that purpose, Capt. Lessig inspected the dam, and saw that it was good. As soon he gave the order to drop the sluice gates, water would begin building up, and the lagoon would drain. Within twenty-four hours, it would be done: Kafra would be open to assault.

Work continued on the diversion canal, which was, in itself, a kind of diversion. He'd planned an unnecessarily long and deep canal, which would take weeks to complete. When his sappers encountered a stubborn outcropping of granite, he'd insisted they dig straight through it, another delay. Of course, he could have saved a lot of time by going around, but for that matter he could have diverted the water to a nearby gulley and forgotten about the canal entirely. Using the gulley would have temporarily flooded some cropland, but with the harvest over, who really cared?

The essential thing is, the royalists must not win an easy victory!

There were footsteps on the stairs. Lt. Radburn arrived, followed by four soldiers guarding Lt. Bardhof, who was manacled. Returning Radburn's salute, Lessig said, "Remove the chains. Lt. Bardhof won't be our guest much longer."

Bardhof seemed surprised and a bit upset at being unchained.

He's crafty. He can smell a trap, but he doesn't know what kind.

Bardhof made a show of rubbing his wrists. "Have you finally seen the light, Lessig? Given up your aristo sentiments? Written off all those ancestral estates?" He was deliberately using the old Covenant dialect, scorned by the aristos as unrefined.

Stay calm. He's testing you.

"That's all ancient history now. We have more important and immediate concerns."

"Strange, it seemed rather important and immediate when you locked me a storage room. Has something changed?"

"A great deal has changed, but for you, the main item is that your investigation is no longer relevant."

"Unless the royal house has been overthrown, I don't see how it could be *irrelevant* that one of your men sabotaged the shoe on

Prince Krion's horse!"

Lessig smiled amiably at him. "What would you say if I told you that was one of Basilius' men in a false uniform?"

"I'd say you were lying!"

Oh, he is a bold one! I wish I had more like him on my side!

"That would have been a reasonable conclusion, last week. But now, I have proof of Basilius' disloyalty. He's declared Prince Krion unfit for command, and named himself the leader of the allied forces."

"What?"

Crafty though Bardhof might be, his shock was certainly genuine. Lessig gave him a copy of the proclamation.

"I apologize for the enforced vacation, but I couldn't allow you to raise suspicions of the loyalty of Covenant troops with your unfounded allegations. Our position here is most delicate. We could easily have been caught between two Akaddian factions, as indeed, Gen. Singer and his Free Staters have been."

Bardhof looked up from the document. "I don't know what they're talking about here. Who is this witch Erika they refer to?"

"You don't remember her? A woman by that name visited Prince Krion in his tent a couple weeks ago."

"Yes, I remember that now, but she wasn't a witch, she was the wife of Gen. Singer!"

"Basilius claims she was a witch, and that she laid an enchantment on Prince Krion. He accuses the Free Staters of a conspiracy. Gen. Singer supposedly made an anti-royalist speech awhile ago."

"That sounds strange. The Prince just promoted Singer, so why would he suddenly turn against him?"

"I thought so too. Who knows what he really said in that ridiculous language? Singer is just a green lieutenant and much too dull-witted to hatch such a plot. But he's off besieging Barbosa, in obedience to his orders, so he can'tanswer to the charges. Meanwhile, Prince Clenas was manhandled by Basilius' men and has declared him a mutineer."

"What?"

Bardhof was visibly shocked a second time.

Good gods, these turncoats take insults to the royal family so seriously!

"Prince Clenas rejected Basilius' claims and attempted to prevent the arrest of Lady Erika. He was seized and roughed up in his own headquarters."

"Disgraceful!"

Clenas' bloody nose means more to him than his own week in captivity!

"Prince Clenas has declared Basilius a rebel and withdrawn the Royal Light Cavalry to the north. I rather thought you might want to join him."

"Where is Krion?"

"I don't know. He's not been seen nor heard of since Basilius assumed command."

Bardhof was getting that sly look again. "How do I know any of this is true? This piece of paper could be a forgery!"

"Could be, but it's not. You'll find them posted all over the place. Why don't you go and ask Clenas about it? I have a message for him, by the way.

"We have had our differences in the past, but that's over now. No responsible officer can accept such a blatant usurpation of power. I have sought and received pledges of support from every Covenant commander, that is, of three companies of pike, two of crossbow, the heavy assault group and, of course, my sappers. All have sworn to support Prince Clenas in any confrontation with Gen. Basilius. You can count on it."

"That sounds very good of you, but again, the proof is lacking."

"Go ask them for yourself, if you wish. None have been reckless enough to commit anything to paper, and neither shall I. However, it's urgent Prince Clenas be informed of this as soon as possible. Since you're well known as a true royalist, you're the best man to convey this message."

Bardhof went to stand at the edge of the parapet, as if to glean fresh clues by looking at the distant forts and encampments around the lagoon. "This is all a lot to absorb in so short a time. A little while ago, I was a prisoner locked up and in chains."

"Again, my apologies for that. I did what seemed necessary at the time. Had I acted otherwise, we might be in much more serious trouble now. Covenant officers would make more plausible scapegoats than the Free State rabble."

"Even if Covenant does pledge its support to Prince Clenas, does that change anything? Most of the army remains under the control of Gen. Basilius."

"Not as much as you may think. The Brethren are confined to quarters. They refuse to take orders from Basilius. The Ragmen, also, will only hear commands from Prince Krion. The Free Staters, too, may well declare for Clenas, when they hear of the insult to the General's wife. In any case, the royal house *must* know who stands beside them in this crisis."

Bardhof reached a decision. "Very well, I'll do as you ask. You need not urge me to speak to the other Covenant commanders. Be sure I'll do so before reporting to Prince Clenas." He was no longer using the old dialect, Lessig noticed.

"I expect no less. There's a horse waiting for you below."

Bardhof saluted.

"May the gods spur you to victory!" responded Lessig.

As Bardhof's horse departed, Lessig stood by the parapet, watching him leave. Radburn came to join him. "I didn't understand your decision to spare that royalist rat, but now I see you're playing a deeper game."

"It's the only game we have, now that the assassins have failed us."

"'It will look like an accident,' you said."

"Well, we shan't make that mistake again."

"You really believe the royalists will attack each other?"

"Count on it. Clenas is a craven little milksop, but bloody his nose, and the royalists will forget all about that. He's a royal prince! A village destroyed here and there is nothing, but a bloody nose on a prince means war.

"And you don't lay hands on his women. If he cares about nothing else, he cares about them.

"On the other side, Basilius is a brutal old cutthroat who has seen a hundred battles, and would like to see a few more. They don't call his men the Twelve Hundred Heroes for nothing."

"One thing I don't understand is this witchcraft plot. Where the hell did that come from?"

"I don't know. Some princeling back in Akaddia probably set it in motion. Worked out pretty well for us. Now, I'm a leader of the royalist faction, and even that ass-kisser Bardhof is running errands for me."

"Just don't forget we're fighting for the independence of our country."

"You can stick a knife in me if I do."

"Count on it."

20: Raeesha

Raeesha sat on the ground and studied the letter, trying with her inadequate Hallandish to make the strangely formed words reveal their secrets:

To Capt. Pohler
Headquarters, Free State [. . .]
Jasmine House, Chatmakstan
URGENT

Inform Prince Krion [. . .] the following: Barbosa has fallen. No [. . .] on our side. Barbosa is a [. . .] fortress, well [. . .] and easily [. . .] against any attack. Our force is [. . .] here, awaiting further orders. Full report to follow.

For your [. . .]: Sgt. Raeesha is known to you as "Rajik." She can't simply be [. . .], because of [. . .] services, but her presence here is [. . .]. Assign her to light duties. Inform at once if she becomes [. . .]. She is [. . .] to a sergeant's pay.

Gen. Singer
Commander, Free State [. . .]

Raeesha had opened the letter with a feeling of dread, not wishing to repeat Umar's mistake. The contents, so far as she understood them, were not reassuring.

She'd awakened shortly before noon, in a pleasant, erotic daze, and found Singer, already in uniform, standing over her, with the letter in hand. "This is a very important message," he'd said brusquely. "I need you to take it to Capt. Pohler at Jasmine House immediately. Leave as soon as you're ready."

With that, he was gone.

And gone from her life, it seemed, the glorious young General, who only yesterday had praised her before the assembled officers, promoted her to Standard-bearer and then taken her to his bed . . .

Don't cry.

She cried anyway.

How can he do this?

It had to be the Witch. Despite all of her precautions, the Witch had gotten to him, perhaps even while he was lying in her arms. She had tried to protect him, but she had failed.

Going back to Jasmine House was out of the question. There was nothing for her in Jasmine House, expect perhaps a mat on the kitchen floor. She wasn't going anywhere until she had Singer back, or the Witch was dead.

She got on her hands and knees, and crept to the edge of the hill top, the same position lately vacated by Sgt. Littleton and his siege crossbows. From here, she could see the distant, tiny figure of Littleton assembling one of his war machines among the machicolations of a tower.

The demons had been assigned a place in the courtyard. Capt. Stewart's men were guarding the gate, turning away sightseers and anyone without orders. In the open area around the castle, there was now a tent city, where thousands of soldiers were killing time.

She'd already scouted the area, and felt sure there was no entrance but the main gate. The spikes Singer had driven into the wall had been removed. She considered her options: Trying to sneak past Stewart's guards didn't seem like a good plan, and neither did scaling the wall without even the help of iron spikes. Bribery probably wouldn't work, even if she had the money. Her face was too well known for a disguise.

The only plan that seemed feasible was to watch and wait. Surely, not even the Witch could make the General disappear from the middle of his army. First, she'd have to separate the two. So, either the army would be leaving, or the General would. Then, she'd have her opportunity.

Hours went by, but nothing happened. The watch was changed. The men were called to supper, then assembled for the evening roll call. Torches were lit. Men sat around campfires, swapping stories. The distant lights and voices only made Raeesha feel cold, lonely and confused.

If he's leaving, it will probably be in the darkest part of the night. If I stay awake, I may catch him.

It was getting very dark. The men unrolled their bedrolls. A faint starlight illuminated the landscape, giving everything a ghostly look. Raeesha rolled herself up in her blanket and tried to keep her eyes on the gate, now merely a featureless black square in the distance.

If he does leave, will I even see him?

She was having trouble keeping her eyes open. She chewed on some of the tasteless dried rations to give herself strength, but before she'd finished even the first disgusting mouthful . . . the rising sun struck her in the face.

I fell asleep! He could be gone already!

There seemed nothing to do but stay where she was and hope for the best. Below her, the men were going through the familiar routines: rolling up their bedrolls, washing, having breakfast, assembling for roll call . . .

There he is!

Gen. Singer had emerged from the gate, on a white horse. Behind him, on a second horse, was a dark-clad figure who could only be the Witch. For a moment, Raeesha considered shooting her, but the range was extreme, and she'd have to pass through half the army to get closer.

As she watched, the two riders turned and proceeded northwards at a brisk trot.

Why are they going there? There's nothing to the north but . . . the Madlands! She's taking him to the Madlands!

No one ever returned from the Madlands. All Raeesha knew about them was rumor and legend. Supposedly, the Madlands were full of fierce demons. Supposedly, there were dead people walking around. Supposedly, anyone who set foot there went insane.

There didn't seem any way to catch them. If she went galloping through the army encampment, someone would surely stop her. And anyway, Singer already had a head start. There was, however, a dry creek bed nearby. If she led her horse up the creek bed, she could probably walk past the encampment without anyone seeing her and cross Singer's path, if not before, at least not long after he'd passed.

The creek, when she found it, was floored with large, smooth stones that her horse had trouble getting over. She hurried it along as fast as she dared; it could easily be lamed in a place like this. The creek bed wound back and forth more than she remembered, so it was late in the morning before she came to a ford with fresh hoofprints leading north.

I'll have to hurry if I'm to catch them!

There was an ancient cobblestone road heading north, covered here and there with patches of soil and dry grass. It led upwards through a canyon between high cliffs of stone, until it came to a narrow pass. At first, Raeesha thought someone very big was standing in the pass, but as she got closer, she saw it was a stone pillar, some ten feet high, square in cross-section, and covered with inscriptions.

I guess this must be a boundary stone.

Looking closer, the inscriptions were in some language she didn't recognize, or perhaps several of them. It was hard to tell, because the stone was so worn: there were places where she couldn't have read even her own language.

On the side facing her, however, was something she immediately recognized: The shape of a centipede was scratched into the stone, a close match for the one she'd seen in the ruined Kano city. Passing her fingertips over the marks, she saw they were only a day or two old.

Is this a welcome or a warning?

It didn't seem likely the Witch had stopped here to make this sign. Perhaps it was intended for the General. Wasn't he wearing a bracelet shaped like a centipede? Whatever it meant to him, it was a mystery to Raeesha, who turned to contemplate the view from the top of the pass.

It was disappointing, in a way: From here, the Madlands looked like the other side, a barren, hilly country crossed by many gullies, almost featureless . . . except for the big stone fortress that blocked the road . . .

Raeesha blinked and rubbed her eyes, in case it was an illusion, but no, it was still there: a castle bigger than Barbosa, but it was ruined. One corner was smashed so flat, it looked like the sky had fallen on it. The rest was full of huge cracks and holes big enough to ride a horse through. The towers leaned at strange angles, and some of the walls, too, looked ready to fall over. It seemed miraculous it *hadn't* fallen over. The walls were over twenty feet thick, she saw, but they were resting at impossible angles

How could this remain standing for a thousand years?

Perhaps some sorcery was still propping it up, or perhaps it was an engineering feat of the ancient Indos. They had plainly intended it to stand here for a long time, perhaps forever, but despite that, something had crushed it like an eggshell.

She studied the castle for a minute. It seemed to be completely deserted. She thought, for a second, to glimpse some motion in a high tower window, but it didn't repeat itself. Otherwise, nothing was stirring.

Was that a bird I saw?

There had been pigeons cooing in the eaves of Barbosa, and buzzards were always circling here and there in the Area of Effect, but there were no birds of any kind in the Madlands. So far, unless something was nesting in the tower, she hadn't seen a single one.

Just because I haven't seen something, doesn't mean it isn't here. I better get moving!

The road turned left and, skirting the edge of the fortress, then turned right, into something that was apparently once a gate, but was now merely a heap of rubble. Cautiously, she dismounted to peer around the corner . . .

It was standing there, in the middle of the road, a hairy ape-like creature taller than a man and at least twice as heavy. It was snarling at her, with its ugly mouth full of sharp teeth, and it had a huge club, long as a man's body, raised over its head.

Shocked, Raeesha didn't move a muscle.

Neither did the demon.

After a minute, when her heart was not pounding quite so strongly, she saw it hadn't even blinked once; it was frozen in that threatening pose. She picked up a pebble and threw it, so that it struck the demon on the right knee. It still did not twitch.

Moving slowly, she readied her bow and took aim at the creature's head. Instead of a solid *thunk*, there was a *clink*, as if the arrow had struck a stone. It fell to the ground. Still, the demon had not winced.

She studied the road for tracks. Had Singer come this way? Yes, and the Witch too. Evidently, this demon had jumped out of the ruins, and, before Singer could do anything courageous, the Witch had turned it into a statue.

Killing the Witch may be harder than I thought.

The horse didn't want to go near the demon. Coaxing it with her voice and soothing it with her hands, she led it past, while staying as far as possible from the threatening club. She didn't dare to touch the monster's hairy side, nor pick up the arrow lying at its feet.

Once past the castle, she mounted and spurred the horse into a gallop, hoping to put as much distance as possible between her and any friends the demon might have. The road was deserted. It wound its way downhill, through canyons and past unremarkable heaps of stone.

At one point, she had to wade across a stream, where a small stone bridge had collapsed. She let her horse drink its fill before she tried the water. It was clean, though with a slight mineral aftertaste. It seemed the Madlands had no more surprises for her this day.

It was getting dark, and she was already seeking a campsite, when the road turned a around a bend, and she found herself looking at a walled city. No ruin this: As she watched, lights were appearing in windows and in the streets. Staring at it from an elevation, she could make out eight major avenues and numerous side streets, lined with two- and three-story buildings.

This is bigger than Kafra! There must be thousands of people! But how can they all live in the Madlands?

She tried blinking and rubbing her eyes, but the city was still there. As she sat gawking, a thin sliver of moon appeared on the horizon. Not trusting the dim light, she dismounted and walked her horse in the direction of the city.

It took a couple hours to cover the distance. In the meanwhile, she'd passed several dark, ruined buildings, perhaps barns or farmhouses.

This is strange. How can the city be populated, while the countryside is empty?

The gates to the city, she now saw, were standing open, despite the late hour. As she got nearer, she could hear the inviting sounds of laughter and music.

What kind of place is this? There isn't a watchman to be seen! Is no one afraid of the demons?

A hundred yards from the gate, she stopped in the middle of the road, reins in hand. Through the open gate, she could see buildings hung with colorful banners, as if a festival were underway. Singing and dancing could be heard, but there was not a soul in sight, not even a single guard at the gate.

What city is this, that has no people in it?

She slapped herself in the face, but the scene remained the same. This was the Madlands, she remembered. She should expect no friendly faces. Whoever lived here was not likely to offer hospitality.

I wasn't invited to this party.

She turned around and walked back the way she came. When she could no longer hear the sounds of revelry, she picked one of the ruined buildings beside the road, a roofless two-story structure with most of the first story still intact, and led her horse in through the gaping door. It was very dark inside.

Darkness is good, darkness is safe. Let me hide in the darkness. Nothing will find me here.

Behind the house was an enclosed area. It looked like an over-grown garden. There was even a fountain in the middle, full of stag-nant water. She released the horse in the garden, taking a moment to curry it and soothe its nerves, before spreading her own bedroll.

In the morning, she found she was lying on a pile of dead leaves. Similar detritus lay inches thick inside the building. In back, the horse was complacently cropping the abundant grass. As she led it outside, she glanced in the direction of the city . . . but there was no city, just a huge pile of rubble, dotted with weeds, and in some places, with sizeable trees.

I guess the party's over. Good thing I didn't spend the night there!

The road held the tracks of her horse and . . . she gasped as she looked it. There were no footprints, only a big wavy line, as if from an enormous serpent. The tracks lay on top of hers, coming from the phantom city and then returning to it.

I was invited to the party after all! And when I didn't show up, the host came looking! Good thing he didn't find me!

There was no sign of Singer and the Witch. She must have lost their track. Mounting the horse, she backtracked, studying the ground as she went.

Within an hour, she found the trail that ran along the base of the hills to the northwest. She must have missed it in the dark. She had no idea what would make a trail in such a place, but at the moment, there were only two sets of hoof prints on it. Near the crossroads was another stone with the centipede symbol.

Someone is showing them which road to take, or perhaps lur-ing them on.

Today, the Madlands were being nice. The sky was blue. There was a fresh, cool breeze blowing. The path twisted around in the foothills, without passing anything more sinister than a ruined farm-house or fallen watchtower.

Only the horse was being contrary. It kept starting at shadows. Twice, it left the path to make a detour around some menace Raee-sha couldn't see.

It's like invisible goblins are plaguing it.

She noticed she herself was feeling a bit light-headed. Now and then, she thought she saw something moving in the corner of her eye, but when she turned to look, it was gone.

Something in the water, maybe. No wonder the horse is acting so strange.

She was almost ready to stop for lunch when she saw the Ban-deluk cavalry patrol.

Is this another lost squad, like Olgun's? What are they doing here? Be brave! Ride right up to them!

"Mertkan, sergeant, Khuram Bey's Palace Guard," said the leader. He was a tall, pale-looking man.

"Rajik, private, Sheikh Mahmud's Home Guard," she answered automatically, before thinking:

Did he say Khuram Bey? He died long ago! Is this a joke?

"We seem to have gotten a bit lost," said Mertkan, in a hoarse voice. "I've never even heard of Sheikh Mahmud."

"That is just as well," said Raeesha frivolously. "You probably wouldn't like him anyway."

"I think I might like him better than Khuram Bey. We were looking for the road to Hillineh, but we must have taken a wrong turn." He loosened a scarf to scratch a rash on his neck.

Hillineh? This had better be a joke! Play along with it.

"I just came from the direction of Kafra." She pointed to the south. "Hillineh would be over there," she added, pointing to the east.

But hundreds of miles away!

"Wow, if we're near Kafra, we're really turned around," said another soldier. He also had a hoarse voice and a rash on his neck.

"This isn't any place I've seen before," said a third. Added a fourth: "Everything looks ruined. We haven't seen a soul all day." Both of these men had hoarse voices and red rashes on their necks. All of them were pale as corpses.

Raeesha felt a sudden chill.

Those aren't rashes, those are rope burns! They look like they were hanged!

Swiftly, she drew her sword and used the well-practiced stroke to cut Metkan's throat . . . or, that is what she tried to do. The sword met no resistance, it just passed through Mertkan without leaving any mark.

Mertkan seemed to be only mildly annoyed. "Hey, what did you do that for?" he said.

Men are brave, but not this brave!

"HYAA!" She struck the horse's flank with the flat of her blade, causing it to break into a gallop. From behind, she could hear a babble of hoarse voices:

"Hey!"

"Where are you going?"

"Come back!"

She'd travelled over a hundred yards before she dared to look back. No one was there. Studying the path, she saw only two sets of tracks, already familiar to her. There was no indication anyone else had passed.

Of course they didn't! They left their bones in Hillineh!

Were these phantoms sent by the Witch to scare her off? Obviously not: The Witch didn't know about the soldiers of Khuram Bey. She must have created them herself somehow, conjuring them up from her own mind.

This really is the Madlands! I must be going crazy!

The fear of insanity was

worse than demons, worse than anything. She felt a churning in her stomach, as if it wanted to turn inside-out.

Maybe I'll see Umar next, or Samia the courtesan! If I find Singer, will I recognize him? What if I shoot the Witch and then see it was really Singer?

She looked around, but everything was as before: The sky was blue, the air was fresh, there was nothing alarming in sight. She could either take the road forward or go back. There was no point in staying here. But going back would mean abandoning Singer, giving him up forever. It was better to go mad. Then, she probably wouldn't even know what she'd lost. She spurred her horse into a trot.

About an hour later, she saw another demon standing by the path. This one was scaly, like the foreigners' pets, but shorter and hunched over. Instead of a silver mask, it had a big, ugly snout full of sharp teeth. It was reaching for something invisible with its claws.

She studied it a minute, without noticing the slightest motion. Then, she drew her bow and tried the arrow test.

Clink.

This had to be another demon statue, one of the Witch's creations.

I hope she runs out of demons before I run out of arrows!

A little further, there were bodies lying on the ground.

Singer!

Her heart seemed to stop a moment, but then she could see she was looking at a dead horse, a white one. Nearby were two more of the scaly demons, lying in their own purple blood. One had its neck hacked through, the other still had a dagger hilt sticking out of an eye socket. There was no sign of Singer or the Witch.

Maybe I worry too much about Singer. It looks like he can take care of himself.

She was about to go on, when she noticed a small, shiny object on the ground. Dismounting, she picked it up: a metal ring, like those used to make armor. It was broken and smeared with fresh, red blood.

"HYAA!" Almost before she knew it, she was galloping down the road. Here and there, she noticed drops of blood, not yet dry.

She'd gone hardly a mile, when she saw Singer lying by the road. His armor was on the ground next to him. He had bloody bandages on his chest. The Witch was kneeling beside him. Drawing her sword, Raeesha rushed to them.

"I can't stop the bleeding," the Witch said listlessly. "We can go no further. I have failed."

"What have you done!"

The Witch looked at her earnestly. "Please don't step on the pelican," she said.

It was then the giant centipedes came swarming over the hill.

21: Rajik

What in the name of all devils is going on!

They were trying to confiscate his *pamuk*. He'd tried to explain to the strange officer that the army sacks marked "horse fodder" in the shed behind Jasmine House were not horse fodder, nor did they belong to the army, but the man spoke no Bandeluki and no Hallandish either. Apparently, he thought Rajik was just an officious stable boy, and was calling a couple muscular-looking soldiers to remove him, when Rajik, in desperation, slashed a sack, brought out a double handful of *pamuk*, and shoved the fluffy material in the man's face.

The officer stared at it in astonishment, as if he'd never seen such a thing before, then offered a handful to his horse, which sniffed once and turned its head away. He gave Rajik what sounded like a few sharp words of reproach, in his incomprehensible language, before retreating, with exaggerated martial posture, in a display of dignity.

I just started learning the foreigners' stupid language, and now they have a different one!

He'd awakened to find the village swarming with strange soldiers, and he'd caught a glimpse of Prince Clenas, with his face bruised and apparently in a foul mood, entering at the gate. Then the silver-black flag of the foreigners was lowered and replaced with a gold-green one he hadn't seen before. The Chatmak guards were shooed away and replaced with new ones, who spoke no language he could understand and were not interested in anything he had to say. He'd gone to the shed to check on his property and found some soldiers hauling it away.

He sat for a minute on a sack of *pamuk* and thought about it. The *Lady* was not here to explain anything. Clenas was here, but he was shut up in Jasmine House, surrounded by soldiers, and apparently not interested in *pamuk* at the moment. Also, they didn't speak the same language. There remained only one possible source of information.

A date palm stood nearby, and next to it, one of the ladders used in the harvest. Rajik placed it against the back wall of Jasmine House, climbed up and peered inside. He was looking into the garden, which was empty. So far, so good. He climbed on top of the wall and found he was in danger of falling into the fish pond. He edged along the top of the wall until he could jump into a more comfortable pile of mulch. Then, it was only a short distance to Pennesey's office.

Pennesey was madly scratching away with a goose quill and a pen knife, removing some items from a ledger and adding others. He seemed to be surprised and annoyed to see Rajik.

"These damned Akaddians are taking inventory," he said. "I managed to buy a couple hours to update the books, but if anything is missing, there will be hell to pay. And if they find the silver, I'm done for."

"There's a mulch pile out back," said Rajik. "Who would take an inventory of mulch? Hide it there.

"A good thought. What is it you wanted?"

"Just to help an old friend," said Rajik, producing his knife. "Did you know you had a leaky roof? Give me five minutes and a pitcher of water, I'll put a leak wherever you want one. You can't be held responsible, if there happens to be water damage to the records."

"Rajik, you are amazing! How did you know I was worried about that spot in the corner, right there, next to the wall? It would be too bad if the requisitions log got wet. That cheap ink they give us is so damned runny."

Five minutes later, there was water dripping from the roof, possibly from last night's rain, and Pennesey was in a more sanguine mood. "So, what is it you *really* wanted? Not to fix the leak, I hope?"

"I just want to know what's going on."

"Oh, of course. That's quite a long story, but the short of it is, Erika has been arrested for treason and witchcraft."

Rajik's eyes got very round.

"Yes, I know, it's ridiculous. But nonetheless, Prince Krion is apparently under a spell of some kind, and Gen. Basilius has taken command. Clenas has declared him a mutineer and withdrawn his troops to Jasmine House. Also, he's occupied the depot at Massera Bay and cut off the army from supply."

"This is bad, very bad. What happens now to the war with the

Emperor?"

"I don't know. Maybe we just go home. It depends on what Gen. Singer does, but he's off in Barbosa, and it will take days to get him a message. Meanwhile, Capt. Pohler has suspended militia training, because he wants to keep them out of this, but the Illustrious Knights have already declared for Clenas. So, to make it short, things are confused, or in other words, a royal mess."

But I have all my money invested in pamuk . . . *who will buy it now? And if the foreigners leave, I'll have to leave with them, if they let me on one of their ships . . . and then I'll have to scratch out a living in a foreign country, where I don't even speak the language!*

Rajik thought about it for a minute. "So, they're all fighting over a woman?"

"That's one way of looking at it. Basilius threw her in the clink, but Clenas wants her back, and Singer, poor sod, still thinks she's his blushing bride."

"I guess that's all I need to know, then. Ask Prince Clenas if he'd pay a hundred thalers for the *Lady*."

Pennesey looked confused. "I'm sure he would, but why do I have to ask him?"

"Just ask him. Trust me, money is always important."

Near Jasmine House, there was a barracks, which was home to the military trainers, Ebrahim, Husam and the others, who had been recruited by the foreigners. Rajik found them sitting around a table loaded with copper coins, engaged in a heated game of cards. He kicked over the table.

"Hey! I was winning!" said Tariq, who had deserted even before the battle.

"The hell you were!" said Ebrahim.

"You shouldn't play with Tariq anyway. He cheats," said Rajik.

"Not as well as I do!"

"Friends, forget this silly game for copper coins. I have a better game, for gold and glory, and for a beautiful woman!"

"How much does it pay?" said Ebrahim.

"Is there any cheating?" added Tariq.

"Enough of both for even the greediest," said Rajik.

One evening a few days later, a crew of wagoners dressed as

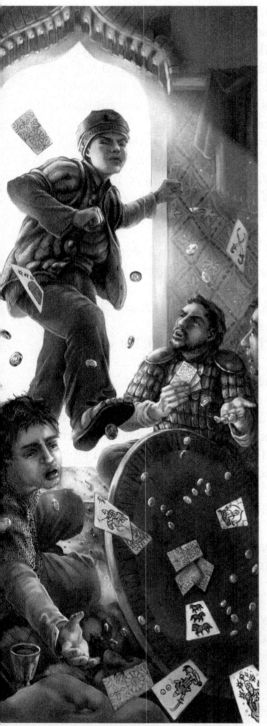

Chatmaks led some supply wagons laden with horse fodder up to Jade Towers, the confiscated Bandeluk mansion which served as headquarters of the Twelve Hundred Heroes. One of them produced a crumpled and dirty manifest showing they had a delivery of horse fodder. The guards at the gate attempted, using loud Akaddian, spoken with many gestures, to tell them the shipment was to be unloaded at a pasture down the road, not at the headquarters itself.

Nodding as if they understood, the wagoners began unloading heavy bags of horse fodder in front of the gate. Frantic, the guards called the officer of the watch, who shouted at the wagoners in his weak Bandeluki. The uncomprehending response of the wagoners suggested they spoke even less Bandeluki than the officer. While the officer yelled and gesticulated, and the wagoners milled around in confusion, picking up bags of fodder and dropping them again, the gate was blocked. A small crowd gathered, none of whom noticed the four wagoners who disappeared around a corner.

Rajik was in the lead, followed by Tariq and Husam. All were armed with daggers. Ebrahim, in the rear, was carrying a bundle of extra equipment.

"How do we even know she's here?" said Tariq.

"Because Hikmet said so, and the servant we bribed said so, and so shut up before they hear us," said Rajik.

Curse all Bandeluks, we can't stop talking until they cut our throats, really, we can't!

According to the information they had, there was a courtyard in the back of the compound and the steps that led down to the cellar where the prisoners were kept. However, all of that was on the other side of a blank ten-foot wall, and there were no convenient date palms in sight.

Rounding another corner revealed only the back wall, which was just as high as the rest. There was no obvious way of climbing up. Rajik picked a spot near the middle of the wall and, whispering, told Tariq and Husam to raise him on their shoulders, and then told Ebrahim to pass him the bow.

The layout here, he saw, was different from Jasmine House and the other country estates he was used to: Instead of being divided into sections, each with its own little courtyard, Jade Towers had one big courtyard surrounding the central building. This would make it harder to break into, he reflected.

In the rear were the well, some water jars and tubs for washing clothing. There was also a rack of fresh washing, set out to dry. No one was in sight. Rajik was about to give the all-clear, when he heard boots approaching from around the corner of the building. He crouched as low as he could, waiting to see who was coming.

It was a lone sentry, looking extremely bored, with a halberd resting on his shoulder. Rajik could see his bow had no chance to penetrate the man's heavy armor.

I'll get only one chance at this, so I better make it good!

As the man, suspecting nothing, walked by Rajik's position, he heard a voice above him saying, "Hey!" Startled, he looked up just in time to see a bow loosed. The arrow caught him in his gaping mouth and passed through, the arrowhead emerging behind his neck. He turned, as if to run away, and then collapsed, with his back to the wall, the halberd falling across his knees. His fingers twitched once or twice, and then he lay still.

Rajik passed the bow back to Ebrahim and asked for the rope. He was looking for a good place to let himself down, when he heard another sentry coming.

Two of them! Don't they trust anyone here?

There was nothing to do but press himself against the top of the wall, the coil of rope in his hand, as the second soldier came closer. The armored man paused, apparently confused by the sight of his comrade sitting in an uncomfortable position by the wall, and called to him. Not getting any response, he came closer and bent over the still figure. Rajik could hear a sharp intake of breath, as he noticed the arrow sticking out of his neck.

That was the last breath of air he ever tasted, because a noose fell over his neck and was promptly pulled tight, as Rajik jumped off the other side of the wall.

"Pull! Pull!" His friends obeyed, until the sound of heels pounding against the wall stopped, and still a minute longer, just to be sure. Rajik climbed back on the wall and waited, bow in hand, but no third sentry appeared, so they crossed into the courtyard.

The door was where the bribed washerwoman told him, behind some steps near the back north corner of the building. Moving softly, Rajik descended the steps and tried the latch. It was unlocked.

If the door is unlocked, there must be guards inside!

Charging in with daggers would be a bad idea: Even if they killed the guards, there would be too much noise. Sneaking in was too risky: What if someone was watching the door? Rajik went back and started filling one of the jars with water from the well.

"What are you doing?" said Husam.

"Shut up and keep away from the door," said Rajik.

A minute later, a sleepy guard, who was seated facing the door, looked up to see a Chatmak boy enter, carrying a water jar. He grunted and gestured toward the back of the cellar, where a number of cages had been constructed. Rajik could see the soldier's helmet on a table in front of him.

Smiling and nodding compliantly, he walked past the soldier, then turned and bashed him on the head with the jar. The soldier fell to the ground, amid a shower of water. Rajik watched curiously as the body went into convulsions.

Is that what I did when they broke my head? I hope you survive this, friend, because I've already killed enough people for one night.

He opened the door for the others, then took a key ring from the unconscious guard and went to look at the cages. The first prisoner he noticed was a pretty, but bedraggled-looking blonde woman in a dirty, blue satin dress.

"Rajik! However did you . . ."

"Shut up, you can thank me later!" he answered, trying the keys on the cage door until it opened. He was turning to leave when she grabbed him by the shoulder.

"There's someone else you should save, more important than I am." She pointed to a cage on the other side of the cellar. Seated on the floor was a miserable-looking prisoner, in a filthy, ragged uniform, unshaven and manacled. He was simply rocking back and forth, paying no attention to the drama in the cellar.

"It's Prince Krion," the *Lady* said. "He's completely mad. They chained him up because he got so angry when they cut off his finger, but it didn't help, because the spell was on him, not the ring . . ."

"Shut up," said Rajik, testing his keys to see which one would release the commander-in-chief of the allied forces in Chatmakstan.

Women are even worse than Bandeluks!

The open cage door didn't seem to interest the Prince at all. He continued rocking back and forth on the floor. "What's wrong with him?" asked Rajik.

"I'm not sure," said the *Lady*. "He was obsessed with my sister Rosalind, but he keeps getting worse, and now you'd hardly know . . ."

"Shut up." Rajik had noticed a flicker of attention from the madman: He'd briefly turned his head at the word "Rosalind."

"Tell him we're taking him to Rosalind."

The *Lady* said something in the bizarre language of the Akaddians that Rajik couldn't understand, but the Prince did. At the word "Rosalind," he stood up and turned to look at them.

Rajik removed the manacles. Pointing at the door, he said simply, "Rosalind!"

Trembling and swaying, the Prince made his unsteady way toward the door. The *Lady* scurried to assist him.

Rajik was again turning to go, when a voice from another cage stopped him in his tracks: "Hello, son."

The man in this cage was twisted and stooped, as if his joints pained him. His fingers were mangled, and there were bloody, oozing sores where the fingernails had been. He was so beaten about the face, it would have been difficult to recognize him, but Rajik knew him at once.

"You're mistaken," he said. "I have never seen you before."

"But you've seen me?" said a voice from another cage.

Although he was thin and pale, and someone had cut off his long, black beard, Rajik saw it was Hussni, his father's watch captain.

"That would depend," said Rajik.

"Do you play cards?" said Ebrahim.

"Sometimes."

"Do you ever cheat?" said Tariq.

Hussni shifted uncomfortably. "Only when I really have to," he admitted.

"Then you can join the party," said Rajik.

As they left the cellar, Rajik heard a sound he'd never imagined and would never forget: his father sobbing.

22: Lamya

"You will be dead in a week," said the old man with the body of a centipede.

Lamya smiled and nodded politely. This was Lord Shayan? He (or it?) claimed to be Lord Shayan, and it didn't seem wise to contradict him. Anyway, he was wearing the monitor, a blue gem set on a silver necklace.

No wonder that thing isn't working right!

"The Madlands are contaminated with many toxic substances," Shayan continued pedantically. "But here, there is one in particular, which will inevitably destroy your liver."

"Hopefully we won't be staying that long," said Lamya. "But these toxic substances, do they cause hallucinations?"

We certainly saw some strange things on the way here!

Shayan frowned. "They can and often do, though in the Madlands, it's sometimes hard to tell. But not here. The only real danger is to your liver. I call this place New Iram. Beautiful, is it not?"

Lamya looked around at the bluish valley and at the stream, full of multi-legged larvae, which flowed between rows of doorless, pear-shaped structures, where the centipedes were crawling around and interacting with each other, under a blue sun.

So this is real, and the birds of my childhood, who returned to visit me, were illusions? Give me back my birds!

"It's lovely. But I seem to remember another woman with me."

Or was she just an illusion?

"Oh, the excitable young female specimen with the unfortunate sword. I was forced to sedate her, she had become quite agitated."

"Being kidnapped by giant centipedes can do that."

"I apologize for the abruptness of your arrival. I had noticed the life readings from the wrist monitor becoming faint, and, as you weren't far away, I sent some of the anamorphs to fetch you. You seem to be taking it quite well."

"Abandoning all hope for the future tends to put these things in perspective."

"Well, there's no need for that now, I should think. Would you care for some tea?"

One of the smaller giant centipedes appeared, grasping a tea tray with its frontal claws. Besides the teapot and two cups, there was a plate of pastries. Out of curiosity, Lamya tasted one. It was sweet and flaky, with a slightly bitter after-taste.

Maybe I can just pretend to nibble without eating much.

"The tea is one of my favorite blends. The pastry is my wife's creation," said Shayan. "She's the chair of our agricultural committee."

"What, you actually married one of these . . . creatures?"

Shayan made a sound that could have been chuckling, or perhaps he was only clearing his throat. "Nothing so bizarre as that. Dareia and I were wed before the Populator incident, and we were both caught in the disaster. I couldn't have survived without her."

"I had no idea such a person existed!"

"That's not surprising. She lost her monitor in the tragedy, but I managed to retain mine. It's rather attractive, don't you think? It reminds me of my former existence. I'll introduce you to Dareia when she's finished seeing to your man."

"How is he doing?"

"Out of danger, Dareia tells me. She's the head of our medical department. He is undergoing a restorative infusion. Aside from the loss of blood, he appears to have suffered no great damage."

Lamya cautiously sipped her tea. Whatever they made it from, it wasn't tea.

Better not drink any more of this!

"You don't care for the tea?"

"I think it may be an acquired taste."

She was already starting to experience a pleasant, tranquil feeling from the small sip she'd taken. Shayan, she noticed, had already drained his cup.

"I'm rather proud of all the work we've done here. Perhaps you'd care to see our museum? We constructed it for the benefit of visitors, but we get very few."

"I would be delighted."

The museum was a circular stone building with a dome and central skylight. Lamya recognized the style from a book she'd seen on Kano architecture. In the center was a statue, she presumed, of

Lord Shayan in his younger days. He was in the pose of casting a spell. Around him were displays of ancient sorcerous equipment. The walls were decorated with murals.

"You like it? Dareia is quite an artist. I think the statue flatters me a bit, but that is how she wanted it. Dareia really is my biggest admirer.

"On the walls, you'll see a record of our history. The first scene shows our stealthy entrance into enemy territory. Then comes the summoning of Populator. The third scene depicts the disaster, as the unfortunate secondary effect of the weapon engulfs us. In the fourth scene, Dareia and myself are thrown into a reality pocket, one of many dimensional anomalies which appeared at that time. This is our beautiful New Iram, but it was initially a bleak and unwelcoming place. Also, it was highly unstable, threatening constantly to implode and hurl us into a distant dimension.

"The fifth scene shows us drawing remotely on the energy of Extinctor, which was unaffected by the disaster, in order to stabilize the pocket, establishing the boundaries of our little world. In the sixth, we're surrounded by anamorphs, which you refer to as giant centipedes. At first, they were hostile, but they became

quite docile as we learned their little secrets. Dareia calls them her children.

"In the seventh, we're sick and despairing, having discovered the pervasive toxin in this environment was slowly killing us. In the eighth, we're engaged in frantic experimentation, trying to save ourselves. At first, we thought we could modify the liver to filter out the toxin, but that would have necessitated changes to the renal system and the circulatory system as well, too many modifications to consider in the limited time left to us. In the ninth, you see the spell of transference, which created the very practical and useful bodies we enjoy today."

Lamya studied the ninth panel, which appeared to show a man's body merging with that of a giant centipede.

Horrible! But fascinating, too.

"I've never seen anything like this," she said.

"Oh, transference is a rather esoteric branch of thaumaturgy. I don't suppose it's much practiced these days. I'll have to arrange a demonstration sometime. In the tenth scene, we're repelling an incursion of Indos, who were seeking to escape the chaos outside our New Iram. Then follows the construction of wards and perimeter defenses to prevent similar incursions . . ."

Lord Shayan's lecture went on for nearly an hour. He described numerous improvements to his home, works of sorcery, engineering and agriculture in which, Lamya noticed, Dareia seemed to be doing most of the actual labor. No cook was as proud of her casseroles as Shayan was of the incubator for centipede eggs, though it was Dareia who had polished the solar reflectors which made the thing work.

No wonder all those expeditions failed. These two have walled themselves off in their own little world, where they can play at being gods. So why are they so eager to receive visitors now?

It was a disquieting thought. To her surprise, Lord Shayan raised the subject: "As you may know, I was part of the original team that summoned Extinctor, and I have preserved a link to him, which I used to stabilize our New Iram. Lately, though, I've been much concerned this link has developed some unfortunate fluctuations, which could endanger our work here. I was hoping you could cast some light on this."

No reason not to tell the truth. It's what I came here to do.

"The stasis spell is very old and becoming unstable. The base at Barbosa is not as you remember it. We are now very few, and cannot possibly renew this powerful spell. Therefore, I propose using the key to dismiss Extinctor before he's released and causes more destruction."

This didn't seem to surprise Lord Shayan. "Yes, I was afraid it was something of the kind. Still, I can't dismiss Extinctor without discarding all of the progress we've made here, a thousand years of hard work! I'll need a little time to consider this. Oh, look, Dareia is here."

The creature entering the museum looked a lot like Lord Shayan, but in this case, the centipede body supported the head of an old woman with stringy, gray hair. "I hope my husband hasn't been boring you too much?" she asked timidly.

"Not at all. I'm amazed by your accomplishments here. May I ask how Gen. Singer is doing?"

"Oh, is that his name? He's responding well to treatment. He should be up and around tomorrow. Are you ready for a bit of dinner?"

"I would be, except that Lord Shayan just explained everything here is permeated with a deadly toxin."

"That it is, but the food is no more dangerous than the air or the water."

"In that case, I might as well try it."

"I hope you won't be uncomfortable dining in the museum. It's the only building intended for visitors, and I fear you'd find our own quarters rather disagreeable. Or would you prefer to eat outdoors?"

Out there under the blue sun, amid the swarms of giant centipedes and the wiggling larvae.

"Here will be fine."

"Excellent, I'll call the children."

A few minutes later, some of the giant centipedes had set up a table and decked it with steaming plates of food and cups of wine. Lamya regarded the offerings with misgiving, complicated by hunger.

A portion of the food looked like rice, but was gooey and tasted more like eggs. There were also small strips of meat that looked and tasted like fried clams, but much more chewy, and something like shredded turnip greens, only reddish in color.

Don't think about it, just eat it!

The wine was strong as brandy and had an herbal flavor. After a couple sips, she felt dizzy and her right eyelid suddenly developed a twitch.

This is strong stuff!

She looked to see how her hosts were taking it. Both drank the wine with gusto.

A few glasses of this wine would probably kill me! Either they're addicted, or those monster-bodies give them some sort of protection.

Neither Lord Shayan nor Dareia seemed to find anything peculiar about the meal. Both were picking at it enthusiastically with their frontal claws. They had, however, forgotten to supply their guest with silverware.

I guess that's what fingers are for!

"You're an excellent cook," she told Dareia after the meal, licking her fingers clean.

"Am I?" said the old woman modestly. "My husband often says so, but I fear he may be biased."

"Nonsense," said Lord Shayan. "You're clearly and objectively the best cook in New Iram! Why don't you have the anamorphs remove the table, so we can do that demonstration I was talking about."

"Yes dear," said Dareia, and went to fetch her "children."

As the centipedes were removing the remains of dinner, Lord Shayan began explaining his next project: "I earlier promised you a demonstration of the transference process. This is a very good thing to know. We've found it extremely useful. And as it happens, I have an excellent subject for the spell."

"What would that be?"

Ignoring her question, Lord Shayan continued with his lecture: "The first step is a fumigation to remove unfortunate influences which could disturb the process or contaminate the specimen."

Taking a censer from the display of sorcerous implements, he set it alight and began swinging it around the room. The smoke made Lamya cough and her eyes run.

Am I one of these "unfortunate influences?" He seems intent on driving me out!

Satisfied with the thick cloud of irritating smoke, Lord Shayan shut the censer. "Once the area has been prepared, we can safely bring in the subject. Ah, here it comes now."

At this point, Dareia entered, pushing a gurney which held the unconscious body of Gen. Singer.

Lamya stood up in surprise. "WHAT!"

"Stand where you are!" Lord Shayan's command was imperative. Lamya felt her body frozen in place. She could move neither her fingers nor toes, nor any part of her body. Lord Shayan came and peered at her, poking her here and there with his claws.

"Now, that went very well," he said. "As a fellow professional, I should tell you that you're under a modified form of the stasis spell. I've articulated it so as to leave your mental facilities intact, in order to witness the demonstration. Ingenious, is it not?"

This creature is insane!

"I have observed this specimen for some time." Lord Shayan pointed to Gen. Singer, who was being wheeled into the center of the museum, directly under the statue.

"I believe he's ideal for my purposes. It's hardly surprising he also attracted your attention, but that he brought two companions with him, I can only describe as a fortuitous event.

"It's high time I took charge of the base at Barbosa, which has plainly suffered centuries of neglect. I'll be bringing Dareia with me. There's already a suitable specimen for her in the clinic."

Dareia, behind him, was apparently paying no attention to this speech. She was setting up sorcerous equipment around Singer's recumbent form. Lamya noticed she'd also focused an instrument of some kind on the stone statue. She couldn't tell exactly what the human-headed creature was doing. Nothing the Old Woman taught her had prepared her for this.

They're both completely delusional!

Lord Shayan continued with his exposition: "I'm entrusting you with our operation here. You'll find detailed written instructions in my quarters. I call particular attention to the propagation of the perimeter flux field, which must be adjusted at least once weekly, or the consequences will be most unfortunate.

"You needn't worry about the toxin. I've already selected a healthy young anamorph to provide you with a suitable body. I'll perform the transference before I go."

He's going to make me into a monster like himself!

Thinking quickly, she tried to remember the sorcerous lore the Old Woman had drilled into her: conjurations, incantations, charms, enchantments, curses and counter-spells. All of it required some preparation, and she couldn't even stir a finger. Whatever Shayan was doing, she wouldn't be able to prevent it.

Meanwhile, Lord Shayan had turned around to see Dareia had completed her preparations. The sorcerous equipment was faintly humming and filling the center of the room with a blue light.

"Ah, excellent, we're ready for the first transference, namely my own. I shall now loosen your tongue momentarily, in case you have any questions. Take care not to utter any words of sorcery, or I shall be forced to seal it again."

He touched her briefly on the head, and she found she now had control of her face.

"You're making a big mistake," she said.

Lord Shayan regarded her with mild amusement. "And what would that be?"

"You can't simply walk in and take over Barbosa. There is an army of five thousand barbarians. They will be quite angry if you fail to return their General."

Lord Shayan chuckled. "You seem to be missing the point of the joke. A simple glamour will convince them I *am* their General."

"But you don't speak the language! And you don't understand the military etiquette! Etiquette is very important! You won't get past the first sentry if you don't know the appropriate greeting!"

"I think you are exaggerating these difficulties. But in any case, I've heard enough. If you have nothing productive to say, you may remain silent."

He touched her again, and she felt her face freeze in what could only have been an expression of horror. As if in a nightmare, she saw him turn and scuttle on his centipede claws to the center of the room, lying down beside Singer.

"You may begin the process whenever you're ready," he said.

"Yes dear," said Dareia, pressing a polished silver knob. The humming from the sorcerous implements now became louder, the light much brighter. Lord Shayan's centipede body seemed to ebb and flow, rippling like a reflection in water. There was a faint *clunk*, as if a heavy object had fallen from a height, while a brilliant flash momentarily blinded Lamya.

When the dancing dots in her eyes no longer obscured her vision, Dareia was turning off the equipment. The humming and the blue glow faded away. On the ground, where Lord Shayan had lain, was the headless corpse of a centipede and a small block of stone, which was the head of the statue. The statue had a new head, a fleshy one, its eyes staring and its mouth open in an expression of surprise and panic.

"Ah! It is done!" said Dareia, clapping her frontal claws together. "I am free at last!"

She crawled up the side of the statue and gave its new head a tender kiss. Then, she touched it with one of her claws, saying, *"Be what you should be!"* and the fleshy head was turned to stone. She picked up the silver necklace with the blue stone from the floor and draped it over the neck of the statue, then scuttled back a short distance to admire her work.

"That is how I shall remember you, dear Shayan, as the brilliant and kindly young marvel I fell in love with so long ago! Forgive me, but another thousand years enslavement to the aberration you became would be more than I could bear. I had only this one fleeting chance, and I took it."

She turned to Lamya and spread her claws, as if appealing for sympathy. "You must not think he was always this way. Shayan was brave, enterprising and inventive, a master who put all others to shame. It was only over many centuries he lost his focus . . . Oh, I forgot, you can't speak."

She reached over to touch Lamya with one of her claws, saying, *"Be as you were!"* and suddenly Lamya could move again.
Free!

She rushed to Singer and checked his pulse. It was normal. His breathing was heavy. She peeled back an eyelid and saw how the pupil contracted in reaction to light.

"Don't worry about him," Dareia said. "He'll be able to walk around tomorrow, and so will the other one. The sooner you make your escape from this poisonous valley, the better. Don't get trapped here, as I was."

"But what about you?"

Dareia looked down sadly at her monstrous centipede body. "I'm too old to start over. There's no place for me anywhere but here. I will remain with the children and share their fate, for better or worse. Don't concern yourself with me.

"But wait, I have something for you."

From one of the displays, she drew an ancient, leather bound book, which bore an inscription in the ancient Kano language: "Field Manual for the Practice of Military Sorcery, 3rd Ed."

"Take this with you," she said. "I have no more use for it. It contains powerful spells which were known to very few even in the old days, and I've added some notes of my own."

"That is a great gift," said Lamya, "and I shall treasure it. But what I really need now is the key to the spells on Extinctor."

"Oh, oh, of course. What was that, it was so long ago . . ." Dareia pondered a minute before brightening. "I remember now, it was very simple, just three words: 'Not For Ourselves.' That is all you need to know."

23: Erika

It was plain from the smell that the Prince's diaper needed changing again.

I don't know how much longer I can handle this.

Erika was exhausted. Since Clenas was so short-handed, he'd asked her to "look after" his hopelessly bewitched brother, who was curled up in a fetal position and no longer responding even to the word "Rosalind". This meant feeding him, rolling him over to prevent bed sores, and also changing diapers.

Hasn't anyone noticed he's twice as big as I am?

Normally, she'd have called a brawny soldier to assist her, but everyone was out "skirmishing," which, as Clenas explained it, was a kind of game where each side probed the other's lines to assess their strength. ("It's rather like the foreplay before the main event.") Almost the only soldiers in Jasmine House at the moment were the wounded, and she was supposed to be helping them, when she wasn't looking after the Prince.

They'd laid two mattresses together on the floor and covered them with sheets, and provided him with blankets and pillows. However, they hadn't provided any diapers, which she had to make herself out of some sheets. And then, of course, they had to be changed.

I guess being a woman is enough to make me an expert on changing diapers!

Lifting him was out of the question. She laid a towel on the mattress and then tried to roll him over onto it. The doctor had showed her how to do it: You kneel down and push on the hips. However, the doctor was much stronger than she was, and he didn't have to put his hands on soiled diapers.

I need some gloves!

The Prince didn't resist her, but didn't help her, either. He was just a dead weight on the floor. No matter how hard she pushed, he wouldn't turn over.

I've got to straighten out his legs somehow.

Tugging as hard as she could, she managed to straighten one leg, but as soon as she reached for the other, the first one curled up again. Frustrated, she sat down to study the problem.

This Prince is a royal pain! What would Rosalind say?

Maybe she could get one of the wounded to help her. But which one? Not the one who had been shot in the chest and kept coughing blood. The doctor didn't expect him to live. Not the one who had taken a lance wound in the thigh. He couldn't even walk. Not the one who had lost his right hand. He just lay there, looking at the ceiling, so pale and grim she was afraid to bring him his tea.

Besides that, there were only the guards, who were forbidden to leave their posts, and the kitchen help, who were not supposed to leave the kitchen. Capt. Pohler had moved the Hallanders to a new headquarters down the road. And she couldn't get the Bandeluks to help her, because Clenas had put them on the payroll and sent them scouting.

What would a princess do? A princess wouldn't be asked to do this kind of work. No, it was worse than that, a princess would graciously *volunteer* herself wherever she was needed. A princess does what a princess has to do.

Of course, everyone does what they have to do. . .

She went into the back room where the wounded were lying. The man without a hand had been languishing there for days, saying nothing, although there was nothing physically wrong with him, except for the hand. He was one of the Illustrious Knights of Tremmark, which meant he spoke an archaic dialect of Hallandish. The Tremmarkers disdained the Hallanders and others who spoke what they considered a mean and debased language.

She walked up to where he was lying, staring indifferently at the ceiling, and cleared her throat before saying, "Prithee, good sir."

He looked at her with interest. "Yes, m'lady?"

Oh good, he talks!

"Good Prince Krion lieth in yon chamber, sore afflicted, and I have not the strength to succor him."

"What ails the good Prince?"

"Alas, a foul ensorcellment hath robbed him of his wits, so that he hath not the power to move nor cleanse himself, and yet his doughty frame yieldeth not to the might of a woman."

Grimacing slightly, he got out of bed. "Fear not, gentle maid. Sir Gladwood is no sluggard when duty calls."

This guy is a real knight! Lucky me!

Ten minutes later, the diaper was changed, and Sir Gladwood

was plaguing her with questions about the military situation, questions for which she had no answers. "Alack, I am not apprized of Gen. Singer's whereabouts. We have had no word for weeks!"

"No tidings are ill tidings, then. I misdoubt that Prince Clenas can muster the strength to humble Basilius and his toadies."

Are those hooves I hear?

"Hearken, Prince Clenas doth return, and with him a goodly host."

Rushing to the front gate, she almost bumped into Gen. Singer, who, in full panoply, was just riding in. She gaped in astonishment.

"Gramercy, thou art here! I well nigh held myself forsaken! Is aught amiss with thee?"

Singer looked at her strangely. "I'm well, and happy to see you, but why are you jabbering like that?"

Great, now he thinks I'm an idiot!

"Excuse me, I was just talking to a knight of Tremmark."

"I see," said Singer, as if he really didn't see at all. As he dismounted, a dark-haired woman in a black leather riding outfit rode in behind him.

I've waited so long for this, and now he has a woman with him, and I'm standing here in a dirty, smelly smock and my hair in a bun! And Clenas could return at any moment! Should I rush joyfully into his arms or what?

Singer decided the question for her by taking her hand and kissing it with a stiff courtesy that held no trace of affection. Switching to Bandeluki, he said, "Erika, may I introduce Lamya, a sorceress who has offered to assist us with Prince Krion."

"She's a Witch!" protested a young Bandeluk, who, to Erika's surprise, rode in after the Witch, carrying a banner.

"I've never been too clear on the difference," said Singer. "In any case, people who consort with demons can't afford to be picky. We should count ourselves fortunate she's offered us her services, and, as it happens, I already owe her a debt of gratitude."

"It's I who owe you!" said, Lamya, blushing.

Erika noticed the Bandeluk threw her a jealous look.

This is so confusing! Have I a rival, and if so, which one? What has Singer been up to?

"If you can help Prince Krion, we will all be much in your debt," said Singer, and turning to Erika, "Where's the Prince? And

Prince Clenas? What of this civil war?"

Riding in behind the Bandeluk, there was a tall man, whose blond beard partially covered a shining breastplate bearing a golden sun.

"I better tell the kitchen to put on some tea," said Erika.

Soon, they were seated in the garden, sipping tea and exchanging news. Erika was only mildly surprised to learn the Bandeluk who was apparently now the army Standard-bearer was actually a woman named Raeesha.

When so much else is happening, I think I'll have to let that pass without comment.

She was pleased to see how angry Singer became when she told him how she'd been locked in a cage.

He may not love me, but he's deeply offended by the disrespect to himself and to his commander. Singer will do what he has to do.

The conversation was mainly in Bandeluki, but they had to pause occasionally and translate for Baron Hardy, the blond cavalry commander. The rest of Singer's army was strung out on the road, and most wouldn't arrive for a couple days, she learned.

After they'd been talking for over an hour, Prince Clenas came in with two officers: Lt. Bardhof and the Tremmark commander, who bore the name Col. Sir Rendel, Thane of House Syndor. They had to repeat all their news, this time in Akaddian. Col. Sir Rendel contributed some interjections in archaic Hallandish, while the others tried to conceal their annoyance.

"If I understand you correctly," Clenas said finally, "you saved us all from a menace we didn't even know existed."

"He says we saved the world from something we didn't even know existed," Singer translated for Lamya.

"What does he mean, we didn't know it existed? Of course, we knew it existed! You saw it!"

"I should have said, *they* didn't know."

"Of course not, why is he telling us this?"

"What is she saying?" said Clenas.

"Nothing of importance. Perhaps I may have a word with Col. Sir Rendel?"

"As it may please thee," said Rendel in Hallandish.

"It pleases me to speak Akaddian," said Singer in that language.

"I have had no reports from you in nearly a month. What have you been up to all this time?"

"I might well ask you the same question."

"I have just summarized my activities for the last few weeks. More than that need not concern you. I am your superior officer, and I require a report."

"You may be sure you will get one when anything of note transpires."

Singer was getting red.

Looks like these two are about to butt heads!

"Nothing about the pacification of a restive province, nor your intervention without orders in a civil war strikes you as worth mentioning?"

Rendel seemed to be looking down his longish nose at Singer, who he plainly regarded as an upstart commoner. "I have done nothing more or less than what my honor required of me."

"And you want me to guess what that means? In the future, you will appoint a liaison who will report to me regularly."

"I cannot spare even one knight for such inconsequential duties. As you may be aware, we are in daily contact with the enemy and can at any time expect a decisive battle."

Angered by this insubordination, Singer stood up, and Rendel did as well. Clenas got up and moved between them, as if he were afraid they'd attack each other.

Quick, do something!

"GENTLEMEN!"

Everyone turned to look at her.

"I believe I have the solution to your problem. There is a knight of Tremmark here, Sir Gladwood, who lost a hand in battle, but is otherwise recovered. I believe he can serve as your liaison."

There was a brief moment of silence, as they thought about it.

"I'd quite forgotten him," said Rendel. "A valiant knight, but no longer able to hold a lance or sword."

"I'll take him," said Singer.

"Then I suggest we adjourn," said Erika. "Prince Krion is in need of our attention."

Seven people had crammed themselves into the small room where Lamya was examining Prince Krion, and more were crowd-

ing in to watch from the hallway, until Bardhof shut the door. The Witch peered at Krion through a green gem, which she pressed against various parts of his body, muttering to herself concernedly as she did so.

At last, she stood up and announced: "This appears to be a simple philter, but with some unusual attributes. For one thing, it's a keyed spell, which means I can't do much with it until I learn the key. For another, there are no limiting conditions on the spell, no temporal or intensity or spatial restrictions, meaning the enchantment will progress until the subject is dead."

"So it's a murder spell?" asked Singer.

"More like a botched attempt at a love spell. An experienced sorcerer wouldn't use a philter to kill someone. There are better ways."

Erika looked at her own ring with some alarm.

Where did Aunt Gwyn get this?

"Where did you get the ring?" Lamya asked her.

"I had it from my sister Rosalind, who received it as a gift from my Aunt Gwyneth, who was married to a sorcerer of Westenhausen."

Lamya frowned. "So this sorcerer in Westenhausen has the key?"

"I rather doubt it. They parted on bad terms. To put it plainly, she vanished one day in a cloud of smoke and was never seen again."

"It sounds like she was projected to another plane."

"You mean, like a demon?"

"Not exactly. Demons are summoned from distant planes, and when dismissed, return to them. But your Aunt Gwyneth was neither summoned nor dismissed, she was projected, and we need to find out where."

"You mean, she might still be alive?"

"That would depend on your uncle's intention. A list of every plane known to sorcery would fill many volumes, but the list of those which can support human life is rather short. If she was sent to the plane of the fire demons, she didn't last more than a minute, but if she was sent to some more familiar plane, she may well be alive."

"So how can we find her?"

"We need first to identify her. Her name is a good start. It would also help if you have anything that belonged to her."

"I had this ring from her. It looks the same as the ring she gave to Rosalind."

"Put it on the table, I don't want to touch it. Are you consanguineous?"

Am I what?

"Um, my Bandeluki is pretty good, but not that good."

"I meant, how are you related to your Aunt Gwyneth?"

"She's my father's sister."

"Then I'll need a few drops of your blood."

"You shall have them."

"I don't have my usual equipment here, so I'll have to improvise. I need an object which is consecrated in some way. That means, after it was made, it was set aside and not subjected to daily use. It needn't be expensive, but you shouldn't expect to see it again."

"I think we have something like that," said Singer.

"I'll also need an empty room."

While Singer went to find a consecrated object, Erika summarized the conversation for the Akaddian speakers, then showed Capt. Pohler's old room to Lamya, who said it would do, once the furniture had been removed. She was already drawing chalk circles on the floor when Singer returned with a wooden case.

"How is this?" he said, opening the case. Inside was a gilded statue of Theros.

"That's one of your gods? How do you think he'd feel about being used for sorcery?"

"He's the god of war, patron of soldiers. His virtues are courage, loyalty and perseverance in adversity. We are being courageous, loyal and perseverant. Theros would approve of us and our actions."

"Then there is no conflict. We may proceed."

She took the statue reverently between her hands and placed it in her circle. Holding the ring on the end of a wand, without touching it, she placed it next to the statue.

"Now the blood. We need only a little. Let it drip on the statue."

Ouch!

Pricking her thumb with a knife, Erika let a few drops fall on the statue.

"Enough. Now leave me, I must work without interruption."

They went outside and closed the door, standing in the hall and looking at each other without daring to speak. There was a faint smell of incense, and the sound of chanting, though no one could understand the words. For a time, Erika thought she heard more than one voice.

That's not possible! I must be mistaken!

After a few minutes, there was a *pop* and, shortly afterwards, Lamya opened the door. On the floor behind her, there was no sign of the statue or the ring. She was holding the green gem in her hand and looking at it thoughtfully.

"I've sent out a probe. It will pass, on a fixed course, from one plane to the next, until it arrives at the one holding your aunt, if she still lives. When that happens, I'll know it at once. Until then, we can only wait."

"How long will it take?" asked Singer.

"It could be hours, or even days. The probe goes first to the closest and most familiar planes, then to the more remote ones. As a rule of thumb, if there's no result within two hours, we should presume she's dead."

"What do we do when we find her?"

"Then I'll try to summon her . . . Oh, look!"

The green gem in her hand was glowing. Lamya stared at it intently. "That didn't take as long as I expected. The probe didn't have to travel far, so the plane must be one quite familiar to sorcerers and presumably to her husband.

"I must now prepare the spell of summoning. Do not disturb me. This spell will take longer than the other one."

Once again, her companions were left waiting in the hall, smelling the reek of incense and listening to a prolonged chant, which seemed to grow in volume. Erika thought she could hear Lamya arguing with someone.

There's definitely someone else in the room!

The argument, if that was what it was, had gotten quite loud, and those waiting in the hall were looking at each other nervously and wondering whether to open the door, when they heard a loud *POP*, followed by a louder *SCREAM*. Singer threw open the door.

Lamya was on her knees, as if resting from much exertion. Standing beside her was an old woman, dressed in tattered clothing and clutching a broom. She was looking around in great confusion. It was evidently she who had screamed.

"There's a witch if I ever saw one!" said Clenas.

"*Bzzz bzzz bzzz bzzz?*" said the old woman.

"She sounds like one of the damned *fui* demons!" said Singer.

Lamya pulled herself unsteadily to her feet. "At a guess, she's just now parted company with them."

Erika stepped forward. "Aunt Gwyn, it's me, Erika. Don't you recognize me?" she said in Hallandish.

"Erika," said the old woman, "you've gotten so big! You're a grown woman now! How did you get here?"

"I didn't go to you, Aunt Gwyn. It's you who were brought back to us."

"To us? What do you mean? Who are all these strange people? And why are they wearing armor?"

"They're my friends, and I'll introduce you, but first I'd like to hear about you, where you've been and what you've been doing all these years."

"That is a lot of questions. I think I need to sit down."

"At first I thought they were going to kill me, but they said that would be incorrect," said Gwyneth, sipping her tea. Since she'd forgotten most of her Akaddian, she spoke Hallandish, necessitating many pauses for translation.

"That does sound like the *fui* demons," said Singer.

"That's what you call them? They call themselves *bzzz bzzz*, I mean, the 'Clever Ones'."

"Haughty vermin!" said Rendel.

"Yes, it can certainly be difficult to deal with arrogant vermin," said Singer.

"They were very nice. I asked them what I should do, and they told me to sweep up. I've been sweeping up for a long, long time . . . years and years . . . It's good to be home."

"You're not quite home yet," said Erika. "We're in Chatmakstan, a province of the Bandeluk Empire."

Gwyneth looked around in bewilderment. "What are we doing here?"

"It's quite a long story," said Erika. "We really have a great many things to talk about, but there's one item which is particularly urgent. Do you remember the rings you gave to Rosalind and myself?"

"Yes, I hope you haven't lost them. You really were such dizzy little girls."

"Can you tell us where you got them?"

"Why, from a jeweler, of course."

"How did they come to be enchanted?"

"Oh, that was rather clever, I thought. My husband was in one of his moods, so I just went in his library and found a book titled 'Universal Compendium of the Sorcerous Arts' and looked it up and followed the directions. It isn't as hard as they make it out to be."

"And you added a key."

"Yes, I was very particular about that. The rings were for the one person who was to love you only and always."

"Do you remember what key you used?"

"Goodness, I couldn't forget that. It was perfectly simple: 'For Me Alone'."

24: Hisaf

No Bandeluk truly hates horses, but Hisaf was getting sick of these. Every one of the thirty pampered steeds in Amir Qilij's stable ate more grain daily than his entire family. Each had to be exercised, curried, bathed and clipped. As the most junior groom, it was his responsibility to muck out the stables, which meant dumping a daily mountain of dung outside the gate, where hungry children picked through it for undigested grain kernels. The rest was eventually dried out and burned as fuel, one of the few sources available to the citizens of Kafra.

It had taken an outrageous bribe to get him a job in the palace, but it was worth it. Now, he got a double ration, plus all the hot tea he could drink, and besides, he could smuggle out some grain to feed his family. He also had the privilege of sleeping in the hay loft, which was more comfortable than the mat at home, where he'd shared a tiny room with four younger brothers and cousins.

Everyone in the palace took bribes. Half his salary went to the stablemaster who hired him, and another slice to the guards who were paid not to inspect him too closely as he left the palace with a small bag of grain hidden in his clothing. Every official, high and low, had to share the take with his boss, so the best part of it eventually landed in the pockets of Amir Qilij, who Hisaf thought of as the biggest thief in the city.

He could have set up a side business himself, selling his horse dung by the pound, and probably have made a lot of money, but the idea of extorting coins from starving people was repugnant. He'd rather play the role of a kindly, if unthanked, benefactor. In a city which had so little, the horse dung, at least, was free.

He'd been here over a week and still had no plan to kill Amir Qilij. The Amir was locked away in his personal residence, and the only entrance was guarded day and night. No one was allowed in except for a few old women, longtime servants of his family, who brought food and did the washing. The wives, courtesans and small children in the harem were never allowed outside.

Besides the residence, there were four major buildings in the walled palace complex: the Temple of Justice, with its commodious underground prison (from which muffled screams could sometimes be heard), the barracks of the palace guard, the kitchens and, of course, the stables. He had full access only to the stables, and sneaking into the residence was out of the question.

Like the rest of Kafra, the palace was built on the ruins of an ancient Kano city, which had long ago sunk into the lagoon. But the palace was on the highest point and held the only intact building left from ancient times, the Amir's residence, a circular, domed structure with a skylight in the middle. The skylight was open, but the sides of the building were covered with gilded tiles, too sheer and slippery for even a lizard to climb.

Having delivered the afternoon's load of dung to its eager recipients, Hisaf returned with his little dung cart to the stable to take a fresh look at things.

You need to think about this. Look around. What is here you can use?

There was all the equipment normal to a stable: saddles, bridles, halters, curry combs, brushes, blankets, shovels, buckets, rakes, scissors, tools for hoof care and for shoeing . . . That coil of rope could be useful to lower himself through the skylight . . . if he could figure some way to get up there in the first place . . .

If this is all I have to work with, I'm in trouble!

He started to climb up to the loft for another look at the residence . . .

Hello! The ladder!

On closer inspection, the ladder was nailed firmly to the wall and couldn't be pried loose without alerting everyone in the stable and, most likely, the entire palace.

Think again. What do we have up here?

In the loft there was a lot of hay, and also the rope and pulley used to lift it. Looking out the hay door, he could see the side of the residence, which was higher than the stable and about twenty feet away.

I'm not high enough, nor close enough, and there's nothing higher than the residence itself . . . except the flagpole . . .

Sticking his head out the hay door, he could see the flagpole, which stood next to the barracks.

If I tried to climb the flagpole, I'd surely be seen, and still would be nowhere close enough.

From here, he could see a foot patrol coming in. As he watched, the officer unlocked the armory door, so they could put away their weapons. No one in the palace was allowed to carry any weapon larger than a knife, unless they were on duty.

All those lovely weapons, so close: swords, spears and bows . . . That's it! But how am I going to break into the armory?

He'd gotten to know the people who worked in the stable. Some of them, like himself, came from well-to-do families and had gotten their jobs through bribery. One of these was Munib, the plump son of a spice dealer, who was not used to physical labor and liked to sleep late. Hisaf sometimes took over his job of walking the horses, because this gave him an excuse to look around the palace.

Early the next morning, he was leading the Amir's black Recaihan mare on its rounds, when he noticed a foot patrol opening the armory door to get its weapons. The key the officer used, taken from a ring on his belt, was one of the heavy, old fashioned kind. It reminded him of the one Uncle Davoud used for his wine cellar.

How does this help me? I'm no locksmith. Uncle Davoud's key is no good here. Is there some way I can separate one of these officers from their keys?

He considered it as he led the horse around for a second lap. He couldn't think of any way to approach a guards officer. They were much too conceited to socialize with a lowly groom, and no bribe would persuade one to part with his precious keys.

As he passed the armory again, he studied it more closely: a smaller building adjacent to the barracks, old, but solidly built of mortared stone, with little, iron-barred windows and a heavy wooden door. It had a plain, clay tile roof. Behind it was a big pile of trash, which had been accumulating since the siege began.

That roof looks interesting, but I need some way to get closer without anyone seeing me.

Clouds had been coming in from the west all day, and by midafternoon, they looked quite dark and threatening. As he was taking a load of dung to the gate, fat drops of water began falling, and by the time he got there, a downpour had begun.

Several people were waiting at the gate to grab an armload of horse dung and run home before it turned into sludge. Down the street, he could see women putting out pots and pans to catch the precious rainwater, which was considered safer to drink than well water. As he turned back toward the stables, he noticed that the guards were pulling up the hoods of their felt cloaks as protection from the rain.

Right now, they can't see or hear anything more than ten feet away. If I'm going to break into the armory, I'll have to do it now. Who knows how long this rain will last or when there will be another shower?

As he passed the armory, he ducked around the corner and climbed on the trash pile in the alley behind the building. The palace gave birth to a lot of trash, about as much, he guessed, as the rest of the city combined: There were heaps of egg shells, bones, tea leaves, dead flowers, worn-out rags, broken pots, fruit rinds and a lot of things he didn't care to identify. Despite the siege, the Amir was not denying himself any luxuries.

A rat ran away squeaking as he clambered up to an unsteady perch under the eaves. There were always plenty of rats around the palace, though elsewhere in the city, they were becoming rare.

Even the rats are starving . . . or being eaten!

The roof was a type familiar to him: plain clay tiles laid overlapping on a simple wood surface. No great expense had been wasted on this building, which was seldom occupied. Experimentally, he tried to pull one of the tiles loose. At first, it seemed solidly in place, but when he pulled harder, it suddenly gave way, landing him on his butt in the garbage.

He turned over the dung cart on top of the trash heap to give himself a better perch and had another look at his work. A narrow strip of the wooden roof had been exposed.

I'll have to work fast to finish this before the rain stops.

Pulling vigorously, he tore off one tile after another until he'd laid bare a broad section of planed timber.

All I have to do is remove that, and I'm in!

He tried to lift up a board by the edge, but it was impossible. The wood was old and cracked, but whoever had nailed it to the beams had done a good job.

I need a crowbar.

There was no such tool in the stable and no time to look for one. The rain wouldn't last much longer, and he couldn't risk being seen. Desperately, he looked through the heap of garbage for something he could use, turning it over with his feet, until the toe of his shoe hit the stone flagging beneath.

That's what I need, it's right under my feet!

The flagstones were big, rough and square. They were lying in a bed of sand. Taken a potsherd, he scraped the sand away from one of them until he could pry it up with his fingers.

This is damned heavy!

The flagstone weighed at least twenty pounds. He swayed unsteadily as he climbed back on the overturned cart and raised it above his head.

It's now or never!

He brought down the stone.

KRUNCH!

The sound was so loud, he assumed someone must have heard, and he stood there with his heart pounding for a full minute, but no one came.

The rain is letting up! Move fast!

There was now a hole in the roof, which he expanded by tearing away the broken pieces of wood. It was dark inside. With a light patter of rain still falling on his head, he cautiously lowered himself into the hole.

His feet touched a smooth surface. Looking down, he saw he was standing on a stack of shields which wobbled dangerously with his every movement.

If this falls over, everyone will hear!

He reached over to grab a rafter and dropped the remaining distance to the floor. As his eyes adjusted to the dim light, he saw he was standing between a rack of scimitars and another of spears, which would have impaled him if he'd landed just a little to the right.

Truly, the gods are favoring me!

The armory held a great treasure of weapons for aspiring heros: swords, shields, spears and axes were in abundance, some in racks, some on the walls, some in barrels and some (the more expensive kind, he assumed) locked away in cabinets and chests.

There was no time to admire the weapons. The sound of rain on the roof was dying away. Someone might come by at any moment. It took him only a minute to find what he was looking for, a bow and quiver of arrows, and toss them out through the hole in the roof. Then, he boosted himself onto a rafter and climbed out after them.

The rain was over. He had to do something quickly about the hole in the roof, because anyone who opened the armory or stepped in the alley would notice it, and then there would be an outcry and a search of the whole compound. Hastily, he laid the broken boards back on the beams as well as he could and covered them with tiles. It was sloppy work, but hopefully, no one would look too closely.

Then, he had to hide the bow and quiver. For this, he decided, a few handfuls of trash would suffice. He was just turning his dung cart back upright, when he heard footsteps coming around the corner. There was nowhere to run and nowhere to hide. Thinking fast, he turned his cart over again, as if he were dumping a load of garbage. A kitchen maid, carrying a basket of offal, discovered him in this pose. She turned up her nose, then quickly emptied her basket and fled.

Hisaf, you stinking muckraker, you're so filthy, even the scullery maids won't look at you!

He'd stolen a knife from the kitchen, a long, straight blade without a point. Knives like these were used for slaughtering goats, and this one was sharp as a razor. He'd tested it on his own beard.

A knife like this is only good for cutting throats. Exactly what I need.

It would have to be tonight. He couldn't afford to wait. Someone might notice the hole in the roof or the missing bow and quiver. Besides, people were dying every day in the streets and in Heroes Square. Things would only get worse if he waited.

Tonight he dies, or I do!

The hard part was finishing his work in the stables, and the rest of his daily routine, as if nothing had happened. He felt terribly nervous. Every time someone glanced at him, he thought he was about to be denounced. Fortunately, no one paid much attention to the grooms and stable boys, so long as they were doing their jobs, and he did his with vigor.

With evening, he collected his loaf of bread and drank six cups of tea as he ate, then retired to the loft, where the other grooms, tired from the day's exertions, were lying. They chatted with each other for a time, mainly about the siege and, in worried tones, their families in the city. Hisaf kept to himself, hugging his dark secret and waiting for the others to fall asleep . . .

He awoke in the dark with an urgent need to piss.

Why did I have to drink so much tea?

Groping around, he touched the hilt of the knife, which he'd hidden beside him in the hay.

Oh, that's why.

He lay there a minute, listening to the sound of regular breathing, before he was satisfied the others were asleep. Then, he got up and stuck his head out the hay door. The night was dark and quiet. He could hear crickets chirping in the distance. There were guards stationed at the gate and the entrance to the residence, but they wouldn't leave their posts until dawn.

A wonderful night for a murder.

Having relieved himself, he went to get the bow and quiver. There were several rats in the alley; he could hear them moving around, but they ran off squeaking as he entered. Searching the trash, it didn't take long to find the bow and quiver. The leather quiver had been gnawed by rats, but the bow was intact. The damage to the quiver didn't matter. He wouldn't need more than one arrow.

Returning to the stable, he opened the stall where he'd hidden the ball of twine, which he'd collected from the bundles of hay. He had chosen the stall of a gentle old mare, who whinnied softly as he entered.

Easy!

He stroked her neck for a moment, whispering to her with his familiar voice. The horse fell silent.

Next, he hid the bow and quiver temporarily behind a washtub in the corner, before taking the coil of rope and climbing back into the loft. No one was stirring. Swiftly, he tied the rope to the pulley, with what he hoped was a good, solid knot before letting it fall to the ground below.

THUMP!

The heavy coil of rope made a much louder noise than he expected as it fell ten feet. One of the stable boys was stirring. Hisaf lay down and pretended to be asleep.

The stable boy was sitting up. It was Azad. A whiny, pimple-faced boy, he'd been given the job through the influence of his uncle, a court official.

If he sees the rope, I'll have to kill him!

The rope, though, was outside the hay door, dangling from the pulley, and was not visible from where Azad was sitting. Azad yawned, rubbed his eyes and went back to sleep. Hisaf gave him a couple minutes more before creeping to the ladder.

Now, things were getting tricky. He tied the rope to one end of the twine then unrolled the twine, so that it lay in big, loose loops.

Let's hope it doesn't get tangled!

He selected a long, straight arrow from the quiver and tied the twine in front of the fletching. Experimentally, he nocked the arrow and pulled back the bowstring.

Damn! I forgot the thumb ring!

There was no thumb ring to be found in the stable and no time to go searching for one. He pulled back on the bow as far as it would go with his fingers, gritting his teeth against the pain, Taking aim at a point high above the middle of the Amir's residence, he loosed. The arrow disappeared silently into the darkness, dragging the twine behind it. There was a faint *clink* from the other side of the residence, as the arrowhead hit something solid.

He waited a minute to see if anyone had heard the arrow, but the palace remained quiet. Moving cautiously, he returned to the trash heap, and hid the bow and quiver.

It doesn't matter if the rats chew on them now. Eat up, little friends!

Now, he had to creep as quietly as he could, around the back of the residence, searching for the arrow. This brought him near the kitchen, which was as dark and still as a mausoleum. The last, tired scullery maid had apparently gone to bed. If the kitchen followed its usual routine, there would be no one awake until the bakers heated up the ovens before dawn.

There were only a few stars in the sky. Groping his way in the dark, he ran one hand over the gilded tiles of the Amir's residence, hoping to find the arrow and the vital piece of twine. Soon he was almost to the Temple of Justice, and he still hadn't found it.

Did the arrow miscarry? Was this all in vain?

He turned around and went back, this time raising his hand as high as he could on the wall. He hadn't gone far before his fingers touched something cold and sharp, the arrowhead.

It didn't miscarry. It's hanging down from the top of the residence, only a bit high and to the side.

He began pulling in the twine gently, meanwhile moving back to where he judged the middle of the residence to be. After a couple minutes, he was standing in a pile of twine, and his fingers were grasping the rope. He took in the remaining slack and gave it a tug, to make sure the knot was tight. Then, he cut loose the twine, rolled it up and stuffed it in his sash.

This was it, the rope was in his hands, and the dark, looming expanse of the residence stood before him. He checked his knife. It was secure in his belt. He had no other weapon.

Now, I find out if I'm as clever as I thought!

Scaling such a steep, slippery surface was not easy, even with the help of the rope. He kicked off his sandals to get a better purchase. He still made no headway until he wrapped the rope around one ankle, holding it in place with his other foot. Now, he had a firm grip, but it was still exhausting to pull himself up, inch by inch. After a long struggle, he reached point the where the dome was flat enough to crawl around on.

I've barely started, and already, I'm tired!

He gave himself a minute's rest. There was a deep, inky chasm in front of him, the skylight. He crawled slowly to the edge and looked inside. It seemed to be absolutely black. Stare as he might, he couldn't see a single thing.

He'd never been in the residence and had no idea what lay under the skylight. There could be a courtyard or a fountain or a fish pond or a weapons rack or . . . anything. Possibly, someone was sleeping down there, directly where he had to put his feet.

I knew this would be dangerous. The gods have favored me this far. I'll have to trust them a little longer.

He lowered the rope slowly into the hole. If there was someone underneath, it wouldn't take them long to notice it. After a couple minutes, the line to the pulley was taut, and there had still been no outcry. He gave the rope a tug to make sure the knot was still tight, then began lowering himself into the darkness.

For a moment, all his weight was on his hands, and it seemed he'd surely fall, but then he remembered the trick of wrapping the rope around one ankle and was able to lower himself slowly. The rope swayed back and forth. He couldn't see a thing. For awhile he thought there must be a wall in front of him, a foot from his nose, but when he reached out to touch it, there was nothing. The darkness itself was like an impenetrable wall.

I should have brought a candle!

Suddenly, something soft touched his foot. He gasped in surprise, but when nothing else happened, he realized he must have brushed against something, a plant perhaps. Then, the plants were all around him, touching him from all sides, lasciviously caressing him as he descended. The center of the building must be full of shrubs and small trees, all reaching up toward the light.

Calm down! The plants won't hurt you! Just try not to make any noise!

Looking up, he could see in the round skylight, the stars were being obscured by branches and leaves. Presently, he was standing on soft, moist earth, probably a flower bed. He could feel shrubbery all around him, but he could see nothing.

This is how it is to be blind. How do blind people get around?

Reaching out with his fingers, he selected a flexible branch that seemed long enough and cut it with the knife. Then, he peeled off the twigs and leaves until he had a switch about four feet long. He poked around with the switch until it struck something solid with a slight *click.*

That must be a flagstone marking the edge of the garden. That's where I must go.

He wriggled his way through the plants, trying hard not to break any dry twigs, until his feet were resting on a cold, smooth surface.

Now what? I still can't see a thing!

How could he find anything in the dark? He could easily get lost and wander around for hours!

Wait! What about the twine?

He tied one end of the twine to a branch and began playing it out, feeling his way with the switch in his other hand. Before long, there was a *click* as the switch struck an upright object, a stone column. He wound the string around the column and kept going, in what he hoped was a straight line.

It felt as if he were crossing a vast, empty space, though really it couldn't have been more than a few feet before he ran into a wall. Experimentally, he ran his hands over it. The wall seemed to be covered with tiles, like the one outside.

And probably gilded too!

The wall curved slightly to the right and the left. He went left. After a few steps, his questing fingers touched a wooden surface, a door. He tried the latch, which was unlocked.

Dare I open it? What if I end up in the harem? It might be safer to look around some more.

He left his twine tied to the latch and kept going. After awhile, he was standing before another door, much like the first and also unlocked. He mentally labeled it Door 2 and continued moving to the left.

Door 3, when he reached it, was different from the first two: set in a more solid frame, and it was made of iron. Also, it was locked.

If he's in there, he's safe. I'll never get past this door!

He kept going. Door 4 seemed the same as Door 1 and Door 2. It was also unlocked. After that, there was another expanse of tiled wall before he encountered the twine he'd left tied to Door 1.

This is hard! If I open the wrong door, someone may notice, and then I'll have to cut my own throat before the guards catch me!

He could forget about Door 3, because he had no way of opening it. It was probably just the treasury. Everyone knew how rich Amir Qilij was. Where would he keep his money but here?

One door probably went to the harem and one to the entrance hall. The other was to Qilij's chamber. But which one?

He put his ear to Door 1, but could hear nothing. He moved on to Door 2 and listened there. Still nothing. He passed Door 3 without stopping and went to Door 4. It was as quiet as the others.

As he was turning away, he ran his fingers over the door and noticed something different about it. The surface was slightly uneven. He scratched it softly with his nails. There seemed to be slight ridges and bumps on it.

This makes no sense! The wood should be polished flat! Why isn't it like the others?

It took him a couple minutes to realize he was touching an inlay. The wooden door was set with bits of gold or ivory some other precious material to create an ornate pattern, which, because of the darkness, he couldn't see.

Qilij, your vanity has undone you! You've marked your own door for the assassin!

He opened the door. There was a light inside . . . and a man with a knife was blocking his way! He stepped forward, knife at the ready, and the stranger did the same . . .

A mirror! I almost gave myself away because of a mirror!

The room was full of mirrors. He could see himself – a fierce ruffian – looking back from every wall, but otherwise it was empty. He closed the door.

Inside the room was a beautiful, polished table with several chairs, and one particular large and gilded chair, doubtless for Qilij himself. On the walls, between mirrors, hung paintings of Qilij, looking younger and more handsome than he did in real life: Qilij the Warrior was flourishing a sword. Qilij the Pious was on his knees praying, Qilij the Bountiful was distributing alms . . . there were several others.

The mirrors, he now saw, were cleverly arranged to multiply the images. Qilij had a hundred faces and was staring at him from all directions.

Qilij is everywhere in this room. This must be where he receives guests.

There was only one other door. This time, he could see the inlay pattern. It was, what else, a mosaic of Qilij, looking particularly stern and commanding.

That picture is looking at me, as if it knows what I'm doing!

He hadn't come this far to be intimidated by a picture. There were many candles in the room, but only one was lit. He took it and approached the final door . . . and then he thought of something that made him pause.

What if there's a woman inside?

If she saw him, she'd scream, and if she screamed, the guards would come. If she were asleep, though, he could simply cut her throat . . . but that might awaken Qilij.

Whatever else happens, I have to kill Qilij! I'll kill him first and worry about the woman later.

He opened the door. The next room was hung with silk and lace curtains. He could hear soft breathing from somewhere, but where? Everywhere he looked, there was cloth: sky blue, pink, ivory or golden. It blocked his view. Behind which curtain was Qilij hiding?

He must love his privacy. Even the woman who brings him tea in the morning must not see him lying in bed. But if the tea stand is here, then where's the bed? It can't be far away!

He sheathed the dagger and pulled out the wooden switch. Some curtains gave easily to its touch; they were hanging from the ceiling. Others didn't give at all; they were hanging on the wall. However, a large, red satin curtain to one side would move only a short distance; it was blocked by something behind it.

This must be the bed!

He cut a slit in the red satin and peered inside. A big, fat form was lying under some sheets on the bed. This was where the breathing sound was coming from. There was no woman to be seen.

You love your privacy too much, Qilij: You sent your courtesan away when you were done with her.

He cut away the red satin and then he was looking at the great Amir, curled up with his butt sticking out of the sheets. He was facing away from Hisaf.

Now what do I do? I can't reach him like this. Maybe I should shake him and say, "Wake up, it's time to die!"

Lying there so peacefully, Qilij looked harmless, a big fat man who would never hurt anyone. Killing him in his sleep seemed cruel. But waking him up would be too dangerous.

Qilij would never spare me if he were awake. To hell with this, kill him any way you can!

The best way, Hisaf thought, was to grab him by the hair, pull his head back and slit his throat. Before he could even wake up, Qilij

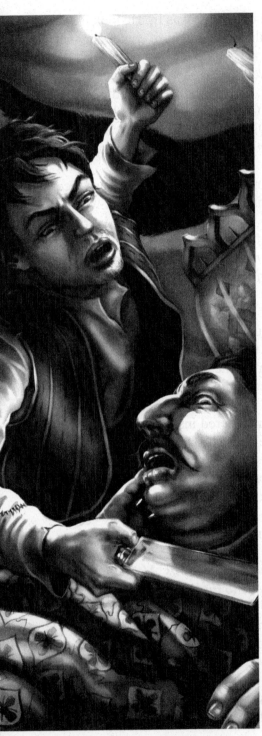

would be dead. But to do that, he'd need both hands, and at the moment, there was the knife in one and a candle in the other.

There was a half-burned candle in a holder above the sleeping man's head. As Hisaf bent over to light it, he noticed a drop of wax forming on the candle in his hand, about to fall. He jerked his hand back, and then it did fall, directly on the Amir. As the hot wax touched his cheek, Qilij started and reached up to touch it. Then, he turned, and for an instant, they were looking each other in the face.

The only thing Hisaf could think was:

I never noticed he had blue eyes.

25: Krion

My officers are such idiots!

Why were they crowding into his tent this way? He hadn't summoned them! He recognized Clenas and Singer at once, but was startled to see an armed Bandeluk with them . . . and then there were these women!

He sat up and pointed a finger at Erika. "I gave orders that no women . . ." He paused. He'd suddenly noticed the ring finger of his right hand was gone. He stared at the disfigured hand, stupefied.

His aide, Lt. Bardhof, stepped forward. "We're no longer in the camp at Kafra, my Prince. We're in Jasmine House. You've been under an enchantment. Gen. Basilius has seized control of the army. It was only with great difficulty that we removed you from the cage where he was keeping you."

A cage?

He stroked his beard. It was obvious he hadn't shaved in many days.

"What is the military situation?"

"We have the Royal Light Cavalry and two Free State squadrons. The Free State infantry is marching from Barbosa, but it won't get here before the vanguard of Basilius' force, which numbers at least ten thousand. He's advancing up the coastal road. We have secret pledges of support from Capt. Lessig and the other Covenant commanders, but they're still in the siegeworks at Kafra, along with the Brethren and the Ragmen. We can also muster a company of Chatmak militia, but they're green recruits and wouldn't be of much use against Basilius."

This doesn't sound good!

He stood up and discovered he was wearing only a diaper.

A diaper?

No matter, time to take charge: "Everyone out of the room but Clenas and Singer. Bardhof, get me a uniform and a razor. I want a detailed report from Prince Clenas, followed by Gen. Singer."

At least, I know who I can trust now. But I wish there were more of them!

Half an hour later, he was fully dressed and shaved and staring at a map of Chatmakstan.

"Basilius is using the coast road, because it gives him space to deploy his superior numbers against us," Clenas was saying. "If we take the interior road, we'll be able to pick up the Free State infantry and arrive in Kafra before Basilius can turn around. Once we've united with our supporters in Kafra, we'll be able to meet him on equal terms."

Not bad. Clenas is not as stupid as I thought.

"What do you think of that, Gen. Singer?"

"I think it provides Basilius too many chances to detect our movements and intercept us. There are places where those narrow hill roads could be blocked with a single company of pike. Once we're immobile, Basilius would lose no time in surrounding us."

"And your preference would be . . .?"

"Ascend the Stairway *here*. A handful of men can defend the Stairway against any number. Cut across the Area of Effect *here*, then approach Kafra from the north. Basilius is not prepared for an attack from that direction."

Even better. That appointment was a lucky stroke. Now, they want to hear my decision, but they'll have to wait.

"What time is it now?"

"Just after midnight."

"Take a few hours rest, but don't oversleep. I want your men mounted and ready to go at the crack of dawn."

"And the militia?"

"They won't be needed."

This is my favorite time of day, when I'm awake, and my enemies are still sleeping.

The first glimmers of dawn were lighting the eastern hills. Jasmine House was surrounded by two thousand cavalry. Sleepy men and sleepy horses were taking their places in formation. Officers were calling roll. Birds, alarmed at the activity, were making anxious noises. Krion had gathered his commanders by the gate.

"You have a native guide?"

"I do," said Singer.

"Bring him here."

The native guide was the same Bandeluk he'd seen earlier. Krion raised his eyebrows when told it was a woman named Raeesha, who was also the Free State Standard-bearer.

Sometime, I really must talk to Singer about his choice of subordinates. But for now, let's see what she can tell us.

"What lies directly south of here?"

After Singer had translated this question and heard the reply, he said, "It's mainly open farmland. There are no roads, only paths through the fields. The Crane village is about five miles to the south, and other villages beyond it."

"Since the fields have been harvested, there will be nothing to prevent us from riding right through them. So, no need for a road. We'll be moving in column. Hardy's Company will take the lead, followed by the Royal Light Cavalry, and after him, the Illustrious Knights. Does everyone understand?"

Rendel, looking flushed, said, "I must protest . . ."

"Do it later. I have no more patience for officers whose sense of honor prevents them from following orders. I will be on point with Lt. Bardhof as my Standard-bearer. Gen. Singer, keep yourself and your Bandeluk close by."

About an hour later, they were approaching the Crane village. There was a footbridge here, over a little stream. Barking dogs announced their presence. Raeesha pointed to the stream and said something in Bandeluki.

"What is she babbling about?"

"She says the streams are also roads, when one doesn't wish to be seen. It's an old Bandeluk trick."

Cautiously, Krion rode down into the streambed. The banks were eight feet high, but there was only a foot of water in the stream, which had a gravel bottom.

"Ask her where this stream goes."

"She says, it goes to the place you originally landed, the Southern Landing Zone."

Yes, I seem to remember a stream off on the flank. This fits nicely into my plans.

"Tell her she's a clever girl, and if she remembers any other old Bandeluk tricks, to let me know. We'll be following the stream. Tell the Standard-bearers to furl their banners."

Sloshing down the stream was slow work, but there was no

great reason to hurry. After two hours, Krion noticed a cloud of dust to the southwest. He halted the column and climbed up the stream bank for a look.

In the distance, he could make out a large body of cavalry moving up the road at the trot. From the red uniforms, he identified them as the Twelve Hundred Heroes. Morning light flashed from their armor and weapons.

They do make a fine display, the Twelve Hundred. How foolish of me to leave Basilius in charge of them!

There was no indication they'd spotted his column, still concealed in the streambed. He reflected that Basilius would probably want to secure Massera Bay before pursuing him. With any luck, then, he'd stolen a day's march and a huge tactical advantage.

History will record my brilliance in using a stream to outflank the rebels. There will be, of course, no need to mention the Bandeluk girl.

Krion's column continued moving down the streambed. After a couple hours, the dust cloud that marked the Twelve Hundred Heroes had vanished to the north, followed by that of another mounted formation. Krion now came to a bridge. The sound of the sea and the calls of gulls were in his ears. A third cloud of dust was approaching from the south.

Now I've cut off Basilius' vanguard from the main body. His best, most reliable units were doubtless leading the column. Let's depart from this congenial stream and see what the rest of them look like.

"Unfurl my banner, Gen. Singer's and Baron Hardy's. Leave the others furled. We'll be moving south along the road."

If the commander of the oncoming formation was surprised to see a cavalry force suddenly appear in front of him, he didn't show it. Krion could see the mounted troops turning to the right and left, arraying themselves for battle.

Prompt and precise, as if they were on parade. Are these the Royal Household Guards? I think I recognize the helmets.

"Should we assume battle formation?" asked Singer.

"No. Remain in column. No man is to draw his weapons."

The Royal Household Guards was an elite formation entrusted with the protection of the royal family and often trotted out in their polished armor on parade. Their commander, Col. Grennadius, was a greybeard and one of Basilius' cronies, but he had once been Krion's riding master.

Elite veterans, but most of them past their prime. Haven't seen any real combat in years. It would be a shame to massacre them. Let's see how they feel about attacking the royal family instead of protecting us.

There was some nervous shuffling among the Guards as Krion approached. The banners they were looking at weren't the ones they expected. Krion's banner, in particular, caused consternation. There was much craning of necks to see if this was really the Prince, or just some ruse.

Let the suspense build awhile longer.

Krion advanced at a non-threatening amble, but behind him, more and more troops were pouring out of the streambed.

Pretty soon, they'll see they're outnumbered. If Grennadius is going to charge, he'll have to do it at one or two hundred yards. Anything short of that would be too late.

At three hundred yards, Krion could see the Guards were talking to each other and pointing at him. The neat line of raised lance points was shifting and rolling like a wave on the sea, as each man leaned over to consult with his neighbor.

Where are you, Grennadius, my old teacher? Hiding behind your troops? How unlike you! Do you wish to keep some personal distance between us?

Krion removed his helmet, so everyone could see his golden locks, made more obvious by the fact they hadn't been cut in weeks. He thought he could hear a collective outcry from the Guards, above the sound of the sea, whose breeze was playing with his hair and whipping his gold-green cloak about to good effect.

They aren't speculating anymore. They know. But how is "Uncle" Grennadius going to react?

At two hundred yards, there still had been no order to charge. Krion could now hear an excited confusion of voices from the Guards, saying, he supposed, "The Prince is here!" or some words to that effect. Behind the battle line was the Guards banner and next to it a massive form which could only be Grennadius, mounted on that great stallion he called his "destier". It was the only steed that could handle his ponderous body. Krion turned his horse in that direction.

At one hundred yards, Krion waved, as if he were on parade,

greeting his loyal subjects. Bard-hof yelled, "MAKE WAY FOR THE PRINCE!" and they did, parting in front of him, without waiting for a command from their own officers. Krion rode directly toward Grennadius, Hardy's company in column behind him, effectively splitting the Guards in two. Many of the latter were turning to see what transpired, their ordered ranks becoming a jumbled mess.

Grennadius sat staring at him, completely flummoxed. His lips moved as if he wanted to say something, but nothing came out.

"Hello, Uncle, forgotten how to salute?"

Grennadius saluted. He still had not managed to say anything.

"I don't mean to scold you, Uncle, but I really must inquire as to why you've left your appointed position in the siegeworks. I don't remember giving such a command."

Grennadius finally found something to say: "On orders from Gen. Basilius and the military council, we are advancing to Massera Bay, to take the supply depot there."

"Take it from whom? Not from me, I hope?"

Grennadius, red faced, was now searching his confused mind for an answer. "Gen. Basilius was appointed commander pro-tem because of your infirmity," he said finally.

"Infirm? Do I seem infirm to you?"

Without waiting for an answer, he removed his gauntlet and held up the maimed hand, so everyone could see it. There was a collective gasp from the Guards.

"I have, to be sure, suffered an injury for which, you may be certain, those responsible shall be duly punished. You're not one of them, I hope?"

"Not at all! I was very much against that!" Now that Grennadius' mouth had opened, a flood of excuses and apologies was coming out: "Basilius said you were rendered incapable by an enchantment! Diomedos confirmed it! I only signed the document they handed me, everyone signed . . ."

Krion nodded understandingly. "Enough! I can see you were not at fault. The orders to advance on Massera Bay are countermanded. You are to return to your position at Kafra. You shall have the honor of leading the van. Get moving, Colonel!"

Grennadius saluted and gave the order: "FORM TWO COLUMNS! FOLLOW ME!" He turned his horse south, and, moving smartly, his men fell in behind him, taking their appointed places in the formation.

They certainly do look sharp, these parade troops! With the Royal Household Guards in front, I don't think we can expect much trouble from the rest. I must remember to give Grennadius a promotion . . . and an early retirement, at the first opportunity. He's earned them both!

By sundown, he'd added four more companies. His following now numbered over six thousand. He'd sent swift couriers ahead, with written orders for the rest of Basilius' force to turn around. By morning, the news would have reached Krafra.

Of Basilius himself, there was no sign. It was unclear if he even knew what had happened to the rest of his force, though by now, he must surely be wondering why the Royal Household Guards hadn't arrived at Massera Bay.

Basilius' vanguard was presumably still somewhere to the north. It no longer mattered much what he planned to do. They'd reversed positions: Now it was Krion who had the numbers on his side, who stood between Basilius and Kafra.

I've won, and I did it without a drop of blood spilt.

He pitched his tent on top of one of the small hills that dotted the plain. As he stood by the entrance, with only loyal Bardhof beside him, he studied the many circling campfires.

This is the best thing in the world, to be victorious, with thousands of swords around me and not an enemy in sight. Nothing can touch me now!

But of course, that was not quite true. Something *had* touched him, in the middle of his camp, with his soldiers all around, and it had come in the form of a woman.

Now would be a good time to settle that account.

"Bardhof, go find the woman Erika. I wish to speak with her alone."

She looks nervous. She's afraid of what I might do. And she should be.

"It is generally believed you're my brother's lover. And still, you claimed to be Gen. Singer's wife. Which is it? Or is it both?"

Erika blushed. "Forgive me, my Prince, I did tell you a fable, but only with the best of intentions. I just wanted to . . ."

"Answer the question."

"The simple truth is, neither the love affair nor the marriage has been consummated."

"And yet I'm told the honest General regards you as his bride, and my promiscuous brother follows you around like a devoted puppy. How is this possible?"

"Gen. Singer and I are betrothed. I am assisting your brother in a project for the economic betterment of the province. I wrote a report . . . I mean, he wrote a report . . ."

"I've seen it. Is it on this pretext you wander about in a combat zone, interfering with military affairs?"

"It is not a pretext. Chatmakstan is one of the poorest provinces in the Bandeluk Empire, but potentially, it's one of the richest. There are great, unexploited resources here. Surely you didn't conquer this place only to leave it a neglected backwater?"

Oh, she is clever, for a woman.

"There are quite a few provinces I'm interested in conquering, and I can spare neither Gen. Singer, nor my brother. I require their services, most urgently."

"I had no wish to deprive you of anything, my Prince."

"And yet you managed to reduce me to imbecility and stir up a mutiny against me."

"And for that, Gen. Basilius locked me in a cage!"

"Which is the only praiseworthy thing he's done here. Madam, you are a disaster! You leave a trail of chaos and disorder everywhere you go. Out of respect for your nominal husband and misguided lover, I give you two weeks to tidy up your affairs here. After that, you'll take a berth on the next ship back to Halland."

"But my Prince . . ."

"No more words! I am offering you a pardon, and you'd be well advised to take it before I change my mind! Now leave me!"

Erika gave him a despondent curtsey and left.

Why did I give her two weeks? I should only have given her one! Theros help me if she causes another disaster!

There was a forest of banners outside his camp. The vendors had all been cleared away, replaced with commanding officers and their standard-bearers, who lined the road to greet the returning Prince. It was quite an impressive show.

How nice. Everyone seems to be here, except for the Twelve Hundred and the Winged Horsemen . . . and Singer's infantry.

Returning one salute after another, he made his way to the gate, where Lt. Mopsus was waiting.

"My Prince! I am overjoyed . . ."

"Later. Any news on Gen. Basilius?" he asked.

"You haven't heard? Basilius encountered the Free State infantry north of the Stairway. He tried to force a road through the hills and was driven back with heavy losses. Gen. Basilius has stabbed himself. The rest are waiting for you to accept their surrender."

Dead? Basilius is dead? How can he be dead?

Basilius was his father's oldest and most trusted officer. He always stood a head above the others. Since he was a child, Krion had always looked up to him. It seemed impossible he'd kill himself. At worst, if he were captured, he could look to the King for a pardon.

He was certainly my father's friend, but was he ever mine?

He tried to picture Basilius as he'd seen him years ago, when he was riding back with the king from a victorious campaign. He could remember every detail, the uniforms, the banners, the bouquets. He even remembered the bay horse Basilius was riding that day. But the man himself, he could not remember. His face was just a blur. Basilius was a mystery.

I need to find out who was supporting him in the capital. Basilius would never have tried something like this without a powerful ally: a member of the royal family, or someone close to it. And he wouldn't have killed himself unless he were hiding something important.

But that would have to wait. "Tell Capt. Lessig to report to my tent."

One of the Ragmen was waiting outside the tent. As he entered, it followed, taking its normal place in the corner without comment.

The interior of the tent was a mess. Someone had dumped the map box and scattered the contents. His clothing was lying about on the floor. The cashbox and the box of mirrors were missing, and probably among Basilius' possessions. His bed was filthy: There were leather straps tied to the bedposts and the blanket was soaked in blood.

He pulled off his right gauntlet and examined the maimed hand.

So this is where they did it, in my own tent, in the middle of my army! A pretended remedy for a real problem! Diomedos is either incompetent or complicit, and in either case, he will have to go, along with those others. But where am I to find a sorcerer in this place? Didn't Singer have a witch of some kind with him?

Lessig was at the entrance to the tent. Krion motioned for him to enter, which he did with an expression of great satisfaction. "My Prince! On behalf of the entire Covenant force, I'd like to congratulate . . ."

"Later. I need a report on the dam."

"The dam is complete, but the diversion canal . . ."

"Doesn't matter. Close the gates. I don't care if it floods half the province. Do it today."

Lessig seemed confused. "Is that necessary, my Prince?"

"What do you mean?"

I thought he was loyal! Why is he questioning my orders?

"No one has told you? I thought you knew . . ."

"Knew what? Out with it!"

Wordlessly, Lessig turned around and went to the entrance to the tent. He gestured for Krion to join him.

What is he doing? This better be good!

Lessig pointed south across the lagoon, to where the roofs of Kafra were visible. In the place where Krion was accustomed to seeing the crimson-silver Bandeluk banner, a flag of purest white was flying.

26: Raeesha

"I need a volunteer."

No one moved. The Blue Bandeluks just sat there, looking at their feet.

Raeesha gritted her teeth in frustration. These were *her* men. She had recruited them and led them across the Area of Effect, all the way to Barbosa. They'd explored the ruins together and fought a demon. She'd brought them safely through every danger, and now they wouldn't even look at her.

Men are so stupid!

It was all because she was a woman. A mere girl had outwitted and humiliated them before the world. They were sent to get Raeesha, and Raeesha had gotten them. They felt robbed of their honor. Their manhood was in danger of ridicule. Some surely wanted to kill her. Only blood washes away dishonor.

She tried again: "This is an important mission. I need your help."

Nobody looked up.

I'd rather argue with the demons! At least, they don't care if I'm a woman!

"The General needs this done. The whole army is counting on us."

Olgun looked at her angrily. "Then they should have asked me! I am the leader here!"

"But you're not the right man for this job."

"And you think you are?"

"Yes. This is a delicate mission."

"I AM DELICATE AS ANY DIRTY BASTARD IN THE ARMY!"

"As you say."

He'd strike me down right now, if he dared.

She pulled out the leather purse and jingled the coins inside. "There's a reward."

"How much?" said Lufti.

"This is it?" said Lufti, looking skeptically at the boat. By his tone, he clearly wanted to be told this was *not* it, that there was a much larger and safer-looking boat awaiting them somewhere else.

"I'm afraid so," said Raeesha, no more enthused than Lufti.

Though natural horsemen, Bandeluks make awkward and queasy sailors and generally prefer letting someone else handle the boat. In this case, the boat didn't inspire much confidence, having been made of bundled reeds by Chatmak fishermen, who refused to sail in it themselves.

"Have you ever paddled a boat before?" she asked.

"No."

"Then you can get in first."

Cautiously, Lufti put one foot in the boat, which immediately started to roll over.

"Put your feet in the middle, not on the side," Raeesha advised him.

If I'd chosen someone for this job, it wouldn't have been Lufti.

Lufti was young, impulsive, full of unwarranted confidence, and eager for new experiences, qualities which made him a willing volunteer and a dangerous person to share a boat with. At the moment, he was making holes in the reedy bottom.

"Are those high-heeled riding boots? Take them off!"

"My feet will get wet," he grumbled.

"You can dry them later."

She held the boat steady, while Lufti, seated in the front, clumsily took his boots off.

"Why do I always get the worst jobs?"

"Because you volunteer? Hold the boat steady while I get in."

"Hold it how? There's nothing to hold!"

"Take a paddle and stick it in the mud until it won't go any further. Then hold it tight."

So far, I look like I know what I'm doing. Let's hope he doesn't see I've never been in a boat before!

Having set her pack in the middle and herself in the back of the boat, she told Lufti to retrieve his paddle. Then, she pushed them away from the shore, noting that the boat seemed willing to keep moving for a moment without further pushing.

This is going to take some practice.

Experimentally, she dipped her paddle in the water on the left side of the boat and pulled it back, as she'd seen the boatmen do.

Now, the boat was moving faster, but also turning to the right. She moved the paddle to the right side, but paddling there made it turn to the left.

"Why aren't you paddling?" she said.

"I don't know how!"

"It isn't hard, just watch me!"

If I paddle on this side and he on the other, then we can get somewhere.

After the first few strokes, Lufti thought himself an experienced sailor, and soon was splashing water around with enthusiasm.

"Hey! You're getting the pack wet! Be careful!"

"Why did we bring that thing anyway?"

"None of your business. You aren't being paid to ask questions!"

"Maybe you should pay me *not* to ask questions . . . What's that?"

The boat had bumped into something floating in the water. It was a vile yellow in color. It was bloated, and it stank.

"Never seen a dead man before?"

"Not like this!" said Lufti, disgusted. He pushed it away with his paddle.

"Better get used to it."

Now that they looked, they could see dozens of dead people floating in the lagoon. They were bound to hit some more before they reached Kafra.

"You aren't paying me enough!"

"Here's some advice: Volunteer for the missions where they're alive and trying to kill you. Those pay better."

"What happens when we reach Kafra?"

"Then we find out if the white flag is just a joke."

"And if it is?"

"Shut up and paddle."

There were tents standing in the place of the washerwomen. No one was visible, except for one old woman who was sitting in a washtub. On closer inspection, she was dead: There was a cloud of flies buzzing around her.

"What killed all these people?" said Lufti.

"Hunger and disease, I expect. Some drowned. And Qilij the

Cruel probably executed some of them."

Lufti stared at the dead woman, who stared back with her sunken eyes. "I'm not going there!"

"You don't have to. Just let me out. Then, you can go back and tell the General there was no resistance."

"There could be soldiers hiding in those tents, or in the buildings."

"In a minute, I'm going to kick over a couple of tents and walk down the street between those buildings. If some soldiers jump out and kill me, tell the General it was a trap."

"How much are *you* getting paid?"

"Not nearly enough."

There was no one in the tents except a dead child, curled up as if it were asleep. There were more tents in the street. From the stink and the flies, Raeesha guessed several were similarly occupied.

Probably some dead people in the houses, too, but no need to look. Dead people will do me no harm.

And then:

A few weeks ago, seeing so many corpses would have made me sick. What has happened to me?

Everything had changed. The familiar, quiet world of Jasmine

House, the only world she ever knew, no longer existed. The tide of war had washed her away and dumped her on a foreign shore, and there was no going back.

I'm not going back to Singer, either. He could've told me he was engaged to another woman!

It was only a bit worrisome that her period was so late this month.

She waved to the departing boat, to show she was all right, shouldered her pack and began to pick her way through the tents that cluttered the street. The stink was terrible. Garbage and filth were everywhere. There was not a living soul to be seen.

Down the street, beyond the makeshift shelters and heaps of trash, she could hear a murmur of voices. Turning a corner, she found herself staring at a huge mob of people, who were milling around in Heroes Square. Some, she saw, were Chatmaks, and a few were foreigners, but most were Bandeluks, all walking around or talking excitedly with each other. There were at least a thousand.

What's happening here? Who's in charge?

Across the square from her, there was a pole that bore a human head, wearing a turban.

Is that who I think it is?

Searching the improvised campsites in the street, she found a heavy wicker basket, about two feet high, the kind used to carry laundry. She flipped it over and stood on it for a moment. It was a shaky perch, but it held her weight.

This should work.

She picked up the basket and entered the square, moving toward the pole. People turned to stare at her. There was a big crowd between her and the pole.

She drew her sword. "MAKE WAY!"

Seeing the sword, people began hastily to move, ebbing away from her like the outgoing tide. She waved the sword to encourage them.

"MAKE WAY!"

Now, she was in the middle of a staring mob of a thousand people, all whispering to each other, but keeping a safe distance.

What's happening? I am! Who's in charge? I am!

She'd reached the pole. Just as she thought, it supported the head of Amir Qilij, mustached and wearing a fine linen turban with a glittering diamond and three peacock feathers. Qilij the Cruel was staring down at her with his mouth open, as if he were flabbergasted to find himself in this position. In front of the pole was a neatly lettered sign that said, "I was a tyrant."

Oh, my fiancé! How very nice to see you here!

She sheathed her sword, put down the basket and stood on it, and taking the proclamation Singer had given her from the pack, began to read:

"PEOPLE OF KAFRA!

"YOUR PART IN THIS WAR HAD BEEN CONCLUDED! TROOPS OF THE ALLIED FORCES WILL BE ENTERING KAFRA TO ESTABLISH PEACE AND JUSTICE! WE COME AS CONQUERORS BUT NOT AS OPPRESSORS!

"PRINCE KRION OF AKADDIA PROMISES TO YOU, AND SWEARS BY ALL THE GODS, THE FOLLOWING:

"NO LOOTING OR RAPINE WILL BE PERMITTED! ALL VIOLATORS WILL BE SEVERELY PUNISHED!

"NO REVENGE WILL BE PERMITTED AGAINST CITIZENS WHO BORE ARMS HONORABLY FOR THEIR COUNTRY!

"ALL PRISONERS OF THE FORMER GOVERNMENT WILL BE FREED!

"THERE WILL BE A PUBLIC DISTRIBUTION OF GRAIN! MEDICAL CARE WILL BE GIVEN TO THOSE IN NEED! REFUGEES AND DISPLACED PERSONS WILL BE OFFERED SHELTER!

"GO TO YOUR HOMES! OUR WAR IS NOT WITH YOU! FROM THIS DAY FORWARD, KAFRA IS AT PEACE!"

She turned to nail the proclamation to the post behind her. . .

I forgot the nails!

She drew the foreign dagger and used it instead, driving it as deeply in the wood as her strength would allow. And turned to go. . .

But the mob of people had not dispersed. They were moving closer, and many were shouting questions:

"Is it really true?"

"When do we get the grain?"

"Can I go back to Clover Meadows?"

"My father is dying! Can you get him a doctor?"

She looked from one anxious face to another, but she had nothing to say. Singer had given her the proclamation, and she'd read it. She had no way of knowing whether the foreigners would keep their promises, or how or when. Prince Krion had signed the proclamation, but it was Singer who had written it.

All warfare is based on deception, the General said.

There was nothing she could do for these needy and importunate people. She held out her empty hands in a helpless gesture, then noticed something from the corner of her eye. Glancing down Dock Street, she could see something white fluttering.

A sail!

"LOOK! THE FOREIGNERS ARE COMING! CLEAR THE STREETS! DON'T LET THEM FIND YOU IN THE STREET! GO HOME!"

The needy mob suddenly became a frightened mob. What would happen if the foreigners caught them in the streets? Something dreadful, perhaps! People started making tracks in all directions. In a few minutes, Heroes Square was empty.

Sometimes, it's better to be feared than to be loved!

Looking again down Dock Street, she saw only some laundry flapping in the breeze. The ships had not arrived. She had no idea when they'd come.

Behind her, someone cleared his throat. "That was a very entertaining performance," said Hisaf.

Uncle Davoud looked down at her through the open door as if she were a stranger. He obviously didn't recognize her.

"Look what I found in Heroes Square," said Hisaf.

Raeesha removed the helmet, and Uncle Davoud started, as if he were seeing a ghost. "Is that you, Raeesha? You look so strange!"

"I'll take her any way I can find her," said Hisaf. "Out of so many dead, this one is alive! She was lost and is found!"

He dragged her into the entrance hall, shouting, "LOOK WHO'S HERE! RAEESHA IS BACK!"

She heard the sound of many feet on the stairs, and then they were all around her, their clothing and hair in disorder, the sisters, aunts and cousins she thought were gone forever. As each woman entered, she paused, astonished to see Raeesha wearing armor and carrying weapons. They stood there in a semi-circle, silently looking at her, until the last and littlest of them, Shirin, who was no older than six, came running in and, without pausing, rushed forward to give her a hug.

That broke the dam. All the women began talking at once:

"Raeesha! Where have you been?"

"What has happened to you?"

"We were so terribly worried!"

"You must tell us everything!"

"That's a long story," Raeesha said. "Why don't we go to the living room? I have some things for you."

In the living room, she began laying out the contents of her pack on the table: There were four big loaves of the army bread, a wheel of cheese, a bag of dates and smaller packages containing tea, sugar, salt and spices. There was also a pouch of tobacco for Uncle Davoud.

As each item appeared, it was snatched by eager hands, poked, sniffed, commented on and finally laid out on the table. As the last item emerged, she heard another set of footsteps on the stairs.

That must be Mother!

Suddenly, she felt weak.

If a fierce demon were coming down the stairs, I'd know what to do, but what can I do with Mother?

Her mother looked thin and frail. She was neatly dressed in her best clothing and had put up her hair.

Even if the house were on fire, she wouldn't come down until she was properly dressed!

The room fell silent as they waited to see what Mother would say. But Mother said nothing, merely walked up and gave her a peck on the cheek, the same empty ritual she'd followed every day for many years.

As if I never went away!

At this point, the boys came in from the back room, ooh-ing and ah-ing over the display of food. Little Jabah went straight to the bag of dates and began opening it.

"Wait!" said Uncle Davoud. "Before we eat, we must thank the kindly gods who have brought us through so many hardships and dangers."

"Yes," said Raeesha. "Let us pray."

Notes

Names

Names are invented or borrowed without any intended reference to historical or literary figures. Any resemblance is purely coincidental.

Free Staters have northern European names, while Akaddians have southern European names, suggesting cultural differences which it would be tedious to enumerate. Covenant names are peculiar to that region. Natives of the Bandeluk Empire have Middle-Eastern names; no reference is intended to any particular nation or culture.

Languages

Akaddian is the language of the Kingdom of Akaddia. Most citizens know no other language. In Covenant, a dialect is spoken which other Akaddian speakers find archaic and hard to understand. Members of the educated classes also speak the main dialect.

Hallandish is the language of Halland and is also spoken in pure or dialect form in all of the Free States. Dialects of Hallandish may seem quaint or rustic, but all are mutually comprehensible. Educated Free Staters also speak Akaddian and sometimes Bandeluki as well.

Bandeluki is the official language of the Bandeluk Empire. Outside of the Bandeluk heartland, a variety of languages and dialects are spoken, none mutually comprehensible. The Chatmaks, for example, speak Chatmaki, and most know no more than a smattering of Bandeluki. Provincial languages like Chatmaki are generally little known outside of their home region.

Religion

The religions described are purely imaginary. No references to contemporary religions are intended. Efforts have been made to avoid any association with Islam, for example, by making the Bandeluks heavy-drinking idolaters.

The predominant form of religion is polytheism. Akaddia, Covenant and the Free States have a common pantheon, which includes Narina, the goddess of mercy and Theros, the god of war. Bandeluks have a different pantheon, which includes Savustasi, the god of war and Paralayan, the sun god.

Local temples serve the spiritual needs of the populace and also play an important social role in the community. In times of war, religious observance may become haphazard and is often reduced to oaths, curses and prayers of desperation by the combatants.

Religious conviction among the educated classes is often tepid.

Military Organizations

These are not nearly as uniform as on 21st Century Earth. The lowest level of organization is the squad, consisting of 8-12 men, led by a sergeant. A group commonly consists of ten squads and is led by a lieutenant. A company is a unit of variable size, generally about a thousand men, and led by a captain. Companies of cavalry are often smaller than infantry companies and are also referred to as squadrons. The largest permanent military organization is a regiment, usually 3-5 companies, led by a colonel. An army is a temporary grouping of various units, depending on the available forces, led either by a general or a member of the aristocracy.

To complicate matters, officers may be promoted for valor without being assigned to a larger unit. Thus, a colonel may frequently be found in charge of a company, or a general commanding a regiment. (However, Singer's sudden promotion from lieutenant to general is highly unusual.) Staff officers (of which Singer was one) are not usually found in command of a combat unit, but are assistants to the commander and may be of any rank, subordinate to him.

Demons

They are not the hellish creatures of the Christian imagination, but visitors, often unwilling, from other dimensions. These are summoned through the science of sorcery and persuaded or compelled to serve the sorcerer, who may choose to sell them or rent them out.

Demons are not native to this world, and they generally find the climate harsh, the human culture alien, the language difficult and the food barely edible. They are often assigned duties which are disagreeable or even dangerous to humans.

Some demons come from places where conditions are so extremely different that they burst into flame or even explode when released from stasis. This lends itself to military applications.

Outside of the professional sorcerers, few people know much about demons or care to associate with them. Superstitions abound.

Named Persons
(Includes Spoilers)

In Chatmakstan (a province of the Bandeluk Empire):
Sheikh Mahmud's Family
Sheikh Mahmud – the head of the clan and aspiring father-in-law to Amir Qilij
Raeesha – his rebellious daughter
Rajik – her younger brother; Raeesha also uses his name
Umar – their slow-witted elder brother
Alim – an elder brother, not seen since the Battle of Massera Bay and presumed dead

In Kafra (the capital of Chatmakstan):
Amir Qilij – the tyrant of Kafra, and prospective husband to Raeesha
Davoud – Raeesha's uncle, a wine merchant
Hisaf – an elder brother of Raeesha
Shirin – a younger sister of Raeesha
Jabah – a younger cousin
Ferran – a baker
Munib – a stable boy to Amir Qilij
Azad – a stable boy to Amir Qilij
Nazif – a stable boy to Amir Qilij, deceased
Samia – a courtesan to Amir Qilij, deceased

Elsewhere in Chatmakstan:
Hussni – watch captain to Sheikh Mahmud
Harim – a peasant from the Fallingstone village
Faisal – a peasant from the Seven Pines village
Rahat – a fletcher in the service of Sheikh Mahmud
Abdul-Ghafur – a groom in the service of Sheikh Mahmud
Ebrahim – an outlaw
Tamira – his wife

Javid – a peddler
Hikmet – a former cloth merchant, servant to Prince Clenas
Husam – a Bandeluk deserter
Tariq – a Bandeluk deserter
Mubina – a shopkeeper
Nabil – a blacksmith
Khalid – a potter
Sea Wind – Sheikh Mahmud's horse

In the Area of Effect:
    Olgun's Squad
    Olgun – sergeant in the Kafra Light Cavalry
    Yusuf – a soldier
    Navid – a soldier
    Lufti – a soldier
    Arif – a soldier

In Barbosa:
    The Old Woman – a sorceress, the legendary Witch of Barbosa
    Lamya – her apprentice
    Deva – a servant girl
    Jessamina – a servant girl
    Extinctor – an ancient and terrible demon

In the Madlands:
    Shayan – a sorcerer
    Dareia – his wife
    Populator – an ancient demon, creator of the Madlands
    Mertkan – a soldier of Khuram Bey

Invaders:
    Akaddians
    Prince Krion – commander of the allied forces, third son of
        King Diecos
    Prince Clenas – his younger brother, commander of the Royal
        Light Cavalry
    Nikandros – a pseudonym used by Prince Clenas
    Basilius – commander of the Twelve Hundred Heroes
    Grennadius – commander of the Royal Household Guards

Diomedos – a sorcerer
Mopsus – an aide to Prince Krion
Parsevius – a captain

In Akaddia:

King Diecos – the aging king of Akaddia
Prince Vettius – his eldest son, retired from politics and
　　　devoted to his family
Prince Chryspos – his second son, a notorious boy lover
Duchess Thea – their sister
Duke Claudio – husband to Thea

Invaders:

Hallanders (Free Staters allied with Akaddia)
Hinman – commander of the Halland Company
Singer – his adjutant
Pohler – a lieutenant
Fleming – a lieutenant
Osgood – a lieutenant
Beecher – a lieutenant
Ogleby – a lieutenant
Pennesey – the quartermaster
Littleton – the engineer
Father Leo – the chaplain
Doc Murdoch – the company doctor
Blaine – a crossbowman
Halverson – a crossbowman
Eckhard – a crossbowman
Kyle – the bugle boy

In Halland:

Erika – fiancé to Singer
Rosalind – her younger sister
Wartfield – their father, a cloth merchant
Houghton – a cousin and commercial rival of Wartfield
Brandworth – Houghton's son, a notorious drinker

Invaders:
  Other Free Staters (allied with Akaddia)
  Stewart – commander of the Thunder Slingers, of Kindleton
  Baron Hardy – a mercenary commander employed by the
      Free State of Dammerheim
  Sir Rendel – commander of the Illustrious Knights, of
      Tremmark
  Sir Gladwood – a knight of Tremmark
  Twenty Three – spokesman of the *fui* demons, in the service of
      Westenhausen

Invaders:
  Citizens of Covenant (a protectorate of Akaddia)
  Lessig – commander of the Covenant Sappers, of the
      aristo class
  Radburn – his lieutenant, an aristo
  Bardhof – aide to Prince Krion, a pleb

In Covenant:
  Moullit – a cloth merchant

Elsewhere:
  Gwyneth – sister of Wartfield, aunt of Erika and Rosalind
  Khuram Bey – a dead tyrant

CPSIA information can be obtained
at www.ICGtesting.com
Printed in the USA
LVOW13s1459110417
530417LV00012B/1015/P